The First Lie

A SELKIE MOON MYSTERY

VIRGINIA KING

Be sure to visit www.selkiemoon.com for insider information, character bios and author updates. Subscribe to *Myth & Mystery* for exclusive news and events.

BOOKS BY VIRGINIA KING

Selkie Moon Mystery Series:
The First Lie
The Second Path
Book Three (Coming Soon)
Laying Ghosts (www.selkiemoon.com)

The First Lie

A SELKIE MOON MYSTERY

VIRGINIA KING

Celestial Hedgehog

§

To Selkie – thanks for the adventure

Glossary

Selkie – sea creature from Celtic folklore that takes the form of a seal in water but can take human form on land.

Hawaiian words:
Aloha – traditional greeting meaning welcome and goodbye.
Aumakua – ancestral spirit guide, in animal form.
Grinds (pidgin) – food.
Haole – Caucasian.
Ho'ohihi – interconnectedness.
Kahuna – wise person, sorcerer.
Lanai – veranda.
Lei – garland of flowers or shells, worn around neck.
Lolo – crazy.
Luau – traditional feast.
Mahalo – thank you.
Mai tai – cocktail of rum, grenadine, lemon and pineapple juices.
Makaukau – ready, to dance the Hula.
Malihini – newcomer.
Menehune – legendary little people who achieve huge projects in a single night.
Muu-muu – long loose-fitting dress.
Pali – cliff.
Pele – volcano goddess.
Pilikia – trouble.
Shaka – welcoming hand gesture with the three middle fingers. folded down.
Shape shifta (pidgin) – supernatural being that can change form.
Tutu – grandma.
Uli – goddess of magic, also known as the heavenly mother.

February 1979

It happens on a beach.

A little girl is splashing in the shallows. Falling over, getting up again. Squealing. A woman in a sundress watches from under a hat, while a woman in a swimsuit plays with the toddler.

Suddenly a big wave comes from nowhere and pulls the child away from the shore. It tumbles her over and over and she waves her little arms and legs at the sky.

The woman in the swimsuit laughs. "You're a mermaid."

But the other woman is screaming. "What are you doing? She's drowning."

"It's just a wave. It's saying hello."

The woman in the sundress rushes into the water and pulls the child back from the grasp of the sea. "Look at her, she's crying. She's coughing up sand."

"That's what happens at the beach."

"She could have *drowned*."

"The gods called her Selkie because she's a mermaid."

"You and your stupid fairytales. She isn't safe with you. She isn't *safe*."

Everybody, soon or late, sits down to a banquet of
consequences.
—*Robert Louis Stevenson*

Chapter
One

I'm falling off a cliff towards the rocks and the sea, when these words ring in my ears.

Someone is trying to kill you.

They reverberate like a call to prayer. Clear. Insistent. Almost musical.

The meaning rattles me to consciousness and I sit up with a start. But as I wait in the semi-dark for the words to repeat themselves, there's only an aching silence. As if they never happened. Except their shape has left a shadow on the wall of my mind and my body has started to tremble.

I reach for my bathrobe and wrap myself against the sudden chill, wishing I wasn't alone. It's a familiar feeling. All by myself in the middle of the Pacific Ocean. Without a life raft.

Unless Wanda crept back after midnight, but across the room her bed lies untouched. No telltale lump under the covers. And no whirring of her blender from the kitchen. She's stayed out all night again. It usually makes her the perfect flatmate.

Of course I've had bad dreams before. Often the same one. I'm trapped underwater, tangled in something so my arms don't work, and wake up to find it's only the sheets. But never anything like this.

Because it wasn't just a dream. It was a message. Seeping into my brain. Someone. Is. Trying. To. Kill. You. As graphic as stumbling across a gravestone in a churchyard inscribed with my name and today's date.

For the first time I notice the quality of the silence. Complete. The bedside clock isn't ticking. The water pipes aren't clunking. Even the whispering sea is absent. I pull the robe a little closer and focus on the steady movement of my chest. I'm not dead yet.

And the message makes no sense. Who would want to kill me? After only three months I'm still a stranger here, and there aren't many murders in this part of the world. It's why people come to Hawaii. To play it sunny and safe. And anyway, I'm not the kind of woman to inspire that kind of violence. Although my ex would disagree. Andrew still can't believe I've swapped opposite corners of the ring for opposite sides of the globe.

Where did the message come from? The remnants of the dream? But it sounded like...a disembodied voice. With that thought an invisible presence seems to fill the space.

Something...spoke to me.

My eyes scan the walls and dozens of eyes stare back. Wanda's artworks, fashioned from dead fish. In garish colours with painted lips. They might ooze an excess of character but they don't speak. Although with Wanda's gift for hocus-pocus it wouldn't surprise me.

Any other possible culprits? A naked shop dummy sits on a chair at the end of Wanda's bed, her plastic legs akimbo. Doris. For the first few weeks I kept jumping out of my skin every time I caught sight of her. Wanda has dressed her in a Hula skirt and peppered her torso with nails, like a woman in a Dali painting. She drapes her with anything from net bags to headbands to *leis*. Today Doris is wearing a straw hat even though she doesn't have a head. No head, no voice, right?

The room is a tribute to Wanda's eye for other people's trash, and my few belongings barely make an impression on the menagerie. A large Buddha head with four faces forever contemplating his split personality. Two fairies shadow-dancing on an art-deco tray. A parrot made from nuts and bolts poised on his own perch. In childhood these creatures might have spoken to me, but my stepmother, Stella, banished imaginary friends long ago.

On the ledge above my bed my Shona sculpture is just a head and shoulders. I brought her with me when I took off from Sydney with two business suits and not much else. A chunk of black and silver rock from Zimbabwe, her profile is as enigmatic as ever. And as silent. But she's no whisperer. If Shona had a warning for me she'd come right out with it, face to face.

The presence is still here. A kind of touchless stroking against my bare skin. Seductive but unnerving. It's making me as rigid as Doris but my eyes keep darting back to the slash of early-morning light spilling through the bathroom doorway. Is it coming from there?

When I was a child I used to feel things like this, invisible things. Stella made me stand in the bathroom until they were gone. I'm still a bit afraid of bathrooms, their cold unwelcoming surfaces gleaming my wild-eyed stare back at me. So it's all I can do to get off the bed and tiptoe towards the doorway.

There are no doors to hide an intruder. And no shower curtain over the bath. When I start hyperventilating about Janet Leigh in *Psycho*, I tell myself to get a grip. No-one would bother breaking in here. The address might be Waikiki, but that's where the glamour ends.

The sun through the window bathes me in light and I scan the empty bathroom with relief. Only my imagination playing tricks. But that's when I see it. In the mirror at the end of the bath.

A face.

It's a woman, just her face, but I'm sure she's naked and reclining in the tub. She's looking straight at me as if she's been waiting, her eyes so piercing they latch onto mine and won't release me, even when I try to pull away. For a long breathless moment our gazes are locked together and I'm lost in the depths of an emotion I can't name. Then she lets go and the recoil spins me towards a window full of light. Now I'm blinking at the bath. Empty. Still empty. And when I spin back to the mirror she's gone.

It takes me a few seconds to come to my senses because it feels like I've been doused by some unbearable sorrow. Then I'm back in my body, splashing my face at the basin, stumbling back to the bedroom and flopping on the bed.

The bedside clock begins to tick, its rhythmic beat counting the seconds like a metronome. The hands are showing six. They haven't moved since the message woke me – surely at least five minutes ago. And the sun doesn't rise this early, not in February. Does that mean the last five minutes didn't happen?

It doesn't matter how early it is, I'm phoning Wanda. She's the one who put that stupid mirror there. After a dream, she insisted that the bath needed to see the sky.

"How can it see?" I asked as she propped the mirror with great ceremony against the wall at the end of the bath. "Bathtubs...don't have eyes."

"We're talking spiritual eyes. Put yourself in her place, staring at a blank wall all day. Soul-destroying. Like being paralysed. But if we put this mirror opposite the window, see? The sky's reflected and she's reconnecting."

"Reconnecting with what?"

"Her wild nature."

There's a lot of that kind of talk around here. Wanda

thinks everything's got a spirit, every rock and insect, even our old ball-and-claw bath.

"Let's ask her for hotter showers," I said. Just one of the reasons this flat is cheap.

"Out of her control. She's the vessel, that's why she's female. She receives. Contains. Transforms. The mirror's special too. It reflects female energy."

Its silver frame is curved like a woman. Narrow at the waist, wide at the bust and hips.

"But we'll notice a difference in other ways," Wanda said. "After a bath, we'll be radiant."

It all seemed like a bit of fun. I've been waiting for Wanda to give the bath a name and paint its toenails red. But now because of that mirror I've looked into the eyes of...a woman who wasn't there.

Confusion drives me outside onto the walkway where dawn is breaking and the air is fresh. As my fingers fumble with the phone, it feels good to inhale. If Wanda's in bed with her new man it can't be helped.

No answer. I leave an agitated message and start pacing.

I've got to get dressed and go to the office but that means going back inside. I close my eyes and try to calm my breathing but the woman's face appears. This time it's just the memory, her gaze caught in freeze-frame, and one of Stella's phrases gallops up the long tunnel from childhood: "It'll cause you trouble, your imagination. Just like your mother. If you can't touch it, it's a figment, and figments can carry you away." My stepmother has a way of creeping up on me, just like she did when I was a child. I might have left her on the other side of the world but she's still living inside my head.

My phone rings. "Sorry I couldn't pick up, Selkie. Up to my armpits in mullet." Wanda's at the docks judging by the hubbub. "Hang on."

Now she's talking to someone and a man is laughing. One of her fishermen, no doubt.

They give them to her – dead fish – because she's an art student. (Her long legs and short shorts have nothing to do with it.) She presses the corpses into squares of soft resin, adding shells to make borders. When the moulds harden she paints them and sells them at the markets as Art.

"OK. They're in the cooler getting acquainted.Something must be up if you're calling this early."

"It's that mirror." My voice is croaky. "The one at the end of the bath."

"You didn't break it, did you?" Pause. "Oh my God, you saw something."

"A face. I saw a face. A woman...who wasn't there."

Spoken out loud it sounds delusional but Wanda is taking it seriously. "OK, keep breathing. Let's eliminate the temporal. It wasn't...your own face."

"I do know what I look like, Wanda. Even in the mornings. And I wasn't peering into the mirror. I was standing in the doorway, looking at it from the side."

"So it could have been at the window. That's the angle. Sometimes kids climb up trying to get a look at one of us under the shower."

It's the first I've heard of it, but it wasn't a kid. "It was definitely a woman. And she wasn't at the window, she was in the bath. Until she wasn't."

"OK." She thinks for a moment. "What do you want me to do, call in an exorcist?"

"Hell, no. Just move the bloody thing." Into a dumpster on the other side of the island.

"You can move it. Turn the mirror to the wall and it

loses its power."

"No way. And I'm stuck outside in my bathrobe. How am I going to get to work?"

"If she disappeared she's gone for now. It's safe to take a shower."

"I'm not going near that bath."

"OK. Go into the bedroom and throw on some clothes. You can do that. And meet me in an hour. At your office."

Holding my breath, I open the front door and rush inside, but the air feels clear as if the presence is long gone. I toss off my bathrobe and pull on my red suit and heels. Hair and makeup would mean looking in another mirror so I throw a few things into my tote bag and slam the front door. Not quite my usual transformation to corporate warrior.

On the concrete walkway that connects each flat it's obvious how the boys can climb on each other's shoulders and peer through our bathroom window. A 1960s' design flaw. And thanks to Wanda, the bloody mirror propped opposite has been giving them an eyeful. Our shower doesn't get hot enough to steam up their phone lenses so we're probably circulating in cyberspace. But right now I don't care.

It's three floors down to Koa Avenue, past rails groaning under towels and surfboards. When I reach the pavement I break into a run, scattering the sprinkling of early birds – beach babes and students and tourists. At the corner it's a right into Kaiulani Avenue, then at Kuhio I cross to the bus stop where I finally begin to feel normal.

This is where I wait every morning, beside the bag lady who lives in the bus shelter. She's hard to miss in her tent-sized *muu-muu*, her flabby feet resting on a large checked bag. According to Wanda she's a *kahuna* named Coral, available for roadside prognostications. She's usually asleep when I'm here but today her eyes fly open and she gives me a *shaka* salute and a knowing nod. It's the first time she's greeted me and suddenly I wouldn't put it past her to teleport herself into our mirror. Just because she can. I start to back away until I realise she's too enormous to fit in our bath. And way too ugly – and happy – to be the woman I saw.

***

The bus arrives, but as soon as I'm gazing out the window the morning's events come rushing back. *Someone is trying to kill you.* A frisson of fear prickles my skin. The woman was warning me, calling out from the bathroom mirror. But who is she? And what does she know about me?

I get off the bus and walk past concrete towers and groomed gardens. This city's struggle to tame paradise always seems a bit naive – against the rugged hills on one side and the raging sea on the other. But today the sight of all this concrete and glass feels almost reassuring. Then I'm turning into Merchant Street and the canvas sign on my building comes into view. *Space to Let.* Another message.

My office is up three flights on the top floor.

It's two steps from the door to my desk and I've just put the kettle on when Wanda's tall figure appears in the corridor. She comes in and throws her backpack on the floor.

"Can't stay long. My fishy friends are still down at the pier and they've got an appointment with the freezer."

"Thanks for meeting me. I couldn't wait to get out of there."

"Yeah." She looks me over. "You didn't even comb your

hair."

"Couldn't look in a mirror." Still can't. "Do I look...deranged?"

"More like you weren't sure who you woke up with this morning and left in a hurry by the fire escape."

"I wish."

When I offer her a teabag, she pulls a plastic bag out of her pocket and drops some herbs into one of the mugs. I pour the boiling water, then with our respective brews we sit down – me on the desk, Wanda on the only chair.

She blows on her mug and gets straight to the point. "OK. This face, did you recognise it?"

That stops me. Did the woman seem familiar? I'm not sure. But surely I'd never forget those eyes. "It's your mirror."

"True. A present from my grandmother. *Tutu.* Just before she died. Real silver. I've had it for a while but something must have stirred it up."

"Stirred up...what?"

"I don't know, but Tutu was a *kahuna.* That's where I get my Hawaiian blood, from her. She saw things. In her mind. And in the mirror."

"Things?"

"You know. The future. Predictions. Visions." She stops. "Now you've seen one."

"I saw a face, that's all. A face that...stared at me." But the hairs on my neck are standing up.

"OK, don't call her a vision, but she was something, right? Something unreal. What did she look like?"

"I don't know, I was looking at her eyes. Not young, not old. But her eyes... They were wild, Wanda. As if she was angry. Or lonely. No, something worse." Betrayed? "Whatever it was it was breaking her heart."

"Did she speak?"

The message. Did I really hear it? "Why would she...speak to me?"

"Well, the mirror was Tutu's, right? So the woman might be one of my ancestors, an ancestor with something on her mind. Because if she was staring you down she wasn't just passing through."

Bloody hell. "Passing through what?"

"The crack between worlds. Mirrors can do that, act like a window. Then you would have seen...the back of her head, a flash of white, even a footprint on the inside of the glass. But this dame wasn't going anywhere, so she wanted to communicate something. Are you sure she didn't shoot something into your mind? It sounds like she wanted to."

No, I'm not sure. "Like what? What would it look like?"

"I've never got one, but Tutu said messages from the other side are...always truthful. And they've got an atmosphere about them. Loud and clear. And you can't ignore them even if you want to."

"So if she sent me a message...I'd know."

"Yeah, that's about it. You'd know."

She waits but I say nothing.

"Are you freaking out, Selkie?"

"What do you think? A face in the mirror, not my face. Ancestors and footprints and messages. I've almost got used to Doris. And your fish, the way their eyes follow me round the room like Rembrandts, but this... This is spooky. Things like this don't happen in Sydney."

"That's probably why you left. Your soul was after a roller-coaster ride."

"Roller-coasters make me throw up."

She laughs. "So you're getting more than you bargained for." Then she takes pity on me. "Look, I'll move it when I get home, OK?"

"Thank you."

She finishes her mug and goes, but that doesn't feel like the end of it. Far from it. What happens now?

I keep a jar of fortune cookies on my desk, just in case of emergencies. It was a fortune cookie that gave me the courage to finally walk out on Andrew. *There is no way to both stay and go*, it said. I went. It's as near as I get to soothsaying because their guidance suits my style. Enigmatic. They don't tell you what to do, they propose a cryptic clue and invite you to make your own decision.

My hand's still shaking as I choose one that's squashed against the side. Seems appropriate. I crack it open and unfurl the tiny paper strip.

To find the right answer, ask the right question.

At first I'm disappointed. It feels like any other riddle. But then the words begin to make sense. I scribble down the possibilities, but in the end there are really only two.

Who is the woman?

What does she want?

I write them in big letters. Then photograph them with my phone. These are the questions that need answers. But how do I do that?

It takes a bit more introspection, but an answer finally comes. The only answer possible.

Investigate.

Chapter

Two

Feeling burdened, I type *Hawaii* into Google, with different combinations of other keywords: *woman, spirit, mirror, message.* The number of hits is huge and the stuff I dip into reminds me of Wanda. This place is full of paranormal sightings. It must be something in the water.

There are lots of names from Hawaiian folklore – *Uli,* the heavenly mother, and *Pele,* the volcano goddess. The *menehune,* little people like leprechauns who come out at night and do good works, and the *Night Marchers,* prowling spirits of ancient Hawaiians. I don't feel a connection to any of them but I open a file and paste in their descriptions just so it feels like progress.

Thousands of other strange sightings come up. Like the faceless woman who appears in the mirror of a public restroom at Kahala Mall. Countless women standing at the basin have seen her combing her hair behind them, and when they turn around she isn't there. But my sighting was in a private bathroom and my woman was all face and no body. It isn't her.

Someone else describes levitating off her bed and almost being sucked into a mirror. She was just able to resist, and afterwards a team of ghost-busters rid her apartment of evil spirits hiding in the sculptures and statues. Wanda is removing the mirror, but I wonder what her menagerie might be hiding. Except they've only ever seemed eccentric, not at all sinister.

After an hour I'm on a feng shui site: *Don't put a mirror*

opposite the bed in case you get trapped in the in-between state between sleeping and waking. The mirror wasn't opposite my bed, but I'd just woken up. It's possible I was still in that in-between state when I saw the woman. Then the sighting would just have been an extension of the dream.

A dream where I was plunging into the sea.

Shit.

As long as I can remember it's been with me, my fear of the sea. After a big wave nearly drowned me as a toddler. Stella says that afterwards just the sight of my little bikini made me scream so they kept me away from the beach. Until I was older. And by then it was too late. I've lived with it. After all, swimming isn't like breathing, it's more like horse-riding – you can go your whole life without ever having to do it.

Then late last year I won a green card and all fifty states were at my feet, but every time I closed my eyes and stuck a pin in the map, it landed on Hawaii. I kept dismissing it, but it kept turning up, even when I spun the map around. Then my research showed it was the perfect place to start a seminar business – a magnet for the conference crowd, the heady mix of paradise and business guaranteeing success even for a small operator with the right skills and a good website. Hawaii became my ticket for leaving Sydney – and Andrew – in a cloud of dust. But when the plane descended into Honolulu...the image is still there in my mind, a tiny dot of land in the middle of all that...ocean.

A face appears in the mirror above my desk and I gasp out loud before I realise it's Derek.

Derek Delaney, freelance writer and new-age tragic. We met in this corridor the day I arrived with a chair and a flatpack desk. In the last three months he's gone from stranger to neighbour to friend. The big sister I never had.

When I turn around he's propping up the doorjamb. Or is it the other way round?

"Are you jumpy or do I look that scary?" he asks.

I breathe out. "Not scary, more like...'scenic'." His brown hair has formed a volcanic-style peak and his lime shirt resembles the crumpled hills behind our office. "While you've been sleeping on a park bench, I've been...perfecting my telephone technique." Almost true.

"Puh-lease. That's the kind of talk that gives me a headache."

"And staying out all night's got nothing to do with it?"

"You know I hate clairvoyance this early in the morning."

Wrong. He loves clairvoyance any time of day.

"You make it so easy, DD. Your clothes are crumpled, your chin is sandpaper, your eyes are bloodshot...and you're clutching a coffee...in each hand. Been doing anything you can tell me about?"

Derek's the inventor of a variation on the traditional *luau* which he's renamed *gay grinds*. The partying and feasting usually ends after dawn at his current 'crash site'. It explains why he doesn't work from home. He needs an office to fake a professional image.

He yawns. "Updating the twenty-four-hour restaurant guide for *Lonely Planet*. A night of tax-deductible gluttony." He takes a slug of coffee from each mug. "The only hitch is the deadline. Close of business today."

"Good timing, leaving it till the last minute."

"Yeah, but I do my best work under pressure, remember?"

"Only if you're awake. Come on, leave the coffee, what you need is a power nap."

Like a trusting toddler he lets me lead him next door

and settle him into his armchair. He keeps a blanket in the filing cabinet because the old air conditioner runs on high or not at all. Most days Derek huddles over his keyboard like King Kamehameha in his cloak.

As I tuck him in he opens one eye. "You don't look so well-groomed yourself."

"Just a bad hair day. I'll wake you at two."

Back at my desk I abandon Google. How dare this woman intrude on my life and in such a confronting way. I've got plans. To make a name for myself on the seminar circuit, not delve into unexplained appearances and uncorroborated threats.

I start on Derek's coffee and flick to my inbox. Several emails have come in overnight from the Moonshine website. The name Moonshine came to me just after I arrived, and the hint of something illicit generates a good hit rate – but after three months of solid follow-up, my conversion to paying customer is zero. It keeps me awake at night, my shrinking bank balance, as the weeks slip by without an income. I'm in danger of believing one of Andrew's early jibes:

You're not brave enough to succeed on your own.

Speak of the devil there's a new message from my ex this morning.

If you come back NOW, I'll forget it ever happened.

It's been like this ever since I left. We were childhood sweethearts, and he can't believe it's over, can't believe I've slipped through his fingers and started a life without him. He had plans for me – for us – until I walked out, changed my name and humiliated him. But instead of asking himself why I ran away, he's turned his hand to cyber-stalking.

Back to the web enquiries. Last night I came up with a new idea – a money-back guarantee. If they sign up for my

Goals for Gold seminar and don't get their money's worth they get a full refund, no questions asked.

In spite of the wasted morning, there's still time to catch the western half of the mainland before their day ends, then there's China and Japan. I pick up the enquiry list and the phone.

***

As I'm popping downstairs for some sushi, Derek throws off the blanket and stretches, then sits at the keyboard and starts mumbling. "You know how it is, ravenous at 3am. And Honolulu doesn't disappoint; you just need to know where to look…"

I suspect he's been composing it in his sleep.

I catch up on updates from Sydney friends. It's what I usually do over lunch, to manage my time, but today it's keeping the woman and the message at bay. Because the incident hasn't faded. Instead it's exerting a pressure on me, a pressure not to ignore it.

The phone offers another diversion until I hear who's calling.

"So you're not dead," a woman says.

My stepmother. "Hello, Stella."

"Your father and I have wondered."

"I've been busy." I sound defensive. Stella always turns me into a child. "I'm sure Dad understands why I haven't called. A new business always saps your time." And a new country.

"Yes, you're still his favourite. Until Gretel has the baby. You can't compete with a grandchild. Especially now you've walked out on Andrew."

"It's just my selfish streak. Taking after Mum again."

That shuts her up. Even though they were sisters, Stella's never had a good word to say about my mother. Prunella died when I was a baby, then Dad married her sister, Stella, and they had Gretel. It means Gretel and I are half-sisters – and cousins.

"Why are you calling?" I ask. "I know when Gretel's baby's due."

"If you care you'll be here, I suppose. Not that I'm holding my breath."

"How is she?"

"What, you haven't spoken to her either?" She clicks her tongue.

"I follow her updates."

But Gretel and I get on together like our mothers never did, so why haven't I been in touch?

Stella cuts to the chase. "We don't have an address for you. In case of emergencies."

I give her the address of the Waikiki flat. And then regret it.

***

At four Derek's back at my door. "I'm done. The editor doesn't deserve me." Don't get him started on editors.

"Two hours, not bad."

"I channelled it."

"The restaurant guide? The astral traveller edition, is it?"

He grins. "How about you? Landed anyone yet?" He knows all about my lack of enrolments.

"Still no luck." I tell him about the money-back guarantee.

"A no-risk seminar wrapped in a tax-deductible vacation. What's not to love?"

"You tell me, but so far no-one's going for it."
"You're trying too hard. Call it a day."

***

I barge into the bathroom before I lose my nerve. But there's no sign of it. The mirror's gone and the woman and the message with it.

"I've taken it away," Wanda says as she comes in behind me, "but say the word when you want it back." She throws her headband on Doris and makes for the fridge.

"Why would I want it back?"

"Do you think she's gone because the mirror's gone?"

"I hope so." I'm counting on it.

"But you don't know. There's a lot you don't know, Selkie. About this woman. Why she appeared to you, a *malihini*. And I hate to tell you, but the mirror is your channel."

I've got a Chinese takeaway, so I sit down and start eating straight from the container. Wanda makes one of her macrobiotic smoothies, putting bananas and yoghurt in the blender. She watches me begin on a bottle of wine.

"It's organic," I plead. "From Chile." I show her the label. "Someone riding a bicycle so it must be natural."

"Yeah. And think how much carbon went into transporting it."

Wanda believes in eating local. As well as the sprouts she grows on the windowsill she's a regular at Hi-Fibes, the health-food store in our basement.

I sip my wine and remember the woman's eyes, the raw emotion of her gaze. Wanda's talking about the guy who rents her the garage where she creates. How she's fallen into bed with him, as I suspected. It just happened, because she's always there at odd hours with the door open and he strolls in and watches her bending over her fish. She's obviously happy, happier than I've ever seen her, but with my troubles I'm not in the right space to listen.

"Are you getting free rent?" I ask, then wish I hadn't.

"Because I'm sleeping with him?" She puts her hands on her hips. "You don't know me very well yet, do you, Selkie? I'd never prostitute my art."

When she goes out my mind returns to the woman. Wanda's right. There's a lot I don't know. Everything. And if I don't know who the woman is, why she's targeted me, how can I dismiss her message?

My fear of the sea is always with me, but the woman has stirred up something else. Something personal. I came to Hawaii to escape my old life, not land myself in deep water.

Chapter
Three

Tuesday morning. I oversleep, but my dreams were uneventful. No messages. And when I stumble into the bathroom, no mirror either. As I stand under a cool shower the blank wall at the end of the bath almost dispels my unease.

I arrive late for work and my office phone is ringing. I race along the corridor, fumbling for the key, convinced the caller is a human resources manager who wants to enrol twenty staff members in a goals seminar. My seminar. He has to allocate the forty thousand dollars by ten o'clock. And I'm going to miss him.

But the caller hangs on and gets my breathless greeting. "You sound like you're selling phone sex," he says. "Good idea. More money, lower overheads...and you get to keep your gear on."

The Texas twang is unmistakeable. It's Guy Morrison, my business advisor. Since he's waived his fee in favour of a percentage I've got to put up with his jokes. He's supposed to be improving my bottom line and he's convinced Goals for Gold is the problem. Not 'quirky' enough. But since when does 'quirky' look credible to a business audience? I keep seeing myself in a silly suit, like a performing seal.

"How's the seminar going?" he asks. "Any enrolments yet or do you miss every call like you near as hell missed mine?"

"Not yet, but I'm going for twenty. Something modest to cut my teeth on."

He has the courtesy to whistle. "At two thousand bucks a ticket..."

"...that's forty thousand." I wish.

"Look, Selkie," he's suddenly impatient, "when can we talk? I've got a scheme to make you millions."

"Don't taunt me, Guy. Hundreds of thousands will do."

"I mean it. Leverage your expertise, really leverage it. I'm very excited about it."

"Do I have to wear a silly suit?"

He roars. "I've never been asked that one before. But I thought you'd know what leverage means. Silly suits are kinda optional."

"I know – working smarter not harder – but guessing games are hard work so just tell me."

"Better if we meet. You free at one?"

Lunchtime. Probably fitting me in between clients who pay. I pretend to consult my diary. "Fine. Here in town?"

Guy's got a house on the North Shore with a *lanai* overlooking the surf. It's where I agreed to share thirty per cent of my future profits while the thundering sea numbed my ability to negotiate.

"Jimmy Ho's. I've already booked a table. You know where it is?"

The most expensive restaurant in Honolulu. "Er, yes, but it's a bit beyond my budget." My annual budget.

"My treat."

"I can't let you do that, Guy. You get the ideas, I get the lunch." Now I decide to talk tough. "But it means it has to be...a noodle bar."

He laughs. "Why not? I don't mind slumming it. You know somewhere, do ya?"

"Chinatown. More private for a meeting too." Like no competitors at neighbouring tables.

I give him the address of the Pearl. It's been my second home ever since I tumbled into a taxi at the airport looking for a friendly face. The cab driver turned out to be Chinese and dropped me at the Pearl. I'd left Sydney in a hurry and was soon downing a bowl of noodles and trying not to panic about being homeless and friendless in a foreign land.

Wanda's advert was lying face up on the floor, covered in footprints but legible. *Bed to let, long-term, cheap.* A number to call. She answered after three rings, and I had a roof over my head and a flatmate before the sun fell out of the sky.

Guy's call doesn't make the world look different. Millions. With so many big clients it's the only number he knows, but there are too many noughts for me to visualise. Especially after the struggle to get even one client to take me seriously. Have I got anything to offer that's worth that kind of money?

I decide to concentrate on the forty thousand, chunked down to the first two thousand. If I can just get that first enrolment before lunch, my relationship with Guy will feel more equal.

***

Chinatown's not everyone's favourite Honolulu location but I adore peering into the open-fronted shops and inhaling the oriental wisdom, hoping some business acumen will rub off.

As I walk down Maunakea Street, the red happy coat that does service as the Pearl's sign is flapping its welcome. Next door the *lei* stall is displaying its wares, and on the other side the vegetable market spills boxes of produce into the street. With its concrete floor and mismatched chairs the Pearl could be any café in any Hong Kong backstreet. The whole front wall opens up with a roller door as if the place was once a lane that's been roofed over.

I check my reflection in a window across the street to make sure I'm looking corporate enough, since the venue screams exactly the opposite. At least today my hair's combed and my face is made up. But I'm not going to think about that.

Guy breezes up looking like money on holidays. Something to do with this term: custom-made. He brushes his big red moustache along my cheek before we step inside.

The interior is dark after the glare outside and the place is doing a brisk trade. I catch a glimpse of Eugene in the kitchen, and Suzi is standing behind the laminex counter.

"You wan' special?" she asks.

Suzi knows I always have the special. It's easier than deciphering the menu and I figure they use the freshest ingredients and I'm putting them to the least amount of trouble. But today I'm entertaining Guy. I tell him about their Beijing duck with pancakes but we both decide on the handmade noodles with shredded pork and hot and sour sauce.

A table becomes vacant and Guy grabs it, no doubt the way he snatches up all of life's little opportunities. I should be taking notes.

"Got ya first enrolment yet?" he asks as we sit down.

It's the question I've been expecting. "Not yet. But I'm not giving up till I get twenty." Just so he knows how tenacious I am.

Guy leans forward. "How about three thousand?"

"What?"

"Participants."

"Don't tease me, please."

He lowers his voice as if the room might eavesdrop. But it's so noisy I have to lean forward till his moustache tickles my ear. "Three thousand participants, paying one hundred bucks a head. That's three hundred thousand. Ten seminars a year..."

"Three million. I can 'do the math', Guy. But since when do you get three thousand people at a seminar?"

"If you're a success guru you do. And the hundred-dollar gigs are just the teasers – cheap half-day shows designed to sell the big weekend workshops at five thousand bucks a go. I've done the research and a spreadsheet and got you earning ten million a year. Part-time."

He hands me a printout. I peek at the big number at the bottom but I'm not buying it.

"In case you haven't noticed, Guy, I'm not a success guru. I'm one of the nobodies on the seminar circuit."

"Just a matter of promotion."

"And who's going to promote me?"

Not Guy. He's made that clear.

"Lester Sloane. Managing Director of Top Notch. He likes you, that's what you'll be. Overnight."

"Lester Sloane?" I almost choke.

Everyone's heard of Sloane. A big-shot promoter always jetting in from somewhere with a model on his arm.

"He promotes all the big names," I say.

"Uh-huh. He's got a shitload of top speakers doing the circuit. All men."

"But I'm a woman –"

"I've noticed that."

"– and I'm not in their league."

"Yet."

Eugene serves our noodles and Guy begins to slurp. He couldn't do that at Jimmy Ho's. It gives me time to steady my breathing and suppress the sensation that I'm treading water.

"All the somebodies started out as nobodies," he says. "Till they got discovered."

"Is Sloane looking for a woman guru?"

"Always. Impressive women are rare."

"So now I've got to impress him. I knew there'd be a catch."

"Invite him to your next workshop," Guy is saying. "An attractive woman of the right age presenting a leading-edge seminar with panache. He won't be able to sign you up fast enough. I should have thought of Sloane weeks ago – saved you all this poverty."

So it's obvious how broke I am? Of course it is – we're eating at the Pearl.

"But my next seminar will only be a small group," I say. Assuming I get any enrolments at all. "I can do that standing on my head, but wouldn't I need to convince Sloane I can handle a group of thousands?"

"Size of group is irrelevant to a gifted speaker. He knows that. And he's used to spotting potential talent. He discovers people, Selkie. It's how he created the most respected agency in the country."

"But what about Moonshine? If Sloane discovers me, that'll be the end of it. I'll be his girl."

"Yep. Big choice. Ten million bucks a year – or a business worth less than squat. Your call, babe." He wipes his moustache between mouthfuls. "Any other reasons you're not going to cut it? Spit 'em out, get 'em off your chest."

His eyes wander to my cleavage.

I consider upending my noodles on his head.

"OK, here's a teensy one. My seminar's about goals,

remember? Not quirky enough, you said. A complete yawn, you said. Gurus have got to say something new, Guy. Their seminar is their signature. Instead of impressing Sloane I'll bore the pants off him."

Guy doesn't miss a beat; after all, he's got money riding on it. Big money. "We're selling you not the seminar. Afterwards we'll come up with something quirky. That hasn't changed but now we're *motivated*. As a woman you'll get away with it. Sloane will go for it."

"It sounds like we're winging it, Guy. Where's the plan?"

He puts down his chopsticks and looks me in the eye. "Fuck the plan, shred the manual. I thought you wanted to be somebody, babe. The somebodies of this world are into freefall."

I remember the cliff in my dream. Shit.

"You're scared as hell, that's all. Good."

"Good? That's easy for you to say. You're at the back of the room counting the money. I'm the one up on stage with no clothes on in front of three thousand people."

He laughs. "So it excites you."

Does it?

"Scared *and* excited." He smiles. "I think we got ourselves a guru."

My noodles are getting cold but for once I'm not eating. My name on billboards all over the country, equal billing with all the big names.

Selkie Moon.

Someone.

***

"I've just signed up twenty people," Derek says as I walk in.

"What?"

He's sitting at my desk holding a pen. "In your seminar. Twenty people from the one company."

"What?"

I'm gazing at him like an idiot. Is all this really happening?

"Your phone kept ringing so I used my initiative – and my key."

Twenty people. From the one company. As I readjust my world view from three thousand back to twenty, Derek vacates my chair so I can collapse into it. His face says it all. He knows how important these enrolments are. He's been with me all the way.

"Twenty? That's..." I nearly say magic, "...awesome."

"They just need a special price for twenty."

"Sure. Of course. But how did you do it, DD? Twenty! Did you have to use any...tricks?"

Derek hates marketing ploys although he knows most of them. He would have played it straight. But how did he manage to land twenty when after all these weeks I haven't got even one?

"That's just it. The guy's a property developer. Oliver Katsuya."

"Japanese."

"Yeah. And a real tough bastard by the sound of him. So I wasn't about to talk him into anything. He wanted to speak to you personally but when I said you were at a business lunch he condescended to speak to your minion. He wants to put his staff through a goals program and he's already decided Goals for Gold is the one – if you give him a discount for twenty, he was insistent on that. So it was nothing to do with me. I just took the call."

"It must be the website." Not that it's worked with

anyone else.

"I said you'd call him back with a group discount. He'll probably try to screw you."

"You bet. I'd be suspicious if he didn't."

Derek moves towards the door. "There's just one thing."

"What? A catch?" Please don't let there be a catch.

"Maybe. And you're not going to like it."

"Look, DD, you've just handed me my first seminar. The whole audience. After three months of banging my head against the nearest wall. I haven't even thanked you yet so don't spoil it."

He hesitates. "Something doesn't feel right. About Katsuya."

"Out with it."

"I don't trust him. The guy's...a shark. And you're a minnow. He could tear you to shreds."

"But I want those twenty enrolments." I tell him about Sloane. "It's a perfect coincidence, DD. Don't ruin it with premonitions."

He sighs. "It must be destiny."

Derek leaves and I look at the note he made. Oliver Katsuya from Skape, both names I don't recognise. After a few pencil calculations I pick up the phone and Oliver Katsuya takes my call. A self-made man with an American accent and an edge to his voice, a man used to getting his own way. I imagine a mature unlined face with a mean mouth and a heavy gold bracelet at the wrist. I don't bother to schmooze him.

He goes in hard on every point – timing, price, content, quantity. Just as well I've just had lunch with Guy because Katsuya is small fry compared to Sloane. At first I knock off five per cent, then ten, but in the end I let him beat me down another two thousand dollars to seal the deal. A drop in the ocean.

"Your website boasts about a money-back guarantee," he says.

"Correct. If I don't deliver the course I've promised I refund the unhappy participant, no questions asked."

"I'll need that in writing."

"And I'll need full payment in advance."

Thirty-four thousand dollars. Not as much as it sounds, with the overheads for this cupboard of an office, plus Moonshine has to pay me back for the website and three months of unpaid work, then there's my loan from Dad.

But this win isn't only about money. It's about arriving.

As I flick to my bank account, hoping to see the payment come through, Derek texts from next door: *Time to celebrate.*

But I've got work to do. Because now I've booked twenty people, an outline isn't enough. It will take days to create all the activities and case studies. Weeks. And if Sloane and the guru thing turns out to be a delusion it's still big – my first seminar. When I was on the marketing team for the telco, I ran hundreds of in-house seminars for staff. But this is different.

This is mine.

For the next couple of hours I immerse myself in the seminar, dredging through past experiences for practical exercises and case studies, anything that brings goal-setting to life in real ways. It's something I've always been gifted at – creating educational experiences that work. A mix of teacher training and a love of commerce and marketing landed me my first corporate training job and it grew from there.

When Derek knocks on my door, I'm surprised at the

time.

"It's after five," he says. "You've been hard at it all afternoon. What happened to celebrating?"

"A *mai tai* at the Lava Flow?"

But he's got other ideas. "A haircut. A fresh new look for the successful you."

"I've had this style since I was sixteen, DD."

"Exactly. And don't tell me, Andrew never let you cut it."

"How did you guess?"

"I've seen how he operates. It's a girl's style, it keeps you naive. Perfect for his control agenda. But you've shed his shackles, so embrace your womanly power."

I laugh. Derek turns everything into a psychodrama. He's already lined up his friend Jerome, who's opened a frock salon called House of Knaves but still does hair on the side for friends. Jerome can fit me in this evening.

House of Knaves is tucked away behind a humble shopfront in Chinatown. I retrace my steps from a few hours ago and dodge the local pedestrian traffic. Merchants and customers in baggy garments and *rubbah slippahs* push trolleys backwards and forwards from illegally parked trucks. Just a few doors past the *muu-muu* factory I knock on an unmarked blue door.

When it opens, the interior swallows me up and I'm standing in a Roman ruin.

Concealed lights illuminate fading frescoes and crumbling pillars. Vines crawl through niches, and faux mosaics lie unfinished at my feet. On the back wall a trompe l'oeil window overlooks a virtual courtyard where the Mediterranean sun always shines. Derek prepared me for Jerome's creative masterpiece but now that I'm here a strange emotion is rising in my throat. A kind of longing I've never felt before. It's making me wander about like a blind person touching things.

Jerome must be used to this reaction. He leaves me to explore for a while before guiding me to a large mirror fragment opposite a real chair.

"What are we having?" He throws a cape over my shoulders. "A new look, Derek said." He grabs my fringe and flips it back so we're both staring at my bare forehead. "Like this."

I flinch. "What? No fringe?"

"You've got the face for it. Look."

But when my naked face looks back at me, the woman from the mirror flashes through my mind. What was it about her eyes that's haunting me? But I'm hallucinating. The face in the mirror is my own.

"With these bangs," Jerome is saying, "you're stuck with half your face covered."

"But I've always had a fringe."

"*Always* is a word we shun in hairdressing. Along with *never*."

"I wouldn't feel like...myself."

He smirks, turning his expression from sleepy to cheeky. "Which self is that then?"

I try for an eye-roll but the man in the mirror is immune to nuance. "The self I've been for thirty-four years. Me."

"Since the womb then. Born with bangs firmly in place like a birthmark." He winks. "And ever since you've been hiding, hiding, hiding. A fawn peering through the foliage. After thirty-four years, Selkie, it's time...to grow up."

This must have come from Derek. Because as a psychologist Jerome doesn't look the part. Mouse-brown hair falls to his waist like a bridal veil, and his jeans and shirt-tails make him look like a folk singer stranded in the seventies.

Without further discussion he sprays my hair with water and picks up his scissors. Then in one slice of the blades a good six inches disappears off the back of my hair. What?

"First we bring the two lengths closer together," he says.

I shut my eyes but in my mind I can see my precious locks poking out between Jerome's bare toes. Tiny tears leak down my cheeks as he trims each straight black strand into a textured edge that tickles the base of my neck. Then he starts on the fringe. Snip, snip, snip.

When he's done, he rubs something sticky through it, then waits. But it's a while before I can open my eyes and face the woman in the mirror. Another woman with a fierce-eyed look. This one has a fringe but it's feathered back to almost nothing and continues right across her head in a crazy headdress. Behind her ears, textured strands poke out, and when Jerome holds up the hand-mirror there's something untamed about the way her hair flies out from the back of her head. The woman looks nothing like me. For a start she's...wilder.

"Magic," Jerome says.

The woman stares back as if she's desperate to bring us together. Meanwhile I'm freaking out about whether there's room for both of us inside my skin.

Jerome removes the cape and brushes my neck with a hand-broom. He hands me a pot of product and says, "On the house."

In a kind of stupor I navigate towards the door between the racks of frocks. Jerome markets his creations to big guys who can't buy their frocks from women's stores – not the right size or shape and not nearly enough bling. As the feathers and flounces rustle against my pencil skirt I understand what's happened. Jerome's given me a haircut as outrageous as one of his frocks.

Outside, I remind myself it's just a haircut, a fresh new look to match my fresh new life. But my hair is thick and without its usual weight I'm light-headed. This is what it feels like to come out into the open. Jerome was right about that – there's nowhere to hide.

As if to confirm it, my phone chirps with a text from Andrew. *If you keep ignoring me, I can play dirty.*

In desperate need of comfort food, I walk to the Pearl and find it empty. That's unusual. And as I step inside it feels like I've entered some kind of time warp – a strange space separated from the hubbub just outside. The shadows feel heavy with portent and the ceiling fans slice the air like they're stirring treacle. I try to shake it off but the sensation remains.

Suzi comes out from the kitchen, blinks at me, blinks again, puts her hand over her mouth, turns and runs back through the curtain. As if she's seen a ghost.

I turn around to see if anyone's come in behind me but there's no-one there. It must be my hair. I know it's different, but is it...alarming?

"It's me," I call, my voice echoing off the concrete floor. "Selkie."

Silence. As if she was never there, but the curtain of plastic strips is moving.

"I just want the special," I say, feeling uneasy.

Now Suzi is peeping out. "Eugene not here."

I try grinning but she isn't grinning back. "You can cook it, can't you?"

It's a moment before she answers. "I cook." She sounds relieved, as if I might be here for some other reason.

But this is the Pearl, a humble noodle bar in Chinatown. Unless they're doing the I Ching on the side. I imagine Eugene's round solemn face reading horoscopes. By contrast, Suzi is rake thin and a bit skittish.

I take a seat, and after some hissing and scraping from the kitchen she slips back still looking spooked. She refuses to make eye contact as she shoves a container across the counter.

"But I want to eat here," I say.

"Eugene back later," she says. "You talk him."

Then she's gone again, but as I retrieve the takeaway she's peering back through the curtain like – Jerome's words come back to me - a fawn peering through the foliage. It must be catching, because after leaving the money on the counter I back out, strangely reluctant to turn my back on her. Her eyes are bright as if she's taken something. She's never been like this before.

***

When I get home I drench my hair, trying to take control, but the cut defies any taming. A lump of Jerome's product - slime green and labelled 'seaweed' - only makes it worse. In desperation I decide to go for a run. To shake off Suzi's odd behaviour and the feeling that my hair is no longer my own.

I'm not much of a runner and I always avoid the beachfront and the track around Diamond Head. Instead there's a path along the Ala Wai Canal. As I pound the pavement outriggers paddle beside me - giant beetles stroking the mirrored surface - and the feeling of longing returns. It stays with me all the way back to the flat.

I'm trudging up the stairs when Wanda overtakes me on her long legs. She's wearing the usual - crop-top, cut-offs and toe-capped boots.

"Carrying the cares of the world?" she asks. "It's easier if you leave them at the bottom."

"Just tired, but I'm glad to see you."

"Well, I'm just going to eat and run, not do any bonding."

We laugh as we take off our shoes and go inside.

"I like your hair," she says.

It's a better reaction than Suzi's. "Why?"

"It's...dangerous."

Like her own. Barely longer than stubble and always swathed in a coloured sweatband, her haircut leaves her face totally uncovered. I decide not to tell her it was Jerome who was the dangerous one, leaving me to feel confused and angry. Or to live up to it.

***

After a dreamless sleep I stumble into the bathroom where the cabinet mirror makes me jump. I've been dreading the return of the woman, but my own face is scary enough. My hair has always been straight and black, but this morning there are silver threads. Has the shock sent me grey overnight?

The headless Doris can't sympathise and we don't have a full-length mirror to show how incongruous it looks. It's ironic that I green-bagged my wardrobe before I left Sydney to create a 'boardroom look' – two identical suits, so there's one to wear and one at the cleaners – never dreaming that a hair stylist could demolish it in one mad cutting spree.

At the bus stop Coral is dazzling in a fresh *muu-muu* – tangerine and black. She beams and makes a scissors sign with her hand. But when I get off downtown I catch glimpses in windows of my new style statement – 'boardroom banshee' – and reach the coffee cart in a state of near despair. As I cringe under the shade sail, wishing I'd borrowed Doris's hat, I decide to reject my usual skinny decaf in favour of a triple shot with extra cream.

Curtis, the barista, raises his eyebrow but he's too polite to probe. Then he looks at me as if he's seeing me for the first time.

"Funky." He hands me my mug.

"Spiky, you mean. To match my personality transplant."

When Derek arrives at the office suspiciously early he pulls me out of my chair and spins me around in a ridiculous pirouette.

"Now I'm as dizzy as I look," I complain.

"Trust Jerome to make a statement. It makes you look..."

"What?" If he says quirky, I may have to kill him.

"Quirky."

He ducks before I can pick up a missile.

"What do you really think, DD? And be polite. At the moment I just feel...violated."

"OK. Here's the truth." He stands back and takes a deep breath. "It's wild. So it makes you look...more like yourself."

He's definitely in league with Jerome. "Like I've been someone else all these years?"

"Someone...called Elkie?"

This is what I get for spilling my secrets to Derek. Selkie is the name my mother gave me. Just one of her extraordinary ideas, according to Stella - naming me after a fairytale, calling me a mermaid, which became a family joke with my mounting aquaphobia. But after a showdown with Stella when I was sixteen - a huge clash that left me reeling - she renamed me Elkie. Just like that. From that moment on she refused to call me Selkie. Andrew was new on the scene and thought Elkie was sexier, and suddenly I was someone else.

When I tried for the green card I used the name on my birth certificate. I still remember how rebellious it felt to change it back. An act of defiance that matched my dream of escape. Everyone in Hawaii calls me Selkie. My real name.

"OK," I say to Derek. "A crazy coif to match my nutty name. But it makes this business suit look...pompous. I may have to resort to a *muu-muu*." And move into a bus shelter.

There's plenty of work to distract me as I toil away at Goals for Gold. At day's end, I even feel satisfied as Derek and I leave the building together. He's busy tonight so we part on the street, but as he walks towards the parking basement I get the feeling I'm not alone. There are plenty of people about, leaving office towers, spilling out of bars, promenading in Aloha shirts in the tropical dusk, but this feels more like a shadow.

I look over my left shoulder, thinking I see something out of the corner of my eye.

But it's just the space where my hair used to be.

Chapter

Five

The odd sensation follows me home. Another text arrives from Andrew. I shouldn't read it but I can't help myself. Each missive is like watching a grown man implode.

This time he's been inspired to write a schoolyard taunt: *Selkie Moon. Barren womb.*

I stare at the words feeling sick. It's alarming how cruel he's become, the man I married. I remember his blue eyes, the way his moody looks always reeled me back when I knew I should run, all the times I ached to leave but felt impotent.

And I've been waiting for this. It's one of the reasons I had to get out. His mounting anger at my childlessness. He wanted a baby and when it didn't happen I wasn't the woman he expected me to be. And unless I go back, his fantasy of a perfect family is in tatters.

I climb the stairs to find a FedEx parcel waiting on my bed. Wanda signed for it before she went out. It's from Andrew. How does he know where I live?

My first impulse is to shove it in the bin but it's probably something I need to see. With a heavy heart I find some scissors and cut it open, then gape at the document inside. Divorce papers. What? We haven't been separated long enough, it has to be a year. Then I see the words he's printed where my name should be:

Desiccated Spinster.

The bastard. My hands start shaking and the words blur. I make it to the bathroom just in time to puke. On and on it goes, my gorge rising, my body convulsing with primal instincts so deep they're way beyond throwing up. Am I dying?

When there's nothing left I drag myself to the basin and try to rinse the revulsion away.

But that isn't the end of it.

As Andrew's barb stabs me again I shred the document, but it's not enough. A gibbering version of me starts racing around the flat. Covers come off my bed, pillows sail across the room. I pull out my little red suitcase and throw its contents everywhere. Even Wanda's things aren't safe. Her bedding ends up on the floor along with anything draped on Doris. I can't undo the knot on her hula skirt, so Doris gets a shove that sends her feet into the air. The clothes on the back of the door go flying, followed by Wanda's vampire novels. Her found friends seem to duck but not soon enough. The Buddha hits the floor and the parrot somersaults onto the bed. In the bathroom I unravel yards of toilet paper and hurl towels into the bath. Just as well Tutu's mirror is gone, as my fury spirals out of control. At the bathroom cabinet a mad woman glares at me and the words of others come back. *Wild. Dangerous.* You bet.

In the kitchenette, I'm about to launch the first plate, when the phone rings.

"Hello," I say, sounding eerily calm.

My sister isn't fooled.

"Selkie, it's Gretel. Are you OK?"

At the sound of her voice I burst into tears. She's used to this and lets me cry. When we were children I cried myself to sleep most nights. Gretel would climb in beside me, then fall asleep herself, so I'd get into her bed. After finding us in opposite beds too often Stella accused me of subverting Gretel and banned it.

Eventually I can speak. "Sorry, Gret. I ignore you for three months, then greet you like this."

"Good timing, I reckon. What's happened?"

I fill her in on Andrew's abuse, culminating in his spiteful document. I leave out the mayhem he's caused to Wanda's flat.

"I didn't think he'd give you up quietly. He's got too much invested in keeping you handcuffed to his arm. Elkie, the trophy wife, beautiful and devoted. Or else." Gretel's never said a word against Andrew and her venom is a surprise. "There's no way you'd go back to him, is there?"

"I hope not. It took me eighteen years to get out of there. But he's messing with my mind as hard as he can go. He knows the words that hurt."

"Plenty of practice. But don't take it personally. He's tamed you before, so he's being lazy. Getting you back in the corral is easier than breaking in someone new."

I laugh. Even though Gretel's younger she's always had more wisdom.

"So it's a waiting game?" I say.

"Pretty much. And I've got my money on you."

"Thanks, Gret. I'll phone you if I need another pep talk. Promise." I find a fallen pillow and lean back against a wall. "How about you? Sorry I haven't called but I've been following Barry's pics of the bump." And dreading the ones he'll post during the birth.

"Yeah, I'm in danger of being mistaken for a beached whale. And there's still four weeks to go."

"You're sure it isn't twins?"

"Just the one, and the ultrasound looks like a girl. Mum's got her heart set on it. Courtney."

Textbook Stella. "You and Barry might want to name her yourselves."

"We like Tayla. You can imagine Mum's reaction." She mimics Stella: "It's a *surname*, for goodness sake."

"And a fish. A bit like Selkie. No wonder she hates it if it reminds her of me."

Gretel doesn't laugh. "I know you think she hates you, and I used to think so too, but she's been so weird since you left. It sounds crazy but she seems...lost."

"Lost without someone to blame for everything. Prunella's wayward offspring, the family scapegoat."

"It doesn't look like that, Selkie, really it doesn't." Gretel never called me Elkie. "She told me she phoned you."

"To get my address."

"To hear your voice, I reckon. Make sure you're OK. Don't laugh but I think she's...worried about you."

I do laugh. "Well, let her worry. Except for Andrew, everything's fine."

"Really? I can see right through your updates, you know. All those *mai tais* on the *lanais*. Tell me the truth. Is it working out?"

"Just beginning to." I tell her about the Skape seminar.

"That takes care of survival,' she says. "But what about everything else? Have you met a man who adores you yet?"

"How could I? Barry's the last of that species and he's blown his chances by getting my sister pregnant."

She laughs. "By the way, I'm hoping you'll come back when Tayla's born. If you can spare a few days. Think about it."

"Don't ask me to mop your brow. Childbirth terrifies me."

"In a way we're both giving birth to new life."

"How do you figure that?"

"Andrew did his best to suck you dry. Now you're re-birthing...your own soul."

"Help, I need an epidural!"

"Just don't leap into the arms of the next total jerk. Leave room for a rare one to turn up. You don't want kids so there's no hurry, is there?"

I swallow. "No hurry at all."

Gretel's call has grounded me and I open a bottle of wine. But as I survey the carnage around me, I can't get our conversation out of my mind. I adore Gretel and I'm glad she's having the baby she's always wanted, but her talk about birthing has unsettled me. 'Re-birthing my own soul'? It might be a poetic way to describe my mad dash for freedom, but it's at odds with my rage and exhaustion, and it feels like added pressure to create something meaningful. First I've got to get Moonshine off the ground. And Andrew off my back. And after his power plays, the thought of 'a man who adores me' has me gasping for air.

And why does Gretel want me there at the crib-side? Selkie the outsider, hovering like the banished fairy godmother, intruding on the happy family scene.

Stella. Andrew got my address from Stella. He knows none of my new friends so it has to be her. She never liked Andrew because he wrested control of my life from her. But leaving him was selfish too. 'Just like your mother.' Then there was my biological clock ticking away, while Gretel was settling down with Barry the respectable doctor and planning when to get pregnant.

When I told Stella about Hawaii she was beside herself. Now Andrew's manipulated her to get the information he wants, information that's none of his business.

Fuelled by another wave of anger, I begin the clean-up of the flat.

***

A phone is ringing. A candle is flickering. The wall of darkness shatters and the flame escapes along a crooked path. The phone goes through to voicemail then starts up again, while the flame disappears in a silent hiss.

When I open my eyes, last night comes back in living colour. I pick up the phone and Derek's in my ear.

"At last. Have we got a Saturday planned for you."

"DD, I've just woken up. And since when are you up at this hour?"

"Ten o'clock? You must have had a big night."

"Yeah." If he hears about it he'll never shut up.

"We're taking you to the Swap Meet. Estate jewellery, knock-off designer stuff, handmade crafts. Have you been there yet?"

It's where Wanda sells her fish. "No. What have you got in mind?"

"Well...you're in the land of florals and flip-flops. And your haircut doesn't work with your power suits..."

"I won't ditch them to match a free haircut, DD." A haircut planned by him.

"I know. Let me finish. You need something Hawaiian for your neck. That would work. And Nigel's got good taste."

Nigel. Saint Nigel by all accounts, Derek's new partner. In a matter of weeks Derek seems to have settled down, and I've been dying to meet the man responsible for the transformation.

"OK. Give me an hour."

When I step out of the shower the phone's ringing again.

"I'm cooking a curry," a voice says. A voice I know.

It takes a moment for my mind to focus. Roger Nightingale is calling me after all these weeks of silence. We met in a bar soon after I arrived and even though he isn't my type neediness drove me into his bed. Then his ex-girlfriend turned up looking for a place to crash and I got sidelined.

"What about Sheena?" I ask.

"Gone to Maui."

"Sounds expensive. Or is this the next leg of her shag-your-way-round-the-world tour?"

He sighs loudly. "Listen to you, Miss Lunatic. Sheena was homeless. I'd have done the same for you, hmmm?" And any other attractive woman in Honolulu. "But you'd already found what's her name."

"Wanda Kadisha Mahala Yavenna Ziegler."

Wanda's name makes most people pause, but not Roger. "And a flat in Waikiki no less. Now, in spite of your grumpy demeanour this morning, I'm offering you dinner. Then, if you're good, a little excursion tomorrow. To the cemetery."

I laugh. "Dinner and the cemetery."

"I have a proclivity for graveyards, you know."

"I'm not sure I'm up for that much fun."

"Very droll. All those angles and textures and shadows." Roger's a sometimes photographer. "Not to mention," he drops his voice to a whisper, "the...inhabitants."

"You can't frighten me with spiders, Roj."

"More than spiders. You'd be surprised who you meet. Around here the interface between the living and the dead...wavers."

It's what Wanda said about the mirror when we were talking about the woman. I wish I could forget about her.

To rub it in, Roger lapses into the local pidgin. "Da

kapa cloth stay thin between their world an ours, an da gods come close for look, see what we stay doin', li' dat."

Roger adores his crazy voices but it's the first time he's gone superstitious on me. *The gods come close to watch us.* Is that what the woman was doing? It's six days now and without the mirror she hasn't been back. But this has got nothing to do with her. Roger's an expert at window-dressing. He isn't even Hawaiian, he's English. He's just trying to divert me from his blatant need for a shag-buddy. And after Andrew's little parcel I'm tempted.

"I'll think about it," I say.

"You're a *déesse*, Miss Moon, but a difficult one."

"A dee...ess?" Does he mean a desiccated spinster?

"*Ma petite déesse*, my little goddess." French accent. "Why do I persist with you, hmmm?"

"Persist?" I laugh. "Your idea of persistence, Roj, is my idea of neglect."

"Opposites. See? No wonder we get on so swimmingly."

CHAPTER
Six

Derek's holding a shell up to my neck and Nigel is nodding.

"Perfect," Nigel says.

"I'm not sure," I say, as if anyone's listening.

Since it's the first time I've met Nigel I don't want to push too hard. And he's a seven-foot beanpole with a shaved head, the kind of presentation that makes people my size polite.

It's the Aloha Stadium Swap Meet where the whole island seems to have a stall. Luckily we haven't seen Wanda because the boys might blurt out the truth about her handicrafts. Sure to, judging by the way they've been riding roughshod over my opinions all morning.

We've been here for a couple of hours looking for a decoration for my neck and when we first arrived I was overcome by the longing again – to find something special, something to call my own. But I've tried on dozens of necklaces and pendants that weren't 'right' according to my new style team.

"It has to be Hawaiian," Derek said.

At least we agree on that.

"And 'interesting'," Nigel said.

Not 'quirky', thank God.

It's hot on the tarmac and I'm feeling like a shrivelled pawpaw. We've drunk the fresh pineapple, orange and guava juice (POG). We've had the shave ice. Twice. Now all I need is a *muu-muu* – or this shell – and my indoctrination will be complete.

"It's not just any shell," Derek says, as if we don't have shells where I come from.

Maybe he's confusing Australia with Austria – all that yodelling and skiing and not an ocean in sight.

"It's a *cowry* shell."

It's gorgeous, for sure. Flawless white like bone china, with a sprinkling of large black freckles. And it's huge, the size of a duck egg, with two holes already drilled in the lips at one end so it just needs a cord. It would make a statement at my neck like nothing else could, but when Nigel holds it up to my ear I realise I can't wear the sound of the sea around my neck like a concrete collar.

I start hyperventilating.

"It must be the heat," Nigel says. "DD, a bottle of water."

Derek disappears and Nigel sits me down on the bench under the stallholder's umbrella. The wizened Chinese woman moves over reluctantly. Her table is laden with the most amazing shells and Nigel starts naming them. I try to close out the information, especially about the poisonous ones. The sea is scary enough without contemplating its deadly inhabitants.

My eyes wander over to the next stall where a woman – a stunning redhead with cascading curls – is doing a line in fashion garments. They're laid out on tables, draped over wire mannequins and on hangers on a mobile rack. Lots of skinny shapes, stunning colours and animal prints. No florals.

As Nigel waves the cowry shell, the redhead looks at me with green eyes that seem to know everything.

Then she leans over and whispers in an Irish accent, "I can make you something stunning, you know, to go with that shell."

Great. Three against one.

What am I going to do? Derek and Nigel have invested too much in this expedition to take no for an answer. But if I buy the shell just to shut them up I'll have to wear it or never hear the end of it. And if I don't buy it, they'll buy it for me and I'll still have to wear it. Better if I buy it myself – less obligation, more control. And I can hide it away before it can ever get turned into something wearable.

I hand over the cash and the Chinese woman wraps the shell in tissue paper.

Derek returns with the water and Nigel makes me finish the whole bottle. Then the redhead leans over and gives me her card.

Davina Kennedy, Designer.

"I have a shop in Kailua," she says.

It's the beach where Derek and Nigel go. On the windward side. Do they know her? But Kailua is a big place.

"All my garments are contemporary and original. Handmade. For you, something slinky, I think…"

I look at her and she seems to read my mind.

"No *muu-muus*," she says.

Derek and Nigel laugh.

It's out of their way but the boys insist on driving me home.

"I know just the cord it needs," Nigel says. "Macramé…"

I take a deep breath. "You've both done enough already. Really. Thank you."

I expect an interjection from Derek, but they take the hint. They ask me about the rest of my weekend and I forget about Derek's opinion of Roger and tell them my plans. 'Curry and coitus' at Roj's place – he adores alliteration – followed in the morning by the trip to the cemetery.

Derek's reaction is fierce. "What? You're going to spend

the night with him after the way he's left you out in the cold all these weeks? That's your pattern, isn't it, Selkie? Sleeping with predators. First Andrew, now Nightingale."

Derek's styled himself as my guardian angel but he cares too much. "Roger's nothing like Andrew. For a start he's charming. And funny."

"They're both attracted by your light. Then they snuff it out."

"I just need some male company with no strings attached. What's wrong with that?"

"No such thing," Derek says. "Ditch him, Selkie. You won't find the right man till you do."

That's how he found Nigel, only a matter of weeks ago. Right after he stopped sleeping around and decided to be alone. "I turned into a whole person," he told me at the time. "Half a person looking for another half a person – the first rift and, bam, you fall over. But Nigel's a whole person so we could *see* each other."

Now Derek's an expert on love.

***

With the cowry shell stashed in a shoebox under the bed, I throw a few things into my little red suitcase. Then on the bus I get to act like a tourist and in a way I am. Thanks to Oliver Katsuya and my new bank balance I can forget about Moonshine for the whole weekend.

Roger lives on the eastern edge of Chinatown. I walk the scenic route past the YWCA and Iolani Palace. The area's a magnet for tourists but the sprawling gardens create a feeling of space in this congested city. Along the way, drinkers spill out of watering holes and my tight jeans turn a few heads.

From Fort Street Mall, I take a left into Pauahi Street. Between a bail bond shop and a pho café a bamboo gate opens onto a path that leads to the Spanish-style building where Roger lives. It was once a grand residence by the look of it, set well back in its own grounds, with tall windows of tiny coloured panes and Juliet balconies on the upper floor. Just a few blocks from downtown, it reflects the former heart of this city. The outside staircases must have been added when the place was converted into flats.

I stop for a moment at the entrance to the path, where I've loitered a couple of times in the past few months, hoping to catch a glimpse of Sheena. Pathetic but true.

Roger likes to boast about the brothel downstairs. Men are waiting outside, alone or in small groups, many of them Japanese. With their Aloha shirts and feigned casualness, they're trying to suggest that a brothel visit is just part of the vacation. As I walk the length of the path every eye is upon me.

I climb the stairs and knock. Roger appears wearing a ridiculous floral robe that shows off his legs to their full disadvantage. Hirsute toothpicks.

"A going-away present from Sheena," he informs me when I laugh.

I don't want to hear about her but I try to keep it light. "Don't the English dress for dinner, even in the tropics?"

"My smoking jacket. Very Gatsby, hmmm?"

"Please take it off."

He complies, dropping it to the floor to reveal his naked self underneath. Someone catcalls from the courtyard.

Roger looks at my folded arms. "I trust you're not going to get boring about Sheena."

"Only if you put that thing back on."

He disappears inside and returns in jeans and an Aloha shirt. Now he looks like the men downstairs. I follow him through the short entrance hall and into the kitchen where saucepans are bubbling on an old stove. He calls it 'Roj's nosh'.

"Smells great," I say. "I'm starving."

"A hungry woman is one of life's gifts."

I leave him to the cooking and wander around the living room, letting my anger about Sheena subside. I've been here before but last time I mainly saw the underside of his sheets. The room is spacious with high ceilings and a sunroom beyond. Slivers of light pierce the coloured glass and make patterns on the parquetry floor. On the coffee table there are three cameras. State-of-the-art SLRs.

It's a charming space but it's almost bare. Odd armchairs in retro patterns, no floor rug, an old bookshelf stacked with airport novels. Along one wall there's a lonely chair beside a floor lamp. It makes Wanda's place with its beaming fish look homely. On one wall a couple of framed photographs show moody graveyard scenes. So he wasn't making it up, he likes cemeteries.

But where are the nudes? All his ex-girlfriends? Roger hinted at a stash when he asked me to pose. It was his opening line as he rushed across the bar that first night like a talent scout. No chance. But in spite of his puny English looks, his zany energy turned me on.

In the sunroom there's a filing cabinet, but before I can snoop Roger calls me back to the kitchen. He's opened a bottle of white and I join him at the table that looks like a reject from the 1950s. He's certainly spent nothing on decorating this place. Maybe it all goes on cameras.

We talk about safe things, like wine. About how the region affects a wine's character. When I mention my

Chilean wine he tells me the story about the lost French Carménère grape, how it was rediscovered in Chile in the 1990s after being mistaken for Merlot for over a century. This is more like it. My prickliness thaws.

"Is there a local wine?" I ask.

"On Maui. But their vintage is small. It's mostly imported."

"No wonder the good stuff's expensive."

My budget means I'm always drinking at the bottom end of the market. And in spite of his knowledge, the chardonnay Roger's opened is an Australian label that's captured the international market with an under-ten-dollar price tag. I never buy it on principle but he's probably chosen it to make me feel at home.

He serves the curry and it's excellent. Chicken – in a cashew and spinach sauce. Yoghurt – the first syllable rhyming with 'dog' in Roger-speak. Potatoes – roasted dry in a coating of real spices. Pappadams. Saffron rice.

"Tell me about tomorrow," I say. "Is it a special occasion?"

"A competition. For serious photographers. Called...*Life and Death*."

A topic that might be haunting me. "Isn't a cemetery a bit...obvious?"

"Only to an amateur. It's the artist's job to accentuate the drama. Transmute the ambience into something...palpable. A solitary gravestone against the horizon...signifying the folly of man's struggle against nature. That kind of thing."

"Right." Roger can be a tad pretentious. "So why do you want me along?"

"Isn't it *obvious*?" he mimics. "I need someone pretty to carry my bags. And waggle her excellent buttocks occasionally."

"I want to take photos too."

He laughs. "You know sweet FA about photography."

"I took a class at school. I take photos with my phone. It's fun."

He rolls his eyes. "*Ma petite déesse*, this isn't about fun. It's a contest for serious talent. And that involves something that can't be taught, at school or anywhere else. *Flair.* You've either got it or you haven't."

"I might have it." I fold my arms. It worked on the landing. "I'm only going tomorrow if you lend me a camera."

He sighs. "All right. You can borrow an old digital. It will do for your...happy snaps."

"Fine. Since gravestones don't move, I'll probably manage. But what if I fluke a better shot than you? How do I enter the competition?"

"Let's not even countenance the hypothetical, hmmm?" He gets up and walks to the stove. "More nosh?"

Afterwards he makes a fuss of my hair and I let him pose me on the chair in the sunroom for some anonymous shots of the back of my head.

"Such a beautiful neck," he cries. "And these shoulders..." He pulls at my shirt to reveal bare skin. "Now turn so I get the curve of your cheek."

He promises to put me in a hair magazine he's designing but I'm sure he's just a master of schmooze.

We drink a bit more wine, and when we end up in the bedroom Roger shows me that he hasn't lost his touch. After years with Andrew he's my first lover and under his fingers my troubles dissolve into pleasure. It's just what I need, to forget the woman and the threats from Andrew, to escape into mindless rapture.

CHAPTER
Seven

It's still the middle of the night when Roger throws me out of bed and into the car along with his cameras. Except he handles the cameras with care.

"Hey? What about breakfast?" I say. "Don't expect me to create on an empty stomach."

He laughs. "We're going to capture the dawn, Miss Sun." During the night it was 'Miss Heavenly Body', more than once. "Then later, if you're good, we'll have a picnic. I've even bought a new rug."

"A picnic rug? How terribly English. A picnic in the cemetery. Brilliant, Roj."

"Sandwiches in the Sandwich Islands. It has a certain poetry, hmmm?"

"And if we die of starvation, we'll be right at home."

As the car creeps down the back lane – so as not to disturb the slumber of the working girls downstairs – he soothes me with details of the contents of the cooler-bag: cheese, tomatoes, salami. We stop at a Vietnamese bakery to pick up some baguettes. It's the only place open and it's full of working girls not yet slumbering. They're busy in their own huddle and I beat them to the last sticky pastry filled with strawberries.

Soon we're racing down the Pali Highway with the windows down. There's something primal about the open road under your wheels, the mist blanketing the mountains, the wind in your hair. The approaching dawn gradually turns the sky indigo, then violet, then palest citrus, but night-time clings to the ferns and the damp scent of jasmine and ginger invades my nostrils.

"Weather to die for," I say, "and you want to celebrate it in the bone orchard. Get a life, Roj."

That just about exhausts my cemetery jokes but Roger isn't taking the bait. The artist is incubating his flair. And he still won't tell me where the cemetery is. All I know is we're heading east, leaving Honolulu far behind.

Eventually we approach the sign to Kailua Bay and I think of Nigel and Derek, and Davina Kennedy. The city sprawls beneath us, a crisscross of coastal homes hugging the curve of the beach. But we're not going into Kailua. Instead we turn right, heading south. After a few miles Roger turns east again onto a dirt track and we bump along through dense foliage, which gives no hint of where we are.

Suddenly the track dwindles into a grassy verge and Roger parks. With camera bags and the cooler slung over our shoulders, he leads the way down a narrow path, under a stone arch and through a ring of palm trees until the cemetery's spreading out before us – an enclave of neglected slabs and headstones reaching up through a tangle of vines.

Then at the furthest edge I see it.

A cliff.

And beyond the cliff, waves. Erupting in fitful gusts.

The Pacific Ocean.

Roger doesn't know about my phobia. I've never told him. And it's too late to tell him now.

He starts setting up his tripod while I fight a strange urge to rush to the cliff and look over. It's always like this when I confront the sea. A kind of hunger overcomes me, a macabre attraction for the dark depths that inhabit my dreams. In the predawn chill I give myself a bear hug and do the only thing possible – I turn my back on the sea.

When I join Roger, he's got other ideas. "Run along and leave the art to the experts."

But I've already decided on a nice safe job. "I'll mind the cooler-bag."

He gives me a suspicious glare. "Over my dead body. Pardon the pun. We'll stash it somewhere safe." He looks around. "Under that angel. Where I'll see you if you attempt a raid, hmmm?"

The angel's expression is suitably fierce. Roger tucks the cooler out of sight before handing over his oldest digital camera. He'll be switching between film and digital, then later we'll develop some 'real photographs' in his bathroom/darkroom. At least that part will be fun. Now he's on his eternal search for the perfect shot, leaving me alone.

I watch him for a while as he gazes around, tilting his head like a stork. It stops me looking towards the sea. But I can hear it, battering the rocks, over and over.

Eventually I pick up the camera. I need the distraction. But not gravestones or angels. There must be some living things around here.

I perch on a low stone wall and watch the entrance for signs of life. If there are houses nearby, there'll be people out for a Sunday stroll. A runner doing circuits or some lovers snatching a few moments of privacy. But there's no-one.

And I refuse to photograph Roger.

I take close-ups of vines and flowers. Spiders. A small tree laden with star fruit. I even play around with focus and composition just to show Roger my artistic side. The star fruit keep my hunger at bay, but the thundering sea never leaves my consciousness.

Then a dog scampers up from nowhere and piddles

against an epitaph. I manage to get three shots in sequence and might just enter them in the competition - a triptych: *Pissing on Death.* Except Roger will no doubt veto it. *Sans flair.*

When I look around the man himself is standing under our angel, waving.

"Picnic time! Please admire my new rug." He swirls it about him toreador-style.

"Why are picnic rugs always tartan?" I ask.

He wraps it around his waist like a bath towel. "Because they make excellent impromptu kilts."

I giggle. As he spreads out the rug and unfolds his limbs across it, I feel a surge of affection for him. I prefer men with more body but Roger's like a teddy bear that's missing a bit of stuffing.

We dive into the cooler and pull out the makings of lunch. He's even brought two beers and they're icy cold.

I sink my teeth into a bread roll. "Are we done here yet?"

Roger shakes his head. "Inspired by Monet and his haystacks I'm going to undertake - pardon the pun - a series of shots from the same spot evolving with the light. Is there a full moon tonight?"

Tonight? "Roger, I've had enough."

"Suit yourself."

I almost choke on a mouthful. "I can't do that. How would I get home from here?"

"Not my problem." He shrugs. "Wait in the car then."

"Fine."

Anger makes me run. It's the healthiest emotion I've felt all morning. I toss away my sandwich and race between the graves, forgetting about respect for the dear departed. But the sun's glare is blinding and it's only when I stop that

I realise where I am. Nowhere near the car. Almost on the cliff.

As if it's just been a matter of time.

The lava rocks are sharp, waiting to be rendered smooth by the waves. Another few million years. But away from the edge, the lumps are carpeted in grass. Keeping my eyes on my feet I walk towards the far boundary where the cemetery ends dramatically in dense jungle. The sun is hot and my anger subsides as the rhythm of the waves lulls me into a timeless state.

That's when I look up and see her.

The woman.

It's her. It's definitely her. But this time she's standing on the cliff. I drop behind a headstone and cringe out of sight, hoping she hasn't seen me. Unless she knows I'm here.

Panic rises but I suppress it and fumble for my phone. Wanda's the granddaughter of a *kahuna*, she can tell me what to do. But it's showing no reception.

After several long minutes of breathless waiting, I peek around the stone, hoping she's disappeared. But she's still there, standing perfectly still. On the edge.

From the safety of my hiding place I stare at her. She's naked. Or appears to be. Just like I suspected in the tub. But her skin is filmy, like a translucent garment that clings. It gives her a sheer substance as if she's not quite real. And she doesn't move. Only the sea is restless, drumming out its rhythm on the rocks below.

She's standing beside a deep cleft in the cliff so she's half-turned in my direction, the sun on her face. But she's not looking at me. She stares with a raw intensity at something else.

Something over the edge.

Is she going to jump? If she was real, it would be my first thought. Because there's a quality to her stillness. A resignation. A sense of loss. As if she's waiting for the right moment, that split second when it's too late for regrets.

But she isn't real.

Wanda moved the mirror but now she's back. This is no coincidence. The woman's stalking me.

The camera. It's still in my bag. With a better zoom than my phone. If I can snap her photo before she disappears, then at least I'll have her image. And if she's some kind of ancestor, it's possible Wanda might recognise her.

Even with the zoom I'm not close enough. So, like a paparazzo stealing secrets, I crawl towards her, stopping behind gravestones to watch her through the lens. It's slow progress across the fallen stones and grass but all the while she stands there like a work of art, a living sculpture, in this garden of monuments overlooking the sea.

As I get closer she looms like a sentinel against the sky.

Her attention hasn't wavered and her intensity acts like a spell. Resisting its power, I stick to my purpose, stop, hold the camera steady and place her in the centre of the frame. But at the moment I press my finger down, she turns her head and looks at me, straight through the lens.

It's the same look as last time, the same searing stare. That's when I get the message, delivered by light waves right into my brain.

Someone is trying to kill you.

Then she's gone, vanished from view. And I'm running again. Across the ledge. Towards the cliff and the sky beyond.

I manage to stop before reaching the edge. It's my worst nightmare come true – the cliff, the sea. But the woman's gone, and if I can't look over and see what she was staring at, then what am I doing here? I have to know.

With crazy resignation I drop to my belly and creep forward. The rocks are as sharp as they look. I can't breathe. Still I inch along, like a caterpillar, a kind of inevitability moving me towards the cleft where she was standing.

At last I'm there. I ease myself forward. But the salt wind slams me in the face. As tears blind me and terror grips my chest, my body slumps like a dead weight and my head hangs over the edge.

Then I do the unthinkable. I make myself look down.

The sea rushes in with full force, then shrinks back. Foam leaps up the cliff wrapping the lava rocks in white. Shearwaters soar on the updrafts just offshore. And I'm clinging to the ledge as helpless as a seal pup.

Was I expecting to find her on the rocks? Proof she was real after all? She was looking at something. Something that was tearing her heart out, something that was...as unreal as she is. Because there's nothing at the bottom of the cliff.

I close my eyes and try to think. The woman might be unreal, but my predicament is exactly the opposite. I'm glued to the cliff edge with an endless view of crashing surf. My arms are pinned to my sides and my breath is coming in short gulps. And I've been here before.

In the dream.

Just before I fell.

I try to calm myself so I don't pass out. I've got to get away from the crash and drag, the deafening boom, the relentless spume. All I need to do is put my hands on the ledge and pull myself back, but I'm tilted forward and the edge is crumbly and if I make the slightest movement in the wrong direction I know I'll fall.

In this state of contained panic, something strange

happens. My awareness slips from my body and floats above the scene. I stare at my empty skin with a bird's-eye view. Trapped in time, paralysed by fear, clinging to the edge of the cliff. Inhabiting the space where moments ago a woman stood. A woman who wasn't real.

And the question comes into my dissociated mind: am I real?

***

Roger finds me. First his shadow, then his fingers touch my shoulders and he pulls me back with a firm grip. Together we crawl across the ledge to safe ground. I'm sobbing my heart out and he tries to hold me but I beg him to take me away.

He drives me home in silence, and I take the stairs to the flat wrapped in a fug of emotion more intense than anything I've ever known.

To find the right answer, ask the right question. The encounter on the cliff has added another question.

Why is she trying to kill me?

Chapter

Eight

As I sit in the dark in the empty flat, my actions trouble me. Why did I run to the cliff edge as soon as the woman looked at me? At the time my reason was compelling - to see what the hell she was staring at - but now, as I replay the incident, I'm sure she wanted me there. That was the spell she wove around me. With her stillness and her searing look, she...called me. And if she was trying to kill me, I played right into her hands.

Wanda comes home and goes straight into the shower without noticing me. She emerges from the bathroom naked and is startled to see me huddled on my bed.

"Didn't mean to give you a full frontal," she says.

She does a gyration with her hips - she's got the gift for Hula, a body-blend of soul and earth, she calls it - then pulls on a nightie and sits on the bed opposite me.

"Shoot."

"How did you know?"

"Just psychic." She grins. "And you're sitting in the dark looking worried so I figure you've got something on your mind."

"It's the woman. The one in your mirror. She turned up again. On a cliff."

"Let's get a drink, then tell me everything. Any of that organic wine in the fridge?"

"I thought you didn't drink wine from Chile."

"I don't *buy* it, but if it's already in my fridge..." She winks.

"That explains why a vegetarian makes art from dead fish. I have wondered."

"Yeah, it's the same. I wouldn't kill for my art, but since they're already dead..." She talks as she gets the glasses and I feel myself relax. "I'm in good company. Take the Buddhists – vegetarians who don't hurt a living thing, right? But if something dies of natural causes it's edible. So in Bhutan they tether their pigs near the cliff, then if an animal *accidentally* falls over the edge...light up the barbecue."

It would be funny if my own escapade wasn't so close to it. She returns with the wine and we settle down on our beds, like teenagers at a sleepover.

"Shoot."

I tell her the bare facts. How the woman materialised then vanished when I snapped her photo.

When I'm finished she says straight away, "Let's see this picture."

I can't believe I haven't looked at it. I open my tote bag and start rummaging, but the camera isn't here. And still isn't after a thorough search. Where the hell is it?

"Look again," Wanda says.

I empty everything onto the bed. "I don't know why it isn't here. I didn't give it back to Roger." I try to remember if he picked it up.

"OK. You haven't got it but you saw her, right? Was she wearing white?"

"Naked. But her skin was pale. Almost white."

"It could be her."

"Who? Shit, Wanda. Do you know who she is?"

"Pele. The volcano goddess. I didn't think of her last time, because I was thinking ancestors, but Pele's always appearing to people. She looks like a normal woman and is usually wearing white."

The volcano goddess. A local mirage. She turned up on my internet search. If Wanda's right, I'm off the hook. 'Always appearing to people' means she's got nothing to do with me. I was just in the wrong place at the wrong time.

But twice?

"It means she's got a message," Wanda says.

I sigh. "What kind of message?"

"For you. She's not just some ghost, right? She's Pele, the volcano goddess, and she's trying to tell you something."

"Like what?"

"Usually it's a warning. You're in danger, you're heading in the wrong direction, you're about to start a project that's going to collapse on top of you. She's telling you to pay attention, Selkie."

"She does a lot of staring, then she disappears. What the hell am I supposed to pay attention to?"

"Cool it. I haven't told you everything I know."

"Sorry."

"With Pele, the location is crucial. You're about to build a house where there's going to be a lava flow or something."

"So, once in the mirror and once in the cemetery. Are they connected?"

"Have to be. You saw the same woman in both places, right? Did you know you were psychic, by the way?"

That makes me laugh. "I'm not psychic."

She shrugs and takes a sip of wine. "Let's join some dots. The mirror and the cemetery – that's the underworld...and death. Did you get any kind of...communication?"

If I want her help I have to tell her everything.

"*Someone is trying to kill you?* Fuck, Selkie. She gave you a message like that and you've been sitting on it like a bomb that's not going to go off?"

Put like that, my denial sounds stupid.

"It's a warning," she continues, "and it's serious so it could be Pele. Roger was with you, right? She might be warning you off him."

"What? Roger is trying to kill me?"

"Probably not literally, but he might be trying to...possess you in some way. Steal your soul or something. Some men do."

I think of Andrew.

"What's he like?" she asks.

"Eccentric. Selfish. A bit patronising. I don't think it's Roger."

"How many other people do you know in Honolulu? Besides me?"

"I think it's the woman."

I tell her about the dream and what happened on the cliff.

"So Roger got to play hero," she says. "Interesting. But if the woman lured you out there, she isn't Pele."

We sip in silence then Wanda gets a thought.

"Coral. The *kahuna*. She'll know more about spirit women than me. But she only speaks Hawaiian and pidgin. Come on." She jumps off the bed and pulls on cut-offs under her nightie, then pushes her feet into her boots.

We make an odd sight as we descend to the street in our nightwear but no-one gives us a second look. On Kuhio Avenue, pairs of working girls are strutting their stuff in hotpants and fishnets as potential patrons cruise by. This is one end of the Track, which stretches four blocks towards Honolulu. When we stop at the kerb, a naked women rushes by, crisscrossing the street in bare feet with a man in hot pursuit. "Put your shoes on," he screams, waving a pair of killer heels above his head like rotor blades. They disappear in a blaze of horns and headlights.

"No wonder we're invisible," I murmur. "We're seriously overdressed."

Coral is perched in her usual spot. Does she sleep in the bus shelter all night? She's massive, so she's not starving, but I promise myself to bring her some food, whether she helps me or not. She shows us what's left of her teeth in a smile and Wanda sits beside her and starts talking. I stand between them, watching their faces and picking up the occasional word, like *pali*. Coral nods and smiles, as if she's lost a marble or two, but Wanda looks serious.

She pulls me forward so Coral's outstretched feet are pressing against my bare thighs. "Stand in front of her feet. That's how she reads things."

I lift my bathrobe out of the way and try not to think about tinea.

Coral looks at me, her eyes full of depth if not intelligence. After the woman, it's all I can do not to look away.

Then she says one word and Wanda translates. "Interference."

"*Pilikia*," Coral says.

"Trouble."

"Interference in what?" I ask.

"The spiritual process. If the camera's missing, someone is trying to stop the woman from connecting with you."

"I probably just left it in the cemetery." Shit. Roger's going to kill me.

"Coral doesn't think so. First you saw the woman in the mirror. You didn't understand what she wanted so she appeared again in the cemetery, and you took her photo. The photo will tell you who she is, right? Then you'll know why she's haunting you, what the message means. Who's trying to kill you. But now the camera's disappeared and the question is: who took it?"

I'm not sure about any of this. What about the woman's attempt on my life?

But Wanda thinks Coral's infallible.

"It's urgent, Selkie." She paces up and down the bus shelter. "You can't put faith in this dame – and her message – until you know who she is. I don't have to tell you how serious this is. You heard the warning and ignored it, so she had to tell you again."

"I know. I just don't see –"

"We're talking life and death, for fuck's sake. *Yours.*"

***

It's all too much for me, I'm exhausted. But as I crawl into bed and drop off to sleep something visits my dreams. Not the woman or the cliff, thank God. But something just as disturbing. First I'm overcome by sadness. Is someone crying? Then my ears fill with a series of sounds steeped in melancholy and longing. Not words, not music. A kind of tuneless singing.

Chapter
Nine

Monday morning. I'm sitting in front of my Goals for Gold program, but I keep seeing myself on that cliff with the sea reaching out its hands. Just like it did when I was a toddler, just like it did in my dream. Wanda's right. I've got to find that photo.

I pick up the phone and call Roger.

"Ah, Miss Lunatic, have you recovered, hmmm? From your little pantomime on the *pali*?"

"Still alive," I say.

"Yes. But your behaviour was…eccentric. Do I detect…a death wish?"

"Roger, your old camera – the one I borrowed yesterday. After you rescued me, did you pick it up?"

He misses a couple of beats. "Have you lost it? I know it was ancient but you might have treated it with a modicum of care."

"It must be in my bag," I lie. Because if he hasn't got it, it's still out there.

"It's not unforgivable," he says. What's happened to his histrionics? "At least you didn't capture anything…artistic."

"No." Only a photo of a woman.

I hang up and return to the screen. The camera is still in the cemetery. Behind a headstone. With my memory card inside. That's when I see the woman again and she's not on the cliff any more. She's trapped. On that memory card. How am I going to get it back?

***

Guy phones wanting the details of the Skape seminar. He's over the moon about the twenty enrolments because now we can showcase my skills in front of Lester Sloane. Suddenly I'm Guy's pet project. He might earn three thousand an hour with his regular clients but with me he's looking at a passive income in the millions.

A few minutes later he calls again. "Done. Sloane's on board. It's up to you now, babe."

"He'll be there? At my seminar?" My mouth goes dry. "Have you got a hotline to his office?"

He laughs. "I got through because he knows me. Knows I wouldn't waste his time with a bimbo. He's very keen to see you in action."

"I hope you didn't oversell me, Guy. What did you say?"

He's in a hurry. "We need to meet. Soon. Discuss tactics."

"Tactics?"

But he's gone. And I'm wondering just what I've got myself into.

Lester Sloane scores lots of hits on Google. The business pages, the social pages, going back years. An article from two years ago announces the completion of his high-rise – *Opening up a moribund area of Honolulu to stylish redevelopment* – a whole building of new apartments that includes his home and his office. The photo at the ribbon-cutting shows Sloane with a broad arrogant smile. Mid-forties, slim, good-looking, wavy fair hair that's longer than mine is now. I look again: the smile might just be confident. If I had his success, I'd have a confident smile too.

I return to my seminar notes, then stop. Goals for Gold suddenly has wider implications than I ever intended. It's no longer an obscure first-time seminar with activities designed for greenhorns. Now it's got to be classy enough to impress Lester Sloane.

***

Derek arrives with coffee for both of us and perches on the edge of my desk. I'm expecting him to notice my introspection and quiz me about my weekend but he's got other things on his mind.

"There's something I want to tell you, Selkie. I've been waiting for the right moment, but it never seems to come."

I'm not sure I've got the energy for more surprises but Derek's always got energy for me. I start on the coffee. "Sounds serious."

He smiles and dives right in. "I've taken up meditation."

After the build-up I exhale with disappointment.

"And it's changed me," he continues. "In ways I want to share with you."

"How?"

"For a start I'm more...serene."

Has his smile become beatific?

"I don't know what to say, DD. You do seem more...settled. When did this happen? I had no idea you've been meditating."

"It started at the Ashram, in the old noodle factory. Nigel took me there for Friday night meditation. They ask you to leave your ego at the door...with your shoes." He fixes me with his dark eyes. "I love it."

Thank God for caffeine.

"There's more," he says. "I'm doing a course with a Buddhist writer in Pearl City, on letting go. Letting go of expectation, going with the flow, writing from the depths of the soul. These days I sit at the keyboard and wait...for inspiration. Then the words just pour out." Like the restaurant guide. "It's magic."

Maybe Derek thinks serenity is catching, but after all this stuff I could clout him with the nearest Buddha. "What happened to good old-fashioned sweat?" I ask. The technique I'm perfecting.

"I'm not explaining it very well. I still do the work, but it's a partnership. I'm not passive, I'm being...guided."

"Right."

At last he notices I'm out of sorts and thinks it must be Roger. It's time to tell him about the woman.

"You've been sitting on this for a whole week and you haven't breathed a word?" He brushes the hairs down on his arms. "I'm hurt you haven't confided in me."

"I kept hoping it was a mistake. That it didn't mean anything."

"This is Hawaii, Selkie. Of course it means something. *Someone is trying to kill you.* I'm going for Andrew. He'll see you dead before he lets you go."

"He's in Sydney. And even at his worst he never laid a finger on me."

"Sydney's only a flight away. And there are other ways to kill you. Like slowly stifling your spirit."

"He can't hurt me now, DD. It's why he's turned into a bully."

Derek doesn't look convinced. "Who else could it be? You're not a very likely candidate for murder."

"Thanks. Wanda thinks it's tied up with the identity of the woman." I tell him about the photo and the missing camera.

"The photo would help, but you've seen her twice.

What did she look like?"

"I'm not sure. Each time I've been mesmerised by her presence, and yesterday I was paying more attention to getting the photo. But she was naked and kind of filmy."

"Close your eyes," he says, "and concentrate on your breathing, then try to see her."

"Meditate on her?"

"Yeah. You'll see things you don't remember consciously. It's as good as looking at a photo."

"Sounds like hypnosis."

"Just the awareness of deep relaxation."

But suddenly I'm scared. I don't want to see her again, even in my mind. All the emotions come back in a rush. The panic, the urge to run to the cliff, my fear of falling, the sight from above of my empty skin. The certainty that she was responsible.

But we're sitting in the office and Derek is beside me. All I've got to do is close my eyes and breathe.

It happens easily. My internal eye sees the cliff, then she appears almost instantly. Standing there, looking down into the sea. But the image is too vivid, the colours too bright, the landscape too sharp. And her presence is more shocking. I shiver. This doesn't feel like I'm remembering her, recreating the scene in my mind, it's more like I'm seeing her in present time. As if she's still there, always there, on the cliff.

I open my eyes, trying to break the spell, but when I close them again she's still there. Like the shutter in reverse. But this time I don't have a camera. This time she doesn't disappear.

"What does she look like?" Derek whispers.

With his words, the fear drains away. This time I really look.

"Spiky hair. Pale skin. Not very tall."

"Sounds like you."

I laugh. "She's standing on the edge, looking into the sea. And she's not afraid, she's...sad."

"Doesn't sound like you. Age?"

"Hard to tell. My age...older. Timeless."

Derek likes it. "A woman beyond time. What do you think it means?"

I open my eyes. "Timeless things aren't real. They don't grow old."

"Good call. And now that you've seen her again, what's your gut feeling?"

I tell him the rest. About my near-death experience. "I think she's the one, DD. The person who's trying to kill me."

I expect him to be alarmed but instead he says, "There might be another explanation."

"What?"

"I haven't thought this through, but the woman sounds a lot like you. The way she looks. So...you found yourself near the cliff and you were afraid. Terrified. And because of your fear, you projected yourself onto the edge. A version of yourself. A phantasm of the psyche. A phobia might be that strong, able to mess with your mind. You were scared of the cliff, of falling into the sea, so that's what you created – your worst nightmare made real. And when you ran to the edge...you nearly fulfilled your own prophecy."

I don't like it, and it doesn't fit all the facts. "That would mean I projected myself into Wanda's mirror. I'm not afraid of mirrors, DD." Not until Jerome cut my hair.

He shrugs. "Then you've got to find that photo. Find out who she is. And why she wants you dead. Have you asked Nightingale about the missing camera? He was the only other person there."

"The woman was there."

"What?" But Derek can see what I'm thinking. "You think she took the camera?"

"She saw me take her photo."

"To destroy the evidence?"

"I know it sounds –"

"No, it doesn't. You might well be caught up in something surreal. We've got to tell Nigel. He's good with this stuff." He picks up the phone. "Me, I just make it up as I go along."

"It's what I like about you, DD. Don't become too serene will you? It sounds kind of...dull."

He grins and makes the call.

"It's no trouble," he says to me after a murmured conversation. "He'll pick us up and we'll swing past your place so you can change. He said we could kayak out to the islands afterwards, but I told him how you feel about the sea."

They're taking me back to the cemetery, a prospect that makes me shudder. But I've got to find the camera and look at that photo.

CHAPTER
Ten

Nigel picks us up at two. At least it isn't rush hour or we'd be stuck in a parking lot masquerading as a highway. At my place he circles the block while I dash inside and pull on jeans and a top.

As we take the same route as yesterday Nigel talks. He works in a dementia unit – a shared 'house' for twenty people who need full-time care.

"Big guys like Nigel get the gig," Derek says, "because some residents can get aggressive and try to 'go home'."

Nigel's obviously proud of his work and his anecdotes distract me, but as we approach Kailua I become more tense. I'm returning to the very place where my nightmare almost came true. Am I playing into the woman's hands all over again?

Eventually we find the unmarked track, then we're riding the bumps before pulling up on the grassy patch where Roger parked. There are no other cars. Just like yesterday. As we walk under the stone arch, the atmosphere is the same – a sense that time has slowed down.

Nigel sniffs the air. "I never knew this place existed. What's it called?"

"I don't know," I say. "There are no signs anywhere."

"These islands are full of old graveyards," Derek says, giving me chicken skin.

We retrace my footsteps and stop near the cluster of headstones not far from the cliff.

"I was crouching around here somewhere," I say,

keeping my eyes on the ground.

We pull back the grass behind each gravestone to see if the camera has fallen out of sight. Then we do it again.

"Are you sure this is where you were?" Derek says. "You might be confused. These gravestones have lost their inscriptions. They all look like blank masks."

I make myself look at the ledge, fully expecting to see the woman. She isn't there and I realise I've been holding my breath.

"This is the place," I say. "She was standing on that cleft in the rock ledge."

Nigel squats so he can get the angle right and parts the grass. "No camera."

Did I drop it when I was running? If it bounced into the sea it's gone forever. Or did someone take it?

After a while we give up. As Nigel and I brush grass off our jeans, Derek does a yoga stretch with his head down.

Then he's shouting and holding out the camera on the palm of his hand.

"Not a wasted trip after all." He can't stop grinning.

"Turn it on." I try to grab it but he holds it out of reach.

We all sit down in the shade on a fallen monument with Derek in the middle. He turns on the camera.

"Nothing," he says.

"There can't be nothing. I took a lot of photos. As well as the woman there were three shots of a dog pissing on a headstone."

"Tasteful. But it isn't here, Selkie. This camera is empty. No photos. Nada."

He keeps pressing buttons, but we all know it's futile. Then he opens the slot for the memory card. It's still there.

"I don't get it," I say. "I know I took those photos. What's happened to them?"

"If you're sure the camera was working," Nigel says, "it might be a simple case of someone swapping the memory cards."

"Someone, meaning...?"

"Nightingale," they chime together.

"It's pretty obvious since he was the only one here," Nigel says. "But why?"

"Because he wanted to swipe Selkie's photos," Derek says.

I sigh. "I don't think so, DD. Roger went on and on about how I'd be taking artless happy snaps. He wouldn't be interested in my photos. And this is his oldest camera."

"Unless he was terrified you'd take a better shot than him," Nigel says. "Stealing your photos fits with that level of paranoia."

Does it? "But why leave the camera lying here?" I ask. "He'd just take it with him. I was in no fit state to notice."

"To make it look like he had nothing to do with it?" Nigel offers. "And if you came back and found it, you'd just assume your photos hadn't worked."

As we walk in silence to the car the upshot of this theory sounds loud and clear in my mind. If Roger took my memory card...he's got my photo of the woman.

***

It's too late for Derek and Nigel to kayak out to the islands. Too late to do anything but return to Honolulu. I get them to drop me near the Pearl. A bowl of noodles will help me forget my troubles.

It's still early so there's only a few patrons sitting at tables. Some old men playing mah jong. Suzi is standing behind the counter, but when she sees me she ducks through the plastic strips. To my relief Eugene's tubby frame emerges, but he's frowning. What's Suzi said about me?

He comes through the hinged door in the counter and guides me to an empty table. We sit down opposite each other and I decide to take the lead.

"Is Suzi OK, Eugene? She was acting weird while you were away."

"Suzi OK," he says.

"Maybe I hurt her feelings or something."

"Suzi OK." He looks at me. "You not OK."

"Me?" For some reason I look over my shoulder. "I'm fine, Eugene. Same as usual."

"Not same. Different."

He's looking past my left shoulder, and I turn around again but there's no-one there.

"You got entity," he says.

The most serious words I've exchanged with Eugene up to now are 'sweet and sour sauce'. I wait a whole minute before I ask, "What's an...entity?"

He shrugs. "Not there last week, there this week."

"Where? Where is it?"

"Riding on shoulder. Like monkey."

I look at each shoulder. "I can't see anything."

He shrugs again. "I see."

This is insane. "Eugene, I don't know what an entity is. Is it something...bad? Why did Suzi run away from me?" And why does he look so bloody serious?

"Might be bad, might not. Depends."

"Depends on what? What is it?" I resist the urge to reach across and shake him.

He frowns. "Part of you, maybe."

"Part of me...is sitting on my shoulder?"

"Maybe. Maybe you broke in many pieces like fortune

cookie, not all put back. Bit broken off, trying to get back."

"But I'm not broken. Look." I stand up and turn around.

"Maybe."

I sit down again. "What's maybe? Is the entity maybe?"

"Not maybe. I can see."

He can see it, and I can't. Is that because he's Chinese?

"What does it look like exactly?"

He shakes his head. "Your entity. You see. Feel maybe. Get message maybe."

I want to scream. "But I can't see it or feel it. I don't know what you're talking about."

Eugene must be able to see the tears about to spill. His expression is kind. "Pay attention."

He says the words as if they're profound. *Pay attention.* To what, I have no idea. I nod to please him, and he seems satisfied because he gets up.

Suzi emerges looking as jumpy as last time. She puts a container on the counter and squeaks, "Special. Sweet and sour fried short soup."

She waves the paper bag with the wontons.

Just like last time, they want me out of here.

Eugene refuses payment and pats me on the shoulder. "Coming back, maybe," he says. "Old friend from far away."

Clutching the takeaway, I step into the street. More confused than ever. I've got an entity. And nothing looks the same any more.

It's like being told you've got a terminal illness. Or finding yourself inside a painting by Salvador Dali. The world tilts. Objects that were solid droop. Things you didn't know existed warp your reality into mayhem. I trust Eugene but he's just dumped a monkey on my shoulder and pushed me out the door.

I catch my reflection in a shop window. Do I even look the same? I square my shoulders and stare at the glass. In my jeans and ballet flats, I look like a street fighter with a takeaway at her side instead of a gun.

And there's not a damn thing on my shoulder.

No entity.

No monkey.

Only a grudge.

Suzi and Eugene should mind their own business.

CHAPTER
Eleven

By the time I get off the bus at Waikiki, I've almost finished the wontons and the full force of Eugene's revelation has sunk in. He's left me with no idea what I'm dealing with. Something invisible inhabiting my personal space, something that might be evil – 'it depends'. Depends on where it comes from, why it's here. And my only weapon against it is to 'pay attention'. Something I'm clearly not very good at since I didn't even detect its presence.

In the bus shelter Coral's bulk looms. Her eyes are closed so she doesn't see me. When I reach my front door the hairs on the back of my neck prickle. I can feel something. My own fear. Fear of being alone with the entity indoors.

I sit on the doorstep, trying to get my courage back. If it really does exist – and no-one's seen it except Suzi and Eugene – it must have been on my shoulder since Suzi's freak-out last week. That means it's been hanging around for days. So I've already been alone with it and it hasn't tried to hurt me.

So much for logic. I consider ringing Nigel and Derek and asking them to rescue me, but that would mean the street fighter was just a mirage. I pull out the last wonton – Chinese courage – and find it's not a wonton at all. It's a fortune cookie. Eugene hasn't left me in the lurch.

When it's time, it's time, it warns.

I'm just wondering what it means when Wanda's head appears on the stairs.

"Did you lose your key?" she asks.

"No, but that's about the only thing I haven't lost."

For the first time I wonder if I'm losing my mind.

Wanda's back for a short session with the blender and some over-ripe mangoes from a street vendor.

"Are you OK?" she says as we go inside.

"Why?" I stiffen. "What can you see?"

"See? I don't know if I can see anything." She peers at me, but shakes her head. "You just seem...different."

"Since when?"

"Since..." She thinks back. "Since you got your hair cut. I'm not saying it doesn't look great. It's amazing the way he's shaped it. And the silver streaks are like moonlight. Moonshine." She laughs. "But a new hairstyle can push you off-centre, right? Especially if you've been hiding behind it forever."

I expect her to ask about the missing photo of the woman but she rushes out again, and I go back to thinking about the entity.

Jerome cut my hair last Tuesday and afterwards Suzi freaked out. My haircut, my entity – sounds like a book title Derek would like.

Back to Google: *entity definition*. Thousands of results to choose from. The world must be full of the bloody things, marching across the astral plane looking for shoulders to perch on. The websites look unreliable but I choose one that's at least succinct:

Entity. A spirit or ghost representing a disembodied consciousness. May manifest itself only to a specific individual, aroused by pent-up stress or created for a special purpose such as psychic protection.

I read the words over and over, hoping for something to resonate. Disembodied consciousness, pent-up stress, psychic protection. Yes, I've been under stress these last few weeks but I've been stressed before. All my life. So that doesn't feel any different. And the rest are things I just don't believe in. I was normal a week ago – and now, after one haircut, I'm surfing the internet looking for manifestations under virtual rocks.

Eugene said something about a message. The entity might send me a message.

Someone is trying to kill you.

It's got to be connected to the woman. It would explain the stalking if she's getting a free ride on my shoulder. She can get in my face whenever she likes. A distressing thought. But then I remember that after I first encountered her, Suzi and Eugene saw me without flipping out. So maybe the entity's got nothing to do with the woman. Why is that a relief?

The singing. I almost forgot about that. I haven't heard it all day, but it's buzzing away again now, like a bee in a bottle. I realise I've been vaguely aware of it since I got home so it's not coming from a dream. But it only started last night, days after Suzi saw the entity. I should have asked Wanda if she can hear it.

Searching for it gives me something to do. I wander around the flat, press my ear against Doris, against the Buddha and the parrot. Even against the Shona sculpture. I'm remembering the story I found online about spirits living in statues. Did the spirits sing? The sound seems to be filling the whole room, not coming from one direction. I make myself pay attention. Does it sound familiar? It's not as sad as it was last night. Today it's got a soothing quality, like dissonant bells chiming. But it also sounds...lonely, the way it seems to echo from far away.

It started right after yesterday's trip to the cemetery so it must be connected to the woman. Does that mean she's still here? I shiver. Everything returns to the woman. And the missing photo.

I've got to get out of this flat and find out if Roger stole my photos. If Nigel's right about his professional jealousy, then the missing memory card is his doing, nothing to do with the woman. I'll just ask Roger to give it back, and if the photo solves her identity then I'll be one step closer to the truth.

I send him a text inviting myself over.

***

He's cooking again. Another curry. And I've only eaten a few wontons. I wait till we're sitting at his kitchen table and he's poured us both a drink before steering the conversation around to photographs.

"Did you end up getting any good shots yesterday?"

"*C'est possible.* In spite of your...antics."

I ignore the jibe. "Show me."

"Art can be very...personal."

I snort. "I was there, Roger. I saw what you saw. A garden of gravestones. It's your interpretation that interests me. And who knows? I might learn something."

"Wait till they're short-listed for *Life and Death.*"

This is ridiculous. I haven't even mentioned my photos. I remind myself that I'm only interested in finding out if he took them. So why am I afraid to come right out and ask him?

After a bit more wine he serves the curry and I get up the courage.

"Roj, your old camera – the one you lent me – it wasn't in my bag. So I went back to the cemetery today and found it."

I pull it out of my tote bag and put it on the table.

He barely reacts. "If it's broken forget it. I never use it."

"It still works, but the photos I took...weren't in it. The memory card's blank."

"A malfunction. *Quel dommage*."

"But I know I took those photos. They were on the memory card and now they're not. Do you...have any idea what happened to them?"

"*Moi*? How could I? I haven't been back there since yesterday."

What would going back there have to do with it? "I just thought my memory card might be...in your camera bag."

"Did you put it there? I'd remember if I did."

"We could take a look. See if it's there."

"No, we couldn't."

"But I took some really good pictures..."

He looks up sharply from his plate.

"...of a dog urinating on an epitaph. I wanted to have a go, enter them in the competition."

"Well, if the memory card's blank you can't."

"I know that. I just want to look in your camera bag –"

"I know what's in my camera bag."

"– make sure the memory cards...didn't get...swapped."

He puts down his fork. "Your pictures are gone. Departed. Vamoosed. And they weren't worth entering anyway."

"How do you know that?"

"For God's sake, Selkie, you seem to be implying that I stole your memory card and secreted it away just so you can't enter your clumsy holiday snaps in a competition for serious art."

Bloody hell.

Suddenly it's all too much and I burst into tears. Roger tightens his jaw and pretends not to notice, then he leans over and puts his arms around me.

"I'm sorry," I say, trying to stick to my purpose. "I just want to see...the photos I took. See if they're...any good."

"Forget about them. We'll do another expedition. And I'll teach you a few tricks and lend you a better camera. As long as you promise not to leave it behind next time."

I nod and sniffle.

We finish our meal.

When we're washing up Roger leaves the room with the camera and I hear the telltale sound of a filing cabinet. So that's where he keeps them, locked away from curious lovers.

A moment later he's back and we talk of other things. The magazine he's designing for a European hair products company, with submissions from photographers all over the world.

"Do you get to feature your own photos?" I ask, remembering the photos he took of my hair.

"One or two. Edgy fashion shots."

"Can I see?"

He hesitates, but the temptation to show off is too great. He leaves the room again and comes back with some sample pages. On top there's a photo of a woman on all fours, almost a porn position, her naked skin covered in a patchwork of animal prints camouflaged against a striped backdrop. Only her face is bare, glaring at the camera like a caged animal.

It's very confronting and I swallow hard. "Wow. You must be an expert...at graphics."

"The best. The publishers headhunted me."

"Who's the woman? She's got an amazing face."

"And body. One of the girls from downstairs. A wannabe model. She stripped and posed for nothing just to get the exposure." He laughs. "Pardon the pun."

When we get to the bedroom, the thought of sex with him after what I suspect him of seems like something I can't quite pull off. But in spite of my misgivings my body soaks up his attentions like a sponge.

As I'm drifting off afterwards my mind replays our conversation. Roger never actually said he didn't have my memory card. Each of his answers carefully avoided it.

***

Three fifty-two on the bedside clock. Beside me Roger sleeps. In the twilight I watch the rise and fall of his chest while I decide if he's out for the count, if there's time, if I've really got the nerve. As I slip out of bed the sheets rustle and the bed slats creak. I freeze. He rolls over and snores once before resuming his heavy breathing.

The bedroom opens onto the living room, and light from the distant street lamps is spilling through the coloured glass. It's enough to see by.

I go straight to the filing cabinet. Locked. So he locked it after opening it last night. Most filing cabinets come with two keys. He'd keep one on his key ring – in his trouser pocket on the bedpost – too messy and too easy to get caught. It wouldn't be pretty if Roger found me searching his pockets. But the second key – it might be hidden somewhere, taped behind something. Like the back of a picture frame.

I begin with the two framed graveyard shots. No key. The sparse furniture doesn't afford many hiding places. I run my hands under the shelves of the bookcase. Then I examine each book in turn. Nothing. The undersides of the coffee table and armchairs come up blank too.

When the bed slats creak again I flop into an armchair and close my eyes. I couldn't sleep – it's true – so I'm sitting here in the half dark. But my breath is ragged.

"Meditate," says Derek's voice in my head.

To my amazement, as Roger goes into the bathroom my breathing slows. I hear splashing in the toilet bowl. Footsteps back to the bedroom. He might still be asleep or he's forgotten I'm here. More creaking. I wait a full five minutes before allowing myself to move.

There's a small gap between the filing cabinet and the wall and the parquetry shows scratches where it's been slid out in an arc. I push my fingers into the gap and run them all the way down one side, then the other. No key. But I can't reach the middle. As the spare key, it doesn't need to be readily accessible, just available for emergencies. I creep into the kitchen and bring back a chair.

Something is taped about halfway down the back of the cabinet just beyond my fingers. I find the corner and start to peel it back, then stop. If it's the key and it drops to the floor, I won't be able to get it. But if I just peel back the top of the tape very slowly...

It seems like an age before the spare key is in my hand.

I try it in the lock. It turns.

I almost cry out at the same moment Roger calls from the bedroom. "Miss Heavenly Body? Time for my early morning wake-up call."

With a pounding chest I return the chair to the kitchen. The clock shows almost five. I've been up for over an hour.

"How about a little...room service, hmmm?"

At least he's still in bed. With the key in my palm I pour two glasses of water and carry them back to the bedroom. I drop the key into my tote bag, without a clue about when I'm going to use it.

"You're as cold as an alabaster tombstone," he murmurs when I climb in beside him. "Have you been dancing with ghosts?"

I shiver. The answer is probably yes.

Chapter
Twelve

Over a hurried breakfast it's all I can do to keep up a normal conversation. The key is burning a hole in my concentration. What if Roger discovers it's missing? With me the obvious culprit? For the first time I'm a little afraid of him.

Under the shower I think about coming back and trying again. But after all my probing questions, if Roger did take my memory card he'll have downloaded my photos by then and wiped the evidence. If he hasn't done it already. Then the realisation hits me - if he downloads the woman's image, he might retouch it beyond recognition, all in the name of art. And if I do find it, I won't be able to trust what it shows.

I've got to get to her photo before he does, but how? Sleep with him again tonight? Or break into his flat?

Halfway to the office I double back before I change my mind. Roger was locking up as I was leaving so he'll be out of the way. The grounds are empty at this hour, so I climb the stairs unobserved. First I knock to make sure he didn't forget something. Then it's the flowerpot for his spare key. Weeks ago he told me where he keeps it, hinting at a threesome with Sheena. I dive my fingers into the pebbles. No key. I rummage around in case I'm mistaken but it's no use. It isn't there.

In extreme frustration I go around the back of the building to find a tap to wash my fingers. Opposite the resident parking spaces three odd plastic chairs cluster around a tin for cigarette butts. A woman in a sarong emerges from the downstairs flat, takes a chair and lights up. She sits with her back to me, blowing out smoke.

A girl appears at the back door. She's Asian and looks like a twelve-year-old runaway. "Gerry," she calls.

Gerry jerks her head around, showing me her face. Her beauty is striking. High cheekbones and disdainful eyes. Eyes I've seen before. Staring out from a photograph taken by Roger, her naked body patterned with animal prints. She sighs and looks at her watch. Then she stubs out her cigarette and goes back inside without a word.

On my way to the office, I wonder if the empty flowerpot means Roger's got something to hide. But there could be any number of explanations. I remind myself that he really might be nothing more than he seems – a goofy Englishman on the outside and a paranoid artist on the inside. And if he did remove my memory card and download my photos it was only professional jealousy, making sure none of my pictures could ever compete with his.

***

Oliver Katsuya chose Thursday and Friday for the Goals for Gold seminar, just over a week away. It still needs a lot of work to lift it above the ordinary, so instead of devising a burglary strategy I pour myself into the task. This morning it's a wonderful distraction from everything that's haunting me – the woman, the singing, the entity. They slip from my consciousness and I start feeling excited about experimenting on twenty guinea pigs. Twenty-one if I count Derek. And he's pressuring Nigel to change his roster and hand out the pens.

"It looks more professional if you've got a support team," Derek explained. "And if anyone gets troublesome Nigel can do his bouncer routine. Except he'll be throwing them out instead of keeping them in."

That makes twenty-two.

Guy rings to arrange a meeting. He's being careful not to mention the 't' word again. Tactics. But it's in the space between us.

"Do you want to have input into the goals seminar?" I ask.

"Nope. I'll leave that to you, babe. But we'll work up something new together, show Sloane the future."

Together. Another 't' word.

"Something quirky," he says.

This is what I get for agreeing to share my profits – another man telling me who to be.

I try to assert my position. "'Quirky' isn't the signature I want to create, Guy. Not if I've got to live it for the rest of my career."

"Let me be the judge of that."

"Maybe Sloane'll fall in love with Goals for Gold."

"I know what he likes."

I sigh. "What do I bring to the meeting?"

"Yourself will do."

Jerome's question comes back unbidden: which self is that then?

Over a break for coffee I check my inbox. Several people are interested in a seminar and now I've got some credibility when I send back a reply. But a new email pops up and I almost faint.

It's from Lester Sloane.

Dear Selkie

> *We won't be meeting until your seminar. Guy is very*

possessive about his role as agent and he's saving you up till then, but thank you for inviting me. I'll do my best to be invisible so you can relax and do what you do. I'm not looking for perfection. I'm looking for spark. And from my experience it's something you've either got or you haven't so think of it as taking the pressure off. Just be yourself and let me do the rest.
I hope you'll let me buy you a drink afterwards.
Cheers

Not twenty-two participants. Twenty-three. How did I forget Sloane? And Guy will be there too, holding up cue cards at the back of the room. I stare at Sloane's words. The man's a big-time schmoozer and Guy's thinking I'm going to schmooze him. No chance. Against this level of charm I feel suddenly defenceless. No wonder he's a millionaire and I'm just a pretender in a power suit.

Should I reply? Probably. But I don't know what to say. And if I spend hours on the wording, trying to sound cool and capable, I'll be doing the opposite of what he recommends. Better not reply immediately anyway and look too eager...

So much for 'being myself'.

Back at Goals for Gold, the words swim. If Sloane was trying to make me relax he's had the opposite effect. He's reminded me how much is at stake and how little my preparation will count. It's all about 'spark', whether I've got it or not.

Just like 'flair'.

***

Guy greets me at his office door, many floors above the harbour. He pecks me on both cheeks, then stands back. "What's happened to your hair?"

I sigh. "It's just a haircut."

But he's looking me over and frowning. "It's feral, babe. Not the look we want to snare Sloane. We need to manage your image now. Down to the last detail."

Manage. I think of Andrew.

"Leave it to me," he says. "I'll find someone to tame it."

"Not another cut."

"A blow-dry," he says.

I shrug and go to the sofa. The sun has just set but the sea is gleaming, so I sit with my back to the view.

"I got an email from Sloane this afternoon. He wants me to be myself, let him do the rest. So there's nothing to do but open that." I nod towards the bottle and two glasses on a side table.

Guy shakes his head. "I've got a lot riding on you, Selkie. We gotta make sure you land this one."

"Sure. But he's coming to Goals for Gold so that should be my focus right now. Another seminar is a distraction."

"Humour me, babe."

He's got no idea the state I'm in. My nerves have gone to pieces. And the goals seminar is refusing to come together, no matter how hard I try.

Guy turns to the whiteboard. "Come up with a new seminar first. Get the benefit of my experience. Then have a drink." He winks. "Something...startling. Original." He writes the words in big letters. "Remember your audience. Hard-bitten business people who think they've seen it all. We need to shock 'em out of their complacency, their old ways. Especially if those old ways are crap."

He begins to brainstorm seminar topics, hoping I'll get ignited and offer something quirky. I'm usually good at this stuff but not tonight. From the depths of the sofa I watch his performance, but his ideas are hackneyed and we both know we'll reject them.

After a while he gets desperate. "An animal theme...what do you think?"

"I think this isn't working."

"Humour me, babe. What animals are there?"

I sigh. "The Chinese want their children to be born in the Year of the Dragon."

"Teeth, fire, scales. Doesn't fit your image. Other animals in the Chinese zodiac?"

"Pig, rooster, dog..." This is insane. "Rat."

"'How to Be a Business Rat'. Catchy. Except most of 'em don't need training for that."

"Monkey." It just slips out.

He pulls a face. "OK. Forget the Chinese animals."

Good idea.

"What else? Say the first thing you think of. Wily as a fox..."

My mouth works automatically. "Brave as a lion..."

"Wise as an owl..."

"Sleek as a seal..."

He stops. "I haven't heard that one before."

I stifle a yawn. "It's my name. From a Celtic fairytale. Selkies are seals that peel off their skins and become human for a while."

"Sleek as a seal." He writes it in big letters. "Sleek, glossy, lean. Sleek in business. Sleek in spending. Sleek in ethics. I like it, I like it."

I curse under my breath. "Sea themes don't really grab me, Guy. And anyway, do I know anything about being sleek?"

"My little seal, you know everything about being sleek. Running Moonshine. A sleek operation if ever there was one."

"But I haven't made any money."

"Yet. Sleek is about hanging in there, never losing sight of your goal, gliding through the choppy waters until success lands in your lap...like a fresh fish." He slaps his hand on his leg. "I think we got ourselves a seminar."

He wipes off everything except the new heading.

"Let's get down a few thoughts to expand later. Then open that bottle."

He starts scribbling. He's thinking faster than he can write. "Seals are curious and cooperative – essential qualities in business. Ride the currents but make quick turns when necessary. Great stuff."

I try again. "Guy, you can't dump a seminar about seals on me. It's too...wacky. And untried. I'd be risking my whole future on some crazy idea I can't even relate to."

"The idea's perfect, Selkie. It's got novelty and charisma. And so have you."

Our eyes meet. He's as smooth as Sloane.

"You make me sound like a magician," I say. "But I'm the one who's got to breathe life into this stuff. You're forgetting I need to be authentic."

He snorts. "For ten million a year, be anything you want. Authentic is just a delusion. You don't think any of the gurus believe what they say, do you?"

"Of course I do."

"That's their charisma talking. All that goal-setting stuff? I bet none of those pals ever set a goal in his life. They just got successful then made up some bullshit to sell seminars. Probably don't even know how it happened."

"But –"

"Success is like sex appeal. Some people have got it, and everyone else wants it, wants it enough to *pay* for it. Enter Selkie Moon – *as sleek as a seal*."

He waits for my reaction. I can tell he's wondering if he's misjudged me. He goes to the side table and pours two glasses, then sits down beside me.

"I don't even like seals," I say after a few gulps. Tears are filling my eyes. "They're slippery, they've got barnacles...and lice."

"You know a lot about 'em."

"I know nothing about them. And I don't want to know. That's my point."

"So go online. Get a few facts. It's called research. Work up an outline. Then warm up the cash register."

He sips his wine. And waits.

"That's all?"

"It's a seminar, babe. On dry land. Not a plunge in the fucking sea."

He knows about my phobia. Of course he does. I mentioned it at our first meeting. As we sat on his *lanai* in front of a wild surf.

I make a decision. I didn't walk out on Andrew, take up the green card, and pour three months of sweat into Moonshine to give up now. "OK. I'll give the seal seminar...everything I've got."

"That's my girl."

He tries to hug me but I pull away. "What do you want me to do?"

"Get a few facts about seals, work up that outline linking them to business principles, knock out one or two activities to try on the group next week."

I nod. I know how to do this stuff. "Anything else?"

"Trademark the name, register a domain – my job." So he's serious. "Let's meet again early next week – see what you've got and...discuss tactics."

I've been staring into my glass, but at that I look up

sharply and catch him grinning.

"Humour me, babe."

***

All the way home the authenticity thing keeps bothering me. How can I teach something so...alien. Then I remember what Gretel always says.

Don't over-think it.

It's always seemed naive to me. How can you sort out what you believe, where you're going, if you don't think everything through? But now Gretel's words come back like a gift.

Because Guy's right. It's just an exercise in research.

CHAPTER
Thirteen

I'm standing on the cliff, trapped inside a door frame, presenting my seminar to an audience of headstones and one living specimen. Lester Sloane. But he's looking right through me because I'm invisible. There's a key in the door, a key that will set me free, but Sloane is looking at his watch as if I've stood him up, and when I open my mouth the cemetery fills with singing.

Then Sloane starts waving a banana and the monkey on my shoulder grabs it. That's when I know the truth. The entity is more real than I am.

The dream dwindles as I stumble out of bed but the singing seems to get louder. Has it been with me all night? Vibrating, beseeching. It's so insistent I race into the shower, hoping to drown it out, but it echoes around the walls until I leave the flat.

Wanda phones to touch base and I ask her if she's heard it.

"What's it sound like?"

"One minute it's sad and wistful. Then it gets rhythmic and almost...joyful."

"No, I haven't heard it, but why would I?"

"Because your grandmother was a *kahuna*. Because you believe in spirits. And it seems to be something in the flat."

Wanda's answer surprises me. "Tutu was a *kahuna*, Selkie, and she taught me everything she knew. But I haven't got the gift. So it must be singing to you."

On the bus, the traffic noise is a welcome respite, but

the texts from Roger aren't. He wants to spend next weekend together and tries to tempt me with a session of *alchemy* in his darkroom. When I don't reply he phones and talks me into dinner on Sunday night. Afterwards I feel sick. I know I've got to get my photo back, but the price is too high. Sleeping with him, raiding his filing cabinet in the witching hours…I'm not sure I can do it again.

***

At the coffee cart I remember the seal seminar. Long before search engines, people relied on waiters and taxi drivers.

"What do you know about seals?" I ask Curtis.

"Hawaii's got its own."

"Its own seal?" I've heard about the turtles in the bay. Wanda likes to swim with them. "Isn't the water too warm for seals?"

He shrugs. "Don't know nothing about temperature, but it's called a monk seal. Monk as in priest. Like they worship the sea." He laughs.

A Hawaiian seal. That might work. And it's less symbolic for me than the Celtic variety.

Derek arrives and I tell him about Sleek as a Seal. He likes it.

"Do you know about the monk seal?" he asks.

"Curtis told me so I looked it up. They're called monk seals because they've got a collar of skin like a cowl. But I don't see how to use that symbolism in a business context."

"Monks devote themselves to poverty, chastity and obedience – doesn't that fit with a business model?"

We laugh.

"Then there's monk-ey business."

Not monkeys *and* seals.

"The Hawaiian monk seal is endangered," I say, "but they still come ashore on the string of uninhabited islands northwest of Kauai."

"Perfect. Just take the Skape people out on a boat and get them to dive for coins."

"Stop it. This is serious."

"What else have you got?"

"Seals are the perfect models for the perfect business person. Adaptable, fun-loving and aggressive when it counts."

"With an insulating layer of blubber."

"Great." I add that to my list.

"So you think Katsuya will go for seals? Him being a shark..."

I pull a face. "He wants Goals for Gold. But Guy suggested trialling one or two of the seal activities on the Skape team. Dip our toes in the water."

He chuckles. "You're taking it pretty calmly, considering your phobia. And your...dice with death on the cliff."

"It's just a seminar, DD." If I say it often enough...

He leaves me to my work and everything starts tumbling into place.

Seals are adapted for life in the sea. With their flippers and streamlined bodies they glide and dive. They're comfortable in their environment, they follow the rules but they also push the boundaries, diving to great depths to find the tastiest food or bobbing to the surface to satisfy their curiosity about people on a boat or on the shore.

How often do we push the boundaries in business? Are we constantly trying new ideas, experimenting to improve our sales, our customer service? Are we curious, like seals, to see how deep we can dive? Or are we complacent about our modest achievements, too frightened to go beyond what we know?

It's that rare joy of creation, breathing life onto a blank screen. Case studies flow into my mind and my fingers glide over the keys as the currents of thought carry me along. And I'm without fear. In fact I'm exhilarated, with energy beyond my own. Synergy of ideas and movement, mind and body, thoughts and actions. Sleek...

Like a seal.

With less than a week to go till the Skape seminar I force myself to put Sleek as a Seal aside and immerse myself in Goals for Gold. When things get complicated I've always thrown myself into my work. It's how I survived the years with Andrew. And why I could never give it up to have his child.

***

The rest of the week disappears in a blur of effort and Goals for Gold finally takes shape. By Friday I can almost relax about Sloane, but the matter of the missing memory card and my upcoming dinner with Roger is weighing heavily on my mind.

Then a phone call from Gretel changes everything.

"I haven't gone into labour," she says. "Can you talk?"

"Sure. But I'm at work. Is everything OK?"

"Yeah, but I've heard something...about your mother."

"What?" The truth about Prunella has always been a secret.

"I was at Dad and Mum's and I overheard them talking."

I can barely contain myself. "What did they say?"

"Look, it was just one word, Selkie. But it's something."

"Tell me, for God's sake."

"Dad said something like, 'If we hadn't rushed into getting engaged, your sister and I –' Then Mum interrupted. 'Don't rake over it, Sheldon. Don't.'"

"Engaged? I don't understand."

"It's the one word I heard clearly. I'd been to the loo and they saw me at the door – I'm hard to miss these days – and clammed up."

"If we hadn't got engaged... Does that mean Dad and Prunella were never *married?*"

"I don't know."

If Prunella had me out of wedlock...was her death something to do with shame? But it doesn't make sense. Not in the 1970s. In the absence of any other information I've always assumed she killed herself, a case of post-natal depression. It explains everyone's silence. Thoughts swirl, snatches of memory. Do I remember her or are they imagination? Someone laughing. Finger painting. Dancing. I'm sure it wasn't Stella so it must have been Mum.

At last I can't stand it. I have a right to know. I pick up the phone and call Dad, hoping Stella isn't on sentry duty, hoping to get him alone. My hands are shaking. I've never dared to ask him about Prunella.

"Hello," he says. "Stella told me she spoke to you."

As my courage deserts me he says something strange.

"Don't be too hard on her. She's done her best for you even though it hasn't always looked that way from your end. Your move to Hawaii nearly undid her."

I snort. "Why? She hates me. Now she's rid of me."

"She doesn't hate you. She just has trouble...showing her love."

Dad's oblivious to the cruelty I endured from Stella – the extremes of control and repression – but he's never opened up before and there are things I want to know. "But she...hated my mum?"

He sighs. "Yes, that's fair to say. She hated Prunella. But she doesn't hate you. What happened wasn't your fault."

For the first time in my life I ask the question. "What...did happen?"

It's an age before he answers. "It's time you knew the whole story, I know it is." Pause. "But I can't tell you."

What? "Why the hell not? It's a long time ago."

"And an unforgivable betrayal. Time doesn't change that."

"Look, Dad, I know you were engaged. Gretel overheard you talking. But I don't understand. Surely it wasn't scandalous for Prunella to be unmarried and pregnant."

"It wasn't that she was pregnant. It was that she was pregnant...to me."

"But if you were engaged, planning to get married –"

Stella's voice comes through the phone. "You promised, Sheldon. She'll get it out of you by stealth. She's as cunning as her mother."

She's been eavesdropping, like she's always done. When I was a child there was nothing I did that Stella didn't know about.

"How did she die?" I ask, urging Dad to continue. "At least you can tell me that."

But it's too late. He's going to submit to Stella. He sounds burdened when he changes the subject. "Have you tried swimming lessons over there?"

I sigh. "They never work, Dad."

"No, they never do. All because of that freak wave. I wondered if you were facing your fear, going...to Hawaii."

"No. Just trying to be my own person." By putting half a planet between me and Andrew. And Stella.

He asks about Moonshine and I tell him about the seminar, that I'm about to start paying back his loan. But my heart isn't in it.

All the way home I keep thinking about it. Stella has always portrayed my mother as some kind of monster, with genetic defects so serious they had to be expunged from her only daughter. Was Prunella crazy? Is that why she killed herself when I was just a baby? Stella would have judged her harshly for being unmarried and pregnant. Did that push her over the edge? And after Prunella died, her more stable older sister stepped in, married Prunella's fiancé and rescued the motherless child.

***

The sound of knocking wakes me from a dream. A key is weeping bloody tears, as if its heart is breaking. It's in my hand and when I put it in my dream pocket the bleeding stains everything red.

A courier is at the door. Another parcel from Andrew. I sign for it before I realise I could have refused it. But he's been quiet for a few days and I need to know what he's up to.

A valuation of the house. A low valuation. Just to remind me that the Sydney housing market is depressed, and after the mortgage is paid off my half won't deliver me much spending money. Does he think I left him for the money? A good story to tell himself. The valuation explains his silence. After the emotional blackmail, he's letting the cold hard consequences of my departure sink in.

It's Saturday in Australia. So I won't be able to engage my own valuer till Monday. Andrew would have planned it that way. A whole weekend for me to stew on things. He knows I'm impetuous but he's hoping that by Monday he'll have undermined me into giving up this silly escapade and crawling back to him.

Saturday is washing day and it helps keep my anger at bay. Not only at Andrew and Stella, but now Dad. Surely my needs should take priority over Stella's just this once.

I take a bath to cool my rage but that only reminds me of the mirror. The woman's appeared twice, told me twice that my life is in danger. But the questions about her identity and her motives remain unanswered. I'm left guessing, just like I am about my own mother.

Late in the day Wanda makes a flying visit. She offers to share her smoothie but I'm living on sauvignon blanc.

I tell her about my failed break-in at Roger's and my dream about the key.

"You can't give up," she says. "Are you ready to look in Tutu's mirror yet?"

I shake my head. "I've read about mirrors."

"Then you've got to get her photo back. It's the only clue you've got."

"That means breaking into Roger's filing cabinet. What if he catches me? And calls the police? I can't afford to get arrested. I've got to protect my green card."

"If he's got your photo, then you're taking back something he stole from you." She puts her hands on her hips. "Why are you being so passive, Selkie? So fucking...*impotent?* Don't you care if you live or die?"

"What do you think? I'm scared stiff. But I'm powerless. About everything. Every direction I go in seems to be obstructed. And the prospect of spending another night with him just to get into his filing cabinet..." I shudder. "Makes my flesh crawl."

"That's because he isn't safe. It's the message from the

dream. That bleeding key belongs to Roger, right? What if he's the one who's trying to kill you? The girlfriend's gone. What if he killed her and you're next? But she didn't have a vision to warn her."

"Or maybe it's Sheena herself. She kills off Roger's new girlfriends one by one so she can keep him." I'm laughing as I gulp some wine, setting off a coughing fit. It's a while before I can speak. "So how do I get the photo back without sleeping with him again?"

She shrugs. "Forget the photo and go back to the mirror. It isn't as dangerous as he is."

***

After Wanda leaves I top up my glass and invite Doris to share my outrage. She's silent on all subjects. Wise woman.

I open the fridge but it's been days since I've been to the Pearl so it's empty of suitable leftovers. As I cruise the kitchen looking for something to eat, a cockroach peeps out from one of Wanda's alfalfa forests bristling its feelers. I know how it feels. I refill my glass, working myself into a fury. The anger feels good but I'm in danger of wrecking the flat again. What I need is an emotional enema. Where's the feather duster?

I'm not much of a housekeeper but cleaning has always soothed my wounded heart. During my marriage the mop and broom were the only things that kept me sane. Wanda isn't much of a cleaner either – she's against all 'chemicals' – but there's a feather duster hanging behind the front door. I look across the room and wonder where to start.

Not in these clothes. I strip off my jeans and top, but don't stop there. Suddenly my knickers and bra are on the floor too. I'm not much of a housekeeper but I usually keep my clothes on. Not tonight!

First a shimmy to get in the mood, then I'm moving around the room, flicking my feather duster like a magic wand. Someone's giggling, little laughs surfacing like bubbles in champagne. Is there anything important I should be thinking about?

Nothing.

The duster slides along every surface, eliminating all my cares with a flick of the wrist. First it's Doris and her spiky chest, then the spines of Wanda's books. I do all four of the Buddha's faces, apologising for my abuse the other night, then I rotate him so his angry side shows. That's better.

Next the fish. There must be one that looks like Andrew. Eventually I find it – a smug expression, jeering teeth and too-blue eyes – it disappears under a flurry of feathers. Then a Stella look-alike – beady eyes and cheeks scored with stripes. I dust all the others and count them as I go. Twenty-seven. Wanda must have sold a few last weekend.

When I reach the shelf behind my bed, the Shona sculpture makes me stop. Her expression is hard to read but there's power in her crude profile. Her shoulders show she's as naked as I am. Wanda would call her a kindred spirit. I run my fingers over her knobbly hair, absorbing the coolness of the stone, and a new resolve strengthens my spine.

Next it's the candle. Silver-grey and as thick as my thigh. Derek gave it to me to harmonise the energy in my office but I brought it home. I'm not really into candles so I've never found a reason to light it – until tonight, if I can find a match. If Derek's at a loose end he might drive over and help me watch it burn. But then I'd have to put my clothes back on. Or get him to take his off.

Nah. This all feels very private.

I switch off the lights.

Night has descended and in the darkness the room is swaying. No, it's me. Gyrating like a reed. Now there's a rhythm happening. It begins in my feet, slowly at first, drumming, drumming. Then, increasing in tempo, it rises through my legs until my whole body is thrumming to a silent beat.

Around and around the room I go, pounding the vinyl with my bare feet. There's something about the rhythm...it's resonating within the depths of me. A dance I know, from somewhere forgotten long ago. Apocryphal, tragic, mournful, suddenly playful. Then bubbling over...with ecstasy.

Somewhere along the way the flat disappears and the wind starts ruffling my new hair. The moon and the stars spill their light and I stretch my arms towards the sky.

It goes way beyond housework. Eventually the drumming consumes me and I lose the feather duster and abandon myself to it. Just me and the silver sky. My whole being pulsing like an orgasm.

But it's bigger than sex.

Deep.

Empty.

As if my heart has expanded to wrap the whole world.

I wake on the floor and discover I'm naked. My eyes are wet and through the tears the room is fractured by prisms. I can hear distant singing and a breeze is blowing from somewhere, making me shiver. I drag myself to bed...

...too dazed to wonder.

CHAPTER
Fourteen

The singing drives me out of bed. This morning it's bouncy and erratic. But overnight it kept up a steady rhythm for a *menehune* – a little boy who worked away on a spinning wheel, creating a mountain of silver thread. Unfortunately I woke before he could weave it into anything useful.

It's Sunday morning and I'm sitting around in my bathrobe trying to make sense of my demonic dancing spree. Anger does crazy things to me. Abetted by too much wine. Luckily, Wanda didn't come home last night.

Someone knocks on my door.

"We're off to the Windward Shore," Derek says, when I open up. "Punaluu Beach. A friend of Nigel's has got a beach house. You need a pleasant distraction so you're coming too."

"No swimming, snorkelling, diving or kayaking," I say.

"Lunch."

I invite them in, and tell them I'll need to be back in time for my date tonight. With Roger.

"Is that wise?" Derek says, after hearing the details. "Stealing his key? What's the plan?"

"Raid the filing cabinet while he's asleep." The thought of it hasn't got any easier.

"And if he catches you? I don't like it, Selkie."

"Neither do I, but after his denials I don't have any choice. It's a whole week since I photographed the woman and I still haven't seen the picture. She might turn up again any minute and I still don't know who she is."

He thinks. "What about breaking in when he isn't home?"

"Tried that." I tell them about the flowerpot.

"Nigel's got a jemmy," Derek says. "And I know how to use it. Let's do it tomorrow when Nightingale's at work."

We leave it at that but I don't cancel Roger because the thought of using a jemmy to gain entry is hard to face. Suddenly the seminar seems easy. Impressing Sloane isn't nearly as heart-stopping as breaking and entering.

While I get ready the boys inspect the fish. They love the one that looks like Andrew, and Derek threatens to draw on a moustache. They move onto Doris and spy the cockroach trap on the floor under her stool – a bowl of red wine with ramps made out of paddle-pop sticks.

"It's very Buddhist," I say. "They're attracted by the smell and accidentally drown." A floating carcass demonstrates.

"Way to go," says Nigel.

"That bottle of red, Nige," Derek says, "the one that tasted gritty? That's what it was. Cockroach strainings."

I ask them if they can hear the singing.

"What's it like?" Derek puts his ear against the Buddha, then the parrot.

"Distant. Rhythmic. Not human. Sometimes lonely, sometimes...expectant. And always very insistent."

"When did you start hearing it?"

"The night after I saw the woman on the cliff."

They look at each other and shake their heads. They're either clueless or bored by yet another mystery. I'm starving. Time to get out of here.

I grab a hat and a jacket. "Ready."

"Not quite," Nigel says, looking stern. "You need your cowry shell."

I don't believe it. They've set me up. "Tell me everything. Now."

Nigel ignores me, but Derek says, "That would spoil the surprise."

"Promise me lunch isn't a lie."

"Cross our hearts."

I could send them packing but I'm desperate for food and company, so I crawl under the bed for the shoebox. Nigel says nothing as he puts it under his arm. While we walk to the car I could swear I can still hear the singing.

***

Derek navigates the sandy driveway of a two-storey timber house, painted grey and white, set back on a long stretch of sand. No garden, just a sprinkling of palm trees and patches of grass.

"I didn't think there was anywhere private on this island," I say.

"It's been in John's family since the fifties," Nigel says. "And they resisted the pressure to subdivide."

"Where's the surf?" Surely everywhere along this coast has surf.

"There's a rock-shelf. You only get waves in rough weather."

So I don't have to worry about cliffs.

Derek parks and a man in his forties comes out to greet us. He's wearing brown drawstring pants and a tooth hanging around his neck. He's lean and tanned, his brown hair cut almost to the skull.

We get out and Nigel hugs him.

"Meet John. He used to work in aged care till he defected to the military."

John laughs. "You make it sound like I fight for a living."

"Don't we all?" I say.

Around the back a low deck stretches across the sand. Through the palms the sun sparkles on still water, but it's a long way off and without the waves the sea is almost silent, just a subliminal shush. And the singing has gone again so I feel myself relax. This is my kind of beach house.

A Chinese guy comes out carrying a tray of drinks. Younger than John, mid-twenties. Another military haircut.

"Thomas is cooking up a feast," John says.

In the far corner of the deck an enormous gas barbecue is already set up with a wok and other utensils. Thomas grins shyly and goes back inside.

We sit down under an umbrella and the guys start catching up over beers. John runs an arts course for personnel at the local Marine Corps Base and he hasn't seen Nigel for a while. Thomas works at the base as a cook. Derek doesn't interrupt. It's the first time he's met them and he's gone shy. Were Nigel and John ever a couple? I don't think so. Their friendship seems genuinely platonic.

Thomas goes past with a tray laden with seafood – crabs, mussels, prawns, fish. He gets busy at the wok and amazing aromas start overtaking the briny smell of the seaside.

"Grandma Wong's congee," John says. "He started on it last night, marinating the rice in spices. We're in for a treat."

"Just as well your phobia doesn't extend to seafood," Derek murmurs to me as Nigel and John join Thomas. "I've seen the way you demolish a plate of fish." He chuckles. "You might have been a seal in a former life."

"It's just a name, DD. My mother fell in love with the

fairytale."

"You've never told me the story."

I pour myself another glass. It's a story I know by heart. "Every full moon the selkies come out of the sea and peel off their skins. Then they dance in the moonlight on human legs."

"On a strip of sand like this?"

"Closer to the shore. Because when they're done they pull their skins back on and dive back into the waves."

"Go on."

"One full moon, a fisherman watches the selkies dancing. He's lonely and their pelts are lying on the sand so he steals one and hides behind a rock. When it's time for them to go back to the sea one of the females can't find her pelt. She's frantic, searching everywhere, but the others have to leave her behind. In the end she goes with the man because he's got her sealskin and won't give it back."

"Wow." Derek brushes his hands down his arms. "He steals her pelt and holds her captive. Like stealing her soul. Does she die of a broken heart?"

"She stays with him for seven years and gives birth to his child. But she's always restless, always pale, never quite herself. Then one day the little boy finds the hidden skin. He takes it to his mother and she can't believe she's holding it in her hands –"

"Like getting her true self back."

"She rushes to the beach and returns to the sea, her home. Taking the boy with her."

"But he's not a seal. Does he drown?"

"She breathes air into his lungs so he can stay underwater until he learns the wisdom of the sea. Then he returns to land where he belongs."

"A happy ending."

"Is it? It always makes me sad. I'm the selkie who can't swim, just like the woman in the story."

Derek looks at me. "Do you wish you could swim?"

"You know, no-one's ever asked me that. Everyone assumes it's a terrible loss, but you don't miss something you've never had."

"So why are you sad?"

Good question. I try to answer. "Because...it sets me apart. When people are swimming I'm left high and dry."

"The outsider again. Just like in your family."

I nod. "And it makes me vulnerable. Andrew exploited it. At pool parties, he'd get the guys to throw me in. It became a regular entertainment, watching me flail and cough." Derek is shaking his head. "Then just in time he'd dive in, to much hooting and applause. As my clothes drip-dried and I fought back tears he expected me to pretend it was funny. I lived in terror that one night he'd be too drunk to play hero ... and I'd drown."

Derek puts his arms around me and I'm glad I've told him the story.

***

Lunch is served. Thomas has thrown the barbecued seafood into the spicy rice and vegetables. I'm in heaven.

Afterwards, Thomas scales a palm tree. He drops a couple of coconuts and they land with a serious thud.

"Never sit under a palm tree," he warns me. "If they fall on your head...you're dead."

I shudder.

Nigel's hand on my shoulder makes me jump. "It's time to get your shell."

His expression says arguing is pointless, and he comes

with me to retrieve it from the car. Then I follow him into the house.

"Show me," John says.

I unwrap the tissue paper. It's the first time I've looked at the cowry since I bought it and in the light through the windows its white surface gleams.

"You're right, Nige," John says, "it's a special one. I've never seen anything like it. Nothing so white. And those freckles look surreal. Valuable too. Luckily the Chinese woman didn't know how valuable."

More likely she did know and wanted to get rid of it.

John goes to a cupboard and brings back a workbox. He sits on the floor and invites me to sit opposite him.

"Hold the shell," he says.

As I pick it up the freckles seem to blink like tiny eyes. And the singing that's just started again gets louder.

John turns the shell around in my hands so the mouth is uppermost and the drill holes are nearest him. Then he takes a roll of black cord and cuts two long pieces the same length. He pushes the end of the first length through one hole and pulls it until both ends are even.

"Hold it firmly." He folds one length across the other, then twists it under in a kind of knot, first one way, then the other way. "Macramé," he says, steadily knotting.

When he's almost at the end he stops and picks up the other length, threads it through the other hole and begins again. The process, at first fascinating, then rhythmic, lulls me into a dream-like state.

When he's finished he takes four small round shells from a jar. They're shaped like fried eggs with a hole where the yolk should be. He threads each one onto a cord end and knots it, then leans forward and knots the cords at the back of my neck. The small shells jangle as they fall and clink against my spine.

When he leans back the shell is sitting against my chest and four faces are beaming at me. The singing has become jubilant, with highlights of exultation. John leaves the room and returns with a large hand-mirror. I don't want to look but I can't disappoint them, and when I stare at myself I'm confused. I'm getting used to the spiky hair but now it's streaked with silver. And the shell is reflecting its freckles into my eyes.

They leave me staring at myself for I don't know how long. The woman in the mirror. Me. Sitting together. Breathing. In rhythm with the singing.

CHAPTER
Fifteen

I'm pretty blissed out on the way back. I should be bothered
- a singing shell. I haven't dared put it to my ear but the
music is loud enough to wrap me in a fug of introspection.

As I gaze out the window the world flies by - the sign to
the Marine Corps Base, the turn-off to Kailua. We should
be going straight ahead towards Honolulu, but Derek swings
the wheel and takes a left.

People are grooming their gardens, tending their ponds
and rockeries, sitting on *lanais* and under umbrellas. Simple
pleasures. It's a very different city from Honolulu, where
relaxation often amounts to 'entertainment'.

We stop in a quiet street. A private house, painted
turquoise and white, with a glassed-in 'shop' in the front
room. The sign on the gate catches my eye: *Sleek and Unique*.
The front door is open, the white Roman blinds pulled up.
Dresses are hanging in the window. Derek parks and Nigel
opens the car door for me.

But this is too much. I just want to be left in peace.

"I've got the shell, Nigel. Why are we stopping at
Davina's?"

"You need a frock," Derek says. "Every woman needs a
frock."

Nigel keeps holding the door.

While this power struggle goes on Davina emerges and
stands by the car. Her green eyes look into mine. "*Aloha*,
Selkie."

How does she know my name?

Derek and Nigel confer. "Measurements," Derek says to me. "Today she just needs your measurements."

"Three minutes," Davina says, winking at me. She knows how to get her way. "But you two have to stay here."

It's the best way to get out of here – give a little. I follow her inside, where the turquoise walls are draped in the most amazing garments – deep necklines, knots and cut-outs, tribal prints. She pulls out a tape measure from under the bamboo counter and quickly measures my bust, waist and hips.

"Just one more," she says. "The shoulder to the waist."

She puts her hand on my shoulder. My left shoulder. Can she see the entity? She stretches the tape measure to my waist. "I see you're wearing the cowry shell."

"A friend of Nigel's just did the macramé." And I just found out it sings.

When she's finished I can't help asking, "What would you charge to make me something..."

"Unique?"

I nod.

She hesitates. "Nothing, nothing at all. I'm not supposed to tell you yet but...those two outside...they've already paid for it."

"For a dress? Before I've even said if I want one?" It's the kind of thing Andrew did. To make sure I wore what he liked.

"I'm sorry," she says. "I didn't know."

"I wondered how you knew my name. They told you."

"That they did. It's a grand name. A magical name."

So she knows about selkies. Of course, she's Irish.

"About the dress," Davina says. "You could accept it as a gift, you know. From your friends."

That softens my anger. They mean well, of course they

do. It's just their delivery that sucks.

"What if I draw up a couple of designs and email them to you? Then you can let me know what you think. No pressure at all. And we can meet up at the Swap Meet to tinker with ideas, choose a fabric, then later for a fitting."

She's making it sound easy and fun. Working on a design together, something made specially for me. My own choice. A gift from my friends. The singing takes on a note of longing and something inside me responds.

"OK."

I say goodbye and return to the boys.

"I know what you've done. She's not very good at keeping secrets."

"You're mad at us," Derek says, biting his lip.

"Furious, DD." I glare at him and he looks terrified. Meditation has turned him into a wuss. When Nigel says nothing, my eyes start watering. "I'm furious because you two are both so bloody...gorgeous. I don't know how to handle it – this level of friendship – so I get angry, OK?"

"Are you still angry about the cowry shell?" Derek asks.

I hesitate. The macramé must have been Nigel's idea. "Only a bit," I whisper.

But is that true? In front of John's mirror I plunged into a deep peace. And liquid notes are calling me back to the peaceful place as Derek starts the car.

***

The Pali Highway is in gridlock. A fall of rocks has blocked both lanes leading back to Honolulu. On an overpass across a valley we pull up behind miles of stationary vehicles. Around us people are turning off engines and getting out to enjoy the view. Far below, ridges and ravines intersect under drapes of green velvet.

Derek turns on the radio. Further on there's a contra-flow onto the opposite carriageway but the Sunday traffic will take hours to clear. A reporter is interviewing motorists who just missed being crushed by the landslide.

"Three Sundays in a row," says a guy whose car was written off. "Pele was standing here at this exact time. Hitchhiking. But no-one was stopping to pick her up. Now this."

The journalist takes the sighting seriously. "Do you think the volcano goddess caused the rock fall or was she predicting it, warning drivers about it?"

"A warning, but no-one gave her a lift so the accident did its worst. She tried for three weeks, *brah*, but was anybody listening?"

"How did you know the hitchhiker was Pele?"

"I've met her before. She's got a...look about her."

"Why didn't you pick her up?" asks the reporter.

"I met her once, I didn't want to meet her again, OK? Lots of drivers going by. This ain't my fault, *brah*."

The reporter moves on and Derek turns off the radio. Nigel pulls some beers from the cooler. At the side of the road some local guys start to dismantle a jeep and others leave their cars to help. In the next lane a family is setting up a picnic table. Japanese honeymooners from a tourist coach start posing in front of the safety rail, but no arranged brides are plunging to their deaths today. It happens. Young women who can't face a powerless future. Just another reminder of the cliff.

"Have you ever seen her, Nige?" Derek asks.

"Pele? No, but someone at work had the pleasure. He didn't buy a house because Pele appeared and he felt a lot of heat. A few weeks later the house got struck by lightning."

"The same kind of story I've heard," Derek says. "She appears for a personal reason. But that motorist assumed everyone saw her. Maybe nobody picked her up because nobody else saw her. It was his car that got crushed. And now we're all caught up in the consequences."

I can't stay silent any longer. "Wanda thinks the woman on the cliff might be Pele."

They turn and look at me as if they've just remembered I'm here. I repeat my conversation with Wanda.

"From your description," Derek says, "the woman didn't look like Pele. Although they say she's a *shape shifta*."

"The warning fits," Nigel says.

"Pele wouldn't try to kill you," Derek adds.

"But is she Pele?" I say. "Until I find that photograph I've only got my sightings to go on. Am I dealing with a murderer?"

"Or a guardian angel?"

"How many times have you seen her?" Nigel asks. "Only twice?"

"Twice too many. First in the mirror at home. Then last Sunday in the cemetery. About a week apart."

"If it's Pele she'll be back. Three times sounds like the number."

"That's what worries me."

To them this is a fascinating puzzle, but my mind keeps pushing me off the cliff as the sea rushes in with arms outstretched. Then watery footsteps tiptoe over my grave.

"Who else could she be?" Nigel is saying. "It sounds pretty personal so there must be some connection."

"But I'm a stranger here."

"In some stories," Derek says, "it's the *malihini* - the newcomer - who brings the truth."

"If that's the case," Nigel says, "your connection won't

be physical, it'll be psychic."

"Try to go back," Derek says, "see if you can pick up anything you missed."

Meditate again. But last time it drew out impressions I'm not getting on my own. As I close my eyes the singing guides me down a long tunnel to a place full of stars. Then I'm back in the cemetery, looking at the woman, experiencing her presence as if it's happening again, seeing her face, feeling her tension. Reliving my fascination and my fear.

"She's looking over the edge," I begin. "Looking for something...important, something she's lost." My next words surprise me. "Something that will make her real."

I open my eyes.

"Last time you called her 'timeless'," Derek says. "If she wants to be real it's a logical development."

"But what's it got to do with me? And it doesn't explain the missing photograph. Or why she's trying to kill me."

"If she wants to be real," Nigel says, "she could be a disembodied spirit...wandering around the fringes of the underworld, looking for a human ride."

"And she jumped into the camera when you took her picture," Derek adds, making it up as he goes along. "Never print that picture, Selkie. If you ever find it. The memory card might be containing her like a genie." He laughs. "Let Nightingale print it. Cosmic payback."

I shiver. I imagined the woman trapped on the memory card. Could printing her photo release some unstoppable force? My insight on the cliff comes back – the aerial view of my empty skin. Was I vulnerable at that moment...to a hostile takeover? Suddenly I'm aware of how attached I am to my body, to breathing. These theories are freaking me out.

"But what's her connection to you?" Nigel sips his beer and thinks. "An entity from a past life? Back to sort out some unfinished business?"

An entity. Did he just say an entity?

"It's...sitting on my shoulder," I murmur to their stunned faces.

I tell them as much as I know. "I can't see it, but I've sensed it at the edge of my vision. A shadow. Eugene called it a monkey."

"You should have told us," Derek says, frowning at the wrong shoulder. "It changes everything."

"I didn't tell you because someone's trying to kill me. And the entity's got nothing to do with it."

"Why do you say that? Surely the entity's the woman – like Nigel said – sitting on your shoulder. Looking to tidy up unfinished business. Getting in your face and warning you. Waiting to be acknowledged, made real. It explains everything."

"No, it doesn't." I tell them how Suzi and Eugene saw me after I saw the woman in the mirror. "The entity wasn't there then. It didn't appear until..."

"When?"

"...Jerome cut my hair."

At the mention of Jerome they share a look.

"What?" I say.

"Jerome's given up hairdressing," Derek says. "He says your haircut was his crowning achievement. When you achieve perfection you don't try to surpass it or even match it. Like Harper Lee after she wrote *To Kill a Mockingbird*."

This is sounding like so much gay histrionics but Derek is serious.

"So who's going to cut my hair next time?" I say. Assuming I decide to stay prickly. "Jerome can't do this to me and then walk away."

"I haven't explained. He'll keep cutting *your* hair, just no-one else's. From now on you've got your own private hairdresser."

Bloody hell.

"The entity must have been hiding behind your hair," Derek continues. That makes two of us. "So it could still be the woman. Can you see it, Nige?" Derek beams at me. "Nigel reads auras."

"It was ages ago, DD. A weekend workshop. And it happens like spoon-bending – when you don't care either way. We've got too much invested in seeing it, so we won't. And," he holds up his beer, "it's a gift that's positively drowned by alcohol."

Derek bites his lip. He thinks Nigel's treating his gift way too lightly but I suspect he's just fed up with my demons.

"Davina probably saw it," Derek says.

"Why would Davina see it?" I ask. She showed no sign of it when she was waving a tape measure in its face. If it's even got a face.

"She's Irish," Derek says. "They've always had a handle on the spirit world. It's their pagan heritage...overlaid with centuries of Catholicism. The Church hates it."

I'm with them.

"Plus she's clairvoyant," murmurs Nigel.

Suddenly I don't want to own one of her frocks.

"Entities," Nigel continues, "are usually created in childhood. To get you through a rough time."

"How does that work?" I ask.

"They act as a haven for bad feelings. Like fear. The entity minds your feelings so you don't have to feel them yourself."

A thought flies past but I can't catch it. Just a feeling of panic. And the colour red.

"You won't know why you've got one till you look," Nigel finishes.

"How do I do that?" Not the mirror.

"I know someone. A hypnotherapist. You need to be deeply relaxed."

"And if I ignore it?" My current strategy.

"That's the coward's way, Selkie. And the fact that it's suddenly shown itself means it might be urgent, don't you think?"

Before I can answer, the traffic begins to move. The dismantled jeep is restored, the honeymooners scramble onto the bus, the family folds up their table, and Derek starts the car. As we creep through the mountain tunnel and out the other side we eventually see the rockfall. It's covered the road and one car.

The contra-flow is in place across the grassy median strip. It takes us a while to reach the crossover point. Then Derek steers between the orange cones and past the traffic cops, but when he reaches the other roadway he spins the wheel in the opposite direction. Back towards Kailua.

"Hey!" I call from the back seat. "Where are we going now? I'm supposed to be going to Roger's."

Too late. We're heading east, past miles of cars still stopped on the opposite roadway.

"The cemetery," Derek says. "If it's a week since you last saw the woman she could be there right now. Waiting for you. But this time we'll be with you while you take another photo."

CHAPTER
Sixteen

Just like last time, we enter the place that time's forgotten. The wind has dropped and the stillness is oppressive.

"This hedge acts like a portal into another dimension," Derek says, wiping the hairs on his arms. "Nigel couldn't find it on the cemetery register, you know. Maybe it doesn't exist."

My chicken skin is back, but Derek takes my hand and the three of us walk between the headstones accompanied by the crashing of the waves.

When we reach the group of headstones where weather and time have obliterated all traces of identity, Nigel pulls us onto the grass so we can see the chink in the cliff. "It was here, wasn't it?"

"Yes," I whisper.

We cross our legs and watch the place where the woman stood one week ago. Empty now except for the gleam of late sunlight on lava rocks.

"What time?" Derek asks.

I look at my watch. "Four fifty-two."

"No, what time did you see her last week?"

"I don't know, DD." The missing photo would show the time. "After lunch. I wanted to leave and Roger didn't. I took off, running towards the car. But instead I ended up here. Then I saw the woman."

"So you were pissed off with Nightingale?"

"To say the least."

Derek nods. "Anger. Plus your fear of the cliff. Did you

hear that, Nige? The sighting was related to high emotion."

"Let's be quiet for a while."

Derek pulls a face. He thinks he's discovered something and Nigel is being dismissive.

"Selkie, watch the cliff," Nigel says, "and think about the woman. We'll act like we're not here."

Derek takes the hint and we sit like the three wise monkeys, watching the sun on the cliff as the shadows swallow up grass and stone.

It could be an experience of deep connection with the souls beneath us in the earth, but the expectation of seeing her again is making me tense. My chest is pounding with the surf, which is all but drowning out the singing shell.

"Breathe," Nigel whispers in my ear.

Suddenly I don't feel safe, even with the boys beside me. They mean well but the woman's got such a hold over me she could easily lure me away from their well-meaning arms. It's one thing to conjure her up behind my eyelids but there's no way I'm going to imagine her back onto the cliff.

Nothing happens. No-one appears. And at last the cliff is deep in shadow.

"She didn't show," Derek says, looking dejected. "We got here too late and missed her."

"There could be a lot of reasons why she didn't show up," Nigel says.

"I didn't want to see her," I say. They need to know the truth.

"That probably did it."

"Why?" Derek asks.

"Because we're playing with something we don't understand. And I'm scared. Of what she'll do to me next time. Last time I nearly ended up on the rocks so I'm not going to call her back until I know who she is, what she wants. It's too...perilous."

On the way back to the car we pass the star fruit tree. I'm reaching for one when Nigel stops me. "Did you eat one last Sunday?"

"Several. Does it matter?"

"I don't know, but the souls of the dead are said to live in the fruit that grows in graveyards."

Bloody hell. "And eating them...?"

"Regenerates the soul that lives there." He sees my alarmed expression. "It's a metaphor, Selkie."

"For what? Getting pregnant with a demon?"

"More like giving birth...to ancient wisdom."

I leave the fruit alone.

***

We return to Kailua Bay and wait out the traffic jam at Kalapawai Market. No-one is hungry so we sip coffees in silence. We'll be back too late for my dinner date with Roger and I'm relieved. After my terror at the cemetery just now the quest for her photo feels dangerous. Is it just a snapshot of her image or something more? Something I don't want to know.

I text an apology but Roger's not taking no for an answer. He'll be in the darkroom all night, he says, and wants me to join him. Any time. When I beg off, his texts become more petulant until I turn off my phone.

It's late when the boys drop me home. On the stairs the smells of a dozen cuisines remind me how long it's been since lunch. When I open the front door Wanda is on her bed with a book.

"There was a landslide on the Pali Highway," she says. "And a rumour's going round it was predicted by Pele." She gives me a meaningful look.

"We were caught in the traffic jam, otherwise it's got nothing to do with me. And we went back to the cemetery but I didn't see the woman."

She starts to speak but stops and stares. "Where did you get the cowry shell?"

With everything else I've forgotten about it. But its voice is still in my ears. "The Swap Meet. The Chinese woman with the shells. A friend of Nigel's did the macramé today."

She watches as I struggle with the knot. "Did they tell you about cowry shells?"

"Tell me what?" That they sing?

"Their special powers."

She's getting glasses of wine. As I make some toast and Vegemite I tell her about the singing.

She puts the shell to her ear and shakes her head. "I told you, it must be for you."

"But I don't understand what I'm hearing. It's just…noise."

"In the islands, cowry shells keep the feminine spirit safe. Because they're connected to the power of the ocean."

"Oceans terrify me."

"Well, I've only heard good stories about cowry shells. So it's singing a spell of safety. That fits with the threat that's hanging over you. And if you bought it from the Chinese woman, it's got Chinese symbolism too. Let's look it up."

The news from Wiki isn't all bad. The cowry is the Chinese symbol of wealth and prosperity. They even used its shape to create their pictograph for money.

Money reminds me of Andrew. His house valuation seems a lifetime ago, but it's Monday in Sydney so I put the shell aside and make a call to a valuer. He wants to view the property inside and out so I supply Andrew's number and warn him to expect fireworks.

Then, with a tummy full of toast, ears brimming with singing and the comforting image of Andrew's face red with fury, I climb into bed. It must be the distance between us that's given me all this courage.

***

The tunnel is long and dark and it ends in the place full of stars. I've been here before but now there's a party going on. All my friends are here, but as I mingle it's clear that I'm invisible. I run from person to person, trying to get them to notice me, suddenly terrified that I'm already dead. Then the stars turn into star fruit hanging from a magical tree. The woman appears and plucks a fruit off the tree. When she offers it to me I don't want to take it, but her eyes are mesmerising and when I touch the fruit it turns into a cowry shell with a thousand eyes and snarling teeth. I scream and try to shake it off, but it sticks to my hand and my gesticulations become a dance. Soon I'm twirling wildly, dancing through the throng on feet that are out of control, and when I look down they're staining everything red. Then the monkey on my shoulder grabs the cowry shell and puts it in his mouth. The music stops but the monkey is giving birth to a demon. I scream and scream but the demon just laughs because my voice is as invisible as I am.

I wake in a sweat, wondering where I am, feeling threatened and alone. It's the old feeling and it sucks the air out of me. Then everything flips and I'm gripped by a hyper-connection to all the weirdness. There's something I'm not getting from this collision of phenomena.

Something...*simple*. The word makes me stop and sit very still, waiting for an insight that doesn't come.

At last I stumble out of bed and remember it's Monday. A new week. My thoughts turn to Goals for Gold. There's still a lot of work to do before Thursday and Lester Sloane. But what's more urgent? The seminar with ten million dollars and all that fame at stake? Or the photo that holds the key to life and death? Yesterday I was afraid to look at it, but today I know I must.

It's early but I phone Derek. He's half asleep but he can't resist the adventure so we arrange to meet at Roger's in a couple of hours.

After breakfast and a shower I spy the cowry lying on the bedside table. It's baring its teeth and snatches of the dream come back – trying to shake it off my hand, dancing out of control, my bleeding feet. It feels like a warning even though Wanda thinks the shell's protecting me. She's already gone so I leave the flat with a bare neck.

On the bus I get my courage up for the task ahead. If Roger's key is back in the flowerpot we won't need the jemmy. Then, as if he's psychic, the man himself calls.

"I'm working *chez moi* today," he says and I want to scream. "And I have a *leetle* surprise for you."

I hesitate for a long moment.

"I know," he says, "you're saving yourself for marriage, you're speed-reading *War and Peace*, you're straightening your pubic hair..."

I wish he didn't make me laugh. "It's my seminar, Roj. It's on at the end of the week and it isn't finished."

"But this is something you need to see," he says, pausing for effect. "A...photograph."

I stop breathing. "A photograph? Why do I...need to see it?"

His laugh isn't pretty. He's paying me back for last night. "That's for me to know. and you to find out, Miss Lunatic."

"I'll be there in twenty minutes."

I try Derek but he isn't answering. Probably already in the car. I text him the changed arrangements, hoping he gets the message.

I take the shortest route through Fort Street Mall. There's the usual mix of office workers and holiday-makers, old men and streetwalkers, but today it feels claustrophobic. Are they breathing the same air as me?

I keep watching every shadow as I try Derek again. No answer. Where is he? Striding up Roger's steps with the jemmy in his hand?

Outside Roger's gate there's no sign of Derek's car. I try his phone one more time. He's forbidden me to be alone with Roger but what choice have I got? Even if he was here he'd have to wait downstairs, and I have to know what's in that photograph. Even if Roger's retouched it, even if I can't trust it, I still have to know.

***

Roger greets me in Sheena's bathrobe. A bad sign. And there's something about his demeanour, a tension that's making his movements stiff. It's all I can do to step over the threshold and maintain a breezy manner. I manage to plant a kiss on his nose.

"Where's this surprise then?" I chirp as something cold wraps itself around my spine.

He takes my elbow and steers me into the bedroom. I try to stay relaxed but my tension must be showing. At the end of the bed we stop and he directs his gaze towards the back wall. But it isn't the woman, it's something worse.

Me.

My anger emerges as a sudden intake of breath. He must have been crouching at my feet because the angle is very explicit. It's black and white. Probably film. And on the old iron bed with only ambient light the effect is quite sordid – a sex worker drunk and out of it between clients. Was I asleep? Or just too blissed out on sex to notice the camera?

It's poster size, too big for Roger to develop at home. Does that mean all the guys at the print shop have seen it?

It takes all my self-control to strike a jokey tone. "This one isn't for the hair mag. Unless they're swapping blow-dries for blow jobs."

He laughs. "For my eyes only, Miss Sun. I captured you," he sweeps his arm towards the photo, "imprisoned you with my lens, and now...you're my most treasured possession."

Every instinct is screaming at me to leave because the man standing beside me is someone I no longer know. As he gazes at the poster his eyes are particularly bright and Wanda's warning rings in my ears. But will Roger do anything more? He's probably just going to keep it for himself – except that's the very thing I can't allow. He's stolen something from me and I want it back.

We gaze at it while my mind races. It looks like film so there's a negative somewhere. In the filing cabinet. I've got the key. But that means getting Roger out of the way. *Now.*

"It's...astonishing," I say, playing for time. "A work of...art."

"*Merci beaucoup.*" He seems oblivious to my real reaction. So far so good.

"Erotic too," I whisper, starting to undo my shirt.

"It has the same effect on me." He plants a kiss on my neck.

I hope my involuntary shudder looks like goose-bumps of passion.

"Bath," I murmur, matching his tone like all the marketing books have taught me. "And bubbles..." I undo another button. He tries to help but I turn him around and give him a gentle shove. "Hot water and lots of it. I've got my own *leetle* surprise."

To my relief he falls for it and disappears into the bathroom. When I hear water splashing into the tub I leap onto the mattress and snatch the poster off the wall. The temptation to tear it up almost wins but there isn't time. I take the key from my pocket. The taps are running and Roger is rattling bottles in the bathroom cupboard. The bubble bath was another gift from Sheena.

I need more noise to mask the sound of the filing cabinet. "*Molto* bubbles, *perfavore*."

He's a sucker for silly Italian and responds by thrashing his hands up and down in the water.

In the living room I unlock the cabinet. The thrashing continues so I know Roger must be bending over the bath with his back to the door. Instinct sends me to the bottom drawer first. Cameras. I don't need them. Next drawer up it's his laptop along with a file-case, a box of CDs and a remote hard drive. There's no more time so I grab them all, hoping it's everything. I'm reassured when the next two drawers contain suspension files of household bills.

It's time to get out of here. I turn away, then remember to lock the cabinet and slip the key back into my pocket. Festooned with loot I glide past the bathroom towards the open front door. By the time I reach the landing, my heart is bouncing so hard I have to slow down for the stairs.

It's another state of high emotion. Is that why I see her? A silvery figure at the entrance to the path. Her face is in shadow but I'm sure it's her. The same intensity. The same stillness. The same filmy skin. She's blocking the gate, blocking my exit, but my feet break into a run. All the way to the gate I feel the attraction drawing me. And all the way I keep her in view, but my hands are full so I can't reach for my phone and snap her again. We're only metres apart and I'm breathing hard when a reflection off a window blinds me, and when I can see again she's gone.

Several men in Aloha shirts are coming through the gate. They step aside with amused expressions as I rush past. But I'm not laughing.

On the street, before I can panic about finding a taxi, someone toots.

Derek.

He's illegally parked with the engine running. He leaps out and opens the rear door while I rush over and throw the booty inside.

Then I'm flopping on the passenger seat. "Lock the doors!"

Within seconds Roger appears at the gate, waving his arms, a silhouette against the sun. As I stare back at him something surreal takes hold of the scene. Like a moment frozen in time he's standing there without moving – a charcoal stick-figure with legs akimbo, pinned against a backdrop of light. Inside his gown he's a marionette, his bones turned to charred wood. And a voice speaks.

Roger's dead.

The message is so real I believe it, even though Roger is running towards us, wispy hair and bathrobe flying. Very much alive.

CHAPTER
Seventeen

Derek takes a series of backstreets before pulling onto the Lunalilo Freeway heading south.

"I got your text then my battery died."

"Thank God."

"Do you want to go home?"

I shake my head. "He knows where I live. But he doesn't know where you live, DD."

We're caught in traffic and I keep looking over my shoulder, expecting to see Roger bearing down on us, semi-naked behind the wheel. He looked angry enough. I'm hoping he hasn't unlocked the filing cabinet yet and discovered the real extent of my theft. It won't be long, but at Derek's he's got no chance of finding me.

Then I remember Wanda. That old block of flats has no security. He could pound on her door until she's forced to call the police. I send her a text suggesting she stays with her man for a day or two. She replies, making me promise to give up the juicy details later.

At University Avenue Derek exits, then loses us in a maze of streets before ascending to the hills behind Honolulu - Makiki Heights and the house he shares with Nigel. For the first time in the last hour I relax.

"You saved my life, DD."

"Is he the one who's trying to kill you? Stop me saying I told you so."

"Not literally."

"Killing your spirit?"

"Something like that."

He raises one eyebrow towards the contraband on the back seat. "His photo files?"

I tell him the sordid story of the poster.

"As soon as I saw myself sprawled on the wall it felt like my life was in danger. My nakedness, my vulnerability. The way he wanted to own me. Like being preserved by a mad taxidermist."

I look at the poster on the back seat. Did I get the negative for that too?

"He's seriously unhinged, wanting to possess you like that," Derek says. "Haven't you sensed that about him before?"

"Only lately. He's always let me think I'm just another shag-buddy. But he didn't let me go, even while Sheena was around."

Derek pulls into the driveway of a white two-storey house. Coastal modern, softened by tropical gardens, with a garage underneath and breathtaking views across Honolulu and the bay. It makes me wonder how a dementia nurse can afford an exclusive neighbourhood like this. Nigel Shaw, another mystery man, like Roger Nightingale.

Together we carry everything inside.

"You might have the photo of the woman," Derek says, nodding towards the loot.

Was she really there on Roger's path?

"I think I saw her."

Derek listens, then shakes his head. "You really need a specialist, Selkie. Someone who understands the spirit world and how it behaves. Especially with dodgy Roger up to his neck in it." He wipes his hands down his arms. "That's twice she's appeared in Nightingale's orbit. Is she's stalking you or him?"

I've got Roger's laptop. And his hard drive. If he's downloaded my cemetery pics, the woman might be here right now. I turn around, fearing she's sitting on Derek's sofa. She isn't.

Derek retells my story for Nigel as I unfurl the poster. I should be embarrassed but these two are my sisters.

Derek is horrified. "Such a violation."

Nigel taps the file-case. "What's in here?"

"His negatives, I hope, including this poster. It's locked." Suddenly I'm grinning. "I stole it all, Nigel. From right under Roger's nose."

"And I drove the getaway car," says Derek.

We look at each other and burst out laughing. It diffuses my dread about Roger's retribution.

"Did you bring back the jemmy?" Nigel asks Derek.

"I could use some matches first," I say.

They let me do it alone. First I shred the poster, then carry the fragments through to the kitchen where Nigel's disabled the smoke alarm.

It takes a long time for the pieces to burn. Tiny pieces of me. Fragmented and vulnerable. As match after match ignites and catches, they curl under the flame and fall from my fingers into the sink.

***

Nigel jemmies open the file-case and leaves me sitting with it on the floor of their spare room. It's red, which suddenly seems significant. Inside I find a series of files, each bulging with negatives and prints. The labels look like nicknames, in alphabetical order. My eyes rest on *Miss Lunatic* about halfway back and I suppress a rising sick feeling as I take in the rest: *Blondie, Bobo, Bonfire, Carol by Candlelight, Flick Me,*

Gabfest, Jelly Wrestler, My Precious, Phanny, She-Girl, Tor, Zaa Zaa. The man's been busier than a leech in a nudist camp.

Holding my breath, I open my file.

But it's empty. The negative isn't here. I cry out in frustration and fear. Roger must be keeping it somewhere else, and after running off with his files I've probably goaded him into some serious payback.

My mouth goes dry as I imagine the photo scanned and circulated on the web for all to see. He's linked into some of my network so he could do some serious damage. But right now there's nothing I can do, so I take a deep breath and turn to the others.

Every print shows a woman. Nude. Sexually aroused. With face obscured. Like the poster of me, they all seem to be candids. He stands at the end of the bed like a wraith with a tripod. Blondie's bush is white and luxuriant, like an unclipped poodle. My Precious has enormous boobs that sag to each side, drawing the eye away from her ample recesses. She-Girl is Sheena and, unlike the others, her face is visible. She looks very young, with almost no figure and shaved pubes. In most shots she's spreading her legs like a kid in a sandpit.

The name Jelly Wrestler catches my eye. She's athletic, with tight buttocks and a glistening vulva. Her face is in shadow but I've seen those cheekbones before. Gerry. Jelly Wrestler. Roger's gift for nomenclature leaps off the page. I flip through her file, finding fashion shots amongst the porn. Is he getting sex in exchange for creating her portfolio? The fashion pics would play into his artistic delusions.

Derek knocks before opening the door. "It's very quiet in here. Just checking you're OK."

I sigh. "You can look if you want. They've already had

their privacy invaded."

Derek notices what I noticed. "Are they drugged?"

"Only on sex, I think. He has the knack of the photojournalist."

"And the paparazzo."

"Yep. Waits till we're preoccupied, uses ambient light. Click."

"What's he doing with all these prints?"

"Besides owning them? Nothing, I hope. If he was posting them on the web he'd be using digital, wouldn't he?"

"Unless he's pretending they're 'art'. Creates them in his darkroom, then scans them and exploits them like any other porn fiend."

"My own negative is missing."

"That's not good. Something tells me revenge is his real art form."

When Roger finally calls, we're in the living room and I put my phone on speaker so the boys can listen in.

"I thought you were different, Miss Lunatic. Special. But you're just a common thief, hmmm?"

"That's rich. You're the one who took that photo without my permission."

"Permission? You don't understand even the basic rules of the paparazzi. The subject doesn't own the photo. As long as it isn't *posing*, it's fair game."

"The subject? We're talking about *me*."

He isn't listening. "I photographed you engaged in your normal business, I'm afraid. Not posing but *exposing* yourself. It's very simple. The image belongs to me."

He hangs up. He's angry but not as angry as he should be, so he hasn't opened the filing cabinet.

I'm breathing hard when I look at the boys. "It's

perfectly legal because I wasn't posing?"

Derek shakes his head. "He just talks about rules so he can drop his pants at them."

***

Fortified with lunch, we turn on Roger's laptop but it's password protected.

I didn't dare ask Nigel to help, but he's already flipping through the CDs. "If these are back-up storage," he says, "they'll be quicker than trying to crack his password. I'll take the hard drive."

We use three computers to triple the effort. Derek and I divide the CDs and start scrolling, looking for anything that might be my cemetery pics. Nigel finds he can access the hard drive so he's got plenty to look at.

"Look for a dog pissing on a headstone," I say. "That should be pretty distinctive."

"Or a naked woman standing on a cliff," says Nigel.

"Unless he's deleted them," says Derek. "Not artistic enough."

"From the look of these files," I say, "he never deletes anything. He composes so many images from different sources, he keeps everything."

Nigel again. "That fits with his ownership obsession. He can't bear to let anything go."

We find thousands of photos from different cemeteries but his system of labelling is idiosyncratic.

"Drop in on random thumbnails," Nigel says, "see if you recognise the cemetery. All those blank gravestones. And who knows? Roger might have photographed the woman himself."

Shit.

It's the first time I've thought of it. Roger was there with his cameras. Did he see the woman? Did he photograph her? A naked figure on a windswept cliff. *Life and Death* encapsulated in one image. It would explain why he swapped the memory cards and made sure I never got to see my pics. Or his. If I entered the same subject in the competition, even if his photo was better than mine it wouldn't be unique.

But if Roger photographed her, that means he saw me running to the cliff and nearly going over the edge. It was ages before he rescued me. Did he leave me there while he swapped the memory cards, with me too freaked out to notice? Such treachery would no longer surprise me.

We continue looking for anything human in the endless images of marble and stone.

After a while, Derek says, "My eyes are still working but the link with my brain is severed. I've got no idea what I'm looking at."

"There are five CDs left," Nigel says. "Let's just do a spot check in case we hit pay dirt."

That's when I find a whole CD of Gerry. Hundreds of fashion shots, many already retouched.

Derek whistles. "This file must be worth thousands. Has she got her own copy, do you think?"

"I doubt it. I think he took them in exchange for sex so he'd have every reason not to hand them over."

"That would be our Mr Nightingale."

It's another half hour before we admit defeat and Derek pours glasses of homemade lemonade.

"He must have a secret stash," says Nigel. "The photos from that Sunday. Why?"

"Because he photographed the woman," I say.

This thought is trounced by a text from Roger. He's

finally opened his filing cabinet and his two-word message oozes menace.

You'll keep.

A wave of malevolence descends like a cloud and envelops me in something dark and airless. In a moment, all optimism is sucked from me and I'm drowning in despair. Images of the cliff, of the woman, of the sea, flash at me. The rhythm puts me into a waking coma where the horror is real but I'm powerless against it. The boys' features blur. Something heavy presses against my heart. I try to open my mouth but nothing happens. No air. No sound. Then blackness.

CHAPTER
Eighteen

Nigel is taking my pulse.

"You just blacked out and fell on your face," he tells me.

I lift my head and take in his frown, then Derek's. Whatever happened, I'm back. From a place I never want to visit again. A dark place. An evil place. A place where the malice was palpable.

"Look around the room," Nigel says, "and name the things you see."

"I'm not having a panic attack."

"Could've fooled me," Derek says.

I gaze around their kitchen. The walls are pristine white, the counter shiny black. Stainless-steel appliances gleam. When I pick up the mug Derek passes me, the coffee tastes good.

"Coffee," I say. "Friends."

"Worried friends," says Derek. "What happened?"

"Probably just exhausted," I whisper, wishing it was true.

***

Nigel agrees to zoom over to my place with a list of clothes and makeup I'll need for the rest of the week. It has to be Nigel because if Roger turns up and starts raising hell he'll be able to deal with him. After an hour he's back. He holds out a coat hanger with my other suit and puts down my little red suitcase.

"Thanks, Nige."

"Everything on the list. Plus this." He slips his hand into his pocket and pulls something out.

The cowry shell.

"It was on your bedside table. With this underneath."

An envelope with my name on it, written in Wanda's handwriting.

We stare at the shell and the envelope.

"Aren't you going to open it?" Derek asks.

Nigel puts the shell on the bed and winks at Derek. "Shouldn't we be in the kitchen?"

"Food in fifteen," Derek says as they leave.

The shell's on its back, showing me its teeth. But I'm hallucinating again. A shell is a shell. It doesn't have a face. And when I look again that's what I see. A cowry shell. It's just like the woman. Unless I find that photo, there's no evidence she ever existed, only my own eyes. Eyes that play tricks.

I rip open the envelope and see one of Wanda's fish – she's made a series of cards. This one looks like Roger. Until I close my eyes and open them again. Now it's just a fish.

In her calligraphic style she writes:

> *Were you listening when I told you about the power of cowry shells? Especially after your text about Roger. The shell is here, meaning you're not wearing it.*
>
> *I told Coral and she's horrified you're ignoring this psychic gift. She says it's no coincidence the shell turned up. It's a sign. You're in danger – that's the word she used – and the shell will protect you from spiritual invasion. But you've got to wear it. All the time.*
>
> *And here's my theory: if you see the woman again, the*

shell might be her messenger. Hold it up to your ear and hear what it's saying.

Do it. Now.

Wanda.

Her writing carries her voice so strongly I pick up the shell and hold it in my hand. The singing gets louder, pulsing through my fingers. And the surface, at first cool, turns hot as the spots begin to glow. Wanda calls it powerful and I can feel it, something fiery filling me up. Could it be channelling the woman? And all I have to do is pay attention? At John's, the singing seemed to creep up on me and slip past my fear, soothing me into a state of peace. If I want to know who the woman is, I have to take a chance.

I lift my hand and press the shell to my ear and hear something I've heard before.

Drumming.

But this time I don't start dancing. This time I collapse in tears.

Derek's been listening at the door and at the first stifled sob he rushes in and takes me in his arms.

"I don't know...why I'm...crying, DD. I listened...to the shell...and started...bawling."

"What did it say?"

"Nothing. It never *says* anything. But the rhythm seems to speak to me and it makes me feel so sad."

"So you've heard it before?"

"Yes, a kind of drumming. But last time...it made me go...wild."

He grins. "Wild is good."

"Is it?" He didn't see me dance. Or see the bloody feet in my dream.

Nigel arrives and I show them Wanda's note.

"Well, you do need psychic protection," Derek says,

picking up the cowry. "But how did it find you? There were dozens of shells on that stall. Spooky." Then he hits on a thought. "That's why the woman didn't turn up. When we went back to the cemetery."

"Because of the shell? But Wanda thinks it could be channelling her."

"Or driving her away. You were wearing it, remember? It was doing its job."

Nigel hasn't said anything. He's fiddling with his smart phone. "See if this app can hear anything."

It's an insane idea but Derek turns the cowry's mouth towards the phone and, to our amazement, it begins to record.

"It's hearing something."

They can't stop grinning and I feel a surge of hope.

The answer takes longer than usual, as if the app is digging deep, but after an excruciating thirty seconds four words appear on the screen.

"*Siren Song*," Nigel reads out loud. "*Artist unknown.*"

I sigh. "Well, we know what a siren is – a seductive woman who destroys men." I wish.

"That's its modern meaning," Derek says, "but the sirens from Greek mythology –"

"Lured men to drown with their singing," I say.

"Not exactly," he says.

Nigel's already on YouTube. He plays several 'Siren Songs' by various artists but they're nothing like what I've been hearing.

"Artist unknown," Derek says. "That must mean the original sirens' song. From Homer's *Odyssey*."

"How could the app know that?" I ask. "Was that music ever written down?"

"I don't think so. The song of the sirens was so

seductive that sailors dived into the sea and swam ashore where the sirens ate them. Odysseus was the only man who heard it and lived to talk about it. He filled his sailors' ears with wax to protect them. But he wanted to hear it so he got them to tie him to the mast so he couldn't jump overboard."

"What did it sound like?"

"He never said. But when he heard the music he tried everything to tear away his bindings."

What I'm hearing is that seductive. And I can't forget my feather-duster boogie, the wild desire to dance until I dropped.

CHAPTER
Nineteen

Tuesday morning. Two days before the seminar. We drive down the mountain to the office or 'descend into the underworld', as Derek calls his daily commute. Against my better judgement I'm wearing the cowry shell after Wanda followed her note with a text and the boys looked so expectant I couldn't disappoint them. And this morning the singing is subdued. That makes two of us.

I throw myself into the seminar. At least with Goals for Gold I can focus on fame and fortune for a while. Less flim-flam than phantoms.

Derek hovers in his office and refuses to leave even for food. "In case Nightingale turns up and gets nasty." He insists on a pizza delivery for lunch.

By five o'clock I'm ready for Katsuya and Sloane with a whole day to spare. Even the seal activities feel perfect. Tomorrow I'll just need to pack my seminar case. After a day of intensity I can almost relax.

Except for my final meeting with Guy.

***

He greets me with an enormous hug, as if our relationship has morphed into something personal. My response is muted. This is strictly business.

"I need an early night, Guy. Goals for Gold is perfect and I've done some great work on the seal seminar. Several activities are ready for trialling. Do you want to preview them?"

"Nope. I trust you to do that. Now it's on the launch pad the rest's up to you." He winks. "Doing what you're good at."

"Thank you. So why are we here?"

He takes my arm and leads me to the sofa. "Tactics."

He goes to the whiteboard and picks up a marker. "OK. Let's brainstorm a list of qualities Sloane's looking for, then take each one and put down how you'll demonstrate it." He thinks for a minute. "Attractive." He writes it down. "Original...quirky..."

He expects me to help but these already sound like someone else.

"...dynamic...successful. Rich..."

"Rich?" That wakes me up. "Does Sloane expect me to be rich?"

"What else? The audience trusts you to know your stuff. That's why they're there. To get a cut of the Midas Touch."

"But I'm broke." One seminar doesn't change that.

"We're brainstorming, babe. Keep going, discuss it later." He turns back and starts again. "Confident, mature...witty, wise..."

I haven't suggested a single word.

"Sexy..."

"I don't believe it."

He stops. "Sex sells, Selkie."

Like the tongue-twister: by the sea shore?

"You're selling yourself to your audience so you gotta be sexy. Keep brainstorming."

"Wait a minute, Guy. Most of the male gurus aren't sexy. I've seen them."

"They don't have to be. But for a woman it's different rules. Sex appeal is mandatory. Old boilers can't be success gurus." He winks again. "Don't worry. You've either got it or you haven't...and you've got it. Now stop interrupting."

He continues with the list but I'm feeling uncomfortable. Of course I want to be sexy. Guy might think I've got it but I haven't forgotten I'm Andrew's 'desiccated spinster'. Then I remember there's only one opinion that counts – Lester Sloane's.

"OK." He's got to the end of the list. Twenty qualities I'm supposed to emulate. "Take each word, write down how you'll demonstrate it, identify any loopholes." He points to the first one. "Attractive – no problem. Just tame that hair and you'll knock him dead."

"Not too dead, I hope. Let's keep him breathing till he signs a contract. But wearing what?"

He shrugs. "What you're wearing tonight."

"A red power suit? Fine, it's all I've got, but what happened to sexy?"

"We'll get to sexy in a minute. And the suit's perfect." He rushes on. "Original, quirky – the seal seminar's got them covered."

He works his way through the list, leaving 'rich' and 'sexy' till last.

"These two work together." He looks at my hemline. "Take that skirt up an inch or three. Distract Sloane from your bank balance."

"That's not funny, Guy."

His face turns serious. "It wasn't meant to be."

"What are you implying?"

"Sloane's a man, you're a woman. A very attractive woman. You've got it, exploit it."

"I still don't know what you mean."

"Put it this way: if you gotta choose between sexy and rich...choose sexy. Rich comes after."

"After what?"

"After you play him like a violin. Have I gotta spell it out?"

When I ask the next question my voice is shaking. "Is Sloane interested in my seminar...in my skills as a presenter?"

"Sure he is. But he's gotta be interested in you first. He likes what he sees, he invites you to the bar. One thing leads to another."

I'm appalled at my naivety. The brainstorming's just a snow job, it's been the casting couch all along.

"Where are you going?" Guy says when I stand up. "I haven't finished with you yet."

"I've heard enough."

His face hardens. The easy-go-lucky Texan has gone. "You need to be more ruthless, babe. Focus on what you want, on who you wanna be. It makes compromising your integrity...effortless."

But I'm walking. It's a pleasure to slam the door.

Guy Morrison, prize jerk. And I never saw it coming. Tainting everything I've worked so hard for. Is Lester Sloane just another mirage?

***

It's one of those romantic evenings with a light breeze. The look-at-me crowd are out and about, jostling and laughing, catching up with each other, carefree and intent on fun. Anger and tears separate me. People stop to stare and their curiosity makes me run. When I stop, I'm outside my office, and by the time I've climbed the stairs, unlocked my door and flopped into my chair, I can think.

Did Guy predict my reaction? Probably, judging by the

way he sidled up to the truth. He didn't want to tell me too soon, but he'll be betting there's still time for the ten million dollars to transform my ethics to mush.

Even after I checked Sloane out on Google and saw how attractive he is, it never entered my head to sleep with him. Now the old joke comes back: if I agree to sleep with him for ten million dollars, then he can change his offer to ten dollars. Because once we've established what I am we're just haggling over the price.

Maybe I'll sleep with him for nothing, for my own selfish pleasure. Rub Guy's face right in it. It's not going to happen but the thought amuses me. A scintilla of power coming from somewhere.

I ask myself if Guy's 'tactics' are his idea alone. I open my inbox and reread Sloane's email, still unanswered. *You've either got it or you haven't.* The same words I've just heard Guy use. Is *spark* just Sloane-speak for the casting couch? Then there's his invitation for a drink afterwards. Perfect for a little seduction. 'One thing leads to another.' So much for my tiny hope that Guy is acting alone.

Sloane is already booked to attend the seminar, and Guy's too ruthless to cancel him even though I've made my attitude crystal clear. If I call the whole thing off just to avoid him, I'll have to return Katsuya's fee and my reputation will be in shreds before I've even begun. If I go ahead and Sloane's at the back of the room, the distraction will be extreme. He'll be testing my ability to stay professional. Big time.

Then it hits me.

I'm not stuck with Guy or Sloane. I can give them both the flick.

I write to Guy first, terminating our agreement as of tonight. In line with the terms, I'll have to pay him his percentage for another five years to cover any profit I make from his advice – as if – but at least the five years start winding down today. I send it as an email, then print it and put it in an envelope. That's one less monkey on my shoulder. The metaphor almost amuses me.

Now for Sloane. This one will be harder. Polite but unequivocal.

Dear Mr Sloane

Thank you for your email and your interest in my potential 'spark'. But we're never going to find out if I've got it or I haven't because I've decided not to go ahead with your assessment on Thursday. Please cancel your plans to attend my seminar. I apologise for any inconvenience this late change may cause you. I've only just decided on this course of action.

I've also terminated my agreement with Guy Morrison so he no longer represents me.

Regards

Selkie Moon

I stare at it for a while, and decide to remove the words *we're never going to find out if I've got it or I haven't, because*...They make me sound petulant – which I am – and why should I care what Sloane thinks since I'm never going to need to impress him, but I remove them anyway. They give him an inkling into my state of mind and it's none of his business. Let him wonder why I've terminated him, along with Guy. Put a tiny crinkle in his confidence. As if that matters either.

After I've taken the phrase out, I change *Regards* to *Yours sincerely*. More truthful. I check my spelling and hit send.

Then I fall apart.

With an arrogant click of my mouse I've done it. Thrown away everything I've worked so hard for. The chance to finally shake off Andrew's judgement and be someone.

Not because I'm not clever. Not because I'm not tough. Not because I can't cut it on the international stage. But because I'm too honourable, too precious, too bloody high-and-mighty...to do whatever it takes.

Derek calls. He thought he was picking me up at Guy's and I tell him where I am. He can hear the desolation in my voice.

"Has Nightingale been there? You shouldn't be alone in an empty building, Selkie."

He arrives and bundles me, sobbing and inconsolable, into his office and his armchair. Then he's rigging up an oil burner and filling the tiny room with fumes.

"Bloody hell, DD. I'm way beyond the powers of essential oils. Haven't you got any bourbon in that filing cabinet?"

"That bad, huh?"

But before Dr Derek will open his medicine chest he insists on a consultation and I'm too far gone to protest. I blubber the story out backwards, trying to unravel why I've plunged into the pit.

Derek summarises. "It turns out to be a high-stakes whoring job. So you tell Morrison to piss off. Then you tell Sloane to piss off. Then you shatter into a zillion pieces."

Just like the shredded poster. I nod.

"But you've put your dignity ahead of fame and fortune, Selkie. This is a victory for honour."

"A victory? So how come I feel like shit? Like I've blown everything that's important to me?"

"You've been under a lot of psychological pressure. Guy's betrayal is the last straw."

"That's not it."

"Come on then, pony up. Tell me what's going around

in your head."

Through streams of tears I go over old ground. How Guy's betrayed me and what a fool I am not to have seen it coming. Then I start talking about Sloane and his email and having spark and being myself and the answer comes out in a rush. "Sloane might have liked me and I'd be on my way to the big time."

Now I'm howling and Derek has to raise his voice. "Worth screwing for, is that it?" His words echo through the empty building. "Making millions would be worth it after all?"

"No," I yell back. "That's not it." I'm shaking my head, trying to think straight. "It's not the money. I don't care about the money. Only Guy cares about the money. That's all he talked about. Landing Sloane and the ten fucking million."

"Of which he gets thirty per cent. So his agenda's a no-brainer. But if it's not the money, what is it? What else is there?"

That's when a light goes on and we say it together. "The fucking fame!"

It's a revelation. The awful truth. And I'm blubbering again.

"You wouldn't sleep with Sloane for the money," Derek whispers. "But you'd sleep with him for the chance to be a star, is that it?"

It's a tough question that only Derek can ask.

"Yes."

He makes Irish coffees. Double shots. He knows what to do in a crisis – get drunk with a friend. We've done it before but the crises were usually his. Nigel's arrival has changed all that so now it's my turn. But we know the routine by heart. He bustles with the kettle and the glasses while I wallow in self-pity in the armchair.

"What did you call it?" I sniffle. "Martyrdom for a principle? Joan of Arc in a *muu-muu?*" Is this how I'm going to die? It feels like it.

"A victory for honour."

"That's it. The pyrrhic victory of a nobody. A serial nobody."

He's got his back to me, pouring boiling water into the coffee plunger. "It wouldn't work, you know. Sleeping with Sloane for the fame."

"Why not? I've seen him. He's not bad. Under fifty. He's probably still good in the sack." My tears have dried but my heart is stone. "Good enough."

"That's not what I mean. It's not just about making it, is it? It's also about *earning* it. And if you screw for it, you're never sure why you made it, if you're good enough. For the rest of your career, every time you step onto that stage you wonder: am I a good presenter, or just a good lay?"

"Maybe being a good lay would be enough." Better than a desiccated spinster. "Or all the applause would drown out my doubts."

"You've got it bad, Selkie. Spinning yourself a web of bullshit."

"Shut up and finish the coffees, will you? I'm in serious danger of dying of thirst."

***

It's a short walk to Derek's car and I lean on him all the way. Luckily I'm not going home, because the thought of being alone terrifies me. In my depleted state, whole hordes of entities might party in my aura. Then who would I be?

It's way past rush hour and an easy drive into the hills.

Then I'm sinking into another armchair - deeper and softer than the one in his office - while Derek whips up some pasta.

"Food and lots of it," he prescribes.

He must do a regular supermarket run if he's got fresh fettuccine and ham and mushrooms and spring onions and pine nuts and sour cream in his fridge. It makes my head spin just imagining it. A fridge full of fresh food. My fridge - empty of everything but Wanda's strange ingredients - demands nothing of me. But a relationship has domesticated Derek.

We eat at the kitchen table. He doesn't seem worried about my alcohol level and opens a bottle of red. Roll on oblivion. The pasta is perfect and I find I'm as hungry as ever.

It's the full belly that does it.

Clears my head.

Makes me decide to ring Sloane.

CHAPTER
Twenty

"Are you sure?" Derek asks over breakfast. French toast and coffee.

I made the mistake of telling him last night before I collapsed into bed. Nigel won't be home for another few hours so I've got Derek and his opinions all to myself.

"What's the hurry?" he says, frowning. "Give yourself time to reflect. Make a decision when you haven't got a hangover. Sloane can always come to your next seminar."

"He'll have forgotten me by then. Found someone else. Chances like this are ephemeral, DD. This way I haven't lost anything, not really."

"Except your self-respect."

I ignore him. "I'll just apologise for jerking him around. Tell him I was terminating Guy and included him in the same action. That I've thought it over, changed my mind, woman's prerogative..."

"And then you'll lie back on his casting couch?"

"Only because it's a worthwhile cause. My own glory." In spite of a throbbing head my energy is back.

"You'll regret it," Derek says.

"You don't know that."

"I know you."

Then he uses his writer's gift to describe the possible scene over drinks.

"Sloane the Sleaze, so rich he can wag his little finger and create an earthquake just for kicks. And out-of-her-depth Selkie, so desperate to impress, Sloane can...smell it."

I remember the charm oozing from Sloane's email like molten kryptonite and the thought of putting myself at his mercy sends a chill down to the tips of my toes.

"The price is too high," Derek continues. "And the rewards too uncertain. It could turn out to be the worst experience of Selkie's life. Worse than the worst. Humiliating, degrading. And then there's the risk of catching something. Syphilis is on the rise and –"

"It's OK, DD. Stop. I've decided. I won't sleep with Sloane for any reason. He's Guy's man, and I'm finished with Guy. With both of them."

He can't quite believe my turnaround. "What about the fucking fame?"

"When you were talking I got it. I don't need Sloane to make me into somebody. That was Andrew's trick. It's my job now. Otherwise I'm just a puppet. I just needed to go almost all the way, to confront the truth."

He hugs me. When he pulls away his eyes are moist. Nigel might be mysterious and a bit tetchy but he's softened Derek.

"I'm starving," I say. "Are you rationing the French toast?"

***

After a lazy morning, it's almost midday when Derek and I head into the office. I could get used to this routine, especially with the live-in chef and driver. And it's distracted me from obsessing about the seminar. Only one day to go.

The light on my office machine is blinking. That's a first. Three calls this morning, all from Oliver Katsuya.

Derek listens in. "That guy's a control freak. I hope his negative vibes don't poison the atmosphere tomorrow."

"Don't worry. I know his type. He's only sending his staff. He won't be there to throw his weight around so he's double-checking everything."

"I hope you're right. His energy coats you like an oil slick."

Derek goes next door and I log onto emails. There's one from Guy, written after I left last night. I scan it for expletives and count at least ten. Tut, tut, the man's broken the golden rule of not sending an email when he's angry. He should get an entity to mind his bad feelings.

***

Derek found the hotel through a contact and the seminar room is perfect. It spills onto a private terrace where small pools trickle water under palms – ideal for small break-out groups, and no bay view to distract me from my notes.

As the people from Skape arrive, Derek and Nigel attend to the registration list and the name tags. They've dressed in matching Aloha shirts with orchids in their buttonholes. I feel honoured. They're mixing vibrancy with professionalism and leaving me free to prepare myself at the front of the room.

When Derek gives me the nod that all twenty people are seated, the noisier-than-usual crowd – because they all work together – suddenly falls silent. This is why I came to Hawaii, just for this moment – to present my own seminar. As a surge of emotion fills my chest I push it down and begin.

To my surprise I'm relaxed and witty, probably because no-one's evaluating me. No Guy. No Sloane. Just me and my audience. They love what they hear and the activities and group exercises flow. All my creativity pays off and the program unfolds as I planned. We break for coffee at eleven and then for a buffet at one. It's clear from the chatter that it's going as well as I'd hoped.

In the late afternoon I even give them a taste of the seal seminar. I'd decided to ditch it along with Guy but it suddenly pops into my mind with a new name – Being Sleek. It's so offbeat and fun that it's perfect to take us through to the end of the day. Pity Lester Sloane didn't happen by. But I remind myself he's history.

My audience is moving out, probably to the bar, and I'm packing up when someone strolls over. His hand on my shoulder gets my attention. He's still wearing his name tag: *Alister*.

"Let me buy you a drink," he says.

I stifle a groan. There's always someone who wants to cosy up to the presenter – usually the most attention-seeking creep – and I'm staying here tonight. Better lose this guy before he becomes a problem. Except he's kind of cute. Have I met him before? I noticed him several times during the day. Attentive, but quiet. Not taking any notes. Now I look more closely. Mid-forties. Longish well-cut curly hair, fair with a touch of grey. White linen shirt and denim jeans. Muscles that make Roger look like Pipe-cleaner Man. Designer stubble and a large infectious smile full of real teeth. I don't recognise his name but something rings a bell.

"Thanks," I say, "but I always decline invitations during the seminar. I know you'll understand." Except he saw me hesitate.

"Looks like I'll just have to cancel that booking on the *lanai*." He adds a wink to the smile. "And it's such a perfect night."

"Do I know you?" I ask.

He puts out his hand. "Almost. Alister Sloane. Also

known as Lester. Long story."

But he doesn't get to tell it. Just as I'm about to fly at him for his duplicity or fall into his arms in a swoon, Derek rushes up and rescues me.

"Everyone's buzzing, Selkie. We don't even need to go to the bar, we're high already. That Sleek stuff – didn't that turn out to be..." He acknowledges Sloane. "Sorry to interrupt."

"That's OK, Derek. Alister is just leaving." I turn back to Sloane. "Nice to meet you." I wait for him to take the hint.

"Are you buzzing too?" Derek asks me. "Or just exhausted?"

"Both. That's why I'm going to say my farewells." I pick up my seminar case, but Sloane hasn't moved.

"See you tomorrow, Alister," Derek says. He doesn't know who he is.

"I hope so. But I'm double-booked."

"Cancel it. You'd be crazy to miss tomorrow. Selkie's on fire."

Normally I'd stop Derek putting pressure on a client, but Sloane's not a real client and I want to hear what he says.

"You're right, Derek. I'll be back." Then he leans towards me and whispers, "And tomorrow I'll insist on that drink."

After he's moved away, Derek says, "Who's Mr Suave?"

"He calls himself Alister, DD. Alister Sloane. AKA Lester. And you let him in."

Derek's mouth drops open and for once he's lost for words. He grabs his clipboard and runs his eye down the participant list. "He isn't here."

"There were only twenty people, I counted them."

"Yeah, I remember. One of the Skape group didn't turn up, then Alister cruised in at the last minute and took his place. Paid cash. I must have been so flustered with the registrations I didn't write down his name. Alister Sloane. Shit."

"It's OK. We didn't expect him to show up. In fact he wasn't invited. If that other guy hadn't been a no-show we would have had odd numbers."

"And not enough pens. Do you think Sloane arranged for someone to drop out?"

"I hope he's not that manipulative."

"He might be. That makes him unpredictable, Selkie. Possibly dangerous."

And as smooth as chocolate.

But he's not going to spoil my evening, my sense of my own success. I decline Derek's invitation to join them and order room service, even breaking my rule about no alcohol during a seminar with a half bottle of champagne. French.

I settle down in front of the view of Mount Tantalus. In the late sunlight the shadows fall into the ravines in sharp creases. Except for Sloane, the day has been perfect and just a glimpse of the Being Sleek seminar turned everyone on.

But what about tomorrow? If he really cancels his other commitment Sloane will be oozing charm all over me and watching my every move. What does he want? With his money and status he's probably not used to rejection and I've told him to bugger off in no uncertain terms. Twice. He's a man who doesn't take no for an answer.

Unpredictable, Derek called him. Dangerous. That's what he said about Roger and he was right.

But I don't have to deal with Sloane until tomorrow. Tonight is all mine.

CHAPTER
Twenty-One

After breakfast, the prospect of Sloane's appraising gaze has me reaching for the cowry shell. Not that I believe in psychic protection, by shells or anything else, but there's obviously something special about this particular shell. And the drumming hasn't happened again so it feels like we've got an understanding.

If Sloane turns up for the morning session I don't notice. Or care.

Because it happens again.

Being Sleek pops up just like it did yesterday except this time it takes over.

I abandon my notes because suddenly I'm in a place where notes are meaningless. Words come from somewhere beyond my mind, pouring out in an endless stream of wisdom - insights I've never heard before and anecdotes that make the audience laugh. Their voices rise with my humour in a wave of buoyant sound. They're carrying me along to a place that's completely new to me. A timeless place.

And it feels so comfortable.

When I'm finished, their applause wakes me as if from a deep sleep. I'm swaying on unsteady feet when someone catches me and guides me to a sofa. As I sit and stare straight ahead a glass of water is put in my hand, but I'm barely aware of anything else. Just a glow in my heart.

"It's a pity 'awesome' is so overused," a voice says, a voice I've heard before. Male. "It's the only word that fits what we've just experienced."

"I prefer 'magic'," says another familiar voice. Derek.

I hear them but I'm not listening. Something is happening to me, something strange and beautiful. My heart is open and the air around me is moving like the sea. I'm floating, bobbing about in clear water, buoyed by the joy of just being here. Each time I breathe, invisible currents flow through my body, opening up every part of me. And I'm alive, acutely aware of every cell.

I look around. There are paintings on the walls and I'm seeing them for the first time. Their colours are glowing, as if they're on fire, moving like exotic fish through the air. I want to go and speak to them, to commune with the colours, but when I try to stand my feet won't support me. This alertness is bizarre. I'm surrounded by three dimensions of untold depth, layers of vibrant colour, every object in the room pulsating with energy. The joy that's bubbling inside me is beyond anything I've ever experienced. Joy without excitement, euphoria steeped with peace. Everything is right, perfect. Just being alive is enough.

"You look amazing, Selkie. Still on a high from your presentation?"

I hear the words and look around. Into the face of Alister Sloane. His real name. A long story. I can see every muscle under his skin. The creases around his eyes are dancing.

"I've called a break for coffee," Derek says. "You should hear what they're saying. Everyone's over the moon."

Sloane chuckles. "I don't think she can hear us." I turn my head. His tongue is moving inside his teeth in slow motion. "She needs more time to come down to earth."

So he understands what's happening to me. But I don't need to understand. I *know*.

A waitress arrives with a tray of coffee. As she places it on a side table the aroma invades my nostrils, my sense of smell as heightened as my vision. Sloane bends over to pour me a cup.

"Just milk," I murmur. And when I put the liquid to my lips, the experience dissolves. Just like that. I'm sitting on a sofa drinking coffee, with Derek cross-legged on the floor in front and Sloane by my side.

"I'll have what you're having," Derek says.

I giggle, still steeped in the memory of it even though it's over. "It's just coffee, DD."

"A great seminar can be like an orgasm," Sloane says. "Ecstatic. Spiritual."

How did I get to be talking about sex with Lester Sloane? But he chooses this moment to get up and leave us in private.

"That's a relief," I say. "He was sitting way too close."

"He caught you when you looked like fainting," Derek says. "I've never seen a man move so fast. Except Errol Flynn in *Robin Hood.*"

***

The rest of the day unfolds with fewer surprises. I return to my notes and Goals for Gold restores normality to our lives. But perhaps because of the morning's euphoria, many participants are inspired to take risks and transform themselves into high achievers, with several sceptics from yesterday more willing to participate and get what they came for.

At the end many people come up and thank me personally. It turns out they were here under duress from a tyrant. At least I won't have to deal with Katsuya again.

It's ages before I can pack up my materials and take my leave. But as I head out the rear door into a hallway, I bump into Sloane. Literally.

"Whoa," he says, stopping me with his body. "We've got a date, remember?"

"Derek tells me you caught me this morning. Thank you. I don't know what came over me. But now I have to go. A date with someone else, I'm afraid." Derek and Nigel.

"Not so fast. I cancelled something to be here today. Disappointed several people. Because I thought this was more important. Correction: *you* were more important. So let me entice you to do the same. Whatever you're doing, cancel it. This is more important."

I wish his eyes weren't blue. The resemblance to Andrew is keeping me alert. "Important to you or to me?"

"Both. Or I'll let you go. Just hear me out for...thirty minutes. Then you'll know whether you want to stay or go. Deal?"

Put like that it would be churlish to refuse. Wouldn't it? "OK, thirty minutes. But not on the *lanai*."

He shrugs and guides me towards a shady interior terrace.

It's *pau hana* – happy hour. But for a Friday afternoon it's surprisingly quiet – the conference crowds must be flying home. We find a private table that's still in full view of other guests. I feel safe enough – and I touch the cowry shell – but that doesn't change how bloody attractive Sloane is.

He orders drinks. Lime and soda for two. It's starting to look like a business meeting after all. But I'm reserving judgement until I hear what he has to say. There's only twenty-five minutes left. Twenty-four.

"I'll put my cards on the table, Selkie. If I can call you that."

Suddenly I feel exposed. "Only if I can call you Alister."

If he knew what the name Lester Sloane does to my imagination he'd agree in a heartbeat. Visions from my dream flash by, of his hand wielding a banana.

He grins. "Only my closest friends call me Alister. You've got that status any time you want."

"Get to the point. Please."

"I know you've dumped Guy Morrison as your agent but since he introduced us he'll have to be included in any deal."

"Of course. He and I have an agreement. What...deal?"

"OK. You gave us a taste of Being Sleek. A quirky idea, underpinned by experience. And a spirited female presenter, if I may say so. It's perfect. I need something fresh for my program of old favourites. Selkie, if you can expand Being Sleek into a one-day program and do what you did today in front of a thousand people, we can make a deal."

So fast. Doesn't he have to sleep on it? Or with me?

"You could go away and think it over," he continues, "but I don't want to risk losing you. Someone in that audience is bound to spread the word. So I've taken the liberty of printing out a contract. The clauses are standard but I've included a sliding percentage as your audience grows and made it for twelve months so no-one feels trapped by today's terms. After a year we can renegotiate."

He pushes a document across the table. Thank God I didn't order anything stronger than soda. Without Guy, I'll have to review it myself.

But wait a minute. Why am I feeling so rushed? Only because Sloane is rushing me. And he's the one who wants me, or so he says. But do I want him? Fame and fortune, the world at my feet. I've already been around that loop and come out with my integrity mostly intact. But I remind myself not to look into his eyes.

"Of course I'm flattered," I say, "but I'll have to take this away and study it."

"Why? Cancel your appointment and we'll go through it together. I've got all night. How about you? Have I convinced you it's important enough?"

Together. All night. Errol Flynn without the moustache. A steamroller wrapped in velvet. Am I making a mistake even sitting here?

But I need to deal with this right now. I'm meeting the boys for a celebration dinner but I can make it an hour later.

"The hotel can find me a work space," I say, "but I'll go through the contract alone."

After an hour or so we meet up again. I'm exhausted, not because it's been a big couple of days but because I've found a clause I can't live with. For a moment there it looked like the big time might be mine after all.

"This clause about creative control," I say, pushing the contract across the table. "Does it mean what I think it means?"

"Top Notch retains creative control. It's the way I maintain the high standard of my seminars, Selkie. Of course I discuss everything with you. You're the presenter."

"But it's my seminar." Being Sleek suddenly feels very special.

"Yes. And no."

"Exactly. That leads us to the copyright clause. It says here that I assign copyright of the Being Sleek seminar to Top Notch. I haven't even written it yet, and as soon I sign this you own it. Then if we decide to part company after twelve months you keep it."

He nods. "It's the only clause I won't negotiate on."

"Why? It's my intellectual property." Roger has sharpened my resolve on this one.

"Mine too, if I promote you."

"But this clause means you own it all. It's tantamount to theft."

He shakes his head. "It means you can't make a name for yourself with me and then, when the money starts flowing, sign on with someone else."

"I understand your position, but if you want me, the copyright clause has to change. Moonshine retains copyright and we license the seminar to Top Notch for the period of this contract."

As Sloane considers my demand, I wonder what would have happened if Guy had been here. He's sure to have sold me down the river just to get his precious percentage. According to our agreement he's getting his percentage anyway, but at least I'm controlling the terms. It's feeling vital not to lose my rights to Being Sleek. Vital and personal. That must be where all this confidence is coming from.

"I can't do it, Selkie. Otherwise a competitor can steal you away after I've invested everything in making you a star."

"Be flexible," I say, not ready to give up. I still want to be a star, just on terms I can live with. "We can extend the contract period to five years to give you more security on your investment. I'm more than happy with the rest of the contract so it doesn't need to be short-term. But I won't sign over my seminar, to you or anyone else."

I'll have to check if Guy registered the trademark to Moonshine or himself. I can guess, but luckily Being Sleek is a whole new name.

Meanwhile Sloane is shaking his head again. "It

happened to me once, in the early days. I lost my best presenter and Top Notch nearly went under. It was a good lesson. Now my presenters stay with me for life and my success has confirmed my policy, over and over again."

"Stay with you because you've imprisoned their souls."

"That's not the way I see it."

"Well, it's a shame," I hear myself say. "We almost had a deal going there."

Then I'm walking out of the hotel bar without turning around, but in a wall mirror Sloane's reflection is gaping after me. He can't believe I'm doing this.

Neither can I.

CHAPTER
Twenty-Two

Celebration time. At Koloa in South King Street. They've got a great menu, Asian-Pacific fusion. Derek orders for all of us and I fall in love with the goat cheese wontons and the tempura ahi rolls. And that's just the appetisers. We sip mineral water as we wait for the champagne.

"Save space for the duck," Derek warns me. *Koloa* means wild duck.

"You realise I'll have to stay the night again," I say.

"No problem. It saves me changing the sheets."

"I get the feeling you're keeping an eye on me, DD."

"Not really. Only on your entity."

My entity. Did it enjoy the seminar? Or sleep right through it? "You can't even see it."

"That's what's got me hooked. An *invisible* entity. If I keep it under twenty-four-hour surveillance it might show itself."

Nigel chuckles. He's in a buoyant mood and he hasn't put any pressure on me to see his friend, the hypnotist.

"I don't believe you," I say to Derek. "You're keeping an eye on me because of the woman."

"There's the woman. There's Nightingale. And the connection between them. When I chose this restaurant I forgot how close it is to his place." He looks over his shoulder.

"He won't come here," I say. "He never eats out. Too stingy. And anyway he's..." I see the image of the stick figure in the gateway. "...*dead.*"

They look as shocked as I am.

"Now you tell us," Nigel says. "For days we've been hovering over you like bodyguards."

"Only wishful thinking," I say.

The champagne arrives and Nigel proposes a toast. "You've created history, Selkie. The first time anyone's turned their nose up at the great man's contract. Here's to Selkie Moon's love affair...with herself."

The bubbles have barely tickled my nose when my phone starts ringing. I hate phones in restaurants and I don't want to talk to anyone anyway.

"Sorry, I'll turn it off."

But Nigel stops me with his hand. "I have a feeling it's important."

Who's got my number? Only Wanda. And Roger. I slip into the street before I see who's calling. Andrew.

"What's your game, *Elkie?*" He spits out my old name like a curse.

"I'm at a restaurant, Andrew. And I've got no idea what you're talking about."

"That valuer you sent. You haven't been listening, have you? I don't want to sell the fucking house, I want you back here where you belong. Now."

The poster on Roger's wall comes to mind.

"You're the one who hasn't been listening, Andrew. There's been nothing in the marriage for me. It's always been on your terms. You don't even know who I am." And *you don't want to know.*

"Everything was so simple till you left. Us, the house. A baby soon. But that wasn't enough for you, was it? You had to make waves. Bloody tidal waves."

What? My hand touches the cowry shell and my voice surges with strength. "You're blaming *me* because *you* can't look in the mirror...and see how ugly you are. Is it that scary to come face to face with the truth?"

"Scary? *Scary?*" His laugh is harsh. "You're the scary one, Elkie. You're the scariest fucking person I know."

He hangs up and I realise I'm shaking. With anger or fear or laughter or a combination of all three. I've never stood up to Andrew before – I could only run away – and the adrenaline rush almost knocks me over.

Back inside there's more to celebrate. Because Andrew is a bigger scalp than Sloane. I tell the boys about his recent tactics as we work our way through the champagne.

"I told you," Derek says, "bullies like Andrew go pop if you stick a pin in their ego."

Nigel laughs and proposes another toast. "Here's to Selkie's weapons of choice – a cowry shell and a hatpin."

The main course arrives, but as I tuck in I can't stop thinking about the cowry shell. It might well be singing a protective spell because I've never felt so powerful.

The duck is delicious – done with macadamia nuts and shiitake mushrooms. We've opened another bottle and I'm mellowing out on self-satisfaction when my phone rings again.

"Bloody hell."

Back outside, I'm hoping it isn't Roger, but it's a number I don't know.

"Selkie," says a voice I recognise. "Do you have time to talk? It's Alister Sloane."

My legs turn to tofu and I almost collapse. For the first time I notice the lightness of his voice, masculine but youthful. It's only an hour since I threw his contract in his face, but now my mouth's gone dry.

"I'm...having dinner...with f-friends...so I c-can't talk." Literally, judging by my stammer.

"Celebrating?"

"Just opened...the second bottle."

"Well, I'm feeling wretched. So I hoped you were celebrating."

My steel is back. "I haven't changed my mind about the copyright, Alister, if that's why you're calling." What a nerve. Did Guy give him my number?

"I'm sure you haven't. I've never seen such unshakeability. It's rare, believe me, especially where status and money are involved."

"Well, I'm interested in status and money – but not at any cost."

"You made that crystal clear. But you want to get back to your friends so I'll make this quick. I didn't ring about the seminar."

I wait. Why did he ring?

"I want you to have dinner with me. Tomorrow night."

My brain tries to decipher what it's just heard. Alister Sloane couldn't be inviting me to dinner, not after the way I treated him. I reach out my hand to steady myself against the wall and touch Nigel's elbow. He's emerged just in time to be my pillar of strength.

"Selkie? Are you still there? Did you hear what I said?"

"I heard. But I don't understand."

He laughs. "It's not rocket science. I'm a man. You're a woman. I'm asking you to dinner. You say yes. Or no."

"Yes...I mean no...I-I'm in a relationship." Do I mean Roger?

"So am I."

Now we're both laughing. Then silence. I look at Nigel but he's minding his own business.

"I could forget that I've met you," Sloane says. "But I'm not going to do that. I want to get to know you better. Over dinner." Pause. "Just dinner."

More silence as I try to figure out how I feel. Just dinner. He's trying to put me at ease but why does he need to? And why did I say yes? I must want to see him again. Does that mean I trust him?

"You're suspicious, aren't you?" he says.

"Well, you wanted the seminar. Badly enough to pressure me. Now you're inviting me to dinner, so you've got an agenda. It's not rocket science."

"I promise not to mention it. A seminar-free evening. What else?"

It comes out in a rush. "Something Guy said…about how to win your contract. It's why I cancelled both of you." But that was someone called Lester.

"Well, Guy doesn't speak for me. So we can talk about it, whatever he said. Clear the air. But from what I saw tonight I'm the one who should be quaking in his boots." Then he whispers, "Take a risk."

That's my line. Straight from the seminar. Suddenly I want to fall into his arms.

"I'll pick you up at seven," he says. "Name the place."

I look at my pillar of strength and give him Nigel's address.

Back inside, Derek voices my doubts. "What happened to the hatpin, Selkie? Wealthy men are rarely trustworthy. They've got too much invested in their egos. And you walked out on him, don't forget. Just like you walked out on Andrew. Sloane's got a better act but what if he's feeling shafted? He may be after revenge."

"It really didn't feel like that, DD. You're overreacting. Anyway, it's only dinner."

"But what does he want in return?"

"The thrill of the chase," says Nigel. "Sloane probably

has women falling at his feet. Selkie's intrigued him. She's not interested in his money or his position. That's a magnet for a man like Sloane who can buy anything he wants."

"Look, I don't want this to spoil our celebration." I pick up my glass and take another sip.

"But what are we celebrating?" Derek says. "You're not free of him at all. One minute you've pissed Andrew off for good, then Sloane moves in to fill the vacuum. I don't like the coincidence."

"You think I've given up my independence just by agreeing to have dinner with him?"

He nods. "You don't have to go just because he's asked you. Call him back and tell him you've changed your mind."

"But I want to have dinner with him, DD. I'm intrigued too."

In fact his voice in my ear made my edges go soft but now's not the time to mention it.

"Ignore him, Selkie," Nigel says, putting his arm around Derek. "He tries it with me too. DD, we're celebrating Selkie exploring her power. Her true self is no longer in the closet. Sloane's call hasn't changed that."

But Derek looks stricken. "Men like Sloane are so shrewd they can snuff out her power...her fledgling success," he snaps his fingers, "just like that."

Suddenly I can see how much Derek cares, how he's watched over me all these months. I reach out and squeeze his hand. "Thank you for being my guardian angel, but it's time for me to take care of myself."

He manages a smile. "My wings are tired."

The dessert arrives – Koloa's specialty called Black Pearl – a scoop of dark mocha mousse nestled in a shell of crusty pastry with passionfruit cream on the side. We dive in with gusto.

Saturday stretches before me. A whole day until dinner with Sloane. I mean Alister. Will I ever be able to separate the man I've met from the man in the dream?

I woke in a panic this morning because he's way out of my league. If he thinks I'm intriguing because I walked out on his contract, then a whole evening in my company is destined to be a serious let-down.

As we stack the breakfast dishes, Derek introduces another problem. "What are you going to wear?"

"Jeans."

He pulls a face. "This is a chance to dress up, Selkie. Nightingale only took you to cemeteries but this is a real date. You might be dining at Jimmy Ho's."

"Jeans are all I've got, DD. I won't wear the power suit, and I green-bagged everything else when I left Andrew. And anyway, last I heard you didn't approve of this date."

"True. I'm confused. But then I remembered Davina. If you've got the right frock I'll be happy."

"Why?" I know he's going to tell me.

"Protection. The perfect dress channels your inner power. And creates an invisible shield against psychic invasion."

Where does he get this stuff? "Well, I haven't heard from Davina. She was going to send through some designs but she hasn't."

"Have you checked your messages lately?"

He's right. During the seminar I didn't want any

distractions. When I open my inbox, sure enough there's an email from Davina.

Come to my stall, she says, *on Saturday.*

"Very cryptic," I say. "And bossy. What's happened to the designs?"

Derek insists on taking me, and when Davina sees us she embraces me like an old friend.

"You don't have to take it," she says.

"What?"

"The dress."

She's pulling a hanger off a rack. It's covered by a large paper bag. Do I want to see it?

"I know," she says, seeing my face. "I was supposed to send through some designs, but something came over me yesterday, you know. A kind of trance. And when I woke up I'd gone into a fine frenzy and the dress was finished. You'll know if it's meant for you."

A dress-designer-cum-psychic. What did I expect? "Is that how you do all your frocks?"

"No, no. I design intuitively, you know, it's how I create garments with meaning. If I have a client in mind I tap into their energetic frequency." She sounds like Derek. "But it's a calm process. Never like this."

She's pulling off the paper bag and Derek is cooing, "Try it on, try it on."

When I see it, I go into a trance of my own.

The dress is narrow and strikingly simple. Charcoal-black with a sheen almost like leather. Skinny sleeves reach to the wrists like long gloves, but they're only joined on at the armpit because the shoulders are bare. Two broad straps from a centre V join behind the neck with a button. As Davina passes it to me the fabric shimmers silver.

It's stunning. And I'm feeling light-headed. I want to be

inside it more than anything. Then something flips and I almost lose my nerve. It looks great on the hanger but what's it going to look like on me?

Davina walks me to the change room at the back of the stall. The trance returns as I strip off and slither into the stretch fabric, then zip myself inside. The fit is perfect. Tight. It hugs my body like a second skin. And the hem sits halfway up my thighs. Still in a daze, I step into my strappy heels – Derek brought them with us – and pull back the curtain.

Davina smiles as I stare at myself in the full-length mirror, watching the way the fabric changes colour as I move, the way it breathes with me, the way it follows the curves of my body, responds to the flexing of every muscle.

"I won't be able to eat if I wear this," I gush at Derek.

They must be able to see the emotions flitting across my face. Joy. Bliss. Embarrassment. Fear. Have I got what it takes to wear it?

Davina comes up behind me and ties the cowry shell around my neck. Derek must have picked it up along with my shoes and he's suddenly avoiding eye contact. The word 'conspiracy' pops into my mind.

But the shell is perfect – bold and dramatic. Even if it's guilty of singing it's a seriously stylish piece. And the spots are glowing again.

Davina ruffles my hair so the silver streaks spike up wildly and the outfit is suddenly complete.

And mine.

I exhale noisily and start to laugh. I'm in a state of rapture. "I'll take it," I say unnecessarily.

"Fine, fine, fine," she says.

Of course, it's paid for already. I steal a glance at Derek. He grins in a rapture of his own as I throw my arms around his neck.

It's time to take the dress off but it's going to be a struggle to give up the way it makes me feel. I've arrived in my own life. For the first time. A sensation I can't explain, because if I haven't been in my own life where have I been? In the privacy of the change room I undress with great reluctance. When I pull on my jeans it feels like I've lost something precious.

Davina puts the dress in the bag and I take hold of the rope handles. "Here's to your grand adventure," she says, as if proposing a toast.

Does she know who I'm dining with tonight? Derek must have told her.

Just as we're moving off a question comes out of my mouth. "What time was it...when you made the dress?"

"Yesterday?" She doesn't think the question's strange. "In the morning, it was. It probably lasted a couple of hours, the trance. I lost track of time."

"Can you remember what happened?"

"A lot of it's gone, you know. I was just wondering why I hadn't had any ideas for your dress, when the next thing I knew I was lost. It was so sudden it was almost like channelling."

I look at Derek then back to Davina. "Did you experience any...visions? Like in a dream?"

She looks at me closely. "Sure. They were so strong I didn't know I was sewing. I do remember one of them. The air was like the sea...and I was breathing in the most amazing colours...like tropical fish. It was grand," she says, "and I didn't want it to end. But of course it did."

It's the same. The same as my trance at the seminar. At the same time.

***

On the way home I say nothing about the twin trances. Derek already thinks the dress has psychic powers and if he got even a hint of this strange phenomenon it would only encourage him.

While we were out Nigel returned to the hard drive but found nothing.

"I have to give everything back," I say. "Otherwise I'm a thief too."

"Propose a swap," Derek says. "All his stuff in exchange for any negatives of you. And your graveyard pics."

"If he goes for it, we'll come with you," Nigel says.

As if he's been listening a text arrives from Roger.

Police taking fingerprints. Gave them your number. Toodle-oo Miss Toony Lune.

Shit. If he's involved the police it's probably too late, but I send the text proposing the swap then turn off my phone.

The afternoon disappears in preparations for my big date and I try not to dwell on the threats hanging over me.

When I go to the mirror to do my makeup the strange sensation that I'm looking at someone else is back. For a split second the woman on the cliff is staring at me. I'm about to scream when my own face returns. The experience is so freaky I keep my makeup to a minimum.

I sit waiting in my little black dress, fighting the urge to perform some exotic gyrations. The shell is drumming again and only the memory of my feather-duster fandango is making me stay put. Something wild and irresistible is trying to take over my body. Is it her? Better to sit here like a waif abandoned at a railway station than succumb to that dangerous rapture.

Nigel coos over the dress, the way it fits me like a sheath, the way it shimmers when I move, and Derek is looking like an expectant father banished to the waiting room.

When Nigel goes to the loo for the fourth time Derek whispers, "Promise me you won't sleep with him, Selkie. He's going to take one look at you and want to eat you alive."

"Your fault," I whisper. "You bought the dress. And now you're giving me ideas."

His face falls and I feel mean for deceiving him. As if I'm ever going to tumble into bed with Alister Sloane.

Just before seven the doorbell rings.

I beat the boys to it and try to eliminate all expression from my face. Like excitement. Or panic. Will the police track me down at dinner?

Derek and Nigel are hovering right behind me. They just want to be included so I invite Sloane in. He's looking pretty cool – and rich – in an open-neck white shirt and a coarse-weave grey jacket.

"Alister Sloane," I say, "you remember my...parents. Derek and Nigel."

He laughs. "A pleasure, gentlemen."

They shake hands and any awkwardness is solved by Nigel. "Have her home by midnight, young man. We'll be waiting up."

It's a relief to escape to the street where he helps me into his car, a BMW convertible. The seats are leather so I can't help myself. I inhale. He smiles – his other women are unlikely to be so gauche.

We haven't spoken since we left Derek and Nigel and as we drive down the mountain I try to think of something to say. The road snakes between hedges of bamboo and taro, reminding me of the cemetery, then the view opens up to the panorama of Honolulu below. Sloane seems content to drive in silence and look across at me every few seconds. My mind is running through all the things I won't be talking about. It's a long list.

I've got an invisible entity sitting on my shoulder. An undead woman is trying to murder me. My former boyfriend has an explicit photo of me that he's probably circulating on the internet. I stole his laptop and the police are poised to arrest me. The shell I'm wearing...sings. Anything else? Oh, yes, I'm starving but I can't eat because Davina had a seizure and made me this stupid dress.

At least the last thought makes me smile.

He catches my sudden grin and thinks it's for him. "I'm glad you've stopped scowling at me. The evening's looking up."

"Do you deserve a scowl?"

"Let's see. I twisted your arm about having dinner. And I'm not number one on your favourites list after that contract. Is there more?"

He's thinking of the Guy issue. That makes two of us. Plus I've just remembered he said he's seeing someone so why are we even doing this?

Instead I say, "If I didn't want to be here I would have cancelled. And not another word about that contract."

"Sorry. I breathe them all day. It will be refreshing to talk about everything else."

"Good." But that takes me right back to my list.

At the Lunalilo Freeway, instead of turning towards Waikiki where I thought we'd be going, we cross over towards Honolulu.

Where does a man like Sloane take a woman like me? Somewhere really posh to impress the pants off me?

Literally? Or somewhere down-market, where I'm less likely to embarrass him by using the wrong fork? I think of the Pearl. It's hard to use the wrong chopstick. But I haven't been there for a while.

"Where are we going?"

"Can I surprise you?"

"Why not? I seem to be into surprises lately."

"Me too."

"Why are you into surprises?"

He thinks about it. "They...demolish old thinking. It's easy to live in a culvert because you're afraid. You talked about that in Being Sleek, about exploring beyond the known." Did I? "If life's too controlled there's less life to control, don't you think? So surprises crack things open and...create new rhythms in the universe."

"That's a big answer. I think surprises just stuff up my plans."

He laughs. "Same thing. You know the joke: If you want to make God laugh tell him your plans."

"So it's God's fault. That's a relief. I'm off the hook."

How did we get to be talking about God? It reminds me I know nothing about Alister Sloane. Just like I turned out to know nothing about Roger Nightingale.

"Surprises are usually more cosmic than we think," he's saying. "Like chaos theory. Just the flutter of a butterfly's wings and the momentum can upset everything."

"So when I walked out on your contract – oops, my fault this time – I created chaos?"

"Several tsunamis. They ricocheted to the edges of the known world."

"I had no idea I was so powerful." But Andrew accused me of making waves. Chaos theory. A good description of our marriage.

"You're very powerful, Selkie. More powerful than you know. So surprise the universe...wisely."

I'm just navigating the depths of this incongruity when he turns into the basement of a high-rise building. His building. When I googled him I saw it. Discordant glass panels fracturing the façade. He must know a charming little restaurant down this way. Perfect for his gauche little guest from Gondwanaland.

He parks in the space reserved in his name. But when we climb out he guides me to a private lift and presses the button.

"We're having dinner at my place," he says to my stunned expression.

"Why?" A silly question. I consider making a run for it, but I'm wearing the wrong shoes. I'll have to knock him down and threaten him with my heels.

"I'm a good cook," he's saying. "And I like cooking for friends. More private than hovering waiters. And a better view." Then he reads my face. "I have staff to help me, Selkie – Ramon and Rita have been with me for years – so we won't be alone."

We step into the lift and ascend in silence. My cheeks flame as I try to recover from being a bloody idiot. Here I am done up in the sexiest dress I've ever owned, freaking out that he might fancy me.

The lift opens into an entrance hall lined with paintings illuminated by spotlights. I recognise some of the artists, especially a lithograph by Salvador Dali. I stop for a closer look. At least it's something to talk about.

A turquoise sky is fading to soft pink on the horizon. Three women on a beach are draped in evening gowns so slinky they might as well be naked. Instead of a head each one has a floral pomander on her shoulders, and two of them are holding musical instruments that drip from their fingers in true Dali style. A piano and a cello. Suddenly I'm immersed in it.

"What's it called?"

"*Three Surreal Women Holding in their Arms the Skin of an Orchestra.*"

"A name as enigmatic as the painting," I say. "Surreal women. And an orchestra that's lost its substance. What's happened here? And why a beach?"

"A typical Dali conundrum."

"I like the colours. He's dissolved a hint of the turquoise sky in the sand. But there's heat in the pinks and browns of the rocks. And it's eerie. Because the women have no faces. They're half real and it looks like some kind of ritual. As if they've stolen the orchestra's skin and they're presenting it...as an offering." I turn to Sloane. "There's something fluid about it. Rhythms rippling through the universe..."

He laughs. "Glad you like it. I find it hypnotic – that's part of its appeal. I can look at it for hours. Even though it's probably a fake."

"Really? I didn't pick you as the type to collect fakes." But so far I've got him wrong on every assumption.

"It's a talking piece. And it might be authentic. But Dali signed a lot of blank pieces of paper before he died. Large numbers of lithographs were printed after his death so the auction houses won't touch them. It's impossible to authenticate this one."

"Did the old man go gaga?"

"A bit of dementia, a lot of arrogance. At the end he was easy to manipulate, I believe."

"Sounds like his minders were holding in their arms the skin of Salvador Dali."

He grins. "I knew you'd give me a different perspective on a few things."

How could he know that?

"So you like talking pieces," I say.

"It's part of why I like it. Reactions like yours." His face breaks into its cheeky grin. "And I have the luxury of only spending time with paintings – and people – I like."

"Which woman is your favourite?" I ask.

He looks back at the Dali. "That's easy. The renegade. The one who's forsaken her instrument so she can dance."

The third woman's arms are outstretched so she could be dancing. But where's her instrument? There's a large shell lying in the foreground showing the intricate folds of its chambers. When I blink, I see it's really a tuba.

We move into an enormous living space overlooking the bay. I turn away from the expanse of cobalt water and take in the penthouse he calls home. At one end a huge arrangement of tangerine lounges surrounds a large square coffee table of finely woven rattan. Scatter cushions in ethnic fabrics and an enormous potted palm complete the effect of an Asian hotel of the colonial era, comfortable and slightly decadent. At the other end a long refectory table – probably a French antique – displays a pair of hand-carved candelabra that might be Portuguese.

In the middle of the room, in front of the view, an intimate table for two has been set with a white tablecloth and wine glasses in three sizes. A candle glows in a crystal bowl that refracts the light.

It feels like he's shunned the decorators and collected pieces himself. Another insight into the man beside me. Just like the room I share with Wanda is an insight into me.

I turn my attention to the view. Full-length windows stretch across one wall, taking in the harbour and the city, now aglow in the remnants of sunset.

"I love this time of day," I say. "The glow looks like satisfaction, another day almost complete."

"That sounds like something you experience yourself. Satisfaction."

"Not often. Too busy trying to create a successful business," and fend off supernatural forces, "to stop and reflect."

"But you must have been satisfied with the seminar yesterday. What did Derek call Being Sleek? Magic."

"I'd call it...surprising," Sloane grins, "since the content was largely...spontaneous. And yes, I was satisfied, but that seminar's off our agenda."

He takes my elbow and steers me towards the coffee table. "Let me offer you a drink. Champagne?"

My tummy is rumbling. And I need to mellow out. But Derek made me promise to stay off alcohol. "Have you got a tomato juice?"

He disappears through an archway and I turn towards the wall opposite the windows. It's lined with a quirky collection of primitive-style paintings. Large and bold. So he's a patron to some budding talents. From the kitchen I hear voices, then Sloane returns with two glasses on a tray and a bowl of nuts. He puts the tray on the coffee table and joins me in front of the paintings.

"I buy works by emerging artists," he says. "It's fun trying to pick who'll be collectable."

"And then you cash in?"

"That was the idea – investment art – until I discovered I couldn't part with them."

Is he another person who can't let anything go? "Why?"

"Because they speak to me. I can't really explain it. Paintings, textiles, photographs. Even jewellery." He looks at my cowry shell. "That's exceptional. I noticed it at the seminar."

"It's not for sale." The words are out before I can edit them.

"I don't want to buy it, Selkie. I'm admiring it. It's clearly something you'll never part with."

"Why do you say that?"

"It looks almost alive, the way the spots...hum."

"Can you hear something?" I need to know.

He thinks about it. "It's visual. You can't see it because you're wearing it, but from here it's dazzling." His eyes meet mine. "Like the woman who's wearing it."

Time to change the subject.

Along the side wall an aquarium sits on a low bookcase. It's empty of water and illuminated with soft lights. Draped over a large rock is an even larger snake.

"Dead or sleeping?" I ask.

"Sleeping. She had a meal today so I won't disturb her. But you can look all you like. How do you feel about snakes?"

"I never judge them till I'm properly acquainted."

"OK. Selkie Moon, let me present Mia the Python."

Mia doesn't respond. She's coiled around the rock. The texture of her skin is exquisite in a delicate pattern of grey and cream. It makes me want to touch her. But her sleek torso is marred by a telltale bulge.

"What does she eat?"

He clears his throat. "You may not like the answer."

"Try me."

"Mice."

I nod.

"*Live* mice."

Suddenly I can see it. A tiny mouse dropped into the

aquarium with nowhere to hide. About to be eaten alive…
Just like Derek warned me.

"Do you…watch?" I ask.

"No. It's the one thing I've never got used to. I tried thawing out frozen mice but she doesn't recognise them as food, even if I warm them up and jiggle them on a stick. So I buy mice one at a time from several pet stores – in rotation."

"So they don't get…suspicious?"

His laugh breaks the tension. "Exactly. If I buy regularly from the same place they wonder what's happening and stop supplying me. I don't blame them."

"Surely you don't drive around Oahu in your BMW carrying a shoebox punched with air holes?"

"Why not? Anything for Mia. If I could catch lizards for her I would, but that would mean digging in public parks and I wouldn't give the paparazzi the satisfaction."

His enthusiasm is infectious and I relax again. We sip our tomato juice in silence.

"Why do you call yourself Alister?"

He hesitates. "It's…my real name."

"A long story."

"Yes." He misses a couple of beats. "But there's a short version." He gazes out the window as he remembers. "At school…I got teased. The other boys liked to call me…Alice."

I didn't pick Sloane as the type to be bullied, but there's pain behind his voice and I sense it was worse than name-calling. Much worse.

"So my dad moved me to a new school and enrolled me as Lester. It stuck."

A change of school and a change of name. Did it make him tougher? Looks like it.

"Only my best friends call me Alister."

I don't know what to say but he's moved on.

"There's a reason I brought you here tonight, Selkie."

Have I been waiting for this? A proposition after all?

"I had a reservation at Donatello's, but I cancelled it because I've got something to show you. Something I picked up this morning. At the Swap Meet."

"The Aloha Stadium?"

"Yes. Sometimes I find an interesting piece, direct from the artist."

I laugh. He's found out about me and Wanda. "Let me guess, it's a resin fish." A fish that looks like me.

"I know the stall you mean. The artist's a character, but her fish are more like craft than art. Not for my collection, but the tourists love them. No, this is something else. A photograph."

My heart does a flip but I manage not to cry out. Sloane walks across the room to the wall beyond the refectory table. On shaky legs I follow him.

"The artist was a bit odd," he's saying. "A skinny guy with an accent and a passive-aggressive manner. He didn't want to sell it to me. But I got it in the end."

"W-what did he say?"

"He told me he took the picture at a hidden cemetery, just a shot of someone he didn't know. But when I said I recognised you, he changed. Became truculent. Said the photo wasn't for sale. Do you make a habit of running through cemeteries, Selkie?"

My legs are still holding me up. Just. I'm staring at a photograph. Of me. Running between the headstones.

"I told him I was having dinner with you tonight," Sloane is saying. "And to name his price. But the photo seemed to mean something else to him and he became...unpleasant."

I'm still staring at the picture, at the proof that Roger photographed me that day. Did he follow me after I ran away? Did he take a picture of the woman?

Sloane turns to get my reaction and sees how pale I am. "Are you all right? You'd better sit down."

He takes my arm and reaches for a chair. And that's when it happens.

Invisible forces grab me and hurl me across the room. Chairs are overturning, cushions are flying, and a wall is rushing towards me.

Thud.

It happens so fast. I'm flipped off my feet, taking flight. Then doubling over and sagging to the floor.

On the edges of my vision Sloane is trying to help me, but the force invades me again and I'm jerking away, this time in a rush of sparking ice. Something hot and jagged is tearing through my body, ripping me apart from the inside. My senses are on high alert. A smell invades my nostrils. Something burning. Acrid at first but then it changes. Almost sweet.

Then I'm losing it. And the room reverberates with a splitting noise.

My scream.

CHAPTER
Twenty-Four

It's the end of a promising evening. I've got no stomach for food – or company – after that performance. At least my bowels and bladder haven't burst their seams. Nor my new dress. Only my dignity is lying in puddles on the parquetry.

Anyone else would have backed away and called the asylum, but Alister straightens a chair, hauls me to my feet in a bear hug and sits me down. Someone appears from the kitchen and Alister presses a glass of water to my lips.

"Thank you," I whisper, still shaking.

It's over, whatever it was. But somewhere deep down it feels anything but finished. The sense of something dark and malevolent is back, a fug of despair enveloping me. I shudder again. But this time it's only from fear.

Alister is crouched beside me and I'm weeping quietly on his shoulder. Suddenly he's Alister, no longer Sloane. Since he's just seen me...in the raw. Whatever it was.

Eventually it slips away but when I try to stand the room sways like the sea. "Dizzy," I say. Then I brush my hand across my crown and wince. "Sore."

He probes the area with gentle fingers. Not quite the intimacy Derek was afraid of. "No blood. Probably mild concussion. You hit the wall pretty hard. Come and lie on the sofa with an icepack."

I'm already plotting my getaway, but since I can't see straight, or walk straight, it has to be the sofa. Do I sleep for a while? A woman puts a plate of antipasto on the coffee table but for once food is the last thing on my mind.

"I need a taxi," I murmur. Alister hasn't left my side. "Please."

He shakes his head. "I'll drive you home."

I'm craving the privacy of the back seat, the anonymous driver, then Derek and Nigel's spare room. But Alister waits until I can stand – it takes a while – then he guides me into the lift.

Once we hit the parking level my head clears and, except for the lingering humiliation, I'm almost back to normal. Just a slight headache. And a burgeoning case of starvation. I barely had two sips of tomato juice and I've eaten nothing since breakfast. Could low blood sugar be the culprit?

"There's a bag of sandwiches behind your seat," Alister says. "Ramon threw them together while you recovered. You weren't touching anything on the platter so I thought you might be hungry."

"Starving."

I reach over and pull out a parcel, rip off the wrapping and sink my teeth into a sandwich. At least I don't have to be polite. My public face has slipped like Dali's orchestra.

Alister drives in silence while I demolish what tastes like pastrami with some kind of pickle. "You know him, don't you?" he says after a while. "The skinny Englishman with the wispy hair."

"Used to know him. Roger Nightingale. Why are we talking about him?"

"He took the photograph."

I'd almost forgotten about that.

"It was meant to intrigue you, your picture on my wall. A surprise. But as soon as you saw it, you flew into that...paroxysm."

"Don't remind me, please. But it had nothing to do

with the picture."

"Are you sure? Your reaction was...almost instant."

Was it? "It wasn't that kind of picture."

"Are there pictures that send you flying across the room and others that don't?"

"I mean the picture wasn't particularly...interesting." Compared to the photos he might have taken afterwards. Of the woman.

"If it meant nothing to you why did you go so pale?"

"I didn't say that. Roger's taken photos of me without my knowledge. That means something to me. You met him, you saw what he's like. I've only just found out what a predator he is."

Pasting posters of me on his wall. Peddling pictures of me at the markets. What else?

"He told me he didn't know you."

"He lied. We went to the cemetery together to take photographs. For a competition. Then he wouldn't show me the pictures he took. Now I know what he was doing behind my back."

"Did something bad happen out there? In the cemetery?"

"Alister, something bad happened...in your apartment."

That was cruel. None of this is Alister's fault. But he doesn't have the right to probe, just because he witnessed something bizarre. We might be closer than we were an hour ago but it's not a closeness I want to encourage. The sooner I can hide in the boys' spare room the better.

But the food is working its magic on my equilibrium and I reach for another parcel. "Ramon makes a mean sandwich."

"It's not quite the dinner I planned."

"Yeah, no candles. But I wasn't expecting to humiliate

myself, so we're even."

"You didn't humiliate yourself."

"What would you call it – a particularly vigorous zumba?"

"A convulsion. Of unknown origins. Unless you know what caused it and you're not telling me."

"No idea."

"Has it happened before?"

"Never." Unless I count the malevolent cloud when I fainted in Derek's kitchen. The feeling was the same. Something evil enveloping me. "It was probably hypoglycaemia. I've eaten almost nothing all day." Payback for wearing this dress.

"I'm not buying it," he says.

"Suit yourself."

He grins. "At least it hasn't changed you. You still know how to put me in my place." Then he gets serious again. "It wasn't low blood sugar. In fact it wasn't anything physical."

"I headbutted the wall, Alister. You can't get more physical than that."

"The headbutting was a result of something. And what caused it couldn't have been physical otherwise you wouldn't be wrapping your mouth around that sandwich as if nothing happened. You'd be...unconscious."

We sit with this while I finish the sandwich.

"It was something...*surreal*," he says.

"Like the Dali women? The wall tried to knock off my head so I could replace it with a pomander?"

"Your humour isn't fooling me, Selkie. Are you in some kind of trouble?"

This is why I wanted to get a taxi. "Look. Just because you witnessed it doesn't make it any of your business."

"That answer tells me that you are."

"What?"

"In trouble."

He looks across at me and I see his concern. And his blue eyes. It would be so easy to tell him everything – the whole list of forbidden topics – then fall into his arms in another swoon. But what would be the point? He couldn't help with any of it. And I'm hardly likely to see him again.

"I just want to bury it, Alister. Call it a dizzy spell. Move on."

"I'm going to call you tomorrow."

"There's no need. Nigel's a nurse. He'll keep an eye on me."

"So you'll tell him what happened?"

"In vivid detail."

We both grin at the barefaced lie.

"And what about Roger Nightingale?" he asks.

"What about him? I'm sorry you've got involved but Roger's my problem."

"Because of me you've found out he's selling photos of you. That makes it my business. Are you going to do anything about him?"

"Yes," I say, as I climb out of the car. "I'm never going to see him again."

***

From the boys' expressions they're assuming the worst about my evening with the rich guy. I go straight to my room to delay any questions. I abandon the dress and the cowry shell in a heap on the floor, to match the way they abandoned me when I needed them. So much for their powers of protection. If I'd hit the wall any harder I'd be dead.

I'm exhausted but not sleepy. I'm too spooked. The

'paroxysm' isn't something I can simply dismiss in spite of what I said to Alister. Not physical, he said. That was just from the outside. He didn't feel what I felt. The malevolence. Something vile drawing my energy, leaving me empty.

Something surreal...

Holding in its arms...the skin of Selkie Moon.

My thoughts go to the entity. Old friend from far away, or something else entirely? An entity with attitude. Hurling me across the room like a poltergeist, demanding that I pay attention.

Or is it the woman? Sending me a message I can't ignore. Letting me know she can get me any time she wants.

And Roger almost certainly took her photo. Just like Nigel predicted. After he photographed me running through the graves. Has he entered it in the competition or is he just selling it at the Swap Meet? And what about my nude photo, is that for sale too? The extent of his betrayal leaves me breathless with rage. I'm impotent against the supernatural but I've got to confront Roger. He'll no doubt be back at the Swap Meet tomorrow so it has to be tonight.

It's still early. Not even ten o'clock. I'm out of my mind with fatigue but this errand feels urgent.

In the living room the boys pour me a glass of wine but the thought of losing control again is keeping me sober. They want to know what happened with Alister and I tell them about Roger's photo.

"That parasite," Derek hisses. "Selling pictures of you. To strangers like Sloane. Why did Sloane buy it?"

"He regards it as art. A woman running for her life through a crowd of gravestones. In black and white it has a certain...surreal quality." That word again.

And he wanted to own my image. Just like Roger.

"I have to take Roger's stuff back," I say. "He hasn't answered my text about a swap so I have to sort him out before he tries to sell more pictures."

Derek's frowning. "He's going to be incensed, possibly out of control. The man's unstable, Selkie. We're coming with you."

***

Saturday night at the brothel. Plenty of comings and goings behind the bail bond shop. The lights are on in Roger's place, but I have a strong sense that no-one's home. I hadn't counted on that. If the key's back in the flowerpot the boys can help me search, but they've agreed to lose themselves in the crowd for ten minutes while I check. If Roger's there he may respond better if he thinks I'm alone.

I lug everything up to the landing. My last visit, I hope, if I leave with what I want. My photos. As I put the file-case down and start to knock the door opens in my face. But it isn't Roger.

She's older than in the photos, but I recognise the spiky haircut, the boyish figure under jeans and T-shirt. She-Girl. Sheena. It didn't take long for her to come back.

She's crying. And when she sees me she starts to scream, then clamps her hand over her mouth. Her eyes have widened as if she's seen a ghost.

"I'm Selkie," I say, suddenly wary. She starts to push past me but I block her exit. "Wait a minute. What's going on?"

She screams, "I knew it was magic." Then shoves me aside with surprising strength.

"Where's Roger?" I call after her, but she's gone, down the stairs and into the night.

And anyway, I already know.

Roger is lying in a puddle on his bathroom floor, surrounded by his developing equipment. He's on his back under a stepladder and his arms and neck are twisted at grotesque angles. His face is a rigid mask of horror.

I don't need to touch him.

He's obviously dead.

CHAPTER
Twenty-Five

Time speeds up. Or stands still. Or spins out of control. I'm frozen in the doorway with the corpse at my feet. Sheena's gone. So is Roger. What happened here? And why am I the witness?

A sob escapes and hovers in the air. A stray emotion for a man I didn't love, a man who exploited me and betrayed my trust. Roger can't hurt me any more but did he have to die?

I take in the terrible tableau. Did he hit his head on the bath? My fingers go to the bump on my own head. Too many collisions for one night. But I'm alive while he's been despatched by something shocking.

Sheena said it was magic. *Surreal...* Alister's word. And Salvador Dali's. And now...*Roger's dead.*

It's dark in here. A darkroom. A place where dark things happen. Something in my chest splits open and a lifetime of my own darkness seeps out into the puddle at my feet.

The floor is covered in shards. Red glass. Something about red. The face of the clock is still. Roger's face stares up at me but *no-one's home.* It's the same thought I had when I arrived tonight. How did I know?

It's time to get the boys, time to call the police. Then I notice a string pegged with prints lying across Roger's body. He was pegging them out to dry when he fell off the ladder, fell against the string, brought his house of cards crashing down. There must have been noise - a clatter, a scream, a crash, a thud – but now there's only silence.

The photos are silent too. But their images trumpet a story. Me running between the graves. Me crouching behind a headstone. Me pointing a camera towards the cliff. Me running towards the edge, then crawling on my belly. Me suspended above the grasping waves. While the woman was trying to kill me, the cool opportunist in Roger Nightingale walked to his tripod and documented it all.

Did he snap her image? Several prints have fallen at an angle away from the door and I can't see them. I slide down the doorjamb, trying not to gag. Now I'm close enough to kiss him, close enough to feel the absence of breath on my sweating cheek. It's all I can do to lean over the leering spectre while my eyes adjust to the dark.

There I am, squatting behind my camera, focused on the cliff.

The empty cliff.

An emptiness with attitude.

The woman isn't there.

In a state of disbelief, I check the other prints. The sequence is here, but she isn't. I don't understand. There was plenty of time for Roger to snap her image with his long lens. Several images.

As I stare past his unseeing eyes my mind starts joining dots. She isn't in the photos, but she was here a few days ago, on Roger's path. Was she here earlier tonight?

Roger stole images of me, and other women, and that's what we did to the woman. Took her photo without her permission. Now she's missing from Roger's print. What if she appears at any time of her choosing but she won't be photographed, won't be captured? She won't be *known*?

The message said I was going to die, but instead it's Roger. As I pull away from his appalling grin he seems to be mocking me. It's his final gesture. As if he knows...I'm next.

I've got to get out of here. Away from mad conjecture and a dead man's stare. My own photos must be here somewhere, in Roger's secret stash. When the police arrive, they'll be lost to me forever. But when I look back at Roger's body I lose my nerve. The woman has disappeared again. Let her stay that way.

***

When I stagger onto the landing the boys are racing up the stairs.

Derek sees my face. "What's he done this time? I'll kill him."

"The universe...beat you to it," I whisper.

They take turns staying with me while the other checks the scene inside. Nigel calls the police and I empty my stomach into the flowerpot. Roger's dead – the cold fact hits me – despatched so neatly. By electrocution.

"He was on the ladder," Derek murmurs as we wait downstairs, "pegging photos on the string."

"And he fell against the safety light," Nigel says, "and got an electric shock."

They think it was an accident. So will the police. But I'm remembering a charred stick-figure against the sun and words seeping into my brain: *Roger's dead.*

Forensics arrive. Then a detective asking questions. Questions about Roger. Questions about Sheena. Questions about the file-box of girly pics that's still on the landing. And all the time, wraiths in Aloha shirts depart the downstairs flat. Nothing like a police presence to empty a brothel.

Then we're driving home, reaching Nigel's doorstep just

before my midnight curfew. I should have been with Alister, wining and dining the night away with a sexy new man in my sexy new dress. But something surreal threw me against the wall.

And on the other side of town, something surreal snuffed out Roger.

I'm so weary I can barely perch on the toilet on my way to my room. When my head hits the pillow I'm already asleep.

The woman is standing on a ladder perched on the edge of the cliff. She's wearing Sheena's bathrobe and holding her arms towards the sky. It's an ancient rite. As her fingertips connect heaven and earth a tempest is raging. Lightning bolts slice off her hair and the wind blows what's left of it into spikes. Waves leap up the *pali*, licking the fallen locks from her feet. Thunder is echoing behind the clouds and flashes of silver light strobe the scene.

I'm hiding behind a headstone, pointing my camera towards the cliff, wanting to capture this surreal spectacle and become famous. But a voice warns me not to press the shutter. If I do I'm dead.

The woman morphs into Roger. He looks at me before tumbling off the ladder and catching fire. His skin lights up from the inside. He's a Halloween pumpkin, a hollow shell.

I'm screaming a silent scream: "Where's the woman?"

But the charred shell that used to be Roger has crumbled into dust.

CHAPTER
Twenty-Six

The police know the time of death. A fuse blew and stopped the clock. "Eight-o-nine last night," the detective named Watkins says into my dozing ear. "Where were you at that time, Miss Moon?"

I sit up in bed and almost drop the phone. He's asking me for an alibi. Have they decided it wasn't an accident?

I tell him about Alister. "He picked me up at seven, and drove me back here around nine."

So that's where I was when Roger's clock stopped, along with his heart.

Watkins wants to call Alister. Just the complication I don't need, because first I'll have to warn him, then try to shake him off.

"I'll have to get his number for you," I say. "He's probably unlisted."

But Alister doesn't answer. And I can't leave a message, not about this. What I do leave is a trail of missed calls. He'll think I'm chasing him when nothing could be further from the truth.

Now that Roger is no longer a threat it's time to go back to Wanda's and leave the boys to their domestic bliss. But as I start packing I'm reluctant to leave this safe cocoon. Just for a moment I'm flying across Alister's living room, colliding with the wall and sensing the dark intent tearing through me in sharp slashes. It's just the memory but it's very real.

While I'm reliving last night's horrors Nigel is back

from a run bearing baguettes and croissants and Derek is brewing coffee. It's all very Sunday at Makiki Heights but the aromas don't dispel the lingering stench of death.

Derek looks at my haggard face. "I prescribe croissants and endless mugs of coffee."

My last meal was a pastrami sandwich, now composting in Roger's flowerpot.

"Toby's Estate," Nigel says. "DD imports it direct from Byron Bay."

Derek shoots him a look.

"He's even supplying Curtis at the coffee cart." Nigel gets another look. "So you won't feel homesick and leave."

Derek Delaney, my guardian angel. But he's powerless against supernatural forces. If only Toby's Estate could numb my memory of them.

"Was that your phone I heard earlier?" he asks.

The man's got X-ray ears. I tell them about the clock.

"Eight-o-nine," Derek says. "You were with Mr Sloane, weren't you? Being wined and dined."

"Yeah." Except for the wining and dining.

"At least you weren't with Nightingale. That death dive wouldn't have been pretty."

"I've been trying to figure out how it happened," Nigel says. "He was at the Swap Meet yesterday and he'd framed prints to sell. Then along came Sloane waving cash but Nightingale didn't want to sell him that photo."

"Alister said he knew me and Roger didn't want me to see the picture."

"OK. If you saw it you'd know he'd been photographing you in the cemetery so he'd probably photographed the woman. He went home in some kind of competitive funk and printed all the others. And while he was doing it he fell off the ladder to his death."

It's an image I can't get out of my mind. His death dive. After I saw the woman I almost fell off the cliff, and when Roger tried to print her photo he fell too.

"He was trying to pay you back for stealing his stuff," Nigel says. "Making a print of you to sell. But it backfired when Sloane bought it. Another man in your life. Proof of his exploitation. Nobody can escape their own character. Nightingale was printing the cemetery pictures with malicious intent, and that made him fall."

"It felt obsessive," I say. "A whole string of images." But why not the nude?

Then I get another thought and it pushes everything else from my mind. If Alister hadn't bought my photo and inspired Roger's fury... Roger might still be alive.

Is that...murder? By your innocent actions triggering a series of events that leads to someone's death? In this case, the late-but-not-great Roger Nightingale.

Not just Alister. Me.

Suddenly I'm seeing all the connections going right back to me winning the green card. Connections that put Roger on that ladder last night and wrote his name on a gravestone months ago.

It's another perspective on the theory of six-degrees-of-separation– by living anywhere but a Himalayan cave we each play a part in each other's destiny. All these connections are like some cosmic map already plotted by the great map-maker in the sky. If you want to make God laugh, tell him your plans.

So why was it Roger's destiny to be on that ladder drying those prints?

Because of his obsessive personality. 'Nobody can escape their own character,' Nigel said. Long before I ran off with his photo files, Roger had taken secret pictures of me.

"He was in a hurry," Derek is saying. "Or he got a shock – in more ways than one – when he started pegging out the prints and could see the woman wasn't there. You're pointing your camera at an empty cliff."

"I suspect only Selkie could see her," Nigel says.

"Or she did her disappearing act just as Nightingale pressed the shutter."

"But if Nightingale saw her too," Nigel says, "then Selkie's connection with her isn't personal. If anyone could see her, she might just be a ghost that hangs around the cemetery. And if we'd gone back at the right time last Sunday we'd have seen her too."

Derek likes it. "It's her job to appear every Sunday on the dot of three o'clock." He looks at his watch. "Today's Sunday."

"Stop it, DD," I say. "We are never going back there. Never."

"But if she's the one who's trying to kill you, she's made a lousy job of it so far. I think you're misjudging her. She's as harmless as me."

Before I can explain my fears my phone rings and I pounce. But it isn't Alister. Where is he?

When I turn back to the boys I must look as wild-eyed as Sheena did last night. "The police want me to meet them at Roger's." If they're trying to unnerve me it's working.

"Take it easy," Derek says. "They'll just want to ask a few questions and get you to show them things."

"What things?"

"Things that relate to his lifestyle, his women, his photography. So they can understand why he died."

"I hardly knew him, DD. They should be asking Sheena."

"Have they found her yet?"

"I don't think so."

"Then it's got to be you."

***

Roger's kitchen feels sordid in the harsh light of day. Without him, the place has lost all character. I've stopped freaking out because it just feels empty. A hole in the universe where Roger used to be.

Detective Watkins's saggy face looks overworked as he asks me about the developing process.

"I don't know how it works," I say. "We were going to develop some photos one night. But it didn't happen."

The other detective, Romero, grabs the baton. He's younger than Watkins, with Latin good looks. "What happened between you? A lovers' tiff?"

"Not exactly."

They listen to the story about the poster.

"When did this happen?"

I think back. "Monday night."

"It didn't take him long to find someone else," Romero says. "Sheena Bradford. We've found no trace of her."

Does he think I'm making her up?

Watkins again. "You said in your statement that you came here and found Miss Bradford leaving."

"She was in a hurry. When she took off I came inside and found Roger on the bathroom floor. My friends were waiting downstairs. One of them rang the police."

He looks at his notes. "Just after ten. What were you doing here, Miss Moon, since you and Mr Nightingale had broken up? You haven't told us...why you came back."

"Haven't I?" They're unnerving me. And what about the division that was fingerprinting the flat? They must know about the theft, unless Roger just said that to scare me. "I'd...borrowed Roger's picture files to look for my photos. I was returning anything that didn't belong to me."

"A bit late for a visit, wasn't it?"

"His files - all those women - made me sick. If you've looked at them you'll understand. I wanted to get rid of them and I thought Roger could be out."

"So you've got a key to this flat?"

"No." I tell them about the flowerpot.

"How well do you know Miss Bradford?" Romero asks.

"Last night was the first time we met. She took one look at me and ran away."

No reason to protect Sheena.

"How can you be so sure who she was?"

"She's in the file-case. Roger called her She-Girl. He was big on nicknames."

"We noticed, Miss Lunatic." Romero's grin makes me glad my file was empty. "So until you saw his other women you thought you were the one?"

What's that supposed to mean? Are they suggesting I had a motive or something? "Am I under suspicion for anything?"

"Just helping us with our enquiries, Miss Moon," Watkins says, making Romero grin again.

But they start treating me with a bit more respect. Do I know how to find Sheena? "If she was here when Mr Nightingale died we need to speak to her."

But I only know she's from Scotland and she came over here with Roger.

Their mistrust stays with me as I walk to Derek's car. They know I wasn't here when he died - or do they? Since I haven't heard back from Alister I haven't given Watkins his phone number. And he hasn't checked my alibi or reminded me about it.

Shit. Their attitude might have been very different if bloody Alister hadn't beamed himself off the planet along with Sheena. Am I that scary? Making everyone vanish? But after my antics in his living room I can't blame Alister. He was all understanding last night but he's had time to decide I'm trouble.

Then there's Sheena. Roger's dead body would be enough to make her take off. Or did she see the woman? She was agitated by something. But when we collided she was only crying. Then she screamed and said it was magic, as if seeing *me* triggered something deep and irrational.

***

Back in Makiki Heights, Nigel has questions of his own as we do another round of coffee. "Was it seeing the photo on Sloane's wall that made you come home early last night?"

It had to come up eventually.

"No," I say. "I had an...accident."

Derek looks up from his mug. "What? You and Nightingale both having accidents? Why is that giving me the creeps?"

"We went to Alister's penthouse. Then after I saw Roger's photo, I...overbalanced and collided with the wall."

I have no idea why I'm spinning this fable.

"A dizzy spell?" Nigel asks.

I don't answer.

"Describe what happened," Derek says. "Or I'm withholding more coffee."

I gaze into my empty mug. I need the coffee. And it's a relief to tell them. "The worst part wasn't my feet flying out. Or my head hitting the wall. Except for this lump it might never have happened."

"What was worse?"

"The feeling of...malice. A cloud of it." Invading my nostrils. Wishing me dead.

Before I can say more, Alister calls.

"Selkie, you've been trying to get me. Is everything OK?"

At the sound of his voice I burst into tears. "Where have you been all day? You said you'd call."

"I'll tell you everything but it's your turn first."

"Roger's dead, Alister. He died last night. At eight-o-nine p-bloody-m."

He insists on coming over. We all sit in the kitchen while Derek brings him up to date. It's drawing Alister into the drama but I don't know how to exclude him. He's the only one who can corroborate where I was last night.

He leaves the room to ring Detective Watkins. When he comes back he says, "OK, they know you were with me. And I've just rung my staff about the timing of Roger's death. Eight-o-nine last night." Three numbers I never want to hear again. "So I checked with Ramon and Rita. They're quite sure." He looks me in the eye. "That's exactly when you had your seizure."

My body starts shaking. At the very moment I was headbutting Alister's masonry Roger was breathing his last. That means the suspicions that should be crazy are suddenly clanging with truth. The two people who saw the woman and photographed her – last night she tried to kill us both.

Alister puts his arm around me. "I warned you, didn't I? Surprise the universe wisely."

My anger erupts. "That didn't make sense last night, Alister, and it doesn't make sense now. This has gone way beyond bloody surprises. Roger's *dead*."

And I came close to joining him. If I'd hit that wall a

little harder...

"Just reminding you how powerful you are," he says.

"Powerful? What, I take one look at the photo on your wall and the resulting thought-bubble throws me across the room and kills Roger stone dead? If I'm that powerful I'd better start putting my head in a sack like Medusa."

"Whoa," Alister says. "That's not what I meant. At all."

What did he mean? Last night he called it *surreal*. Today I have to agree with him, but he doesn't know the whole story so that makes him pretty damn flaky.

Derek thinks he's onto something. "This photo, Selkie. You looked at it just before your seizure?" I nod, still wondering what Alister means by 'powerful'. "It shows you running through the cemetery, moments before you saw the woman?"

"Yes."

"What woman?" Alister asks.

I know Derek's going to tell him everything. Except the part where the woman bumped off Roger and had a go at me. That's my secret. These two are suddenly competing to be my knight in shining armour with no idea that I'm the one who needs the armour.

I leave the room. Somehow reliving the story is tantamount to inviting her to try again. How will she respond to failure?

I could get out of here, catch a taxi back to Wanda's and escape all this attention. But she's hardly ever home and I'm afraid. Afraid of being alone. Afraid of a woman who isn't real.

Because now Roger isn't real either.

***

I'm standing naked on a stage because I've lost my little black dress. Alister is dressed in armour and he's holding a frame in front of me to hide my nakedness, but the frame contains a sheet of glass so I'm even more exposed. A crowd has gathered and people are staring at me like I'm a painting by Salvador Dali. The cowry shell round my neck is calling and my skin melts, slipping me inside it. Suddenly I'm curled up safe and sound in this protective shell. A foetus that never has to be born.

"Selkie." Derek's shaking me. "You need to hear this."

I've been asleep for only a few minutes but in those few minutes the relationships in the kitchen have changed. It's like the reverse of a fairytale where the hero goes to the bottom of the sea for a few days and returns to find centuries have passed in the real world. In this case Derek and Nigel and Alister are now on the same team.

"Alister went back to the Swap Meet this morning," Nigel says.

"I wanted to take another look at Roger. Go through every photo and demand he destroy any pictures of you. He wasn't there, of course. But the woman was."

"The woman?" My breath deserts me.

"Not the woman on the cliff," Derek says.

"The woman who was with Roger yesterday," Alister says. "She was there again today. With Roger's photographs."

Sheena.

"She knew me from yesterday. When Roger got surly and didn't want to sell, she pushed him aside, took my money and handed over the photo. He was never going to part with it but she was all business."

So that's how Sheena knew me. From the photo that Alister bought. Then I turned up on the doorstep just after

Roger printed more photos of me and died in the process. Timing like that would freak anyone out.

"She took off in Roger's car," I say. "All the prints would have been in the back, ready for today's stall."

Another cool opportunist, stuffing the proceeds in her own pocket before the corpse was cold.

"I looked through everything on the stall," Alister says. "There were no other photos of you."

Derek takes all of us to the stadium in his old car. But Alister's interest put the wind up Sheena. The next stallholder says she abandoned her post hours ago. We call the police and they tell us to wait there. They pack up the photos, then ask me for the licence number of Roger's car but I can only remember the colour.

"Keep looking," I tell them. "She's probably sleeping in it."

I want to get out of here and find a shell big enough to hide in, but we're stopping at another stall. Davina's. Derek's idea.

Today she's dazzling in a tiny tiger-print dress, the vibrant orange matching the wild flames in her hair. A macramé belt rides her slim hips and her ballet shoes sharpen to leprechaun points. I'm wary of her. Our twin trances when she made my dress gave me one hell of a fright. What else is she capable of?

Derek introduces Alister, then says, "We need your help, Davina." He's avoiding my eye. "A mystery to solve."

"You know I love a good mystery, do you?"

"Leave it alone, DD," I hiss. "And leave Roger dead."

He looks insulted. "I'm not suggesting a seance. Puh-lease. Seances went out with ectoplasm." He turns back to Davina. "A disappearing woman."

Davina looks at me.

"Not Selkie," he says. "She's still here."

"Are you sure about that?" Davina asks.

What's that supposed to mean?

Now she's looking at her watch. "Where and when?"

"My place," Alister offers. "Tonight. Revisit the scene of the...happening. Eight-o-nine pm."

"A *happening*, is it?" Davina says. "And a disappearance. You've intrigued me now."

Not a happening, I want to scream. A *crime*.

Davina's still looking at me. "What do you think, Selkie?"

"Some things are better left alone."

In case stirring them up leads to premature death. Mine.

"So you don't like mysteries yourself then? You don't...delve into the murky depths?"

I shrug. "I don't even paddle."

She laughs. "But you used to delve. Long ago."

This feels like therapy with an audience but my voice responds anyway. "It's not safe," it says.

Time does its standing-still thing and four pairs of eyes look back at me. Derek's are urging me to let him loose on the mystery. Nigel's are beaming out impatience tinged with strength. Alister's baby blues are stroking me with such passion I have to look away. Into the eyes of Davina. They're deep and clear, watching me without judgement, giving me space.

After last night I'm running scared. A madwoman frantic to escape. But wherever I go the woman will track me down because there's nowhere to hide. Wanda hid the mirror but the woman appeared on the cliff. Roger hid in his darkroom but the ladder still toppled over.

As I look into the eyes of my friends, the woman's

piercing gaze comes back to me. At the time it didn't feel evil, it felt...*desperate*. She wants something with the darkest depths of her being.

Something from me.

"Let's do it," my voice says.

CHAPTER
Twenty-Seven

It's his staff's night off so Alister orders in finger food. Chinese. I'm starving and suddenly impatient to hear from Davina.

She refuses wine. "Not when I'm intuiting, you know."

We all sit on the sofas, and it might as well be a seance because the atmosphere is charged. Davina crosses her legs Buddha-style.

Derek begins, summarising without emotion, and I let him. A few days ago I couldn't have paraded my life like this because Alister and Davina are people I've wanted to impress. But something inside me has let go of all that.

Derek's memory is perfect. It's his skill as a writer or he's been keeping notes. He goes back to the very beginning. To the taxi driver dropping me at the Pearl. Finding the leaflet for Wanda's flat. Jerome's haircut and his bizarre reaction. The singing shell and the app's verdict. The entity on my shoulder. My sightings of the woman, and the camera that went missing and then turned up blank. Coral's thoughts about Pele and the stolen photographs. My trance in the middle of the seminar. Davina's dress.

Strung together they're a litany of paranormal happenings to boggle the mind. And that's leaving out the things I haven't told anyone - the feather-duster boogie, the cloud of menace in Nigel's kitchen, Sheena's scream...

Derek finishes with Roger and his stolen images (the nude poster does it for impressing Alister). Then the event that's the most bizarre and frightening - my seizure in this room only last night, at the exact moment Roger breathed his last.

Davina's listened with unwavering concentration. She has a habit of creasing her brow into two vertical pleats and tilting her head as if she's listening to distant music. Can she hear the shell singing? After the cosy shell appeared in my dream I'm never taking mine off.

We all inspect the photo on the wall. Roger's fast exposure caught me glancing over my shoulder, my face fully visible and both feet off the ground. Behind me, one gravestone shows its inscription but all the others are blank. When I look at the photo again there's a moment of tension, but no repeat of last night's performance even though Alister's poised to grab me. So it wasn't the photo that triggered it.

When we return to the sofa it's Davina's turn. To peer into a crystal or a teacup or something. Her presence is calming but it's a big ask to explain the unexplainable.

Except Derek is reaching into his pocket. And pulling something out. A memory card.

"In the camera under the body," he says.

A camera I managed to miss.

"Don't look at it," I yell. "Roger looked and...he's dead."

"I've already looked," Derek says. "I didn't see the woman but I saw the urinating dog. They're your photos." He notices Nigel's incredulous look. "I wiped my fingerprints off the camera afterwards."

So Derek's survived to tell the tale. But Roger didn't. I can see him on the ladder, leaning over the string, using the viewfinder to compare my photo of the woman with his print of the empty cliff. That's when he fell, dropping the camera beside him.

Davina leans back and closes her eyes. "Let's deal with the woman later."

Her voice is so soothing everyone sinks into their seat. Derek puts the memory card away so for the moment the woman's contained.

"I suggest we work backwards," Davina says.

"My 'paroxysm'," I whisper. "And Roger's death."

Davina begins. "Roger Nightingale liked possessing things, artistic things, beautiful things. Photos. Women. He was incensed when you stole his poster and his precious picture files. And when Alister walked off with the photo of you his emotions began unravel. By the time he went into his darkroom last night he was in a fine fury, I'd say. And hell-bent on further revenge."

A ripple of rage surges through the room. Is it Roger, seething from beyond the grave? Or is it...the woman?

"The prints on the string were designed to hurt you, Selkie. Just like the nude poster exposed your vulnerability – and Roger's power over you – so did the incident on the cliff. But what happened last night isn't about the woman – she's another story, although Roger got tangled up in it. No, this is about Roger, how he was focusing on you. With emotions at the top of the Richter scale."

"It fits," I say, "but how do you know?"

"The message."

"The message from Sheena? She screamed at me, said it was *magic*."

"Ah, Sheena. She's a wildcard, that one. You gave her a grand fright, I'd say. I wonder what she was up to. "

"Did she kill him?"

Davina pauses and sniffs the air. "Not imaginative enough. Up to her own business, I'd say. That's a girl who's after the main chance."

"What message?" Derek asks.

"The message Roger sent to Selkie," Davina says. "A psychic one. You know what I'm talking about, don't you?"

"No idea," I say, and no-one contradicts me.

"At the instant of his death Roger was thinking about you, Selkie. Malign thoughts. His emotions were so strong they connected him to you on a psychic level and you picked them up just as he died."

She waits but I still don't get it.

"Your seizure wasn't a real one. It was a communication. Roger's thoughts were directed towards you, then suddenly he touched a live current and you were zapped too. No wonder you bounced off Alister's wall and lit up like party lights."

"You mean..."

"Electrocution. By proxy. You channelled Roger's dying thoughts...delivered by a psychic dose of one hundred and ten volts."

Shit. Now I'm reliving it. My body jerking and jolting. The acrid burning in my nostrils. A pantomime of Roger's death throes, his last seconds of life. When I glance at Alister I see that he's remembering it too.

"Volts with venom," I whisper.

Davina allows the news to sink in before she asks, "Selkie, has anything like this happened before? Experiences that aren't your own? Because only a skilled channel has the power to receive a message like this."

Wanda said I'm psychic. How the hell did that happen? My confusion is overtaken by a crushing sense of responsibility. Then anger. I don't want this.

"It explains all the weird happenings," Derek is saying. "You're a magnet for the paranormal."

Nigel chuckles. "The reluctant psychic."

"Surprise the universe wisely," Alister murmurs.

He's looking at me but I refuse to meet his eye. Andrew thinks I'm scary. Do I frighten Alister too?

Nigel asks, "If Roger hadn't died, would Selkie have received any message at all? Not from the electric shock but from his thoughts alone?"

"It depends how powerful a channel she is," Davina says. "She might have felt something, a shiver of evil."

The dark cloud in the boys' kitchen. After I stole Roger's files. At the moment he was developing the picture he sold to Alister. The timing fits.

My head is spinning. Is the woman off the hook? Because I'm responsible? Medusa after all? God knows I was angry enough to kill Roger when I saw that picture on Alister's wall. Suddenly I'm scared of myself.

Davina is reading my mind. "You're not responsible for what happened, Selkie. Telepathy isn't voodoo, it's a message. You're just the receiver, the channel. Roger's death was a physical outcome of physical forces. You didn't even know it was coming."

Yes, I did. *Roger's dead* said a voice in my head. A voice that knew the future. Because she was about to...create it.

"What about the photograph?" Alister asks. "Was it a coincidence that Selkie looked at it seconds before Roger died?"

"Now that's the real mystery. Along with the identity of the woman. To be sure, I don't know how the photograph fits. The world is full of coincidences that mean nothing at all, but this one..." Davina pauses and tilts her head. "Unless...something about the image...turned Selkie into a channel just as she looked."

"Can photographs have that kind of power?" I can tell Derek's remembering his genie-in-the-bottle theory. And the memory card burning a hole in his pocket.

"I don't have any experience of it," Davina says, "but a photograph is a form of embodied energy. It captures a moment in time and looking at it can evoke the energy of the original event. Like a song can arouse real emotions from the past. By the way, that's probably what the app picked up – the energy of the shell's song, not the song itself.

"This photo was taken just before Selkie saw the woman, wasn't it?" she continues. "Was that telepathy? Seeing a woman who wasn't there? Not if Roger saw her too. But he might only have seen Selkie's *photo* of the woman – a photo intended for Selkie's eyes alone, like the *kahuna* said, and interfered with by Roger – then when he printed his own photo he discovered the woman wasn't there."

My happy snap trouncing Roger, the great *artiste*. That would push him off the ladder... Clever. She didn't even have to be there.

Davina again. "So it's possible something about the photo on the wall activated Selkie's psychic power."

Power. That word again. And if looking at a photo of myself turns me into a psychic I'd better start wearing that Medusa sack.

Davina goes over to the photo. In the corner, the little star fruit tree is leaning over a gravestone. "Did you eat the fruit?" she asks me.

I look at Nigel. "At least three." More like five.

"In the land of the dead, fruit represents soul food." She cocks her head. "When you ate you might have become akin to the underworld..."

I'm remembering that sweet flesh. After Roger made me go without breakfast.

"So seeing the *photo* of the fruit," Davina is saying, "might have reactivated some deep ancestral knowing." She looks closer. "Who's Raven? It's the only name visible on all these headstones."

"No idea," I manage to say.

"The star fruit tree is living off her grave."

Davina leaves it at that. They're all content with the evening's work. Selkie is a telepath and the seizure is explained. Alister opens more wine and the boys marvel over Mia the python. But I'm not feeling satisfied. Because writing everything else off as the visions of a reluctant psychic is too neat, too convenient. Too impossible.

Davina is standing beside me, sipping her wine.

"The entity?" I ask, feeling like we've only scratched the surface. "If I'm psychic, why haven't I seen it?"

"Only you know the answer to that one. Even though you think you don't. Trust your instincts. The entity will appear when it's ready, you know. Perhaps it already has."

"You mean the woman, don't you?" Another too-neat solution. "But her appearance doesn't match the sighting of the entity. And I don't want her riding around on my shoulder." If I've got any choice in the matter.

"They've got to be connected," she says. "You don't seem to be picking up other people's stories, only your own. Which suggests your story is unresolved in some way."

"I picked up Roger."

"While he was printing pictures of you."

Across the room Alister is showing the boys a cast-off snakeskin and I get a sudden stab in my chest. Bloody hell. Now I'm picking up messages from reptiles.

"If you need to talk," Davina whispers, "you know where I am."

***

Everyone is leaving.

"I need a favour, Alister." He looks hopeful but I'm going to disappoint him. "Would you give me the photo? It was never Roger's to sell and I feel funny about leaving it here."

"Of course."

We cross the room. There I am, trapped in time, running between the graves, oblivious to the watchers. Behind me the star fruit tree caresses the gravestone of someone called Raven, 1960–1995.

"That's where Roger and I are the same," Alister murmurs. "We both want the wild woman with the haunting eyes."

"At least my photo is less trouble than the real thing."

He grins. "It's the trouble I'm interested in."

Our eyes meet. He isn't frightened. Far from it.

"But you've had enough men wanting to possess you this weekend," he says.

"This lifetime."

"That's because you've got something, Selkie. And I don't mean the telepathy."

"Yeah. Something that attracted a loser like Roger." I'm not even going to think about Andrew.

"He was convinced he didn't deserve you. That can drive a man like Roger over the edge."

"You only met him for a few seconds, Mr Freud."

He grins again. "And I saw he was a gifted artist and an emotional dwarf. He knew straight away what I planned to do."

"What?"

"Don't you know yet?"

More possessive talk. A crass joke comes to the rescue. "Yeah, but killing him was a tad unnecessary."

"How did I do that? Magic?"

"Nah, you followed him home and tampered with his ladder."

"Cunning. Make it look like an accident. But why was it unnecessary?"

"A free dinner and I'm anybody's, Alister. You just never got to find out."

He chuckles. "That would be great if my desire was only to make love to you, Selkie Moon."

"What else is there?" I ask.

I lift the photo off the wall.

"What are you going to do with it?" he asks. "Destroy it?"

"What is this, a psychics' convention?"

Davina calls across the room, "A word of advice, Selkie. Don't destroy the picture. It may hold secrets you are yet to uncover."

We lock stares. Her eyes are as green as a shamrock on Saint Patrick's Day. I should be able to read her mind, shouldn't I? But all I'm getting is a prickling apprehension. What else does she know about this photo?

I look at it again. Destroying it seems like such a good idea. The only alternative is keeping it.

"I'll drive you home," Alister says.

Suddenly all this support is too much and I'm desperate to be alone. "Thanks, but I'll get a taxi. And thank you all for everything you've done." I cross the room and press the button for the lift. "Great food too. Best Chinese this side of Nathan Road."

"Not quite the dinner I planned."

"Yeah. No candles."

Derek comes down to the parking level with me to retrieve my suitcase from his back seat. He lets me go reluctantly. "Our spare bed is yours, you know."

"I know. Thank you."

When I reach the street, there are no taxis in sight and a build-up of clouds is threatening rain. As I look up and down the deserted tarmac it occurs to me that none of these events would have happened in Sydney. Is it too late to go back?

I'm just about to call a cab when a car pulls up.

"I'll drive you," Davina says.

She might want to say more about the photograph. From one psychic to another. I decide I have to know. But in the car she's silent. What's she waiting for?

Then she asks, "Did you imagine things as a child?"

Suddenly I'm the one doing the talking. "Only voices. Whispering to me."

"Voices. Tell me more."

"My mother died when I was a baby. It was her voice I heard."

"What did she say?"

"Weird things. Wonderful things." Suddenly I'm telling her everything. "I felt lost without her, so her voice was a kind of comfort. But my stepmother, Stella, needed to know everything. I don't know if she did the same to Gretel but she watched over my thoughts with a ruthless vigilance. One day she heard me whispering to someone and wanted to know what was happening. Then she tried to make me stop. So I started writing them down, the secret conversations."

"What happened?" She knows something did.

"Eventually she found it, the diary. I was sixteen by then. I'd stopped believing the voices came from Mum, they were my thoughts I wrote. Stella was always going through my things but I'd managed to hide it for years." I swallow hard as I remember. "She read it from cover to cover, then burned it. She'd been waiting for me to thank her - for stepping in and mothering me - and after reading *my opinions* she accused me of being ungrateful.

"There was a terrible row. Dad left the house, left me to my fate. Then, as if she hadn't already annihilated all traces of me, Stella renamed me Elkie. She was shouting that she should have changed my name when my mother died, that Selkie was a dangerous name, that she'd never call me Selkie again. Suddenly I didn't exist.

"I felt like I was fighting for my life. For the first time ever I screamed back at her - that I didn't understand why I couldn't keep a diary, why I couldn't have opinions, why it made me ungrateful, why I had to have a new name. But by then she wasn't talking to me, she was only talking to...Elkie."

"What opinions?" Davina asks.

"I don't remember." I'm crying now. "Something in me died with the diary, and so did my memory of everything I'd written."

"You remember nothing at all?"

"Only that the things I wrote amazed me. But Selkie was gone and the voices in my head suddenly stopped. So...Stella won."

"Don't be so sure about that."

Outside my building she puts her hand on my arm. "Big things have blown your way, Selkie. And it's just the beginning. But wait seven days before you take action. It's a good policy..."

Davina makes every shot count, then moves on. I like that.

"And I hope we'll be friends," she says.

"But we don't have anything in common," I blurt. "Except being psychic. And I find you a bit...frightening." Just like me.

"Because I've shown you a gift you could well do without."

"Yeah, a gift I'll be sending back."

She laughs. "I like your sense of humour. Is that enough?"

"And I've just told you stuff I've never told anyone." Even Derek.

"You're not sure you can trust me."

That's all. She's not going to persuade me of her integrity. I like that.

"Well, remember I'm your friend if ever you need one." She turns her green eyes up a notch. "And I think you might."

Something moves in my chest and I realise how important friends are. I've been so focused on escaping from Andrew, on proving myself, on being someone, I've taken my friendships - with Derek, with Wanda - for granted.

I climb the stairs to the flat, clutching the photograph and worrying about being alone. But if I really am psychic then I'm never alone - I'm surrounded by messages and unseen companions, eerie feelings and apparitions. Have they always been with me but I've suppressed them? And now they're bursting through?

The telepathy explains my seizure and why I've heard the woman's voice, why I've felt her pain. But what if Roger's death was a message in itself? If I'm a channel for psychic communications, and a novice at that, then it doesn't protect me. It makes me more...exposed.

I lean the picture against the wall, but as I begin to open

the door a shadow comes from nowhere and pushes me inside. The force of it almost knocks me over but I manage to spin around and fumble for the light. Then I turn around and come face to face...with a woman.

Chapter
Twenty-Eight

Jeans. T-shirt. Spiky hair. Leaning against the doorjamb with her arms folded. Sheena.

"I thought you were never coming home," she says.

Under the overhead light her features are harsh. Bulging eyes that make her look slightly startled, overlarge nostrils accentuated by a nose ring, kitchen-sink streaks in several colours including green.

I stand very still. At least she's real. But her audacity makes me alert. She's trouble. *Pilikia.*

"What are you doing here?" I ask. Roger knew my address. Has she stolen his phone as well as his car? "The police are looking for you, you know."

"So you told them about me. Thanks a million. Or your boyfriend did. The guy with the big smile. Cute. And rich. Bet he's got a few spare rooms at his place. Unlike this dump." She does a great eye-roll. "But any bed will do."

I pick up the phone. "The cops'll give you somewhere to sleep."

"I didn't do anything, did I?"

"No, Sheena. You didn't even call an ambulance when Roger died." I'm sounding braver than I feel because I've got no idea how to get rid of her. "You can't stay here, I've got a flatmate. She'll be home soon. And last night you were afraid of me. Totally freaked."

She shrugs. "After Roj carked it who wouldn't be?"

"You saw him die?"

"Course not. I was watching telly, wasn't I? He was

doing his *alchemy* shit in the bathroom. Next thing there's a bang and the telly goes off."

She should do the eulogy.

"Tell the police. I've got their card here somewhere." I put my suitcase on the bed and open it. "Unless you pushed him off the ladder yourself."

She snorts. "Not guilty. But we've got business, Sel-kie."

As she stumbles out my name her tension shows. She's still jumpy. So why is she here?

"What business?"

She's already hefted a backpack onto the floor. Now she opens a flap and pulls out a photograph and a string of negatives. She hands me the print, but pushes the negatives into her pocket.

It's the poster print. Of me on Roger's bed.

"Where did you get this?"

"Roger's enlarger."

After he died. He was in the process of printing it so she stepped over his body. No wonder she screamed when she saw me. She'd just stolen my photo from the corpse.

"A thousand bucks and it's yours," she says.

I go to the fridge and pour two glasses of wine. At least Guy taught me something about the art of negotiation. She sits down with her glass while I leave the room to pee. And fire off a text to Detective Watkins.

"I only take cash," she says when I return and examine the print again.

"I'll have to see the negative, make sure it belongs."

She pulls out the strip of negatives and holds it up to the light. It shows that Roger took several shots of me that night, from different angles. Of course he did. If I had a lighter in my pocket I could make Sheena let go – and destroy the negatives – all at the same time.

"We'll have to go to a cash machine," I say, playing for time. "What else have you got to sell?"

She tips the contents of the backpack onto the floor. Five cameras. So she went through Roger's things, took anything portable. She only missed the one hidden by his body.

"Five thousand for the lot," she says. "You know they're worth it."

Now that Derek's got my memory card, the cameras don't interest me. I'll never look at my photo of the woman but I know where it is. Safely with Derek. I start turning on the digitals, intending to scroll through the shots and give myself time to think. She watches, leaning back with her wine. But there's not a single photo in any camera.

"Don't tell me you're selling the memory cards separately," I say.

"Course not. I gave them to Gerry, didn't I?" So Sheena knows the sex worker. "She wants her photos. Roger wouldn't hand them over, not while he was getting free sex." This sounds like the truth. "But she didn't find them, did she?"

She didn't find them because I've got them. It's the one CD I kept.

"These cameras are stolen goods," I say. "I can't touch them."

"You didn't mind nicking Roger's laptop."

So she knows about that. What else does she know?

I've run out of stalling tactics but I've got to get that negative before the police arrive. A thought comes from somewhere.

"I knew Roger was dead," I say, dropping my voice to a whisper, "before I bumped into you last night."

The balance of power suddenly shifts.

"H-how did you know?"

"You knew the answer last night."

I can almost see the hairs on the back of her neck stand up. "M-magic?"

I've remembered Roger telling me she's a village girl. From way up in the Highlands. She would have grown up with the selkie stories, before she moved to London, got streetwise and met Roger. Her need for money made her brave tonight but her childhood superstitions run deep. That's why she screamed last night.

"Just give me the negatives and the photo," I say, "and I'll let you take the cameras...before the cops get here."

That makes her jump. "The cops?"

"They'll be here," I sniff the air, "any minute."

The hint of more clairvoyance clinches it.

Keeping her eyes on me, she tosses the negatives on the table beside the photo, packs up the cameras and leaves.

When Watkins and Romero arrive, I've destroyed them and poured myself another glass. The detectives aren't pleased to be called out on a wild goose chase. As they take in Wanda's decorations they seem to reconsider my credibility. I remember how Davina didn't defend herself and do the same.

"Sheena Bradford is looking for all the world like a figment," Watkins grunts.

Stella's favourite word. "She was here," I say, letting them notice the extra wine glass. "Trying to sell me Roger's cameras."

Romero snorts as he takes out his notebook.

"You didn't find any, did you?" I say. "He had at least five."

"There was one. Under the body. Without a memory card." He glares at me.

"Sheena's got the rest."

He shrugs as if it doesn't matter, but I can tell she's a loose end they want to tie up.

"If she tries to contact you again, Miss Moon..."

"I'll be in touch."

***

It's after they've taken my statement and gone that I feel it. The sense that something's missing. I've been gloating about the negatives but now I'm in a panic as I scan the room, wondering what she took. She was only alone for a moment but for Sheena it was enough. Wanda's fish come and go so I can't be sure about them. The Shona sculpture is still here. What did Shona see?

My suitcase is on the bed. Open. And I'm on my knees, doing a clumsy search. There was never much in it. Toiletries, makeup...and my clothes from last night.

I upend it but I already know. My slinky black dress – the dress Davina made me, the dress Derek and Nigel bought me, the dress I wore to Alister's, the dress that flew across the room as Roger died – is gone. And I'm doubled over, sobbing with rage and regret.

Through a blur of tears I pour more wine and try to calm down. After a little taste of telepathy I'm in danger of imbuing every event with cosmic significance. Sure it was special, gorgeous, sexy, but a dress is a dress is a dress. It can be replaced.

So why does it feel like I've lost much more than fabric?

It's when the bottle's empty that I remember the photo from Alister's. When Sheena pushed me through the door it was leaning against the wall. I rush outside, hoping it's hidden by shadows, but it's gone.

The next thing I know, I'm down in the bus shelter pouring it all out. Through all my blubbering Coral presses her feet against my thighs. Has she understood a word I've said?

When I stop, she grins, opens her mouth and speaks.

Just one word of wisdom.

"Pizza."

I call for a delivery and wait beside her in a state of shock. Then, as we share a family-size Hawaiian, I realise Coral really is a *kahuna*. It wasn't just about filling her belly. I'd forgotten my golden rule: food first.

When we're finished she forms her hands into a pillow beside her head. Sleep on it. I agree with her. In the morning I'll know what to do.

***

I wake early from a stolen-dress dream: hundreds of prostitutes in replica frocks were sashaying down the Track in military formation. The consuming emotion is envy. Everyone's got my dress except me.

The dream dwindles but the sense of loss is overwhelming. I've got to get it back. And after what happened with Sheena last night the price is going to be high.

But all these thoughts are sucked from my mind when I swing my feet off the bed.

The vinyl floor is covered in footprints. Red footprints. What?

At first I stare at them in disbelief. Then bewilderment. Then with a growing sense of violation. Because they're too small for Wanda. Fighting back sobs of anger and fear, I crawl to the end of the bed and follow them with my eyes all the way to the front door. They enter, walk the length of my bed and stop beside my pillow.

During the night someone dipped her bare feet in red paint, broke into our flat and walked across the room to look at me. And she's still here.

"What do you want?" I scream.

I remember the local woman who was almost sucked into her mirror and the exorcists who found demons living in her statues. Since Wanda's mirror is gone the woman's found something else to harbour her. Something in this flat. What?

Shona is sitting in stone above my bed and I wonder if she's what she seems. Her face hasn't changed but has she betrayed me? And did she have any choice?

Or the four-faced Buddha, he's ripe for habitation, and the parrot looks shifty with its half-open beak. And Doris, what would Doris do in exchange for a head? And could I blame her? Even Wanda's fish are following me with new eyes.

At least with the mirror I could see the woman. Her invisible presence is much worse.

The shell is on my bedside table. What does it know? With shaking fingers I put it to my ear but the voices are almost silent. I tie the shell around my neck, cursing myself for not wearing it all night, but it's large and lumpy, an obstruction to sleep.

Sleep. The time when you're most vulnerable. The thought of her watching me as I lay sleeping escalates the threat to a whole new level.

"Why didn't you kill me when you had the chance?" I scream.

And what did she do to me instead?

CHAPTER
Twenty-Nine

Things start happening in a blur. My phone chirps with texts. Alister and Davina and Derek. I'm not thinking straight enough to look at them but I pick up a call from Wanda, and when she hears my strangled voice she tells me to stay put then races home to find me marooned on the bed.

"We've got to call Detective Watkins," I scream. "I'm the victim of a...stalker."

But if the woman isn't real why are her footprints? I look at them again, at the way they cross the floor with such confidence, such entitlement. Who else would be so brazen? And why are they red?

"Keep your shirt on," Wanda says. "I can't see them, right? So they're not the kind of footprints to interest the police."

I'm the only one who can see them. I know what that means.

"The woman was here," I wail, "while I was asleep." She's still here.

Wanda puts her hands on her hips. "Have you put your own feet in them?"

"I'm not touching them. They're...red."

Like the shards from Roger's developing light. Sprinkled across the floor...like bloody footprints.

"Show me the bottom of your feet."

I'm cringing under the bedclothes but across the room Wanda opens her backpack and pulls out Tutu's mirror.

"Not the mirror," I scream. "Not again. No!"

Wanda's not listening. She comes towards me holding it up like a shield. Then she grabs the sheet and throws it out of the way as she puts the mirror under my bare feet. "Look."

I've covered my eyes but the mirror has other ideas. Through a crack in my fingers the soles of my feet look back.

"What do you see, Selkie?"

My voice is a whisper. I can't believe it. "They're...red."

"Just as I thought. When you said they were small I thought they might be yours. You made the fucking footprints yourself."

"Shit."

As if that settles it Wanda goes into the kitchen. But I've got to get out of here. Go to the office and try to look normal. Not in my red suit. Suddenly red is forbidden. Unless it's in a bottle. I pull one out from under the bed, but Wanda insists on a smoothie.

"It's eight o'clock in the morning. Wine will only muddle your head."

Like I'm thinking straight.

"Go easy on the wheatgerm," I say, but she puts in extra chia and I still have to eat it with a spoon.

We eat in silence. She's waiting for me to ask.

"I don't get it," I say at last, feeling like a fool.

"Two words. Psychic footprints. It's not the first time they've turned up in Tutu's mirror."

"But those footprints were made by spirits. You told me. On their way to the underworld. I'm not going anywhere. And I'm a real person." But I'm remembering the times when I wasn't so sure. "Was I sleepwalking?"

"If you don't remember you must have been."

"But where did I go? And why did I go there? I didn't even dream about it."

"The soles of the feet are sentient. They must have been out there...feeling things."

"I thought that was just Coral."

"It's another message, Selkie."

***

I go to the office in jeans. The first time ever. And try in vain to push the incident from my mind. On the bus, I remember the texts from the others but I still can't face them. The footprints have humiliated me. Made by my own feet. As a psychic I need L-plates.

Where did I go in the middle of the night? In bare feet? And only a nightie? The streets around the Track aren't safe for semi-naked female sleepwalkers. What happened out there? In the shower I looked for injuries in the obvious places. Nothing.

And why are the footprints red? Something is niggling at my memory. I've seen those feet before. I rack my brain but it doesn't come.

And the mirror's back. Wanda thinks it's time I reconnected with the woman, asked her straight out what she wants, but she agreed to turn it to the wall until I'm ready. As if.

At the office I throw myself into emails, trying to focus on work and forget about phantoms. It's Monday morning, my first day back since the seminar. On the dot of ten o'clock the phone starts ringing so I pull myself together, hoping it's a client, hoping my reputation is already spreading. It's the receptionist from Skape. Oliver Katsuya wants to speak to me. Personally. Surely he's not the type to thank me for the seminar. I'm right. He isn't.

"This paperwork you faxed me," he says. "Your money-back guarantee."

My stomach does a psychic lurch. "Yes?"

"I want a refund for the seminar."

"What?"

"Wrong question, sweetheart. Try 'how many?'"

"H-how many what?"

"Refunds." He's playing with me. And enjoying himself.

"How many of your staff weren't...satisfied...with the seminar?"

"All twenty."

"That's not true!" There must be a misunderstanding. I get control of my voice. "Most of your staff came up and thanked me personally. And they all wrote glowing testimonials. If you give me a minute I'll fax them to you."

"Don't bother. It says here you give a refund 'no questions asked'."

Silence. While the penny drops.

"You bastard."

He chuckles. "Flattery won't change my mind, sweetheart."

"But we had a deal. A seminar designed for your people. It was a quality product and you know it."

"And it included a money-back guarantee, all here in black and white."

"You set me up, from the beginning. You never had any intention of paying, did you?"

Another betrayal. And I never saw it coming. How many is that? I've lost count.

"No questions asked," he says again. "I'm reading it right here off your brochure."

That's thirty-four thousand dollars. Gone, just like that.

My first income in three months of struggle. My first chance to prove Andrew wrong, to be someone. All a sham. First I'm done over by Roger, then Guy, then Sheena – now Katsuya is one too many. Tears are trickling down my cheeks. Another reason why he's a millionaire and I'm just a greenhorn with a green card.

Or am I?

The singing has suddenly become deafening. On my chest the cowry is glowing and a thousand voices are vibrating my spine. The spine that a moment ago was marshmallow is now flowing with molten energy.

"I'll expect your payment by –"

"Wait a minute, Mr Katsuya." He must be able to hear the change in my voice. The confidence. Am I channelling? "Let me get this straight. You're reading from my brochure, is that correct? Requesting a refund for the seminar you attended?"

"My staff attended. Don't get clever."

"So you weren't there yourself."

"You know I wasn't. Look, cut the bullshit and refund my money. And if you don't honour the claims you make I'll report you to the relevant authorities. You can't set up a business in this town and make promises you don't keep. Sweetheart."

But I've reached for a copy of my money-back guarantee. There it is in black and white, just like he said.

The rush of joy makes me so eloquent I'm almost singing too.

"Please note the exact wording: *If a participant is dissatisfied with the seminar for any reason, a full refund will be paid, no questions asked.* You can see the problem, can't you? You weren't a participant so this guarantee doesn't apply to you. Sir."

Silence again. This time it's the silence of the out-played. I'm right and he knows it. And he can't believe it.

"I have a record of all attendees," I add, "so if you involve any authorities in this matter I'll be forced to make a complaint about your practices."

Katsuya can still white-ant me around town but I doubt he will. Instead of his clever story about outsmarting the novice presenter, I've got the counter-story about turning the tables on him.

As I hang up Derek is grinning from the doorway. "Since you got that cowry shell you've morphed into one tough cookie."

He's right. The contract with Sloane, the phone call with Andrew – something powerful is emerging from my usual swamp of emotions. Is it all down to the shell? But I haven't forgotten the footprints. And two hours ago I was cringing under the sheets, feeling doomed.

Derek wants to talk. It's why he's come in early. But my phone is ringing again. It's Davina.

"I've got your dress," she says.

"What?" She's laughing and I'm laughing. "How? When?"

"Come over and get it and I'll tell you how I managed it."

It's her day off so we make a date for this afternoon. By the time I get there I might be able to talk about the footprints.

Derek's hovering with intent, but now there's another text from Alister and this time I read it. Sheena's with him and he's just got the photo back.

So she's offloaded each item onto the obvious target. And kept her distance from me. It makes me wish Mia was venomous.

I fumble a reply: *Don't leave her alone with anything portable.*

But he's probably figured that out.

Derek loses patience. He drops a printout on my table and I hear him stomping down the stairs. He'll be back in five with coffees from Curtis. Toby's Estate. And Curtis has kept his little secret.

I pick up the printout. It's an article from the *Guardian*.

Sirens from Greek Mythology were Monk Seals

A scientific team has investigated an island off the Amalfi coast of Italy known as Le Sirenuse, the Island of the Sirens. Legend says it's where the sirens lured ships onto the rocks with their song, but scientists have now identified a configuration of rocks that amplify sounds coming from the island. Their tests show that a human voice isn't loud enough to reach out to sea, but the moaning of the monk seals is loud enough to be amplified by the rocks.

The sirens from Homer's Odyssey might have been monk seals, supporting the theory that the epic poem was real.

Derek finds me skimming the details.

"Nigel's been through hundreds of articles trying to track down your 'Siren Song'. Mostly they retell the Odysseus story. The wax in the sailors' ears and Odysseus strapped to the mast. He found this one this morning."

"Very interesting, DD. Thank him for me."

"The singing might be a seal song."

"And how does that help?"

"It's your name."

I don't like where this is heading. Derek thinks I'm tough, but he doesn't know about the footprints, how unstable I am underneath.

"DD, I can't deal with any more right now." I tell him about Sheena. "Especially not anything weird."

"But this article is good news."

"It's mythology. Blame my mother."

"But the seals might be calling you."

"From the Mediterranean?"

"The seas are interconnected," he says. "They link everything."

"And why would they be calling me? So I'll join them in the sea and drown? Maybe the seals are in league with the woman."

"You *are* fragile. The shell is protecting you. We thought this article would cheer you up."

I know Derek's addicted to my cause but Nigel's efforts surprise me.

"I appreciate your support, DD. You and Nigel have been amazing. But you didn't read to the end. It says here that historians aren't amused. They think this research devalues the *Odyssey* by trying to turn its mythical creatures into something literal. I'm with them. Selkie is a name. Let's leave it that way."

"Then you won't be interested in this." He hands me a photocopy and takes his coffee back to his office.

When I read the bold print I drop it on the table.

Animal Spirit Guides from Hawaii: Mea Hulu, the Monk Seal

If Mea Hulu calls us, we are being reunited with the ancient rhythms of ancestral knowledge, no matter how out of integrity with our family we have been till now.

Bloody Derek. I try to ignore the words but they intrude on my thoughts. *Out of integrity with our family.* It's what I am – with Andrew and Stella and Dad – but who could blame me?

*****

By midday, it's not too early to ring Gretel. Because I'm not out of integrity with her. She's on the sofa with her feet up and is pleased to hear from me.

"Have you given any thought to that flying visit?" she asks.

"Don't get me wrong, I'd love to see you. But you know I'm not into babies. And where would I stay? Not with you. And I'm pissed off with Dad and Stella."

"More than usual?"

I tell her about my call to Dad. "He said he couldn't tell me about Prunella, even though I deserve to know. And Stella was hovering, making sure he kept his promise."

"The great mystery woman. What do you think happened? You always had good intuition. Until you hooked up with Andrew. Has it come back?"

I'm not going to tell her about the weird stuff. Not in her condition. But I close my eyes and try to focus on my mother. There's not much there. "She feels...black. I don't know why I said that."

"The black sheep."

"Or black-hearted."

"You've been listening to Mum."

"It's hard not to. I used to tell myself Prunella was a saint who died young – and she wasn't around to quash the image. But if she was a good person, a good person who made some bad mistakes, like killing herself, why would Stella and Dad try to protect me from the truth? Especially now I'm an adult. What could be so bad they have to hide it for thirty-four years? If the truth doesn't explode soon I think I will."

She chuckles. "Me too. Any day now."

There's nothing more to say about Prunella so Gretel

asks about the seminar. I end up telling her about Alister. And Roger.

"Electrocution," she says. "It's a hell of a way to solve a double-dating problem. And get this. At the same time you were losing Andrew."

"What?"

"He hasn't blocked me from his updates and I've just seen a photo of his girlfriend."

Andrew with another woman? After the way he's hounded me? For a moment my head spins, then I understand.

"He wants me to know, Gretel. That's why he hasn't blocked you." I tell her about the divorce papers and the house valuation. "He's escalating the pressure."

"Another woman is his last card," she says. Then, "You never loved him, did you?"

I don't know. "I felt...tied to him. And every time I tried to leave and couldn't, I blamed it on love. A destructive love."

"His possessiveness made you impotent. I've always wondered why you married him but while you were together I didn't think I could ask."

"I was so young. He wanted me and I was desperate to be wanted. By someone. I thought that meant I wanted him. Stella hated him, and she was so sure it wouldn't last..."

"...you stayed." Gretel understands but she doesn't judge. She gets another thought. "Look, Andrew might be dating this girl out of spite but it might work in your favour."

"You think he's...replaced me?"

"Someone new to fixate on."

"But he's a psychological stalker, Gretel. I've got to warn her."

"Not your responsibility. You can't fight her battles. And she wouldn't thank you. How credible would you be, his ex-wife?"

She's right. I've got plenty of battles of my own.

***

Davina laughs like wind chimes as she recounts her tale. I'm laughing too. It's been a while.

We're sitting in her beach house behind her shop. The walls are stark white adorned with vibrant wall-hangings. French windows open onto a lush garden, and in the middle of the room low-backed sofas in different fabrics hug a bamboo coffee table.

We're sipping wine. An Italian pinot grigio that's treating my tastebuds to something I can't quite name. A sensation that's got nothing to do with flavour.

"...so I reminded Sheena the dress was second-hand, you know." She wrinkles her nose. "My shop was closed so we met in a café. After she bought me a coffee, I glanced at the dress and offered her ten dollars." My shocked expression makes her grin. "She didn't get to see any price tags so she doesn't know I do one-off originals. Any of the vintage shops in Honolulu would have given her several hundred because of the label, but she'd come straight to me. That was her downfall. She tried to haggle but I told her to take it or leave it. She took it."

I'm choking with laughter. Davina makes hardened negotiators look like pushovers. Then I remember Katsuya and feel a surge of solidarity with her. Meanwhile, the dress is sitting on the floor in a rope-handle bag. A comforting presence.

"That trance you had when you made it?" I ask.

"That *was* curious."

"I was having one at the same time."

"Is that what Derek was talking about? Twin trances, was it?"

I tell her more about the seminar, how I almost fainted and Alister caught me. How I went into the strangest state, breathing in all those colours, feeling an intense peace with myself, with the world.

"It's the same," she says. "But while you were sitting in amazement beside the delectable Alister Sloane, I was here alone working my fingers to the bone." She laughs at the accidental rhymes. "You're wondering how it happened."

I nod. "Were you the telepath, or was I?"

"What's your hunch?"

I think about it. "Well, you were making a dress for me so it's like Roger, isn't it? I must have been picking up your energy as you were creating it, experiencing what was happening to you."

"It happened so fast, it could have been in two directions. One minute I'm wondering why I haven't come up with a design and the next minute it's finished."

"Were you aware of time passing?"

"Over in the blink of an eye. Like those fairytale journeys, you know, to the bottom of the sea? Where the hero comes back after an hour and a hundred years have passed in real time."

I know.

"I've never made a dress in that kind of space. It was as if it was...already made." She's looking puzzled.

"So you think we picked up each other's energy back and forth?" I ask. But why was I in a trance?

"To be sure, I don't know. There's something strange about that dress, don't you feel it yourself?"

"Only that I couldn't bear to be parted from it." I keep looking in the bag to make sure it's really there. "That doesn't happen with my power suits."

She laughs. "I've got my own name for those. They're such grand camouflage, I call them *impotence* suits."

***

Alister phones and suggests we try dinner again, tonight. Tempt the gods to intervene this time. But Davina and I have decided to make a night of it. Just as well. My attraction to Alister might unravel next time I'm alone with him. And his interest is too intense. Especially after the revelations about my 'powers'. I don't trust it. Or him. And I sure as hell don't trust myself.

"I'm not going away," he says. "Dinner is a standing invitation."

"I know."

"And of course the photograph is yours."

"Thank you. Did she drive a hard bargain?"

"I'd call it a quick transaction. She had it with her so I took it and told her to leave."

"With nothing?"

"Ramon made her a sandwich."

I laugh. "His sandwiches are the best."

"It's the salsa, his secret recipe." Pause. "Call me, Selkie. I want to see you again. Soon. I've got something to tell you."

"What?"

"It has to be face to face."

That's all he says and I'm left holding the phone. What could be so bad he has to save it up?

CHAPTER

Thirty

There's a noodle place on the bay front. But it's noisy inside and windy outside so we take our wonton soups back to Davina's. We sit on floor cushions and eat straight off the coffee table, accompanied by another bottle.

That's when I tell her about the footprints.

"Sleepwalking. In the witching hours," she says. "What's your hunch?"

She's making me work. "I don't know. Before I saw my feet in the mirror I was sure it was the woman. Stalking me during the night."

"The same mirror where you first saw her, was it?"

I tell her about Wanda's grandmother, about the way Tutu used the mirror.

"Both times it was a vision," she says. "A reflection. Of the woman, then your own footprints. That's what you saw in the mirror, you know. Not your feet, a reflection of the footprints."

"How does that change things?"

"Everything's a metaphor, remember that. Even the woman. You've sensed yourself she isn't real."

"Doesn't that mean she's...a spirit? From...the other side?" I've been living with Wanda too long.

Davina shakes her head. "If you label her a 'spirit' you close off your options, miss the true meaning of the message. She represents something. Something to do with you. It's your job to play detective, find out what it is."

"Investigate. I've tried that but I'm not cut out to be a detective. I get confused, then exhausted."

"A spiritual detective. It's hard work because the clues are cryptic. And the woman's trying to tell you something you don't want to hear."

"Someone's trying to kill me."

"That's taking the message literally too. Most clues are not what they seem. You've got to dive down behind the words and come up so you can see them from another angle."

"Dive down." I tell her my history with the ocean, my fear that I'll die in the sea.

"The deepest investigations are always the darkest," she says. "But sometimes you have to take the plunge to find out the truth."

Exhaustion rises up but I push through. "And the footprints?"

"Another symbol. What do footprints symbolise?"

I let my thoughts flow. "Walking a path. Going on a journey. Getting lost. My footprints were...coming home."

Two words that have the ring of truth.

"And if they're red?" she asks.

The dream comes back. The link to red feet that's been eluding me all day. Davina listens to the images I can recall.

"I was invisible. And I was afraid it meant I was dead. Then the woman gave me a star fruit but it turned into a cowry shell and stuck to my hand. I remember its teeth and trying to shake it off, then my feet started dancing until they bled bright red."

She nods. "What do you think it means?"

"I was dancing in a frenzy. As if my life depended on it, I'm sure of that. The dance was...killing me."

"Something was killing you, making you invisible, but

what does dancing symbolise to you?"

I remember my manic moves with the feather duster, how exhilarating it felt to be dancing naked. I've tried to hide from it, but now I think I was snatching a moment of freedom.

"Freedom," I say. "It means...freedom." I start to cry.

"Tears are grand," Davina whispers. "They give you new prisms to view the world through. So the dancing in the dream, it was *saving* your life. Red is a paradox, you know. It means sacrifice and anger and murder, but it also means passion and vibrant life."

"I wasn't dead," I cry. "That's why I was bleeding. In the dream I was...truly alive." I give myself over to crying and the tears seem to wash away my confusion. "So last night I was...walking on the wild side."

We laugh.

"Or dancing," she jokes. "Where did you go?"

"I must have gone down to the sea."

Everything comes back to the sea. My fear and my fascination. And it explains why I didn't get raped or arrested. A semi-naked woman at night on Waikiki isn't such an odd sight, and beyond the street lights I might have been hidden by shadows. I'll check my sheets for sand when I get home. I'm sure it's there.

But did I go alone? Or was I...with her? Because my sense of her presence when I woke this morning was so strong. The fear that she'd been looking at me as I slept. Perhaps she had.

Davina's reading my thoughts. "There's something else in that dream, you know."

"What?"

"Only the woman could see you."

"Yeah. And it scares the hell out of me. At least being

invisible feels...safe. But she looks at me and her eyes seem to know things about me I don't know myself."

"You know what that means."

"Investigate," we say together.

I take a sip of wine and notice it again. "This wine. It's giving me a strange sensation. As if...a space is opening up. In my...chest."

"A good space, by the sound of it."

"I'm not sure." God knows I've consumed enough wine to know what mellowing out feels like. And I'm doing that, in spite of the strange talk. But this is something else. I take another sip and recognise it. "It's an ache...in my heart."

"You're longing for something, girl, and the wine is showing it up."

"Probably just another drink." But she's nailed it. The longing has sneaked up on me again. It's never far away but tonight it's taking over.

"Alister Sloane," she says.

"That's just lust." Another 'l' word.

"Are you sure about that? You've slept with him, have you?"

This is what's great about getting drunk with another woman. A woman like Davina. We're practically strangers but already we're down to the real issues.

"There hasn't been time. I only broke up with Roger last week, then he died. And I hardly know Alister."

"Then it isn't lust."

She's right. Against my better judgement I hopped into Roger's bed the first night we met. Driven by longing? Or wanting to be wanted? My old pattern. So even though I've been telling myself the seizure got in the way, if I am lusting after Alister wild horses wouldn't have stopped me. Or him. And we'd still be at it.

"Anyway, he scares me," I say.

"In what way?"

"The money. Terrifying."

"Sure, but that's a no-brainer. What else?"

"Well...he's forty-five, so he's been around the block a few times. He can have any woman he wants and probably does judging by the publicity pics. And he's seeing someone but hasn't mentioned her again, and that hasn't stopped him coming on to me. So can I trust him? What if I'm just his next conquest?"

Why does that bother me? I'm overdue for some fun.

"Keep going."

"You sound like a therapist." But she's got me *delving* again. And the next thought is getting close. "He wants me. And I don't just mean my body. He wants me in a way that's much more terrifying than sex."

"Go on."

"Because..." I take a slug of wine and start coughing. The words won't come.

"Because he might find out the truth? That underneath your act – and it's a grand act for sure – you're really a woman of straw?"

"I'm completely unworthy of a man like him."

The insight sits between us as we sip more wine. And again I'm fighting back tears.

"What if you're wrong?" Davina says. "Have you thought of that?"

"Wrong about Alister?"

"About yourself. Nelson Mandela said it's not our smallness that scares us, it's our greatness. You think your act is covering up your smallness, that underneath you're worthless. But what if that's a lie? The biggest lie of your life? What if it's your act that's *keeping* you small? If underneath you're a woman of...infinite wisdom, a woman Alister can immerse himself in? It sounds like he wants to."

It's why I went for the green card, why I started Moonshine – to escape from Andrew and find the courage to be big. But Davina's metaphors are conjuring images of deep water and I'm flailing out of my depth.

"You're alone," I say, deflecting back to her. "Why?"

"For me it's better this way. I'm too wild. I need the freedom. And the space to be creative. I couldn't balance a man and my work, they'd both get short-changed. But your freedom might look different."

I remember the wild abandon of the feather-duster dance. Could I ever be that free with a man? Andrew controlled me with his put-downs – because I let him, because I believed him. But being with him also felt...safe. That word again. While he's been hounding me all these months I've been playing at being free, knowing he's still there, poised to reel me back the moment I give up. But if he's got another woman...I'm in freefall.

"It's possible to be with someone and still be free," Davina says. "But if your pattern is to choose men who don't *see* you – and Roger was one of those for sure – then real freedom is about breaking that pattern. That's the key."

"Choosing a man who can see me." See what? How afraid I am? Alister thinks he knows who I am but that's at the heart of my terror.

"Maybe I'm longing for something else and Alister's just a smokescreen."

I wish. Then I could ravish him without a qualm.

"What's your hunch?" Davina says.

"Something..." A word comes from nowhere. "S...ilver." I laugh. "I don't know why I said that."

She thinks about it. "Silver, is it?"

"A ring?" That doesn't feel right.

"Or a dress."

"My dress is black."

"And silver."

That's when Davina's hands fly up to her mouth, upsetting her glass on the way. Almost in slow motion wine is splashing like sea-spray.

"Oh my God," she whispers. And she's not talking about the mess.

"What? What is it?"

Did the shell's singing just get louder?

"I found the fabric for your dress...in the attic."

She won't say any more. She gets some paper towel and starts mopping up the spill but her mind is somewhere else.

"You're scaring me, Davina, saying something weird like that and then clamming up. You've got to explain."

"No, no, I've said too much already. Like an eejit."

She starts muttering and I only catch two words: *scared* and *excited*. It's disturbing being in the same room with her, but all I can do is wait until the other Davina returns. And she does. After leaving the room and coming back with her purse.

"That'll be ten dollars you owe me." It's as if the muttering never happened, like a channel coming out of a trance and having no memory of it. "This exchange is very important because the dress belongs to you, remember that." She looks at me. "That's why Sheena stole it."

"What?"

"So you could buy it back."

As if that makes sense. But I haven't forgotten how bad it felt to lose it. As I hand over the money a state of calm descends.

"Go now." She hands me the bag and bundles me out

the door.

For the second time in so many days I'm standing alone in a deserted street. Holding something precious.

***

Nigel picks me up. He sees me waiting for the bus with the bag clutched to my chest. He's on his way home from the Mokuluas – the pair of rocky islands near the reef.

"Kayaking?" I ask.

He nods.

"Why do you go there so often?"

"There's a shearwater colony. You might call them mutton-birds. If you get there just before dark and sit very quietly you're amongst them when they come back to their nests. Hundreds of them, bombing in like meteors."

"Why would you do that?"

"Being in the middle of them gets you here." Nigel taps his chest. "A connection with the natural cycles of life. *Ho'ohihi*, the Hawaiians call it. Interconnectedness."

"Interconnectedness," I say. "With birds. I think I'll stick with my smart phone."

I expect him to laugh but he doesn't. "This is different, Selkie. This is real."

"Sorry, Nige. That was flippant." I think about what he's just said. "This interconnectedness – has it got anything to do with...dementia?"

"In a way. After spending all day with people who've forgotten who they are, I get pushed off balance too. Until the birds restore me."

"When you lose your mind you lose yourself?"

"Yeah, losing is a good word for it. You haven't disappeared, you haven't gone anywhere, you're still the same person at your core, but you've lost the key, if you will, to the room where that person lives."

We drive in silence for a while. I think about not knowing who I am and feel adrift. That old feeling. Is that why I ask the next question?

"You've been an amazing friend, Nige, but...I get the feeling you don't like me much."

He keeps his eyes on the road. "It's a shallow question, Selkie."

"What do you mean?"

"Seeing yourself in terms of being liked. Or disliked."

"But what else is there? Except indifference. And indifference just makes you invisible."

"That's my point. You're used to being abused or worshipped. So you think you only exist in the eyes of others."

It's a confronting image, but I wonder if he's right. Andrew abuses me. Stella. Derek worships me. Roger...Alister...

"Like social media at its most narcissistic," he continues. "Every post screams, 'Look at me'. Because if nobody looks, if nobody notices, the person isn't sure they're really there."

I think about this. "OK. I get that. And you're right. Being invisible terrifies me. But sometimes around me you're irritable and other times you're happy. Aren't they just mini versions of abuse or worship?"

"Nope. That's just my mood. I'm a moody guy. Nothing to do with you."

Nothing to do with me. Do I make everything about me? "So if you don't like me or dislike me...you just...what?"

"See you." It's what Davina said. "And it makes you uncomfortable."

I sit with this for a while. Nigel does make me uncomfortable. If it's because he *sees* me, it's like being naked, the opposite of invisible. Exposed. But also...real. I'm desperate to ask him what he can see and the expectation excites me. But I also know he'll tell me the truth and that feels too scary.

There's only one response, and it's heartfelt. "*Mahalo.*" Thank you.

After a while he says, "You haven't mentioned the photos."

"What photos?"

"Your photos from the cemetery. I can't believe he didn't show you. DD printed them last night after we got home from Alister's."

"What? After I told him not to?"

"He should have waited till you were there. But you know how impatient he is."

Derek printed my photos. Of course he did. "What does she look like?" I whisper.

Nigel hesitates. "You should see for yourself, Selkie. Not get it second-hand. DD was going to show you this morning."

"He tried to but I couldn't cope with any more surprises. Is she...a surprise?"

"Yes. And no."

"I'm not going to look at her. Not after what happened to Roger."

"You really think her photo had something to do with his death?"

"I know it sounds melodramatic but he was looking at it when he fell. I can't afford to take the risk. Not if her message is true."

He thinks about this. "It's safe for you to look. Promise.

I'll take you back to our place."

He won't say any more so I've just got to trust him.

Eventually we pull into his driveway, reminding me of another question.

"You haven't always been a dementia nurse, have you?" Makiki Heights is for rich people.

"No. I used to be someone else."

"Who?"

"A futures trader on Wall Street. Making big money. Until I looked in the mirror one day and wondered who I was."

"What happened?"

"I was looking at a stranger. Without my work, who was I? I didn't know. It was my own dementia moment, if you will."

"The key to the Nigel room was missing."

"Yeah. It brought me to Hawaii where I found this house and took up nursing. And meditation."

"And have you discovered who you are?"

He grins. "I can look in the mirror these days and see myself."

Something I can't say.

"The birds help," he adds. "They give me space to be creative."

"What are you creating?"

"My own soul."

It's what Gretel said about me.

***

Derek is still up and the prints are on the kitchen table. All the shots I took that day – the flowering vines, the spider webs, the stone surfaces grainy in close-up. They're good.

Artistic. Roger would have hated them.

The dog's relieving himself in three frames. First he cocks his leg, then the stream of urine trickles down the stone. In the last photo he's kicking his back legs to cover his tracks.

"These make a statement," Derek says, "even if it's not very fair on..." He peers at the inscription. "*Raven, 1960–1995*. Good God, it's the same gravestone. And the same star fruit tree."

I'm not listening. "Where's the woman, DD?"

He's been holding the last photo behind his back.

It's the moment I've been dreading, but nothing happens when I take it from him. It should be an omen. I look at the image and blink several times in case I'm mistaken. After all this time, here it is, the image I've been waiting to see, the image I took in bright sunlight. An image...

Of an empty cliff.

"Where is she?" I yell.

As much as I've been afraid of seeing her in print, of knowing who she is, of what she might do to me when I look, it's a devastating blow.

We're all silent, as if the woman has died. Derek passes me a magnifying glass. The grains get larger under the lens but the woman doesn't appear. Not even as a ghost.

"It makes sense that she wasn't in Nightingale's pic," he says, "but she should have been in yours. We've been chasing shadows all this time."

"Not even shadows, DD. The woman doesn't exist. She's been a figment all this time."

In my mind, Stella is cackling, *If you can't touch it, it's a figment and figments can carry you away.* She warned me often enough and she was right.

They pour wine while I stare at the gaping emptiness of that windswept ledge. The woman's as invisible as I was in my dream. Everything's a symbol, Davina said. It's my job to play detective. What the hell does it mean?

"Roger died for this picture," I hear myself say. "And there's not a damn thing in it."

"You could try meditation," Nigel says as he drives me home.

"Why?" Since our last conversation we're closer, but the subject still feels uncomfortable.

"When you silence the mind, you see things clearly."

"What things?"

"The truth."

I think about it. "You mean if I quiet my mind, I'll know who the woman is? Why her photo is blank?"

"Probably."

"But that means you're saying...somewhere between what my eyes saw and what the memory card recorded, my mind...got in the way. How could it do that?"

"The mind is a great tool and a great liar. Meditation bypasses the lies, takes you to a place where the mind loses its power to control, where the noise of your thoughts is just that. Noise."

"Sounds...lonely." Like standing on a windswept cliff.

"In a way, but it's a rich loneliness. Sometimes you need to risk being lonely to hear your inner voice."

"Now you're scaring me, Nige. I'm already hearing voices. And I don't like what they say."

"It's not really a voice. It's the truth of your heart."

I try to get my head around this. "So you think the woman has got something to do with the lies...or the truth...about me?"

"If you will. Most mysteries have."

"But how can she have anything to do with me? I'm a stranger here."

"You keep saying that, Selkie, but everything's interconnected. *Ho'ohihi.* Her connection to you might be cosmic."

Butterfly wings causing a tsunami.

"Or psychic."

Symbols appearing in the same mirror.

"Or ancestral."

Unfinished business.

"And you've been there before," he says. "To that still place where the chatter of the mind is silenced. You've been there. At least once."

My trance. At the seminar. Nigel was there. He recognised my altered state.

"A peaceful and amazing place, Nige, and not a bit lonely. But there weren't any voices. Only the most vivid silence."

"Same thing," he says.

***

Wanda is back from a Hula happening and I update her on everything. With the madness over the footprints this morning she doesn't even know Roger's dead. We sit up late and talk, lubricated by another bottle.

"Telepathic," she says. "No surprise there. But it frightens you. All those powers."

"Lots of powers and no control."

"You've got to get yourself some wisdom."

"Yeah. Is there an online course?"

I show her the cemetery photos and she falls in love

with the dog.

"Get these framed. I'll move a few fish to make room. Who's...?" She squints at the epitaph. "*Raven?*"

"Just a grave. I was photographing the dog. But here's the picture we've been waiting for."

She stares at the empty cliff. "What a let-down. You must be furious. What's she playing at? You know what this means, don't you? You've got to go back to the mirror."

"No way, not after the footprints. That was so humiliating."

She shrugs. "OK. You're the boss. You'll know when it's time. But let's at least show Coral. She wanted to see this picture but Roger stole it."

After the pizza I don't feel bad about another consultation. And with Wanda to translate we might learn something useful.

Coral stares at the empty cliff and shakes her head. It was crazy to think she could interpret something invisible. I'm turning away when Wanda flips through the photos and shows her the dog. She points to the headstone and says, 'Raven.'

Coral looks at me and looks at the photo, back and forth several times. Her intensity is unnerving so I stare at her feet. The soles are surprisingly smooth, but then she doesn't walk far. Only to the toilet in the parking lot. And down to the beach to bathe.

Now she's grinning. "*Aumakua.*" She's a woman of few words.

Wanda nods and signals at me to leave.

"What?" I ask on the way back.

"It's an ancestor," she says. "Raven is your ancestor."

I sigh. "I haven't got any Hawaiian ancestors."

"It's not literal, Selkie, it's a metaphor. An *aumakua* is a kind of ancestral spirit, a guardian that protects you and guides you. And it can often take the form of an animal."

She's pleased with her intuition. Showing the photo to Coral was a coup.

"An ancestor that's an animal," I say. In a world where shells sing this should make perfect sense.

"It's more than an animal." Wanda's comfortable with the contradiction. "An *aumakua* is a god too. An ancestor who's become a god and looks out for you."

"But this is a human grave."

"Yeah. But they live in rocks and statues so a headstone is perfect. And they're into shape-shifting. So if Coral's right and Raven's your *aumakua*, then she's the woman. It explains why you saw her. And why she had a warning. First she appeared in human form, then on the cliff she turned into a raven – her animal of choice – and flew away. It accounts for her disappearance and means your eyes weren't playing tricks. Did you see a bird?"

I don't answer. In a sudden rush of exhaustion I can't keep my eyes open. It must be the wine. I've been drinking since four o'clock.

Wanda sees me sway and helps me onto the bed. After that I don't remember.

***

Something wakes me up, some time after two. The cowry shell is singing but that's my aural wallpaper now. It was something else.

The old venetian blinds don't block out the light from the street so I can clearly see the shape of Wanda asleep in her bed. It wasn't her who spoke. It was that other voice.

I sit very still, not wanting to believe it.

Figments can carry you away, it said. Just like...Raven.

CHAPTER

Thirty-Two

"You're looking a tad grey around the gills," Wanda says to me at breakfast.

That's because I was up half the night with Coral.

After the message announced itself, I got the photo out again and went down to the bus shelter. I don't know anyone called Raven, but the message kept repeating itself like a chant.

Coral was dozing. She'd pulled her shawl over her shoulders and I couldn't bring myself to wake her. Maybe if I sat in her presence and stared at the photo it would activate my 'psychic powers' regarding the woman called Raven.

Raven.

A bird.

And an omen.

At that thought Coral opened her eyes and looked at the photo in my hand.

"*Lolo*," she said, then closed her eyes again.

Crazy.

A word guaranteed to keep me awake till breakfast.

Now I'm staring into the empty fridge, thinking about food, wishing I had an army of *menehune*, elf-like versions of Ramon with pointy ears and bells on their toes, who restock my shelves by night. Is that what this longing is all about? Someone to keep my fridge and my tummy full ever after?

Wanda pulls me away from the fridge and starvation

makes me agree to a smoothie. She gets busy with the blender while I tell her about the new message.

"It's from the *aumakua*," she says. "Now that you know who she is, she's feeling safe to contact you."

"But what does it mean?"

"It's your message, Selkie. My impressions might be way off the planet."

"I'm too close to it." And too spooked.

"OK." Today's ingredients include a star fruit but I say nothing. "*Figments can carry you away. Just like Raven...* First, it's about Raven, right? No surprises there. She's your *aumakua* and she's speaking to you. But it's cryptic. That's usually the domain of dreams. What does *figment* mean to you?"

"Something that isn't real. If you can't touch it, it's a figment. It's what Stella always says. She hates anything that smacks of imagination."

"So it's a word you relate to."

"Only because of Stella."

"But you grew up with it, so it speaks to you at the ancestral level. That fits with the *aumakua*. And it's a warning, right? Being 'carried away' is negative. You've lost your perspective, you've stopped being grounded in the real. The message says it happened to Raven and the outcome was bad."

"Well, she is dead."

"Is she? That assumes you can trust the gravestone. And the photograph."

Bloody hell. Is there anything I can trust?

"She might just be mooching space, remember? Like a hermit crab. First the mirror, then the gravestone. Places where she can keep her eye on you."

I should be feeling protected, my own *aumakua*

watching my back, but I haven't forgotten Coral's nocturnal pronouncement. I tell Wanda.

"*Lolo*," she says. "That's bad."

***

At lunchtime I walk the streets to clear my head – the advantage of wearing jeans and ballet flats. I haven't told Derek about Coral's latest verdict because I know how his mind works. He'll be convinced the woman is Raven – my *aumakua* – and she turned herself into a bird at the moment I photographed her. Disappearance explained. He'll say her purpose was to watch over me, to warn me about Roger's rapacious nature by giving me a photograph for him to steal, before he stole something more valuable from me, like my will to live.

But there's more to investigate. Was it just my dreaming mind that put Raven's name into Stella's favourite phrase? Or is Raven connected to me? Connected enough to send messages? Someone I've never heard of.

If I'm going to play detective I've got to examine every clue. And there's another picture of Raven's grave – in the photo on Alister's wall.

He'll be in his office on the floor below his penthouse but Ramon could hand over the photo. That way I'll delay the power of Alister's presence until I can face dinner. But I've got to phone him first.

I feel bad about interrupting him. How many thousands an hour is his time worth? A hundred times more than mine. He doesn't care about that but I do. Our fiscal imbalance.

"Sounds like you're avoiding me," he says when he hears my plan.

"You're a busy man."

"I'd like to give it back to you in person. After all it's the picture I had to own...over Roger's dead body."

"Great metaphor." I should have predicted this. "How did Sheena track you down by the way?"

"My fault. I gave her my business card at the Swap Meet. In case she found any more photos of you."

And she found one at my place. Great.

"Give me ten minutes," he says. "Then ring the bell to my apartment."

Fifteen minutes later he's asking me what I want him to do.

"Hold me." It just pops out.

And he does. Until I stop trembling. Am I trembling for him? Or for myself? Too hard. His arms are strong, and when he lets go it doesn't feel like it will never happen again.

The living room is streaked with sunlight filtered through heavy clouds. We walk to the photograph, back in place on the wall.

"It's the best place for it," he says. "Until you take it back."

There I am, still running for my life as if I've seen a ghost. Or I'm about to see one. And the letters on Raven's grave seem to strobe.

"Do you look at it?" I ask.

"What do you think? I can't stop looking at it. You haunt me, Selkie."

"Why?"

"Look at your eyes. You want something. With such a smouldering passion your eyes are mesmerising."

I look at myself and for the first time I see it. Bloody hell. The woman and I have got the same eyes.

At that moment, a ray of sunlight bursts through the clouds and dresses me from head to foot in silver. I start to tremble again and Alister wraps his arms around me. Then he presses his lips into my hair.

"You could trust me, you know."

But he can't help me. Whatever's going on, it's between me and her.

He lets me go and I hear myself say, "I'm starving. Could Ramon make me a sandwich?"

Ramon does better than that. As the day turns dark and a steady rain dulls the harbour he produces an Italian lunch fit for a mafia reunion.

"Don't you have to go back to the office?" I ask as Alister opens a bottle of wine.

"What? When I've finally got you where I want you, at my table? This weather has been gifted to us for a boozy afternoon. Work has ceased to exist. There's only you and me."

And Ramon and Rita.

"So this cancels the dinner invitation," I say. "That's a relief."

"You're a slippery character. This does not replace dinner and you know it. Dinner is dinner and lunch is lunch. But if my charisma isn't working then Ramon's cooking might."

Alister's charisma is working just fine but at that moment Rita serves the pasta and I get the chance to show Alister what I do best. Eat. And what I do second best. Drink. He seems content to watch this spectacle of gluttony. His face creases with amusement, the understated version of his beaming smile.

But the woman isn't far away.

Why do we have the same eyes? I consider asking Alister

to turn the photo to the wall so I don't have to look at it, just like Wanda's mirror. But for the moment I've disappeared behind the reflections off the glass. A temporary reprieve.

The wine begins to soften my edges. "You talk, I'll eat," I say, to stop any questions about what I'm not telling him. The whole Raven thing.

"OK. I've got a story for you. And I'd better tell it before we get too drunk."

"Are we going to get drunk?"

"Uh-huh."

"I might act up and ruin my image."

"You might," he says. "It's what images are for. Demolition."

Just like Davina said. And underneath my act, I'm...what?

"But let me demolish my image first," he says, "and possibly...spoil your lunch."

"It'll have to be good to put me off my food."

"It is." He picks up his glass and looks at me, and my edges soften a bit more. Then he takes a deep breath. "Her name is Genevieve."

For almost a year he's been seeing her. And her twin boys. A warm widow, an instant family. And on Sunday morning he tossed them over. Because of me.

"But you don't know anything about me, Alister. Haunting eyes on a photograph...they're hardly a reason to dump your lover."

"I know plenty about you. You're the only one who knows nothing about you."

Whatever that means.

"But ditching Genevieve five minutes after meeting me...I don't want that on my conscience. She probably had...expectations. Not to mention the pressure it puts on me. I'm not about to make any declarations, you know."

I'm about to run a mile.

So the man's got everything – except a soul mate. One of those guys on an eternal search for his perfect match. I knew he was too good to be true.

"I couldn't not tell her the truth," he's saying.

"Which is?"

"I don't love her enough. Then she was the one who ditched me, after announcing my faults in language she's never used before."

"Sounds like you got off lightly if she didn't reach for a kitchen knife."

He manages to laugh. "We never got as far as her kitchen. As soon as she opened her front door, she knew. She said she could see it on my face. That I'd met someone. So I had to confess on the doorstep. She wouldn't let me go any further, not even to say goodbye to the boys."

I can't help liking Genevieve's style. "And what did you confess exactly?" Better if it's out in the open.

Alister takes a slug himself. And when he looks at me I see what she saw. And he's got it bad. Poor Genevieve, she knew she couldn't compete with that.

He's about to untie his tongue when Ramon serves the scallopini.

It's enough to change my mind about leaving.

"She already knew you didn't love her," I say between mouthfuls. "She's been waiting for this to happen."

"What makes you say that?"

"The checklist of your faults. She didn't love you either."

"Are you trying to make me feel better? Two people living a charade just so they wouldn't be alone."

"Feel as bad as you want. You were totally dishonourable, stringing her along for your own comfort."

"Now I do feel better, thanks. But it didn't seem dishonourable...until I met you."

"My fault then." Isn't it always? "But she was dishonourable too. So you're even."

He thinks about this. "The money."

"I'd frame it more kindly. The *children*. Two boys to bring up on her own. You're a good catch. Better than good. Handsome, rich, single. Plenty of charisma." I laugh. I can take the moral high ground because I wouldn't sleep with him for ten million. "And here was I thinking you only dated ex-models."

"I employ ex-models to run my office and accompany me to public functions. It feeds the appetite of the paparazzi and keeps my private life...private."

I wonder. Paparazzi are relentless sleuths. I must google Lester Sloane and Genevieve. If I care. "Is it over with her then?"

"For me it is. But for Gennie, I'm not so sure. Her anger verged on the dangerous."

Gennie. The woman scorned. And her financial agenda foiled. She'll be so pissed off she can't think straight. "I get the feeling she isn't finished with you yet."

And I haven't finished with him either.

"Getting back to Sunday, I kept trying to phone you about Roger but you were out of contact for hours. And your encounter with Genevieve sounds brief – unless the list of your defects takes an age to deliver."

He chuckles.

"So something else happened. After you left Genevieve." And before he went to the Swap Meet and gave Sheena a reason to steal my photograph.

He sighs. This wasn't part of the confession. "You're not going to like it."

"That's what you said about Genevieve."

But Genevieve isn't bothering me. If he didn't have someone I'd be worried. Handsome, rich, single – and alone. With a pet python. That would be creepy. I just assumed the steady stream of dizzy models demonstrated his insatiable appetite for non-commitment.

"Where did you go, Alister?"

He tells me.

"The cemetery?" He's right. I don't like it. My old dream comes back: Alister waving a banana and me so transparent I don't exist. "A ramble amongst the gravestones. How...Roger-esque."

The jibe hits home. "It wasn't what you think, Selkie. I thought I recognised the place. All those anonymous headstones. Gennie lives near Bantry's Bluff. So I went to take a look."

"Bantry's Bluff?"

"It's what the locals call that cove – and the cemetery. Some homesick Irishman said the cliffs reminded him of home. The name stuck."

Bantry's Bluff. After Bantry Bay. We've got one of those in Sydney. But I'm being distracted.

"That picture of me is none of your business, Alister. Not enough for you to go snooping around where it was taken."

"Isn't it? Remember, this was the morning after I bought it, the morning after you had your seizure in my living room. I thought the photograph sparked it. That made it my business."

I shrug. "Any...surprises?"

"It's an eerie place when you're alone. I found the spot

where the photo was taken – I took it with me to check the background. I wondered why you were looking over your shoulder, what you were looking at. But there was nothing obvious."

"So you saw...Raven's gravestone."

That makes me shiver. I walk over to the photo and look past my haunting eyes to the inscription behind. If I was hoping for a clue to her identity, there's nothing but the inscription to see.

"Have you found out who she is?" Alister asks.

"No."

"But you weren't interested in her before. What's happened?"

I sigh. "A kind of rhyme came to me last night, about someone called Raven. *Figments can carry you away. Just like Raven.*"

"Something from your childhood?"

"Why do you say that?"

"Rhymes and ravens suggest childhood to me."

I tell him what Coral said. If he knows about *aumakuas*, he doesn't say. Thanks to Genevieve and the cemetery the boozy afternoon is over, so we go into his home office and search the online register of deaths. No Raven. Difficult with only one name. Alister tries a keyword search, but still comes up blank.

"She doesn't exist," he says.

That's what I was afraid of. The grave of a nobody. A crazy nobody.

C H A P T E R

Thirty-Three

Alister wants me to stay for dinner. And beyond. But I'm not ready for that. Davina was right. Lust would be easy but sleeping with Alister would mean a whole lot more. He seems so sure of who I am, of what he wants, but I'm not sure. Especially after Genevieve. And with my relationship with the woman still unresolved I'm not taking one step further in his direction.

As soon as I can politely leave I do, but I can't take the photo away because rain is bucketing down. So he gets to be haunted by me for a while longer.

I walk the wet streets remembering what he said: 'Rhymes and ravens suggest childhood.' Under a shop awning I stop. And call Stella. I've lost track of what time it is in Sydney. I don't care.

At the sound of her voice, the chant tumbles out. "Figments can carry you away, Stella...just like *Raven*."

She's caught unawares and misses a beat. "Elkie..." Then she tries for her usual sarcasm. "Your father and I are well, thank you for asking."

But it's not working. Because I hear something new in her voice. Defeat.

I press my advantage. "Who's Raven?" I'll keep asking till my battery goes flat.

It's a while before she speaks, and her voice takes on another quality that's new. Regret. "You should never have gone to that place."

"What place?" Does she know the cemetery at Bantry's Bluff?

"Hawaii."

I try again. "Who's Raven?"

"You've seen her, haven't you? I knew she'd win. She always did. What's she said about me? Don't believe her."

"Raven's dead, Stella. I've seen her grave."

"Dead?"

It must be the same Raven. "I don't know who she is. But you do."

Her voice hardens. "It's too...sordid. Too...painful."

"I have a right to know."

"You'll regret it. We both will."

"Tell me."

So she does. "Raven was...your *mother*. My sister. Raven was the one who had your father – *my* fiancé – before *I* did. And bore his child."

A child called Selkie.

My head is spinning. The life has gone out of my voice. "But my mother was Prunella."

"She changed it when she was sixteen. Said Raven suited her untamed spirit. Unlike Prunella. And Stella. Names for dull girls. Like me."

Now she's started, Stella doesn't hold back. Years of suppressed bitterness rush into my ear in a torrent. She was already engaged to Dad when Raven, the teenage siren, lured him onto the rocks with her magic.

"She was so young, so captivating. A child in a woman's body. She tempted your father beyond what any man could endure."

Stella was saving herself for marriage, but Raven was driven by other desires: luring Dad away from her prim older sister, having him first, escalating the victory by getting pregnant. That's what Dad meant by 'an unforgivable betrayal'. An understatement. He was up to his neck in that betrayal. No wonder he could never tell me.

I'm sobbing now. "You told me she was dead. But she didn't die till 1995. I could have *known* her, Stella. My own mother."

"You think you wanted to know her, but you didn't."

"Because of you, I never will."

"You'll never understand. It's better this way. She finished with Sheldon, ran off to Hawaii chasing some man, gave you up. I didn't want you trying to find her. You were impressionable, the image of her. I couldn't take the risk."

"Was she that...crazy?"

"Clever too. But after you were born there was a crazy edge to her cleverness. She called herself your fairy godmother so she could shirk the mothering and just have fun, but her games spiralled into recklessness. You adored her, but you weren't...safe."

"When did she...give me up?"

"On your second birthday. It took a while but she got bored with you in end."

***

All the way to Waikiki it pours out of me. A river of sorrow. The fantasy of the perfect mother plucked from life early lying in tatters around me. While I was imagining her whispering secrets from beyond the grave, Raven had run off and forgotten me. Passengers on the bus see my tear-stained face and look away. But I'm beyond caring. I'm getting to the core of things now. The secrets locked away for a lifetime unveiled in all their blackness.

Gradually my tears dry and another emotion surfaces.

Anger. Towards all of them. Stella for lying to me, for escalating her betrayal into my betrayal. Dad for his weakness, manipulated by Raven and then by Stella, with me the innocent casualty. And Raven, the woman who conceived me for her selfish amusement, then abandoned me.

Derek phones from the office to see what's happened to me and gets the whole story.

"It explains everything," he says. "Your mad mother runs away to the islands, lives a wild life, dies too young at thirty-five."

"But how does her...spirit...know I'm here?"

"She's kept a psychic connection with you. After all, she's the one who named you."

Playing fairy godmother. Giving me a crib-side gift. A name as wild as hers.

"Your stepmother resented it, tried to stifle your imagination, changed your name in case you turned out like Raven."

"But why has she suddenly appeared?" I ask. "After all these years? When she was alive she never tried to contact me."

"She's been waiting for you. Calling you. In a voice you couldn't understand, but it had the power to pull you all the way to Hawaii."

Does this explain who the woman is? My long-lost mother, demanding acknowledgement after all these years? Gazing at me from beyond the grave with a look of infinite regret?

I thought I was heading home to wallow in self-pity under the covers, but it's obvious now. I've been on another mission all along.

***

The flat is silent. The scene is set. The mirror is back in place at the end of the bath. I've draped it in a towel and put a kitchen chair in the doorway turned towards it. Inspired by Odysseus and his mast, I've strapped myself to the chair with several of Wanda's leather belts.

Heeding the warnings about psychic protection – if ever I needed it I need it now – I showered first, before putting on my dress and the cowry shell. One belt is through the chair legs and around my knees, another is around the chair back and my waist, and a third one secures my shoulders. If the woman appears as I intend her to, there's no chance I'll be lured to the other side by her haunting gaze.

Before pulling the string I've tied to the towel, I close my eyes and try to calm my breathing. It's ragged. I was so sure this was what I had to do – confront the woman on my own terms and ask her who she is, why she's haunting me, if she's the spirit of my mad mother – but now that I'm strapped in place and powerless, I feel like a sacrifice tied to a stake, a maiden chained to a rock awaiting a sea monster. It's making me panic about 'unfinished business'. Is the black-hearted Raven trying to claim me as her daughter? And what will she do to me if she succeeds?

But the shell is singing in my ears and if I can use its rhythm to slow my breathing and silence my mind, surely there'll be space for the truth to appear.

Somehow it happens. The singing softens. My breathing slows. My heart rate steadies. And I plunge into a vivid silence.

When it's time, it's time, the fortune cookie said.

My fingers tug the string and the towel slips off the mirror. It's the same angle as that first morning. Oblique.

The word seems to comfort me as I await...my fate.

***

Wanda finds me in the chair. I must have fainted and my hands and feet are numb. As she shakes me awake and she sees my bindings, she thinks I've been assaulted or robbed or something worse. Then she sees my face.

"You're radiant, Selkie. What's happened?" Then she chuckles at what it looks like. "I'd recommend a man next time. Four hands instead of two."

"Unstrap me, will you? I've just seen the woman."

When she looks at the mirror and hears it isn't kinky sex, she roars. "Tutu would have loved your inventiveness. And your valour. You've got no idea what you're doing but if it was good enough for that Greek guy with his mast...Odysseus, right?"

"You're the one who brought the mirror back."

"Yeah. That was provocative." She starts to undo the belts. "But I knew those bloody footprints meant you were still in danger, and the mirror always knows where the bodies are buried. Like looking through the keyhole into a secret room. But I didn't think you'd resort to bondage. Tell me what she said. Is she Raven?"

That's when I realise I don't remember. The woman appeared. I saw her face. I looked into her eyes. And everything afterwards is blank.

"You must remember something," Wanda says.

"Nothing at all." And I'm shattered. After all my efforts to get in touch on my terms I don't even know if we spoke to each other. Beyond seeing her face – and one glimpse of her longing look – I remember nothing.

Wanda can see my despair. She gives me a hug and I tell

her what I've learned about Raven.

"Your mother, your *aumakua*. That Coral might have halitosis but she's as savvy as the Delphic oracle."

"Yeah, Raven's my long-lost mother but it doesn't feel good. Stella says she was selfish and arrogant and fickle." An understatement.

"Your wicked stepmother said that? Can her opinion be trusted?"

"I believe her, Wanda. I prised it out of her and she's never sounded so truthful. So I strapped myself to the chair to find out the truth. Is Raven the one who's stalking me? Because Stella agrees with Coral – Raven was *lolo*. What if she's trying to contact me...for sinister reasons?"

"But she's been warning you – *Someone is trying to kill you*, and all that. She's been doing what *aumakuas* do, right? Looking out for the living."

"Knowing her history, she's got...ulterior motives."

As Wanda thinks about this, her eyes widen and she voices my fears. "Your mother's *lolo* spirit masquerading as your *aumakua*? Cunning. When really she's got a crazy scheme to attach herself to her living daughter."

Attach herself. Wanda doesn't know about the entity. "Why would she want to...attach herself?"

"Well, she abandoned you, right? So she regrets it. While she was alive and living it up she probably never gave you another thought. Glad to be rid of you. But now she's dead, and you've turned up here, she's longing to reconnect with her long-lost child."

"But I'm not a child any more. She might have given birth to me, but she left me to Stella, left me to grow up an outcast. Now she's dead, does she think she can pull my strings...from the other side?"

I shudder. *Someone is trying to kill you.* I've wandered into her orbit, aroused her spirit, and now she's hell-bent on...what?

Wanda reads my thoughts. "She'll suck the life out of you, Selkie. Some mothers do it by never letting go. Raven let you go but now she wants you back. And if she's desperate, you're in trouble."

It's what I've seen in her eyes. Eyes that are the same as mine, because she's my *mother*. Shit. For once I agree with Stella. I should never have come to this place.

"I'll go back to Sydney." To Andrew. To Stella. "I was safe there."

"It's too late. You've piqued her interest. You'll never hide from her now. Your only chance is to find out what you saw just now. Truth is power. You've got to look through that keyhole again with your soul eyes. Tutu's mirror never lies."

"It's gone, Wanda. Whatever I saw must have been so shocking my mind blanked it out."

That's when Wanda does a Coral impersonation.

Just one word.

"Hypnosis."

***

"These days, he's called Tejala," Nigel says. "After a guru in India named him. It's Sanskrit, means 'bringing light'."

Bringing light. Moonlight. I see a woman dancing naked, illuminated by a moonbeam. But beyond the light...darkness. Then the image fades.

"Everyone calls him TJ. He's got a place in Kailua."

Several phone calls later, it's done. A session with Tejala Turnbull MD, known as TJ. After hearing the issues he warns me the session might be big. There's the woman.

There's Raven. And there's the entity. How are they connected?

"Come without expectations," he says. "The outcome might surprise you."

And come with a friend, thank God. Someone to witness and comment if asked, but mainly to support me. Davina volunteers, and because we have a psychic connection TJ agrees.

It may take several hours so I'm to eat a hearty breakfast and drink lots of water. The hypnosis will begin at eleven. The day after tomorrow.

Derek wants me to stay over till then, but Davina has offered her spare room and she'll give me the space I need. Derek is almost mollified when I ask him to monitor my web enquiries and attend to an errand for me.

In a strange state of calm I pack my little red suitcase with almost everything I own. Will I be coming back? Wanda and I don't discuss this but she gives me a farewell hug. Then Coral salutes me with her warmest *shaka* as I hail a taxi for Kailua.

The taxi driver is a philosopher. He looks in the rear-view mirror. "You angry, sistah?"

I haven't said a word.

"We all like blame uddah guy fo problems, but you stay angry, then angry gonna find you."

When I don't reply he keeps up his monologue all the way over the range.

"Which way you wanna live?" he asks the ginger-laden air. "Don't fight li' dat, sistah. Take time fo look inside. It's da heart dat knows. Then you make betta choice. Flow round da rocks like water."

It makes me appreciate Coral.

***

"What are you going to do all day?" Davina asks when I emerge from her spare room.

Good question.

"I don't walk on beaches," I tell her. Not when I'm awake. "I won't be paddling out to the islands either. And I'm too spooked for social networking. But I need a distraction or I'll obsess about Raven."

"You could draw."

"I don't draw either. I only run seminars and drink." And occasionally dance nude.

Davina laughs. "Let me show you what I've got in mind. It can take you as deep as meditation but it's fun. And it might prepare you for the hypnosis."

She goes to her bookshelf and brings a box over to the coffee table, along with a pile of old magazines and a large sheet of sketch paper.

"Sit on the floor," she says. "It takes you back to your childhood and gets you into the right space. Playful."

I don't remember playful. "What am I going to draw?"

"Well, you told me about your stepmam destroying your diary way back. So make a new one. A visual diary, you know. Don't plan, just look through the magazines and cut out anything that appeals, write down words you like, draw pictures, glue on the photos from the cemetery. Illustrate all the happenings in your life in a collage. It might be cathartic and you might...see connections."

"But I've never done anything like that. What if I mess it up?"

"This isn't a work of art, girl. This is soul work. Detective work. Once you get started you'll forget about being perfect and start being –"

A word comes to mind. "Sleek."

"You and me both," she says.

She leaves me with her 'box of tricks' – scissors, glue, crayons. I've got the photos from the cemetery so I take them out and look at them.

"Don't be afraid to cut them up," she counselled me before she left. "It breaks your visual pattern."

I stare at all the materials, feeling silly. A grown woman making a collage in the face of imminent peril feels like Nero and his fiddle. But flipping through magazines is something I know how to do, and Davina's living room with its colour and light inspires creativity. Within minutes I come across a leopard and want to cut it out. Then a pair of bare feet. And another pair. Soon I've got disembodied feet bopping across the page.

Before I know it, I'm in that land beneath the sea where time goes so fast that centuries pass without notice and I'm lost in a pictorial geography of my own life. A mirror like Tutu's turns up with curves inside a silver frame. Its angle is even oblique. As I cut it out the answers about it feel close.

Then words and phrases start finding their way into the landscape.

Texture. The art of life. Move. A stunning collision. Authentic. Instinct. Mythbuster.

And through the words all the happenings in my life seem to be forming some ultimate meaning even though I'm afraid of what that might be.

Then a phrase makes me stop: *A mother's love.* Instead of Raven I think of Stella.

"She doesn't hate you," Dad said. "She just has trouble...showing her love."

At some point, I find the fortune cookie message crumpled in my purse and stick it on. *To find the right answer, ask the right question.* Then I cut around all the headstones in my photos, including Raven's, and overlap them in a jagged cluster, followed by the star fruit tree. A virtual cemetery and a virtual cliff. At least in a collage the players are contained. Unless Raven's sitting on my shoulder, a *shape shifta* with more than one animal form. I notice a shadow out of the corner of my eye and feel thankful for the booking with TJ.

With cut-out letters I make a sign for Bantry's Bluff. Named after Bantry Bay. An Irish name. And a Sydney name. *Ho'ohihi.*

Hours pass. Davina comes through from her workroom and makes a salad and a jug of lime and frangipani water. She only speaks to remind me to drink lots of fluids. She doesn't look at the collage. But she gives me something. A small swatch of fabric from my dress – the fabric she found in the attic. The sight of it makes me cry out, breaking my trance. Light is streaming through the windows, like the moment at Alister's when I was washed in silver. Am I going to discover what it means?

Back at the collage I cut out the shape of my dress and stick it on. Then my fingers pick up a crayon and for the first time I write. Words of my own find space between the pictures and almost dance off the page.

Figments can carry you away. Just like...
Selkie Moon.

"*Makaukau*, Selkie?" TJ asks.

It's what the chanter says to the Hula dancers. Ready?

I've been sitting on a swing-seat in TJ's garden, 'emptying my mind', while Davina's been inside getting guidance.

"Is hypnosis anything like Hula?" I ask him.

"Good question. And the answer is yes. Hula is an expression of spirit. And hypnosis...connects you with spirit."

In the therapy room the curtains are drawn and the shelves are decked with candles, all alight. Davina is lying on a massage table with her eyes closed. She's already in a hypnotic space. I lie on the other table and TJ begins to relax me with his voice, deeper and deeper.

Last night he spent an hour in this room showing me what would happen today. Just a state of deep relaxation while I was still awake. I got to cruise through different colours, like my trance during the seminar, and I liked TJ – a plump sandy-haired guy in his forties with a broad open face. No saffron robes, just fluoro board shorts and a white shirt.

"Everything that happens in this room," he told me, "comes from you. You've had experiences that seem to be paranormal in origin, but hypnosis can only deal with your own mind. Whoever we meet under hypnosis is part of you. If we meet the woman, she's you. If we meet Raven, she's you. If we meet the entity, it's you. Like the actors in your dreams they're all parts of you."

"That'll be a relief." Won't it?

"Some people find it terrifying. They prefer to deal with spooks and spectres, not the demons in their own psyches."

I thought about this. Spooks and spectres are comforting. You can put their meddling down to chance. Or bad luck. Nothing to do with you. But a crowd of personal demons would prove I've been *lolo* all along. Just like Raven.

And if she's riding around on my shoulder and won't let go, does that make her 'part of me'? My mother, my entity? I've always longed for a real mother and now I can't wait to get rid of her.

"I have to find out what's going on," I said. And meant it. "The roller-coaster has made me dizzy."

"Good. Be open to whoever makes contact."

"What? The demons get to choose? But they've been calling the shots for weeks. When do I get a turn?"

He laughed. "You need to be open so your mind doesn't control things. To find out the truth you've got to let go and observe."

So today we're going deeper. To the observer space. I'm still awake, still aware of my body, of the room. It's my level of detachment that's different. If someone fired a gun, I'd find it...interesting.

When he's satisfied with me, TJ moves away and brings himself down too. I feel him arrive. Then we're all in that kingdom beneath the sea where time has no meaning, where thoughts are just noise. I see my thoughts floating above on the surface and I'm gazing up at them from a place of deep contentment. They're just bobbing there, like flotsam from a shipwreck, not even interesting.

What is interesting is the sense of my own presence, a timeless stillness. I'm paying attention at last, an awareness that's amazing because it requires no energy, and I never want it to end.

When TJ eventually speaks his voice comes from far away. "Can you hear me, Selkie?"

"I hear you."

"Davina, can you hear us?"

"Yes, I can."

Her voice delivers a rush of support.

TJ begins. "You're going to look in the mirror, Selkie. You're going to go back to the chair. You're going to see the bathroom and feel the straps around your body and you're going to look into the mirror. How do you feel about that?"

Another voice comes from far away. My voice. "I'm afraid."

"You're afraid. That's the truth. I want you to talk about your feelings all the way. You're afraid but you're in a safe place. You're lying on a table in a candlelit room. I'm here. Davina's here. Nothing can happen to you."

"If nothing can happen why am I afraid?"

"Because you were frightened once upon a time. And you're still carrying the fear around, perpetuating the state that created it. It's probably why you blanked out what you saw in the mirror."

"It frightened me."

"Yes. But now you can acknowledge the fear and go back to the mirror."

"Acknowledge the fear."

"You've already done that by being aware of it."

But I want to do more. "Thank you, fear," I hear myself say. "You've kept me safe. We're going to do something scary now, we're going to look in the mirror. But nothing bad can happen to us because TJ and Davina are here."

"OK," TJ says. "Let's begin."

He takes me back to my bathroom doorway and I'm sitting in the chair all over again. I can feel the bindings. And I can feel the fear. But instead of overwhelming me, it's strangely comforting. Like an old friend.

"Now you're going to pull the towel off the mirror. And when you look into the glass, you're going to stay present with what you see."

In my mind I do what he says. I pull the string and the towel slips onto the floor. I gaze into the mirror and wait. Nothing happens.

"What can you see?" TJ asks.

"Nothing."

"Keep looking. Don't take your eyes off the mirror."

Is this what happened last time? Nothing at all? But I'm sure I saw the woman before I fainted. Now she's playing hide and seek, as if she knows the game's up.

"Selkie? Keep talking to me."

"Still nothing."

"Can you see anything, Davina?"

"Selkie is standing on the edge of something. She's gazing...into a black void."

"Yes. Does that make sense to you, Selkie?"

Suddenly I'm screaming. "It's the underworld. She's trying to suck me into the underworld. She's trying to take over my body, she's trying to steal my soul."

"Who?" His voice is calm.

"The woman. She tried to suck me into the mirror with her eyes. She tried to throw me off the cliff. She turned up at Roger's and he *died* trying to print pictures of her. Now I know she's been my dead mother all along."

"Raven."

"A bird. And an *omen*. Ravens are black-hearted. They forebode *death*." I'm standing on the edge of the abyss, almost swooning as the blackness rises up to grab me. If I faint again I'm gone. "Don't let her take me," I wail. "I'm not ready to die."

"Nothing can happen to you here," TJ says in his calm way. Then he asks, "Why is Raven after your soul?"

Doesn't he understand? "She's dead," I scream. "I've seen her grave. She's *dead*. And I'm *alive*."

"But she's your mother."

"She's gone over to the dark side. She wants to take over my life because I'm *family*." A word I've always hated. "She left me for dead as a baby and now she's trying to kill me again. Everything she does is *evil*."

"Do mothers do that, suck the life out of their daughters?"

"Yes," I scream. "It's their job. When she's finished I'll be an empty shell."

Then he speaks so quietly, the words reverberate like thunder. "So why are you letting her do it?"

"What?"

"Raven's dead, Selkie. She abandoned you and you've grown up without her. But you're still holding on."

There's a long silence before I answer. "She's holding on to *me*. She's the one who won't let go."

"How do you know that?"

"Who else would the woman be? Raven died here and now she's stalking me. She looks like me. She's got my eyes. Everything *fits*."

"And whose mind is making them fit?"

More silence. I'm still strapped in the virtual chair, so Raven can't get me. But I can't escape the interrogation either.

"Look in the mirror, Selkie. And tell me what you see."

"I don't want to," a little voice says.

"No, you don't want to. Why?"

"I might see...the truth."

"That's what you saw last time. The truth. Scary, wasn't it?"

"Yes."

We sit in silence. We've come right back to the fear. I was afraid once upon a time and I'm still afraid.

"It's your friend, isn't it?" TJ says. "The fear? It's kept you safe all these years."

"Everyone needs a friend," the little voice says.

"Especially a little girl...who lost her mother."

Someone starts to cry. Me. I couldn't bear it if he took my friend away.

"Let's find this friend," he says. "Let's look in the mirror and find the fear."

Part of me knows it's a trick but I want to see my friend. So badly it hurts.

"I'm bringing you light, Selkie. To help you see."

Tejala means 'bringing light' – I remember that.

Suddenly the black void is swallowed up and my body appears in the mirror, bathed in light. Liquid light. Blindingly beautiful light. I can't help looking. In the middle of the space I see my body, sleek and glowing.

"There's so much light," TJ says, "that any shadows around you will stand out against the brightness."

In my mind I squint. I can see all sides of my body as if I'm the light itself.

"Take your time. And tell me what you can see against the light. Anything at all, no matter what it is."

"I can't see anything," I say.

"Look again."

I start at my feet and rotate in a spiral all the way up to my head. There's nothing anywhere. What am I supposed to see? A monkey? A raven? A naked woman with an evil stare? There's nothing to be afraid of here. But where's my friend?

My voice sounds as distant as TJ's. "I'm floating in white space."

TJ asks Davina, "Do you see anything around Selkie's body?"

"Nothing at all."

"I agree. How do you feel about that, Selkie?"

"How do I feel?" Feelings surge. The light around my body flushes red. I start to shout. "Angry, that's how I feel. Furious. You said I'd see my friend but there's nothing there. You betrayed me. *Everyone* betrays me."

"Keep talking about your feelings."

I start to cry again. Great racking sobs wash over me in multiple shades of blue. "I'm so *sad*," I scream at TJ. It's all his fault.

"Yes, you are. Let the sadness flow."

Sadness I've never felt before gushes out of me and the kingdom at the bottom of the sea is awash with the greyness of grief.

Then TJ asks, "If you could see this friend...who would it be?"

"I don't know."

"And if you did know...?"

Time slows down. Something hidden flips into my mind. "Someone...I've lost. Someone...of my own kind."

"Tell me more."

What my voice says next is a total shock. "My child."

There's a moment of silence before TJ says, "Have you had a child, Selkie?"

"No. Whoever just said that *lied*." More betrayal.

"Have you lost a child before full term?"

"No."

"Are you sure? There's something here. I'm getting very strong energy around this. Around your grief. And your denial. I feel a presence. What are you getting, Davina?"

"An abortion."

"Selkie?"

My voice is very detached. As cool as ice it betrays me. "A miscarriage. In the downstairs bathroom. A very long time ago."

"Describe what happened."

My voice goes on, separate from my will. "My period was late. We were watching TV."

I remember it clearly, sitting on the floor with Gretel and Stella, watching an old movie. Rock Hudson and Doris Day. Rock had already died of AIDS but Stella was in denial.

"There was a rush between my legs. A force I'd never felt before. I didn't understand, only that I had to run. I made it to the bathroom and locked the door."

The bathroom for guests still had a lock.

"It was a long time before it was...finished." I'm back there now, looking into the toilet bowl. "I knew what it was. I saw...more than blood."

"What did you feel?" TJ asks.

From my detached space, it's a strange question.

"There was a terrible mess, my clothes were bloody. I had to clean it up without Stella finding out. She was pounding on the door, demanding I open up. I wasn't allowed to have secrets, not from Stella."

I'm reliving the panic, how I had to think fast.

"I decided to say I'd vomited, to explain why I'd washed

my clothes in the basin and come out in a towel. Then there was an unholy drama about what I must have eaten."

"What did you feel?"

"Relief. I wasn't pregnant. No one was going to find out." My voice emits an evil cackle. "I got away with it."

"What was it you got away with?"

It's a moment before a little voice says, "Can't tell. Secret."

"But it's not a secret any more."

"If you tell, you *die*."

"It's safe here, Selkie. Nothing can happen to you here."

"I'm never *safe*."

"Why?"

Hasn't he been listening? "*Someone is trying to kill me.*"

"Why? What did you do?"

"Can't tell, not safe."

TJ waits, then he says, "That's the secret, isn't it? Not telling. Who didn't you tell? You can just say the name."

If I only say the name it's not telling, is it? "Andrew," I whisper.

"You didn't tell Andrew."

"No."

"You didn't tell him you were pregnant. You didn't tell him about the miscarriage."

"No." Now I'm screaming. "He'd want to keep it. He'd blame me for losing it. I didn't know how to resist him. I hated myself for not loving him."

I'm sobbing now, sitting in the wreckage of my secret, a metaphor for my life. Guilt swirls around me in all its ugliness and I'm ashamed.

"I was only sixteen." My voice drops to a whisper. "The same age as my mother."

"It isn't safe to have babies, is it?"

"If you have babies you *die*."

"Just like Raven," he says.

But now I know that was a lie.

After a while TJ asks, "What did Stella think of Andrew?"

The cackle is back. "She hated him. Because he wanted me. A rival for control of my life." I stop. The penny drops. "It was right after Stella burned my diary, stopped calling me Selkie. I slept with Andrew that first time...to pay her back."

Another secret. This one I'd kept from myself.

"Virtual suicide," TJ says. "We punish the people who've betrayed us by killing ourselves."

"But I didn't kill myself. I killed...the baby."

"Is that true, Selkie? It was a miscarriage."

"My mind killed it. I didn't want it. I knew it was my fault."

"Miscarriages happen every day. That baby wasn't meant to live. But you were part of what happened. Own your part in it."

He gives me time to sit with the truth. To take responsibility for creating that baby. For not wanting it. For not grieving for it. For turning it into a guilty secret. He lets me cry until there are no tears left.

"Denial is a powerful thing," TJ says. "By not wanting him, you kept him."

"Who?"

That's when something amazing happens.

Against the light embracing my body, a tiny shape appears. It begins as a smudge. Then a head takes shape, like a foetus growing, followed by arms and legs.

"I can see him," I say.

A small boy is sitting on my left shoulder. His head is

bowed and his arms are wrapped around his bent knees. But as I watch he straightens his back and lifts his head. When he looks at me I remember him from my dreams.

Words pour out of me. Words I don't expect. "Hello. I'm sorry you've been alone. I'm sorry you've had to hide. I pretended you were nothing but...I love you."

And in that moment I even love myself. Whoever I am. Someone I've only just met.

Guided by instinct I reach out my hand and the boy takes it.

"Your fingers are icy cold," I say. "Where have you been?"

For the first time he speaks. "To the bottom of the sea and back again."

That's the moment when the mirror is lashed by silver light. Under its blinding glow my awareness expands and I understand...

Everything.

I'm coughing up water and a woman is screaming. I'm not safe. I'll never be safe. The message takes root in my soul.

I'm shut in the bathroom for imagining things. Someone is crying. It's the strangled cry of the misjudged. It isn't me, it's another Selkie. She's taken my place while I hide.

Stella sees right through me because I'm invisible. But the fake Selkie knows how to get noticed. By being compliant instead of real.

My diary is missing. Stella's read it and destroyed it. My thoughts disappear forever and the fake Selkie gets rewarded with a name of her own.

My empty shell seeks false refuge in Andrew's bed. When my period is late, I believe my life is in danger and wish the baby dead.

Stella is pounding on the door and I'm standing over the toilet. In that moment of acute relief, an entity detaches itself and soaks up a lifetime of lost emotions.

My terrible secret ties me to Andrew. With my true feelings quarantined, I'm emotionally asleep, abetting his emotional abuse.

Escaping Andrew, I find him in Roger, forever choosing predators so I'm always under threat.

Meanwhile, the tiny entity on my shoulder has kept me 'safe'. Safe from the reality of sadness and grief and joy and love. Safe from the truth of my own heart. While my default emotions, fear and anger, displaced everything else.

"Why did you stay?" I ask the boy. "Your soul was free to go."

"You needed me."

It's that simple. In my moment of acute panic, he wasn't free. By denying him, I trapped him forever. And, forged from denial, he made the perfect guardian for the life force I'd denied – entity and emotions linked forever by the same lie. He even stored them at the bottom of the sea where he knew I'd never find them.

We hold each other's hand and no-one speaks. It's enough that we're together at last. Moments of infinite understanding pass between us. Moments of forgiveness. And love.

"You've done a great job," my voice says. "Thank you."

It's the acknowledgement he's been waiting for. He's done a great job and his job is over. He stands up, and with TJ's guidance I create a virtual bowl. The boy knows what to do. He steps into the bowl.

"Take it in both hands, Selkie," TJ says, "and swirl."

Do I know what's going to happen? I spin the bowl and

the boy goes round and round, getting smaller and smaller. He disappears into the light, just like a dream with the dawn. And I'm alone. Deeply alone.

An arrow of grief leaps from my heart and I cry out in pain. But it bounces off the mirror and douses me in something new.

"He's gone," I say, tears of grief and joy rolling down my cheeks.

"Yes," says TJ.

"I've set him free."

He's free.

And I'm free.

C H A P T E R

Thirty-Five

At Davina's place I sleep. And sleep. Thursday disappears, then the next day comes and goes. When I finally wake the following morning, starving, I can't believe I've lost two nights and a day in slumber-land.

"I don't even remember my dreams," I say when I stumble into Davina's kitchen and she tells me what day it is. Saturday.

"They must have been deep."

She cooks me a serious breakfast. Bacon, eggs, tomatoes, pineapple, hash browns, toast. I also drink about a gallon of water.

"That's better. My bones were going soft."

She laughs. "Any longer and Wanda would have preserved you in resin."

"And Alister would have bought me for his wall."

A resin cast. Less *pilikia* than the real thing.

"But it's the trouble I'm interested in," I hear him say.

I spend the morning with my collage. Trying to include the hypnosis.

There's Raven. As a child I made her beautiful. And tragic. A perfect mother who whispered secrets to me. But when I knew the truth about her I swapped her for an evil mother.

"They're just two sides of the same lie," TJ said in our debrief. "The never-break-free-and-grow-up lie. By eulogising her or demonising her, she's loomed so large in your consciousness that you never had to let her go."

"Raven wasn't trying to steal my soul?"

"She's dead, Selkie. And even if she wasn't, the choices she made are in the past. Whether she was a bad mother or a good mother doesn't influence who you are, the choices you make. Ancestral wisdom helps to shape us, but yours has been distorted by abandonment, heaped with shame, then suffocated by secrets. You needed to know the truth so you can move forward without shackles into your own future."

Figments can carry you away. Just like...Selkie Moon.

When I wrote these words I already knew. And the photo of the gravestone is giving her the right status in my life. My dead mother. We're connected by ancestry, she gave me my name, she let me go, she died young. Knowing who she was would be interesting, but it's no longer my driving force.

And what about the woman? I was too exhausted to return to the mirror with TJ so I still don't know who she is.

"Next time you'll know," he said. "Last time it felt safer to look through your fear filter, but your view was skewed. Without the entity holding a shield in front of your heart, you won't be able to avoid the truth."

"That makes me more afraid than ever."

"Healthy fear. Can you feel the difference?"

The fear felt sharp, poignant and raw. "Scary," I said, "and exciting."

"It's the right space to discover the meaning of the message."

Someone is trying to kill you.

"Stay present," he said, "and the truth will amaze you."

I look at the collage. I can't represent the woman, so I try to show the entity, but my mind tries to control things.

It makes me cut out a baby but the entity wasn't a baby. What was he? A…paradox. Guarding and at the same time stifling my emotional options.

"Where's he gone?" I asked TJ.

"Not far. As your emotional bolthole, he left you living a half life. Now he's reconnected and made you whole."

"'Old friend from far away'." Eugene was right.

"The Chinese description of a memory," TJ said. "And the entity was like a lost memory. It got stuck in the shame of the miscarriage and the dark secret it became."

"He wasn't the soul of my dead baby?"

"He was always part of you. The miscarriage itself was physical, but in symbolic terms it represented a life stalled. The entity was the part of you that's never been fully born, your masculine part. You were on the brink of adulthood when the shame of the miscarriage split you in two. It's meant you've only had your rage to empower you, but rage is a passion that eventually burns you out."

My short fuse.

"Now the secret of the miscarriage is out in the open, the male and female parts have reunited and they'll spark deep insight in your psyche. Just give your male side time to mature and your ideas will be more dynamic, there'll be more energy for action in your life."

That's where those moments of dynamism have come from. The entity was ready to come home.

"He said he's been to the bottom of the sea," I said.

"Travelling between worlds – your present reality and your lost self – weaving away at his creative work while you've been disconnected from his wisdom."

My own dementia moment.

Then TJ said something surprising. "Have you ever used contraceptives, Selkie?"

How did he know?

"My periods stopped right after the miscarriage." Something else I never told Andrew. "I had lots of tests but they couldn't find anything wrong."

"Expect them to come back. Your reproductive regions have been on ice."

While my mind was disconnected, my body's wisdom wasn't. It knew a child with Andrew would mean I'd never be free.

TJ gave me a Sufi prayer: *Shatter my heart and create a new room for a limitless love.* I don't really understand it, but the words are beautiful and I write them down. Then, without the interference of thought, my fingers pick up the scissors and cut a hole in the middle of the collage.

It's my entity departed. An opening, a window, a doorway...

Into what?

***

Derek can't stay away. In the late afternoon he arrives, along with Nigel and Alister so it doesn't look like he's the only one who's crowding me. I'm content to be alone and Davina is giving me space, but the arrival of the others means I get to try out my relationships, to see if they're as different as TJ predicted.

"Your feelings will be sharper," he said, "because your refuge is gone. But don't be a rabbit caught in the headlights. Embrace each emotion head-on."

Derek would like to think he's the one I notice first. But it's Alister. A bolt of raw emotion leaps from my chest, does a circuit of the space he's occupying in Davina's hallway, then bounces back like a puppy on a leash. That's new. I was shut down before, shut down to what he's offering me, and now I'm willing to explore.

He smiles. It goes from his toes past his eyes to the crown of his head and beyond. How can a man smile like that?

"Been surprising the universe at all?" he asks.

"Only wisely." Now I'm overwhelmed by shyness.

Derek pushes past us into the living room. The guardian angel's feathers are a tad ruffled. "It's been *days*, Selkie. We need to be updated before we're killed by curiosity. Poor Nigel's beside himself wondering what happened with TJ. And I haven't written a *word*."

Has he deliberately left Alister out of this summary? Yes. He saw the look we exchanged and he's jealous all over again.

Everyone sits down and waits for me to say something. Derek is voicing what they'd all like to ask but are too polite. And I love him for it, with an intensity that's new. But I don't know what to say. Where would I begin?

"Was it a monkey?" he asks.

That's when I understand what Eugene saw. A metaphor. The metaphor of 'the monkey on my shoulder' – the entity I couldn't shake. Denial of the entity's presence and the feelings he was harbouring left a powerful metaphor for Eugene to 'see'.

"In one way Eugene was right," I say. "I had an entity, and with TJ's help I set it free."

Derek's shoulders sag. He wanted me to 'pony up' but he senses that's all he's going to get right now. "Can we...celebrate?" he says.

Davina gets champagne glasses while Derek opens the bottle he's brought. Bless him.

Nigel winks at me. "Here's to departed entities."

After one sip I stop. When you've tasted the paradise of your own heart, alcohol doesn't do it for you any more.

"What about Raven?" Derek asks.

"Whatever's going on," I say, "it's not about Raven."

"Who is it about?"

"Me."

Four faces look at me. It's as if I'm allowing them to see me for the first time, and I grin at Nigel as I feel myself expand under their gaze. Nothing boastful, just an opening up to their love and friendship. That's new.

Then we're talking of other things. While I've been at the bottom of the sea, the outside world has moved on. The police have closed the case on Roger. Electrocution by misadventure. They couldn't find any foul play even though Sheena is still at large. Nigel's found Prunella Ryan in the records, cause of death not stated. Davina's been invited to enter *Vogue*'s 'new designer' awards. And Derek has handed a CD of fashion shots to a sex worker named Gerry and declined her grateful offer of a freebie. That just leaves Alister, but what he's got to say is for my ears alone.

We move out of range of the others.

"Wonderful things have happened to you," he says.

"And it isn't over yet. TJ warned me something big is coming."

"And you need to face it alone?"

"Yes."

"Well, I'm not going anywhere until I know you're through it."

"I won't forget you're there." Ever.

"And don't go away either."

"Wherever I'm going I'll be back." Because I haven't finished with Alister yet. Not with so much to explore. And there's a seal seminar to develop for Moonshine. "You've still got my photograph anyway."

He grins. "And there's also a small matter of dinner." Pause. "When it's over, Selkie, let's get away and get to know each other. I've got a house on Kauai."

"On the beach?" Why do I know it's on the beach?

He nods. "We can swim with the monk seals." He's remembering Being Sleek and thinking I swim. "If we're lucky we'll see a mother and calf."

That image touches me in a new way.

Then I say, so I don't start blubbering, "Something's happened to you too."

He nods. "You were right about Gennie. She's got herself a lawyer. Breach of promise, he's calling it."

"So it's going to be...public."

"I'm sure it's not what she wants – a humiliating spectacle – and I've had an idea that's got everything to do with you."

"That's scary. Can't you afford your own lawyer?"

He chuckles. "You pointed out that in dating me she was putting her boys first. So I'm going to offer to put money in trust for their schooling."

"To give her the acknowledgement she wants from you...and preserve her dignity. No court case. And you'll know you're doing your best for them. You love those boys, don't you?"

He nods. "Sometimes love sneaks up on you."

His eyes are huge but I don't look away. "When they're adults," I manage to say, "they might get back in touch."

"You're a wise woman."

I swallow. "Just a woman...without an entity."

When he leans over and kisses the top of my head, I realise we've never even kissed. It's still too soon. I'm way too vulnerable. More vulnerable than ever, according to TJ.

Maybe after I've faced the really big one, opening up to Alister won't feel so huge. He seems to understand. And anyway, if we started stealing kisses in Davina's hallway we'd never stop.

***

The others leave and Davina and I are alone again.

"Thanks for keeping the hypnosis to yourself," I say. "I saw DD putting pressure on you to tell all. His curiosity is insatiable."

"It's your story to tell. But I couldn't tell him anyway. I've forgotten it all, you know."

"Really?"

She laughs. "A fine fog it is. Like your episode with the mirror."

"Have you blanked because you were afraid?"

"No, no. It's just gone. And I've been wondering, you know, if that TJ wiped my memory when he brought me back. So I couldn't gossip."

She's laughing but it's having the opposite effect on me. Until this moment it never occurred to me that TJ might be able to manipulate anyone's mind. Not Davina's. Or mine. Everything that happened was bizarre but it also felt...true.

Now I'm doubting it.

Outrage cuts through me with its serrated blade. My anger is back, and I welcome the pain of an old ally. If TJ cleared Davina's mind, what the hell was he doing to mine? Spinning fables? Taking each piece of information I so eagerly supplied and turning it into an elaborate charade called 'hypnosis'? My thoughts were so surprising he could have planted every single one.

The rage escalates as I recall our debrief. How he

cemented my impressions that everything had sprung from the murky depths of my own psyche.

'The entity was part of you. The miscarriage represented a life stalled.' I couldn't even see the entity till he started asking leading questions. 'Shame split you in two. Only your rage empowered you.' He was so plausible, I didn't doubt him for a minute.

Is my life destined to be one betrayal after another? I was conceived in betrayal and ever since it's been my roadmap, every signpost leading me in one direction. Towards the cliff...

Davina knows something's wrong. "What are you thinking, girl? Out with it."

But my one sip of bubbly is coming up again and I rush into her bathroom and lock the door. Now she's pounding on it, just like Stella all those years ago, and I'm staring into the toilet in a parody of the past.

"Unlock this door."

"I need to be alone."

"Not with those thoughts, you don't. What are you telling yourself?"

But TJ's words are haunting me. 'Hypnosis can only deal with your own mind.'

My laugh is more like a scream. He guided me to see things and my mind obliged...by making them up.

I open the door, knocking Davina off her feet. She chases me into the living room but she can't get there in time.

"Don't!" she shouts.

I'm waving my collage, seeing all the symbols for what they are. Magazine clippings. Pretty pictures. An exercise in guided bullshit.

"Try and stop me," I scream.

She lurches at it and it rips in two, leaving each of us holding a piece.

"You're in a fine funk," she shouts. "Talk to me first. Five minutes. Then if you still want to, tear it up."

My chest is heaving. "I can't trust anything, Davina. Think about it. If TJ was wiping your memory clean, what the fuck was he doing to me?"

"I was joking, Selkie. TJ wouldn't manipulate anyone."

"You don't know that because *you* don't remember." Another betrayal. "I was under his control, while you were supposed to be my witness."

Her eyes flash. "I've forgotten because I *was* your witness. I was there and my job's done."

But I'm not listening. My mind is under siege from all the spiritual paradigms this island peddles.

Derek and his psychic protection. Nigel and his interconnectedness with birds. Wanda and her mystical mirror. Coral and her sidewalk soothsaying. Davina and her telepathic trances. Eugene and his entity detection. Even Alister and his ever-so-wise surprises.

Their voices are screaming at me to give myself up, to lose myself in the dementia of delusion, to be like them. Meditation, channelling, psychic powers, spirit guides...

But I'm remembering who I used to be and I'm missing my old self with a passion. Selkie Moon, seminar presenter. With an abusive ex-husband, a hateful stepmother, a fetish for Chinese food, a vacancy for a good man, and an alcohol habit.

Someone is trying to kill you, a voice whispered in my ear. *And figments can carry you away.* Warnings from my own sane mind.

I've been drowning in hocus-pocus.

Davina's eyes haven't left my face. "The real question,

Selkie, is why would my little joke make you doubt what happened with TJ? Was it that *bad?*"

"Bad?" I look down at my torn collage and start to howl. The grief during hypnosis felt as desolate as it gets, but now I'm sinking into darkest despair. I remember gazing into the black void, how it disappeared into white light. And I want the light back.

"Well?" Davina asks.

"It was amazing. Like drinking from a nectar so pure and so clear and so deep that all my fragmented pieces came together...and I experienced myself in four dazzling dimensions, beautiful beyond reason. That's why I can't trust it."

"So that was the hypnosis. But you're back in the real world now and today you've had a test-run with your friends. TJ couldn't meddle in that. You've been let loose with what you learned. So ask yourself, has it felt...true?"

True. That word again. So potent it defeats my resistance in an instant. Because I can never forget how it felt just now, to be with Alister, to be with Derek. To be so open, so vulnerable. So real. TJ said the emotions that were hiding on my shoulder would now be out there 'on my sleeve'. And he was right.

"Today...has felt like...the most honest day of my life."

Bloody hell.

Davina throws her arms around me as I dissolve in tears. "You eejit, Selkie. It's time you trusted your inner knowing, girl. The voices in your dreams. Your maddest ideas. The singing of your soul. Don't give up now. I told you this detective work is hard, that you're hearing things you don't want to hear. These doubts are jewels, they'll give you the answers, but you've got to push through to where the truth lies. In your poor battered heart. Not in that mind of yours. It's the one spinning spells."

I collapse on a sofa. I can't say TJ didn't warn me.

"You'll be stronger and more vulnerable," he said, "all at the same time. Strength and vulnerability are twin states. Your fear was a kind of protection because it limited you, kept you safe by keeping you small. You could shrink to the refuge on your shoulder. Now the entity's gone, and your Raven fantasy too, so you're open, wide open. Your mind won't like that. It's used to being in control and now it's sidelined. So before you learn how to be strong, you're vulnerable to being overwhelmed by...the enormity of who you are...and for a while there's a danger your mind will shut everything down."

The mind is a great tool and a great liar. I've been living the lies for a lifetime and it's hard, so hard, to break free.

"Something big is coming," TJ said. "It's why you've done this work right now."

Something big. I've sensed it myself. Three letters that feel enormous.

Davina leaves me to sit with my torn collage. The suspicion that ripped it apart has sobered me up and I look at the two pieces with shame. It's hard to face such raw contrition, but the pain passes and then I know what to do. I'll take what everyone's offered me, see what I've started through to the end, find my own path through the spiritual smorgasbord and decide what's right for me. Only then will I know what to trust.

My phone rings. I'm not going to answer it but I see it's Dad. Do I want to speak to him?

"Gretel's gone into labour," he says. "She wants you to come back."

I don't even think. Of course I'm going to be there. For Gretel. For me. For an entity from a past life.

For...unfinished business.

Davina rings the airline while I pack my few belongings. Then she drives me to the airport for the 6pm flight.

Dad is there in Sydney to pick me up.

"Stella and Barry are at the hospital. Our granddaughter is taking her own good time to arrive." He tries for a chuckle. "Waiting for Aunty Selkie, I suppose."

His hug is stiff. He knows that I know about Raven, that I was conceived during his sordid affair with his fiancée's teenage sister. Such betrayal is as shameful as it gets.

We don't say much on the long drive. What would we say? At least he's had the courage to face me today. I consider letting him off the hook, making small talk about life in Hawaii as if the truth hasn't hurt me; or battering him with rage about their perfidy. But neither response feels right. Their secret has impacted me deeply, and if I want Dad to bear witness to my pain Stella needs to hear it too.

The insight calms me. I'm here for Gretel and her baby. Everything else can wait.

Dad navigates the motorways to Westmead Hospital. We're going against the morning traffic so we make good time. Then we're parking and making our way to Maternity where Stella's been sitting up all night. That makes two of us. Her lean body is taut with tension as she gets out of the plastic chair and hugs me. Another stiff hug. She's good at them.

I remember TJ's warning about her.

"You'll particularly notice a change with your stepmother. She suppressed you, made you afraid. You had to hide, hide who you are. Now you'll be more open around her."

"That feels scarier than meeting the woman," I said. It made him laugh.

But I can feel it now. Not my usual defensiveness, but a kind of honesty making its way to my throat.

Stella notices my hair. "Reinventing yourself, I suppose."

"No Stella," I say. "Like changing my name back to Selkie, I've just stopped hiding."

Before she can say something snide, Barry comes through a doorway. He's looking dishevelled. The doctor in him couldn't help getting his hands dirty.

"A boy," he says simply. "Mother and baby are tired but fine."

He goes back inside, leaving the three of us to stare at each other.

"Congratulations," I manage to say, feeling emotional. "Your first...grandson."

"A boy," says Stella. "That's what I get for praying they wouldn't call her Tayla."

"Be careful what you wish for," Dad says.

"Don't tell me you're disappointed." I'm ready to get truthful on the subject of baby boys.

"Of course not." She glares at me for misjudging her. "Just surprised. And done in. As soon as we've seen them, Sheldon, take me home."

It's a while before they're ready for visitors. Then Gretel is sitting up in bed with her fair hair slicked back in a ponytail and her forehead glistening. She beams at us from her exhausted but joyful face.

"You made it," she says, winking at me.

"I could say the same about you. You and little…"

I look down at the crumpled red creature in the crook of her arm. He's got a profusion of straight black hair.

"His hair's like yours," Gretel says, seeing my haircut. "Prickly."

She laughs. "How about real?"

"We don't have a name yet," Barry says. "We were so sure he was going to be a girl."

Something about the little guy stirs me deeply. It's a while before I can speak. A name has popped into my head. "You two just had wax in your ears. Not Tayla. Tyler."

Gretel and Barry look at each other. Stella opens her mouth then closes it.

"Tyler," Gretel says. She looks down at her new son. "I like it. It suits him."

Instead of telling me I'm out of line, Barry grins. "Tyler. I wasn't sure why you needed to be here, Selkie. Now I know."

We stay for a while. I keep my distance in case my emotions overflow. The proud grandparents coo.

It's only in the car that I see the parallel. Me giving Tyler his name. Raven giving me my name. Did it pop into her head as she gazed at her new baby? It mellows me out as we drive back to Seaforth. I was going to get Dad to drop me at a hotel but I've changed my mind.

Suddenly I can feel their pain.

We pick up some Chinese at Seaforth Junction. My idea. Better than trying to 'make myself useful' in Stella's kitchen. We've all gone way beyond tired – more like wired. Is there about to be an explosion or are my senses just exploring their new emotional range?

The house I grew up in is just the same with its smooth white render and curved 1950s' façade. It feels significant to be here as we cross the stone paving from the garage and enter through the French doors.

The Chinese don't charge extra for the wisdom that comes with their food. As I fill my face, I decide to give Dad and Stella space to tell me everything in their own way. Raven is their secret. They've been sitting on it for decades. I know what that's like. When a secret is out, it creates a new world order and everyone feels raw.

We eat in silence. They're not going to insult me with small talk either. Then we stack the dishwasher and even though it's still daylight we go upstairs to bed.

***

Jetlag wakes me early. I was dreaming about the key. Shedding more bloody tears. There's something I haven't unlocked. The identity of the woman. The meaning of the message.

It's just light, a typical March morning. A few late-season cicadas are warming up and it brings back memories of long hot days, staying away from the beach. I think of Andrew, of the house we shared. Does his new woman sleep on my side of the bed? If I borrow Dad's car I could catch them by surprise, say I've come to check the house and give Andrew a shock. But that feels like a lifetime ago.

I wander around my old bedroom, noticing how Stella has removed all traces of my former occupancy. It used to make me furious the way she expunged me like a stain, payback for deserting her for Andrew. But what if she'd kept my room as a shrine to my 'happy childhood'? That would have been worse. Is it possible that around me Stella can't do anything right?

I pad downstairs in bare feet, hoping she isn't up yet. In the empty kitchen I get a bowl of cereal and take it down to the pool.

Dad is doing laps. He swims over to greet me. "Keeps the brain active, they reckon. Don't know how it works but it's fun."

He returns to his exercise while I stretch out on a banana lounge, feeling strange to be here, to know what I know. I watch Dad's almost bald head and broad freckled back and try to imagine him at the centre of a love triangle. Impossible. He's sixty-five years old, almost an old man. The passions that drove him seem bizarre even to a vivid imagination like mine.

It doesn't take long for Stella to appear.

"How did you sleep?" she asks. She's being careful not to call me Elkie. Or anything else.

"Well enough to dream."

She clears her throat. "You had terrible nightmares when you were small. Your mother used to sing you to sleep, but I'm no singer. I could never get you to settle."

"What did she sing?"

"Something she wrote herself. She was very creative. Artistic. Beautiful."

We both know Stella hated her. After Raven stole her man or long before?

Dad gets out of the pool and we all walk up to the house. He disappears and returns in a tracksuit. Then we sit on stools in the kitchen while Stella puts on the kettle. The atmosphere is charged. We're like players who've lost their scripts. I'm waiting for the first act to unfold when something unexpected happens.

Stella is pouring water into the teapot when she stops.

Almost in slow motion the harsh lines around her eyes crumple and a sound comes out of her mouth, a sound I've never heard in my life before. The sound of Stella sobbing.

At first Dad doesn't respond. He's as shocked as I am. Then he rushes over, takes the kettle from her hand and wraps her in his arms.

"It's death...by a thousand cuts," she sobs. "After thirty-five years of keeping the lid on it...I'm being humiliated over and over again. And Selkie already hated me. Now she'll despise me."

"Why would I despise you?" More than I do already?

"For lying about her death. I just couldn't," her voice cracks, "I couldn't bear the thought of you looking for her. Finding her and..." she lets out a wail, "comparing her to me – the plain...dull...substitute."

"That's not true," Dad says.

Stella ignores him. "After she gave you up, you were the cuckoo in the nest. You should have been *my* daughter, but you were...just like her. Magical. Wild. Selfish. I hoped you'd grow out of it. I tried so hard to make you normal, to keep you safe." Her voice drops. "It was like holding back a tsunami."

It's as if there's been an exorcism. Demons have been driven out and the air is fresh. Without my entity, I'm picking up Stella's pain like a psychic sponge, this woman who could never have my love. Fuelled by humiliation and driven by every cell of her being, she guarded me through childhood from the wildness she feared I'd inherited. But with every oppressive measure she pushed me further away. And in the end I ran off to Hawaii anyway, following in Raven's footsteps like a prophecy carved in stone.

I wander around the kitchen, looking for I don't know what. A shoulder to shrink to, a shell to curl up in. The room where I used to hide in my psychological house has been demolished. My anger's no longer on tap and I'm desperate to escape this...compassion. It's so overwhelming it shows me how numb I've been for as long as I can remember.

Stella is staring at her hands. Her image is in shreds but I remember something Alister said. Images are meant to be demolished. Underneath her steely act I'm seeing Stella for who she is. A woman betrayed and depleted. She got her man in the end, but she was left holding the baby, literally, and my presence in their marriage has been their living souvenir.

Dad is looking shell-shocked. He hasn't been covered in glory by any of this and he knows it. After the betrayal he was so relieved to be forgiven – and have a mother for his child – that he ignored Stella's heavy hand with me.

I have to find something to do. I finish filling the teapot and pour us all a cup.

Stella rests her head on Dad's shoulder. It's a gesture of solidarity that flips my point of view. For the first time I understand what drove them, how difficult it must have been. I may even forgive them one day, but as always there's someone they've forgotten.

"After what happened," I say, "it must have been heart-breaking to parent me. Being reminded of her every time you looked at me."

They look up as if they've just remembered I'm here.

"But I'm not Raven."

They're frowning. They don't get it. They've been so driven by their image of Raven, they've never really noticed me. They've only ever seen her. All these years I've been wanting them to love me. For who I am. As if without their acknowledgement I don't exist. I feel the familiar pull to keep trying, to keep polishing the rhinestones on my daughter costume until it dazzles them into accepting me, but as I stare at their frozen expressions a voice whispers in my head.

They're never going to get it.

Even if I stay away long enough to reclaim my own sense of myself, in their eyes I'll always be the embodiment of a dead woman.

They sit in silence over their tea while I finish mine in a state of deep awareness. This story is their story. I've been confusing it with my story. Until now. But there's a small matter of unfinished business.

"Did she leave anything behind?" I ask. "For me."

They look at each other and exchange a subliminal nod. Stella leaves the room and comes back with a book. She knew exactly where to find it. *Celtic Folktales.*

"It was her favourite book," she says, then adds, "I've kept it for you."

"But you've never given it to me."

"I decided to wait until you asked." Hoping against hope I never would.

I go into the living room and sit in an armchair by the window. It must be her handwriting on the title page. *Raven.* Just Raven. It says so much about her, just five letters written with a youthful flourish. She loved her new name. She was only sixteen when she changed it, not long before she named me. She didn't know about mothering, she didn't know about fidelity, about love or responsibility, but she knew about names.

I turn to the story I know is here. *The Seal-Maiden.* Did Raven read it to me over and over, the story that gave me my name? I don't remember. As much as I want to lose myself in the words, try to conjure up a glimpse of her lost spirit, this house can never be the place.

I'm closing the book when something falls out. A photo. A young woman and a tiny child are standing on a beach with the sea behind them, squinting into the sun. I've seen an ugly school portrait of Prunella with her hair in plaits. Stella's way of representing her. But in this photo the schoolgirl has become a woman with flowing raven hair. She's wearing a swimsuit and laughing at the camera, but the little girl in the bikini looks tense.

I turn the photo over. And the words written in the same hand swim.

Raven and Selkie. Bantry's Bluff. March 1979.

***

All the way to Sydney airport, I replay the conversation.

"She took you with her," Dad told me. "Stella was already caring for you and Raven was dropping by when it suited her. One day she took you to the park and didn't come back. We hired a detective to track you down."

"We knew you weren't safe," Stella said.

"You were in Hawaii. She was shacked up with a man near Kailua. A beach house of sorts. We flew in and rented a cottage nearby. To keep an eye on things until Raven's attention span ran its course. Stella was sure she and the boyfriend would soon get bored with the sleepless nights and the responsibility."

There was one question I had to ask, even though I knew the answer already. "The incident with the wave, when I got scared of the sea. Did it happen at...Bantry's Bluff?"

Stella looked at the photo again. "This is the day it happened. A few weeks before your birthday. It's why you're looking miserable. You'd been a happy child, but after you nearly drowned and I pulled you out of the waves, you became introverted. You were suddenly afraid of shadows, started having nightmares, and you refused to go near the beach. It helped our cause. Raven thought motherhood should be fun and you weren't fun any more. On the day of your second birthday, she told us we could have you. Sheldon made the arrangements and we brought you home."

Home. Where is my home?

"We never heard from her again."

As my cab pulled away they were standing at the window. Stella might have lifted her hand, but I could have been mistaken.

***

I send a text to Gretel. *Gotta go back. Unfinished business. So glad I came. More than I can say.*

Gretel remembers what day tomorrow is. *Tyler sends hugs for your birthday.*

In the anonymous space of the gate lounge I pull out Raven's book. I know the story already but this time I'm inside it and the ending blows me away.

It was the boy who heard a voice and found the sealskin in the attic. His mother's sealskin. Without it she had shrivelled, lost her lustre. The skin shone black then silver in the boy's webbed fingers and he wondered what it was.

But she knew. Soon she was laughing and taking the boy in her arms down to the sea, where the seals had waited many long years to welcome her back. They knew of the boy, he was spirit already, so she pulled on her sealskin, breathed air into his lungs and together they entered the kingdom under the sea.

They stayed a while. Long enough for the boy to learn the songs of the seals and become a whisperer on the wind.

And for the seal-woman to become glossy and sleek, before returning each full moon to the shore.

C H A P T E R

Thirty-Seven

The return flight is full of holiday-makers but I feel separate. And when I pick up my little red suitcase at the luggage carousel and feel how empty it is, a wave of liberation hits me. Without my usual baggage I'm someone else.

A text is waiting when I turn on my phone.

Time for a trim. Today.

In the past I would have railed at this command, but something has changed. I've changed.

The cab driver is full of the news. Plagues of cowry shells are washing up on beaches all over the islands. It explains why I can hear them. Thousands upon thousands of voices ringing in my ears.

Jerome greets me at the door and guides me through the ruins and the frocks. He drapes me in a black cloak, picks up his scissors and waits with arms poised. He's like a conductor before an orchestra. Can he hear the singing? At a silent signal he begins, chipping away in a trance-like rhythm. As if this ritual is preparing me for...I don't know what.

This time I keep my eyes open. In the mirror, the woman I've become looks back. A woman without an entity, a woman with silver hair, a woman who with every snip of Jerome's scissors is being transformed into...someone else.

When he's done, he presses his hands together in front of his chest and bows to the woman in the mirror.

Namaste.

Jerome's spirit honours her spirit. And she returns the honour.

***

As I walk the streets to the office, the world carnivals around me. The teased and buffed, the casual and carefree, all surge and pulse. But everywhere I'm an outsider. I relish the separateness. My nourishment is elsewhere.

Derek smothers me in hugs and I give him the gift I found at Sydney airport – salad servers fashioned from Huon pine into a pair of hands. A small symbolic gesture to the two men who have guided me with such loving care. He adores them and can't wait to show Nigel. But when he realises what it means he makes me promise to come back.

***

When I call Wanda to tell her I'll be gone for a while, she's distraught. Coral is missing. Last night she went down to the beach and didn't return. The sun came up this morning to reveal a vast gaping space in the bus shelter.

"People are saying she took off on a turtle."

Why do I think it's got something to do with me? My entity departing. Davina forgetting. Coral disappearing. All their jobs...done.

"Did she take her belongings?"

"Still there," Wanda says. "Like they're waiting for her. And have you heard about the cowries? They're invading in the millions. Waikiki is choked. Something's going on, Selkie. Wherever you're going, make sure you're wearing yours."

***

Davina greets me with a hug. She doesn't ask about my trip and she doesn't mention my 'fine funk' in her living room even though I accused her of betraying me. She doesn't bear grudges and she's demonstrating another 'f' word. Friendship.

When I emerge from her shower in my little black dress, the cowry shell at my neck and my silver hair spiking wildly, she hands me her car keys.

It's time.

She also gives me a cooler-bag. Inside is a bottle of water and some sashimi. I ask her about the raw fish and she tells me it's a symbol. It reminds me of her insight about the fabric from the attic. She knows what's going on, and when the time comes I hope I'll know.

I take the food and the keys and go. Out of Kailua, up the hill to the crossroads, then left. I've never driven on the right before, but I manage it easily and the turn-off to the track. The car negotiates the bumps and stops on the grassy verge. I sling the cooler-bag over my shoulder, just like Roger did that day, before walking under the archway and entering that other place.

Today it's just the same. A world that time's forgotten. Full of gravestones leaning this way and that. Some whispering to each other, others shunning each other, like a mirror of the souls beneath.

Everything a mirror.

"Will you return to the cemetery?" TJ asked at the end of the session.

I shook my head. "I'm too afraid."

"This might not be about the cemetery, you know."

"But all these happenings revolve around it."

"And the cliff."

Now I know this isn't about the cemetery but it fooled me for a long time. Nothing to do with Roger, although he had a part to play. Nothing to do with Raven, but I needed to know her story so I could let it go and embrace my own. Everything to do with the cliff and the endless sea pounding out its own rhythm, its own voice. A voice that merges with the thousand voices singing a cappella in my ears.

I find Raven's grave and stand where Alister must have stood. I stare at the engraving on the stone. Just *Raven*. I think of my own name. *Selkie Moon*.

She conceived a child at sixteen. Just like I did. She got a new name at sixteen. Just like I did. We lost each other after the incident just below these cliffs. Then she died at thirty-five, the same age I am today. If Derek was here he'd be brushing down those bloody arm hairs.

I go down on my knees and knock on the stone.

"Thank you for giving me my name," I say. "It's a special name, isn't it?"

Yes, says a voice in my head. *You're about to find out how special.*

"I'm afraid."

That's because long ago a wave called your name.

"I don't remember that."

It's time to remember, to go beyond fear. It's time to find out who you are.

I've brought a posy from Davina's garden and I place it before a blank headstone. A temporary shrine to my entity. Losing him was a kind of death, the death of a soul divided.

I stay with my head bent, letting the grief flow. Am I praying? I'm not sure but the posture feels right.

The star fruit tree seems to bend and offer me its fruit. I pick one. It's time to find a shady place to sit.

And wait.

For the woman.

I didn't bring a camera. It was the camera that got in the way last time. Giving me the means to try to capture her, steal her image. The Roger syndrome. His picture file was a killing room of stolen souls.

But the woman couldn't be captured – the crucial pointer to her identity and I missed it. I was too busy burying lost emotions, setting the effigy of a half life with rhinestones and making it an altar to a mixed-up mind.

I didn't bring my watch either. Because *when it's time, it's time*.

I sit in the shade of the palms and eat the raw fish, the star fruit, drink the water, all the time watching the cliff.

I have no idea what will be asked of me. But when the time comes I hope I'll know.

I find myself slipping down to that deep place of timeless peace where thoughts are just the driftwood of the mind. And the singing of the shells is my own special music.

Then she appears. The woman on the cliff. Not because I want her to but because I want the truth.

It's late. Later than last time. Dusk. And she's gazing again at something over the edge.

We've been here before, she and I, and the image comforts me. But then she turns and looks up, looks right at me with her surreal eyes. And beckons.

No!

The breeze is strong. It's coming in gusts, like my fear. One moment I'm exhilarated, the next I'm afraid. The singing becomes deafening, echoing the fear that's surging in my chest. I remember the cliff, the furious sea. And I'm afraid.

Still the woman beckons. And if the singing could get

any louder it does. There are millions of cowries coming ashore – a plague of cowries, an army of cowries – and they're calling me, resonating through the shell on my chest, making the spots hum like stars blinking in the fading light.

Part of me wants to run away. I might be longing to know the truth but I'm not strong enough for this.

Then the other voice rises above everything else. *It's time to find out who you are.*

The woman lights up. In the last rays of sunlight she's a lightning rod, connecting heaven and earth. But something's missing.

I'm missing.

I don't know what will be asked of me, but when the time comes I hope I'll know.

And the time is *now*.

I leave my bags and run. Just like the picture on Alister's wall, but this time I don't look back. I run like the wind. Across the cemetery. Towards Bantry's Bluff. And the sky beyond.

Is this what happened to Raven? At the age of thirty-five? Did she take off for the heavens, to live up to her name? Just like I'm about to dive into the sea and live up to mine?

Somewhere between the cemetery and the cliff all fear leaves me and I'm completely empty. Just the skin of Selkie Moon rushes to the edge and falls into the arms of the woman, who grabs me and stops me going over.

We embrace. Like old friends. But she's the one who's real while I've become the wraith. I feel the shift in power as she takes hold of me. I almost swoon but she doesn't let go. She'll never let go again. In every way, I'm in her hands.

At our feet there's a cairn of stones marking a path down to the beach. A cairn that wasn't here last time. A path that wasn't here last time. A beach that wasn't here last time.

Or I didn't have eyes to see.

I slip out of my shoes and follow her down the cliff. The path is lit by a runaway flame and with each step into the underworld my conscious mind loses its grip. When we reach the sand the stillness is complete.

Not sand, cowry shells. Cowries in every direction, covering the shore like a carpet from cliff to sea. The waves have ebbed with the tide and they hiss in and out, tame and welcoming.

I've seen this beach before. Not only in Raven's photo. I recognise the rocks, the cliffs, the turquoise sky. *Ho'ohihi*. And now I recognise the woman. She's wearing Shona's head instead of the floral pomander – the one surreal woman who forsook her shell-shaped tuba so she could dance.

But she isn't dancing. Like Dali's painting she's trapped in limbo, waiting for something to make her real.

In the middle of the beach a doorframe stands facing the sea. The woman walks towards it and I follow. Then she stops. And I stop.

So far I've shadowed her every move, followed her step by step, put my feet in her footprints. We've done this before, beyond my memory, but now she turns to look at me.

It's the look she had in the mirror, the look she had on the cliff, a look of such intense longing that it shatters my heart and creates a new room for a limitless love. Last time the obliqueness distorted it. Then the camera got in the way and an entity filtered out the pain. But now I'm wide open and the message stabs me like a lightning bolt.

A crime has been committed. A theft. Long ago

someone stole the most precious thing she possessed and ever since she's been leaving traces of her injury, staining everything red in her efforts to get it back.

We look down at my dress, and I see how it wraps me in the embrace of a long-lost pelt. No wonder it's felt so precious. It was stolen and hidden in the attic, and a spirit-boy helped me bring it back. It belongs to the woman and I begin to strip, but she puts up her hand and stops me. Then she turns, steps through the doorway and disappears.

No!

Too late I realise she's gone but when I rush to the doorway, I come face to face with a mirror. And the woman looking back at me...

Is me.

To get the right answer, ask the right question.

Who am I? And what do I want?

I stare at myself and see the answer. Until I opened my heart, the oblique glimpse of my own greatness made me faint away. But now I see what I've been longing for. To be comfortable...in my own skin.

It's a moment of profound clarity and a shooting star leaps from my cowry shell and takes off across the sky, creating a gust of wind. The doorframe starts to shake and as I reach out to hold it, I see beyond the rippled reflection something else.

My collage.

How can that be? Did I bring it with me? But there's the tear where I ripped it in two, and the words and symbols are already dancing, swirling like a wheel of fortune around the hole I cut in the middle. As I watch, they stop spinning, reform and tumble into place. The story they tell is so startling that I can't tear my eyes away.

It's the story of a tiny baby who the gods named Selkie.

They granted her infinite wisdom, the wisdom of the sea, but shame obscured her ancestral insight, clouded her oceanic knowing. A wave tried to spark her memory, but she was too young, too vulnerable, alone and afraid. The oppression of a fearful love soon overwhelmed her. She still heard the voices and knew she had to keep them secret, but she'd been dragged into another's dance. As her life force shrivelled to a safe place, the connection to soul was severed and the whispering stopped. She struggled, she misunderstood and finally...she forgot.

It's my story and my heart is breaking. *Someone is trying to kill you.* It's been me all along. Wearing a false coat that wouldn't fit without killing me. Dying to comply with others and failing to nourish myself. The insight is so liberating that I fall to my knees in thanks. Thanks for the journey, always blind and clumsy, every mistake another bloody footprint on the path.

The sun has set. The beach has plunged into darkness. The breeze is making the mirror shudder wildly. Soon the waves will come, the frame will droop and the mirror will shatter. And my chance for transformation with it.

It's time to seize the moment but my mind is playing tricks. It's reminding me about playing safe, about living without pain. It's beguiling me with the old effigy of a half life set with rhinestones, telling me the woman is just another figment, that there's more kudos in staying than going. On and on.

Then the moon peeps over the horizon and its silver light leaks into a willing sea. It illuminates the hole in my collage and the singing in my ears becomes words. Words I understand.

Don't be afraid of not knowing, they say. *Come to the bottom of the sea and learn our wisdom. The world will still be spinning when you get back.*

Is this the power of the 'Siren Song'? Luring the unwary to a watery death? I don't have a mast to strap myself to. And my ears aren't filled with wax.

But the sea has become a mirror – everything a mirror – and heads are dipping and diving, heads with silver hair and knowing eyes. They move like so many moon crescents, tiny escaping offspring never looking back. Their pelts flash black then silver, they surface near the shore, then peel off their skins and rise above the waves on human legs.

Suddenly they're running, splashing through the shallows, driven by a wild longing to feel sand between new toes. To dance.

Now a rhythm's happening. Drumming, drumming. It resonates within the depths of me. A dance I know. From somewhere forgotten long ago. Tragic, mournful, then bubbling over with ecstasy.

On and on the passion drives them. Bodies laughing, souls prancing, spirits soaring on moonbeams. Moonbeams that are making a path across the sea, a path from the horizon to my collage, to the hole that's too small for me.

No!

Then a voice echoes across the sea. *The key. The key. The bloody key.*

It's hidden in my secret dream pocket, the key I had to steal so it would stain everything red. Just like my psychic footprints, my reminder never to forget again. It's wet with blood in my fingers, but as I turn it in the lock the bleeding stops.

In a flash of silver light, the split that my despair created rips the collage apart.

There's no looking back. Not this time.

I step through the opening. Peel off my dress. And join

the dance.
The dance of the selkie moon.

Thank you so much for reading this Selkie Moon mystery. I hope you enjoyed it.

Write to me at selkiemoonmystery@gmail.com and tell me what you liked, which characters you'd like to see more of, which countries and folktales Selkie could explore, even what you didn't enjoy so much about the book. I'd love to hear your thoughts and feedback.

You can keep up with the series and all its characters in the following ways:

- Download the free 24-page ghost story *Laying Ghosts* – the prequel to the series: www.selkiemoon.com
- Sign up for the *Myth & Mystery* newsletter for sneak peeks, freebies, giveaways and periodic news about new releases: www.selkiemoon.com
- Follow Selkie Moon on Facebook: www.facebook.com/selkiemoonmysteries

If you think your friends would enjoy the series I'd be honoured if you'd spread the word. Books also make great gifts!

If you feel particularly motivated by your reading experience, please take a few minutes to post a review on your retail site and/or on Goodreads. Reviews tell other readers what's worth reading and I'd appreciate it if you'd leave a few words.

Many thanks,
Virginia King

When a voice wakes you up in the middle of the night and tells you to write a mystery series what's a writer to do? That's how Virginia King came to create Selkie Moon, after a massage from a strange woman with gifted hands was followed by this nocturnal message. Virginia sat down at the keyboard until Selkie Moon turned up. *All she had to do was jump*, the first sentence said. Soon Virginia was hooked, exploring far-flung places full of secrets where Selkie delves into psychological clues tangled up in the local mythology.

Before Selkie Moon invaded her life, Virginia had been a teacher, an unemployed ex-teacher, the author of over 50 children's books, an audio-book producer, a workshop presenter and a prize-winning publisher. These days she lives in the Blue Mountains west of Sydney with her husband, where she disappears each day into Selkie Moon's latest mystery. Bliss.

Acknowledgements

The First Lie began as one sentence: *All she had to do was jump.* A momentous sentence that also applied to me because although I'd written many children's book, this was my first novel. From this sentence the story that I didn't know I was telling took shape, changed shape, became something more than me. Along the way many people have had confidence in me – even when I lost confidence in myself.

Claire Scott-Mitchell introduced me to myths and folk tales and their layers of symbolism. I was hooked. Elspeth Liberty and Akash Kevin Olver looked after my psychology, taking the fear out of 'delving'. Poet Deb Westbury, agent Selwa Anthony, and publisher Jane Palfreyman showed interest in the manuscript, boosting my confidence.

Awesome editor Nicola O'Shea with her magic mix of encouragement and honesty brought *The First Lie* to publication. Nicola and her partner Keith Stevenson at ebookedit.com.au have been my publication team. One day, I hope to meet them.

My writing friend Maureen Lawson read early drafts, giving insightful feedback and encouragement. Maria Curran, Margaret King and Philippa Russell-Brown have shown unfailing belief in me.

Claudia Lane helped bring the series to market with energy and commitment. She also made sure that Selkie Moon is a thirty-something woman, crossing out anything 'a tad 80s' in the manuscript, when what she was noting was really 'a tad 70s' (and before her time).

Others told me about their lives and/or read early drafts: Elspeth Liberty, Maria Curran, Brian Curran,

Sandra Stevens, Lesley Lane, John Hillel, Marc Lane, Laura Brundle, Nicola Styles, Tara Madden, John Morgan, Diana Dixon. Paul Vale informed me on subjects ranging from electrocution to Honolulu. Many people have bought the book, read it, told their friends, left a review, and kept up the support.

Artist Lindena Robb provided creative inspiration. A section of her powerful painting *Looking* became the first cover. Julia Kuris at designerbility.com.au brought both flair and patience (with the author) to the new cover. Damon Baker and Marty Walker created my gorgeous website. Thanks to indieBRAG for awarding *The First Lie* a BRAG Medallion and for supporting quality indie authors.

Many books with psychological layers were essential to my research and inspiration, too many to list. But notably, *The Girl in a Swing* by Richard Adams, *Women Who Run with the Wolves*, by Clarissa Pinkola Estés and *Travels* by Michael Crichton. Google Earth and Streetview brought Hawaii right into my Blue Mountains office.

And finally, my live-in coffee-maker and reviewer Alan Lane has never stopped believing in me and this book. He's listened to every word, then watched as they've been rewritten over and over. He's been there, through the ups and downs of living with a writer. *The First Lie* would never have reached the world without him.